2-

WORLDS OF HONOR

DAVID WEBER

BAEN BOOKS by DAVID WEBER

Honor Harrington Novels:
On Basilisk Station
The Honor of the Queen
The Short Victorious War
Field of Dishonor
Flag in Exile
Honor Among Enemies
In Enemy Hands
Echoes of Honor

edited by David Weber:
More Than Honor
Worlds of Honor

Mutineers' Moon
The Armageddon Inheritance
Heirs of Empire

Path of the Fury

The Apocalypse Troll

Oath of Swords
The War God's Own

with Steve White:
Insurrection
Crusade
In Death Ground

WORLDS OF HONOR

DAVID WEBER

Contents

The Stray

Linda Evans

Dr. Scott MacDallan was, by dint of much sweating and swearing, trying to turn a wriggling, ungrateful little demon of a breech-birth infant for head-down delivery, when the stray arrived on the doorstep.

Mrs. Zivonik had a history of easy births without complications or he'd have done a simple Caesarian, but turning an infant wasn't complicated and the monitors in place showed him neither baby nor mother were in distress, so rather than create an incision and put the woman out of work for several days, he simply took the time-honored step of reaching in for the baby, grabbing it in one hand, and rotating it right-end around instead of wrong-side down. Mrs. Zivonik was doing fine, too, was even cracking terrible jokes despite the sheen of sweat soaking her and the occasional sharp grunts, gasps, and deeper groans when the contractions hit. Scott had just touched the baby's toes and was wondering why he'd ever thought this would be easy—while trying to ignore Evelina Zivonik's sounds of acute discomfort—when a wave of emotional anguish strong enough to knock him cock-eyed rolled over Scott like a naval battle cruiser.

His involuntary grunt and sharp movement drew a startled sound from his patient. "Doc?" Scott blinked, fighting the urge to panic, and managed, "Uh, sorry. No problems, you're fine and the baby's fine." For God's sake, Scott, pull it together! Before your patient thinks you're as loony as your misbegotten ancestors. Some of them had been burned at the stake . . .

Scott blinked as Evelina Zivonik leaned up far enough to

1

peer over the top of her distended belly. "That's good. But *you* don't look fine."

Just beyond the bedroom door of the Zivonik home, Fisher—who had the run of Scott's home and office, but *not* of his patients' homes—began bleeking in acute distress. He'd never heard the treecat make a sound quite like it, in fact, and the emotional wallop he was getting from his companion was enough to shake him into blurting out the truth.

"I'm not fine. Or rather, my treecat isn't."

"Your treecat?" she echoed. A thread of fear colored those two words. Treecats were viewed with awe and no small measure of worry by their human neighbors, who were almost universally uncertain how to respond to their presence.

"Yes. He's upset, very upset, I'm not sure why." *Careful, Scott . . . you're treading thin ice here.* "I've never heard him make a noise like that," he added, glancing worriedly toward the closed bedroom door.

"Well, I'm not actually in serious labor yet," Evelina said uncertainly, the worry stronger this time. "If there's a problem with the treecat, you need to go find out what it is. If he's hurt or sick . . . well, I'm not exactly going anywhere, so you should find out what it is."

His professional ethics would permit no such conduct, of course. Abandoning a patient in the middle of a procedure just to comfort his friend was out of the question. But Fisher's deep distress was not to be denied. Fisher knew how to open doors, of course, and the bedroom door was closed, but wasn't locked. Scott hesitated, torn between the need to reassure himself that a treasured friend wasn't in peril and the need to bring this baby into the world.

"Why don't you call him in here?" Evelina suggested, correctly interpreting his hesitation. "Irina has told us all about Fisher and showed us pictures, but I've never actually seen a live treecat." The hint of wistfulness in her voice decided Scott in an instant.

He flashed her a grateful response. "Thanks. Fisher! Come on inside, Fisher, it's not locked!"

The door swung open and a cream-and-grey furred streak shot across the floor on collision course with Scott's shoulder. He grunted softly at the impact, one hand still trapped in Evelina Zivonik's womb, the baby kicking and moving under his fingers.

"Bleek!" The treecat touched his cheek with both front hands, then pointed urgently at the window.

"What? Is there some danger outside?"

That wasn't the feeling he was getting from his companion of nearly twelve Terran months, now. He was getting better at reading Fisher's emotional "messages" all the time, thanks to an empathic ability of some sort that he carried in his extremely Celtic Scots Highland genes—an "ability" that still scared him silly on a rational, scientific level. The first time it'd happened with Fisher, he'd literally thought he was hallucinating. Only later did the truth sink in—and that was almost worse than a hallucination. On Sphinx, the kind of legacy he'd inherited from a long line of charlatans, parlor tricksters, and other assorted loons was met with mere skepticism and ridicule. But there were human worlds where professing to ownership of anything remotely similar to what his more ... flamboyant ... relatives (all on his mother's side of the family, thank God, so the name MacDallan hadn't been connected with them) was punishable by incarceration for fraud—or outright insanity.

What he was getting from Fisher now was not so much a sense that there was some kind of danger outside as more a sense that something outside was *in* danger. Or distress, maybe. It was also abundantly clear that Fisher wanted *him* to go outside, urgently. "Fisher, I can't go outside right now. I'm trying to deliver a baby."

Grass-green eyes shone brilliant with distress. The treecat made a pitiful sound. Just then, a chorus of childish voices erupted out in the main part of the house.

"Daddy! Come quick!"

"It's a treecat, Daddy!"

"Aunt Irina! Hurry! There's a treecat outside!"

"He's hurt or sick or something! *Hurry*, Daddy! Hurry, Aunt Irina!"

Scott and Evelina Zivonik exchanged startled glances.

"Go," Evelina said firmly. "I've had six babies. This one's going to get himself born just fine, whether you sit here and sweat to death with worrying or take five minutes to go out there and maybe save a life. You're the only doctor for a hundred kilometers. If there's an injured treecat out there, then *it* needs you more than I do right now. Besides," and she gave him a wry, sweaty grin, "I could use a breather from all that mauling."

Scott flushed; he'd continued working to turn the baby even while trying to determine what was wrong with Fisher, and "mauling" was probably what it felt like to poor Evelina Zivonik.

Fisher touched his cheek again. "Bleek?" The sound tugged at his heart, not to be denied.

"Thanks," he said with heartfelt sincerity. "I've never seen Fisher this upset. I'll be right back." He eased his hand out of Mrs. Zivonik's womb, reaching for a towel with the other. That bit about Fisher being more upset than Scott had ever seen him wasn't exactly true; but Scott didn't like talking about the injuries he'd suffered the day he and Fisher had first made one another's memorable acquaintance. The treecat had saved Scott MacDallan's life. The very least he could do was repay the favor to a treecat in trouble.

So he hurriedly scrubbed off and jogged outside, where the Zivonik brood danced around their father and Aleksandr Zivonik's younger sister, Irina Kisaevna. Aleksandr and Irina stood a good twenty yards to the side of the house, peering up into a picket wood tree's lower branches. Scott had no more than cleared the doorjamb than the most anguished sound he had ever heard uttered by a living creature smote him straight through the skull bones. The sound keened up and down like a banshee driven insane, voice torn by more pain than can be endured. Fisher, who huddled on his shoulder, wrapped his tail around Scott's throat and shuddered non-stop. "Bleek!"

Scott broke into a run, even while reaching up to soothe his companion with one hand. "Where is it?"

Aleksandr pointed. Scott peered up into the tall picket wood closest to the Zivonik house, toward one of the long, perfectly horizontal branches that made the picket wood so unusual among trees. "Up there."

Scott had to look closely, but he spotted the treecat near the trunk, sitting up on its haunches like an old Terran ferret, longer and leaner than one of those ancient weasels, yet with a head and certain other characteristics far more feline— except, of course, for the six limbs, a trait it shared with the massive and deadly Sphinxian hexapuma it so closely resembled in all but size. The treecat keening in the Zivoniks' backyard picket wood was larger than Fisher, about seventy centimeters long, not counting the prehensile tail, which effectively doubled its length, yet the little arboreal was far too thin for its length. It *did* look sick—or injured. Its coat was mottled cream-and-grey, like Fisher's, but even from this distance, Scott could see dirt and darker stains that looked sickeningly like blood.

"Fisher?" he murmured, trying to soothe his small friend's violent tremors. "Is it hurt? If I could get to it, treat it . . ."

The hair-raising cries halted. The strange treecat made a pitiful sound, tiny with distance, then moved haltingly down the trunk toward the ground. Scott's pulse raced. He wanted to break into a run, wanted to rush toward it, and was afraid of frightening it away.

"Aleksandr," he said in a low voice, "I think maybe you and Irina should take the children back to the house. If anything spooks it, we may never get a chance to help, and I think that treecat needs help very badly."

Aleksandr nodded. The set of his mouth was grim. "Come on, kids. And no arguments!"

Irina Kisaevna glanced involuntarily toward Scott, concern darkening her vivid blue eyes. Of all the humans Scott had met before being adopted by Fisher, Irina alone seemed to grasp the depth of the bond between himself and the remarkable creature who'd come into his life nearly a full Terran year previously. Widowed when her husband had died in the plague that had devastated the human population of Sphinx, Irina had become a close friend during the past couple of years. Scott enjoyed her company, her quick, incisive mind, and her ability to make him feel rested and at ease, even after a difficult day; but when Evelina's latest pregnancy had turned difficult, she had moved in with her brother on the Zivoniks' farmstead—thus depriving Scott of her delightful company and occasionally intuitive insights into his relationship with his treecat.

"Irina," he said quickly, "I'd appreciate your help."

Warmth flashed into her beautiful eyes. "Of course, Scott. It would be my privilege." She, too, peered toward the slowly descending treecat in the big picket wood tree above them.

Scott waited while Aleksandr herded his youngsters back toward the house. The whimpering treecat had reached the lowest branch of the picket wood, where it stopped, bleeking piteously. Fisher replied, then pointed. Scott made a hopeful guess at Fisher's meaning. "It's okay if I go to him?"

"Bleek!"

He couldn't pick up anything like sense from Fisher, but the emotional response was unmistakable. He hurried toward the picket wood trunk and peered anxiously upward. The strange treecat was shaking where it huddled on the low branch. The dark stains *were* blood, long since dried, matting the once-beautiful pelt in a leprous patchwork. The treecat was far too thin, looked half starved, in fact. Was it an outcast, that no treecat community would help it? Did treecats have outcasts? Whether they did or they didn't, Fisher was certainly urging Scott to help the stranger, so there was no clue to be gleaned from his own treecat's behavior.

"Hello," Scott said quietly, speaking directly to the treecat above him. "Can I help?" He projected all the warmth and welcome he could summon.

The reaction stunned him. The distressed treecat let out a warbling, broken sound, then jumped to the ground and ran straight to Scott, clasping his leg with all four upper limbs and holding on as though life itself depended on the strength of that grip. Fisher swarmed down, touching faces with the stranger and making the soft, crooning sounds Scott recognized from his own occasional bouts of emotional distress. Scott crouched down, offered a hand. The bloodied treecat bumped it with his head, begging for the touch, leading Scott to wonder if this treecat had been around humans before. He stroked the treecat gently, trying to determine from that cautious touch how badly injured it might be.

He found no wounds to account for the blood, not even a sign of swelling or inflammation. But the treecat clung to him and shivered and made broken little sounds that horrified Scott nearly as much as they did Fisher, judging by the emotional aura his own treecat was projecting. Something truly dire had happened to this little treecat—and Scott received a strong premonition that whatever it was, it meant serious trouble for him and his companion. When Scott tried to pick the treecat up, it let out a frightened sound that prompted Fisher to rest both of his true-hands on the other's nearest shoulder. A moment later, the filthy, blood-matted treecat swarmed into Scott's arms, huddling close. Fisher jumped up to his customary perch on Scott's shoulder, still crooning gently.

Irina hesitated some distance away, biting her lower lip uncertainly. Scott nodded her closer with a slight movement of his head and she approached slowly, while Scott stroked the painfully thin treecat reassuringly. When Irina stood beside him, the stray let out a strange, mewling little sound, gazing up at her through grass-green eyes as deep and wounded as a hurt toddler's.

"Poor thing," she whispered gently, offering a cautious hand.

The trembling treecat permitted her touch, arching slightly in Scott's arms as she stroked gently down its spine. But it was Scott the stray clung to, all four upper limbs clenching in Scott's shirt.

"Will you let me take you inside, I wonder?" Scott asked aloud, moving cautiously toward the Zivonik house. "You're hardly more than fur and bones. You need food and water and God knows what else." The washboard ribcage under his hands spoke of a prolonged deprivation and he could see cracked, dried skin around the treecat's mouth, eyes, and

delicate hands, indicating dehydration, as well. Scott stroked
the distraught treecat gently, whispering softly to it, as he and
Irina slowly approached the meter-thick stone walls of the
Zivonik house. The most cursory examination told him the
treecat was male and—thankfully—uninjured despite the dried
blood in its fur.

Irina called out, "Alek, the poor thing's half-starved. Get some
meat scraps for him, a dish of cool water, whatever we've got
left from dinner last night!"

"Karl, drag out that leftover turkey," Aleksandr said, shooing the children inside. "No, Larisa, you can look later, after
the treecat is out of danger. Nadia, go check on your mother.
Stasya, get some water for the treecat. Gregor, run some hot,
soapy water and bring out a handful of clean towels."

"Yes, Papa."

Children scattered.

"Kitchen's this way," Alek escorted him into the house.

Scott moved cautiously inside with his unexpected patient,
Irina trailing anxiously at his shoulder, and entered a brightly
lit kitchen just in time to see Karl, their oldest son, setting
out a platter with an enormous, half-stripped turkey carcass.
The boy set it down on a broad wooden dining table built to
accommodate a growing family.

"Dig in," the boy addressed the bedraggled treecat shyly,
cheeks flushed from excitement. "Help yourself." Stasya, the
Zivoniks' middle daughter, was carrying a basin of water to
the table, eyes round with wonder as Scott set the thin treecat
down. It paused for only a moment, as though making certain the offer were genuine, then tore into the carcass with
ravenous hunger. The children hung back, staring raptly at the
wondrous creature on their kitchen table; very few humans
had actually *seen* one in person. Even stolid, broad-shouldered
Aleksandr Zivonik hunkered down to watch the starving treecat
tear into the carcass with surprisingly dainty hands, visibly
entranced by the sight of his diminutive sentient guest.

Scott smiled gently. "Fisher," he said, reaching up to stroke
his friend, "I have to go back and help deliver that baby now.
Can you stay with him?" Scott had no idea how much his
treecat actually understood of what he said, but he and Fisher
generally had little trouble communicating basic things. Fisher
simply swarmed down his arm and jumped to the table, crooning softly to the battered treecat, which was busily stuffing
strips and hunks of turkey into emaciated jaws. Scott hauled
his dirt-streaked shirt off, smiling gratefully at Irina when she
carried it toward the laundry room, then scrubbed his arms

with hot, soapy water and disinfectant at the kitchen sink and hurried back to check on Mrs. Zivonik.

"Mama's doing fine," Nadia, the oldest of the Zivonik daughters said at once. "How's the treecat?" she added anxiously, edging toward the hallway.

"Eating your turkey dinner. Go on, see for yourself."

The girl darted for the door. Scott found his patient nearly as apprehensive as her daughter when Evelina gazed up at him. "It wasn't injured?" she asked anxiously. Clearly, Mrs. Zivonik was as worried over the sudden appearance of an ailing treecat on their doorstep as her husband. So little was known about treecats, the abrupt appearance of a *healthy* one was often enough to upset the most steady of settlers; a starvation-thin one with blood in its fur was genuinely cause for fright—and Evelina Zivonik wasn't the only one afraid of the reasons for that treecat's condition. Scott was considerably disturbed, himself, despite nearly a full T-year of daily contact with a treecat to accustom him to their sometimes startling habits and behaviors.

And the last thing Evelina Zivonik needed during a breech-presentation, difficult labor was to fret over this unexpected development. He tried to reassure her as he resumed his interrupted work with the baby. "No, I didn't find any actual injuries. Of course, I can't hazard a guess when he last had a solid meal and anything to drink, but he's wolfing down turkey as fast as he can tear it off the bones, so there's nothing wrong with his appetite."

"Nadia said it's covered with dried blood?" Worry still knotted her brow into a deep furrow.

"Yes, but none of its own. Whatever's happened, we can't communicate with treecats very effectively, so I doubt we'll ever know where the blood came from. The important thing," and he gave her a firm, reassuring smile, "is that your little neighbor is doing just fine, so there's no sense in worrying about it. So I want you to relax for me and let's see if we can't get this baby of yours born, eh?"

Evelina Zivonik gave him a wan smile and nodded, then dug her fingers into the bedding and groaned as a contraction rippled across her distended belly. Scott reached once again for the recalcitrant infant attempting to get himself born feet-first and scowled in concentration, moving by feel and instinct. After several minutes of awkward squirming, during which Evelina grunted sharply only a few times—a stoic woman, Evelina Zivonik—Scott's effort and sweat finally paid off. "Ah-hah! Gotcha!" Scott grinned as the baby under his groping hand finally cooperated enough to turn around inside his mother's uterus. "Head down and rarin' to go. Okay, Evelina Zivonik, let's see if we can't get this latest son of yours born!"

Humanity had discovered the existence of the Sphinxian treecats only fifteen Terran months previously, when eleven-year-old Stephanie Harrington had caught one raiding her parents' greenhouse—with several bunches of purloined celery strapped to its back in a neatly woven net. No one knew why treecats were so hyped on celery, but ever since that first, fateful encounter, treecats had been popping out of the woodwork, so to speak, all over Sphinx, importuning their new friends for all the spare, stringy stalks humanity's kitchen gardens could grow. The sheer number of treecats who had abruptly come calling suggested a far-flung and quite sophisticated communications system of unknown origin, all the more remarkable because the treecats had succeeded in hiding from a high-tech civilization for fully half a Terran century.

Enter one eleven-year-old genius with a camera and a battered, shattered glider, and fifty years of secretive observation from the treetops had ended with treecats exploding onto the scene, seeking out human companions in the same way little Stephanie Harrington's crippled treecat had come to her rescue, leaving its own kind to live with her family. While the adoption rates were not very high compared to the overall human population—perhaps one in only a million or so—compared to fifty T-years of total secrecy, during which humanity hadn't even suspected the treecats' existence, the sudden switch in tactics on the part of the treecats was startling.

Clearly, the treecats were as insatiably curious about people as humans were about treecats—yet humanity still knew almost nothing about their newest neighbors. Not even their level of intelligence could be accurately determined, although Scott had begun forming his own ideas along those lines. Thanks to his somewhat bizarre genetic legacy—one he'd sooner have been slow-roasted over coals than reveal to anyone, let alone the xenologists here to study the treecats—Scott was somehow "tuned in" to the emotions of a sentient alien, one that was, he was beginning to suspect, a whole lot smarter than any human on Sphinx had begun to guess. He also suspected that eleven-year-old Stephanie Harrington wasn't telling the full truth about *her* treecat, either, not if Scott's experiences with Fisher were any indication. And he was beginning to suspect he knew the reason for her silence.

One of the most intense feelings close association with a treecat engendered was an overwhelming protectiveness, an almost subliminal sense that *whatever* an adoptee learned about his or her treecat, it should under no circumstances be made public knowledge too quickly. Treecats clearly needed the help of their human friends to avoid the fate of so many other indigenous, low-tech, aboriginal populations throughout human history. Caution and secrecy seemed the better part of wisdom until more could be determined about the simple basics of treecat biology, sociology, and culture. Not to mention how humanity was going to react in the short-term, never mind the long-run.

And that was a difficult job, even for an adoptee. Even one like Scott, who had the somewhat unexpected advantage of his ancestors' irritating tendency toward "second sight" flashes of empathy or whatever it was that Scott experienced on a daily basis with Fisher. That the treecats possessed some level of telepathy or empathy was obvious from the reports made by any "adopted" human. But no instruments existed to measure a thing like telepathy, much less an empathic trait. Understandably, the xenologists were massively frustrated.

At the moment, so was Scott MacDallan.

The "stray," as the Zivonik children had christened the emaciated treecat, had filled his cadaverous little belly and promptly gone to sleep. After the successful delivery of squalling young Lev Zivonik, the stray had graciously suffered Scott to plunk him into hot, soapy water to remove the caked blood and dirt. But he—for the stray was definitely male—would not let go of Scott afterward, no matter what enticements were offered. He simply held onto Scott's shirt, which Irina had thoughtfully laundered for him while little Lev was getting himself born, and shivered.

And Fisher displayed an urgent desire for Scott to go outside. Scott suspected that Fisher was relaying what the stray was feeling; or perhaps Scott was also picking up a sense of urgency from the thin treecat clinging to him, but what he couldn't fathom was why the treecats wanted so earnestly for him to hike into a picket wood wilderness after a long, intensive delivery that had left him tired enough to want to go directly home and collapse for the evening.

Each time he quietly suggested they might go back to town and return later, however, Fisher grew nearly frantic and the strange treecat emitted choked, mewling sounds like a kitten being mauled in the jaws of a killer dog. Scott swallowed hard and tried to sound a reasonable note. "But Fisher, it'll be dark in a couple of hours and I really need to get some sleep. I don't want to fly after dark, not as tired as I am."

"Bleek . . ."

Aleksandr asked, "Can you get a sense of how far away they want you to go?"

Scott shook his head. "I can't get that kind of detail. Nobody can. All anyone can really pick up is a sort of subliminal sense of intelligent feeling," he lied through his teeth, aware of Irina's sharp glance. "Well, occasionally, sign language and pantomime can convey a pretty clear meaning, but it's maddening, trying to communicate with a sentient that can't speak your language, knowing you can't possibly learn how to speak its language, either." He considered the problem for a moment. At length, he suggested, "Fisher? Could we fly there?"

He received a bewildering flash of confused emotions, closed his eyes to try sorting them out. Anxiety, sharp fear, rage . . . Scott blinked, stared at his friend. *Rage?* Fisher huddled on the table in front of him, looking forlorn and solemn.

"I'm not sure why," he said slowly, "but I don't think the treecats want me to use the air car. They're afraid of it. Not Fisher, I mean, he's flown with me dozens of times, but if I'm reading Fisher's reaction right—and that's a big if, I'll grant you that much—I'd say the stray's scared witless of the idea."

Alek lifted one shaggy brow. "Really? Well, we could set out on foot now and if we haven't found anything in an hour, we could turn around and come back, put you up in the boys' room and get a good night's sleep, then start out again tomorrow."

"Bleek!" Both treecats spoke in unison.

"I think they approve." Irina smiled.

Alek added, "I've got a spare rifle. It's not likely we'll run into a hexapuma, and peak bears don't generally come down this low in a valley, but I don't go hiking without a good rifle in my hand."

Scott glanced up. "No, I don't blame you. I've seen what hexapumas and peak bears can do to a man inadequately armed. I've got a rifle of my own in the air car, though, thanks." He scraped back his chair, offered his shoulder to Fisher, who jumped lightly to his accustomed perch. "Let me just get it."

The stray wouldn't go near Scott's air car. Scott retrieved his gear, casting uneasy glances at the emaciated treecat who sat in the nearest tree, bleeking in terrible distress, and wondered why the treecat reacted so violently to air cars. Surely nobody would have harassed a treecat colony from an air car? The 'cats were protected by the Elysian Rule and the fiercely protective reaction of their newest neighbors, most of whom earnestly wanted this most recent and personal of interspecies relationships to get off on the very best of feet. But Scott couldn't imagine any other reason for the treecat's reaction, which caused him a great deal of concern as to who might be guilty of "buzzing" a treecat colony from the air. All sorts of dark thoughts ran through his mind as he gathered up what he'd need for even a short hike into Sphinx's wilds.

Irina Kisaevna volunteered to go with them and Scott seriously considered agreeing; she'd been of immense help during the early months of his adjustment to Fisher. But Evelina Zivonik was still recovering from the delivery and Aleksandr was uneasy about leaving her alone without an adult in the house, so she reluctantly agreed to stay.

"Be careful out there, Scott," she said urgently before returning to the house. "We don't know what's happened or what the treecats want you to see out there. I'm worried."

Scott nodded, kissing her gently. "So am I. Believe me, we'll be very careful."

"Good." She smiled up at him. "Go on, then. Solve our mystery for us, Scott. I know you're anxious to be off."

He rubbed his nose sheepishly. Irina Kisaevna knew him too well. "We'll com you if we find anything, all right?"

"I'll sit by the speakers and wait," she smiled, kissing him again.

They finally set out a quarter of an hour later, with Aleksandr Zivonik in the lead. His oldest boy Karl, who at fifteen T-years was a keen marksman, covered their rearguard. Scott drew the relatively safer middle position, with his own rifle and his medical pack strapped to his back. He'd learned the hard way to carry a well-stocked medical kit with him wherever he went—particularly on hikes into the wilds of Sphinx's picket wood forests, which were a tangle of interlaced, interwoven branches and nodal trunks, thanks to the picket wood's bizarre method of reproduction.

The picket wood tree propagated itself by sending out four long, straight branches parallel to the ground at a height of about three to ten meters, radiating out like spokes from a primitive wheel, at close to right angles from one another. Periodically, these branches put down "roots" which grew downward and formed a new nodal trunk, with perfectly ordinary, randomized branches growing above and below them. A single picket wood "tree" could grow to hundreds of kilometers in length and breadth, an unbroken green carpet that ran through river valleys, climbed partway up mountainsides, and spread out lushly across flatlands, with thousands of "individuals" genetically identical to one another. Consequently, hiking through a picket wood forest was an adventure in orienteering, since the interconnected system prevented one from holding anything like a reasonably straight course for more than a couple of meters at a time. It was a crazy way to reproduce, but it provided a perfect habitat for the arboreal treecats. The picket woods created a kind of intercontinental "super-highway" system that, so far as could be determined, inhabited every corner of Sphinx that would support the trees.

The treecats had taken to the tangle of branches the moment Scott and the Zivoniks entered the forest; they raced ahead, pausing impatiently to let the humans catch up, then raced on as the sun descended steadily toward the horizon. Scott wasn't a professional woodsman, but he enjoyed fishing with a passion and had done his share of hiking to some of Sphinx's remoter spots, having emigrated here from Meyerdahl only three T-years previously.

Sphinx didn't possess "true" fish, at least, not like Terran species, but wherever there was water, there were things that lived and swam in it, things that would glom onto a hook dangled temptingly in front of whatever they used for mouths, and that was all a born fisherman could ask of life. Scott loved the dense picket wood forests, loved the scent of their leaves and the slanting sunlight that filtered down through the dense green of the canopy, loved the clear, rushing streams and wild rivers that poured through these forests, and the fresh colors of spring as the land came back to life after the unimaginably harsh winter snows, fifteen Terran months of them, even this far into the subtropical zone of the planet.

Thanks to Sphinx's long year, spring—Scott's favorite season—also lasted a marvelous fifteen T-months, which meant it had *been* spring for the entire time he and Fisher had been companions, for the entire time humanity and treecats had been getting to know one another, for that matter. There was something satisfyingly appropriate about the growth of new ties and friendships with a brand new sentient species while the whole planet they shared was coming back to life again.

Hiking through the burgeoning picket wood forest now, Scott breathed in the wild scent of a world coming alive all around him, and smiled. Then he glanced upward, where two treecats waited impatiently, and felt the smile run away like bilge water. Whatever the treecats wanted him to see out here, it wasn't likely to inspire smiles. What in the world could have happened, to leave the strange treecat so cruelly wasted with hunger and thirst? Where had all that blood come from? And why was the treecat so afraid of air cars? For that matter, he'd clearly been wary of humans in general until Fisher had showed up with Scott in tow, refusing to come anywhere near any of the Zivonik family. Why would a treecat be afraid of people, yet broadcast its presence so vocally—and when a human turned up in treecat company, cling to that person like a leech and insist they go with him into trackless wilderness?

Despite the overwhelmingly positive reaction of the Sphinxian human population to their arboreal neighbors, Scott could think of several unpleasant reasons why a treecat might be afraid of any number of people, given the history of human race relations, even amongst its own species. While the colonists were, on the whole, good people, there were always troublesome, unpleasant individuals in any population and there had been occasional grumbles about sectioning off large parcels of previously choice real estate as sacrosanct treecat preserves.

None of the darker thoughts occurring to Scott as they hiked deeper into the forest inspired any confidence that this trek would have a happy outcome. So he gripped his rifle, watched and listened for any sign of hexapumas or peak bears, and tracked the passage of time as the sun lowered gradually toward the treeline. By the time the one-hour limit expired, Scott was flagging behind Aleksandr, an increasingly footsore hiker—he wasn't wearing his hiking boots and civilian shoes weren't manufactured with Sphinxian picket wood systems in mind—and was more than ready to turn back. As his watch alarm sounded, he called a weary halt and shut it off.

"That's an hour," he said, unnecessarily.

The treecats burst into a frenzy of bleeking, racing along the horizontal picket wood branches overhead to dance agitatedly just above them, then turning and racing back in the direction they'd been moving steadily for a full hour, now. The urgency he was picking up from Fisher increased at least threefold. He also received the distinct feeling that they were very close to whatever it was the emaciated treecat wanted them to see.

"Five minutes," he agreed reluctantly. "Five minutes, then we turn back."

"*Bleek!* Bleek, bleek, bleek!"

Fifteen-year-old Karl Zivonik grinned. "Five minutes, huh? Just how hard is it to say 'no' to a treecat, Dr. MacDallan?"

"Watch yourself, youngster," Scotty smiled, "or one of these days some pretty little lady treecat might decide you're exactly what she's looking for—and then you'll find out!"

The boy's eyes went round. "Really? Do you think I might ever get adopted?"

Scott chuckled, then slapped the youngster's shoulder. "Frankly, I have no idea. The treecats can't share their criteria for picking friends, after all, since they can't talk to us."

"Have any girl 'cats adopted anyone?"

Scott frowned slowly. "That's an interesting question, Karl. Come to think of it, I haven't heard of any. I'll have to check it out. Maybe the xenology team that arrived to study them will know."

They forded a shallow creek, work boots and Scott's low-topped shoes squelching in the mud, and climbed the opposite bank, heading deeper into a thick tangle of picket wood trunks. A couple of minutes later, Scott noticed an increase in the light falling through the canopy, a familiar sort of increase he'd noticed several times before while hiking to a promising fishing site, where occasional natural clearings in the forest allowed in more light. Such clearings often marked the presence of small lakes or old forest-fire scars or a change in topography or soils that discouraged picket wood growth. Another minute later, they rounded a thick tree bole and emerged at the edge of a small clearing, just as he'd surmised they would. But when he got a good look at that clearing, Scott rocked to a halt. So did the Zivoniks.

It was not a natural clearing. A ragged hole had been forcibly torn through the forest canopy, leaving a debris trail ninety meters long. Something large and man-made had plowed through the tangle of branches and upper-level trunks with massive, splintering force on its way to the forest floor. Bits and ribbons of metal lay in torn, jagged shreds in a path arcing downward along the trail of broken branches and clipped trunks. More metal fragments had embedded themselves in unbroken trees on either side of the path of devastation, where the force of impact had flung them. Scott's gaze followed the trail of ruin down and to their left, aware of a sick tension in his muscles as he sought what he knew he must inevitably find.

And there it was, nearly a dozen meters to their left. A massive cargo carrier had come down at what must have been a terrific rate of speed. The hulk had finally smashed against a picket wood trunk too thick to snap off, about two meters above the forest floor. The metal frame had crumpled like fragile tissue paper around the picket wood, then slammed down to the forest floor at an insane, twisted angle, a complete ruin.

Scott swallowed hard.

How many people had died, inside?

The treecats uttered shrill, sharp sounds and raced away through the tangled, broken branches, making for the wreck. Scott caught Aleksandr's glance. He considered suggesting that Karl stay behind, then thought better. The Zivoniks were pioneering folk, farming a hundred klicks from their nearest neighbor. Sheltering the boy wouldn't do him any favors. Colonists needed tough hides. The look in Alek's eyes told him the same thoughts had gone through the farmer's mind, as well. Aleksandr nodded sharply, then broke trail through the ruin of debris and splintered trees. Young Karl said nothing and looked rather pale, but followed his father without pause. The medical pack Scott had strapped on before leaving the farmhouse felt useless, a superfluous gesture in the face of violent death.

They climbed over fallen limbs and shattered tree trunks until they reached the wreck, then Aleksandr said, "Let's see how stable she is before we go looking for the hatch."

Scott nodded. The big farmer studied the way she lay, looked at the broken tree limbs under the hull where she'd dug partway into the ground, then shoved at the battered airframe and hung his full weight from it. She was wedged in solid as a mountain, from the look of things. As they hunted across the twisted hull for the access hatch to the pilot's compartment, Scott dreaded the sight which awaited them. He found a vaguely familiar, battered logo on a badly dented section of hull, a stylized picket wood tree with its trunk formed from the double-helix spiral of a DNA molecule. The paint was so badly scraped, the name had been completely obliterated, leaving only about half of the double-helix tree. Aleksandr Zivonik noticed him peering at it and looked over his shoulder.

"That's a BioNeering company logo," the farmer said quietly. "They've got a research plant out here somewhere, but it's a long way from our farm."

"I thought I recognized the logo, I just couldn't place it."

Overhead, the treecats emitted a sharp whistling sound and jumped down onto the uptilted end of the wreck, scampering across the side to pause halfway down.

"Looks like they found the way in," Karl said nervously. The boy was swallowing hard.

"I begin to suspect," Scott said slowly, "that the stray 'cat knew whoever was inside." He couldn't imagine any other reason for the treecat to behave in such an agitated fashion, or for the 'cat to have been in such a wretched state. Had the stray adopted the pilot, perhaps, and been left behind when the air car took off for its cargo run? Just how long had the air car been down? It would take days to run that much weight off a treecat. The thought of Fisher struggling across miles of wilderness trying to reach *him* brought a thickness to his throat. Scott started to climb cautiously up the dented, twisted hull and found, not the hatchway, but the shattered windows of the pilot's compartment.

One look and Scott swallowed sharply. It was not difficult to determine where the blood all over the treecat's fur had come from. The pilot's compartment had been awash with it, before the spatters and puddles had dried to a rusty brown scum.

"The hatch is back here," Aleksandr said off to Scott's right. "The frame's bent pretty badly around it, but the latches popped under impact." Bending metal shrieked in the unnatural stillness, a desecration that couldn't be avoided. Scott edged his way around to help pry it further open. The hatch shrieked in protest, but finally gave way. Scott ducked through first. The stench of decaying flesh gagged him. He paused to cough and wipe his mouth, then fumbled for a mask from his surgical kit to tie around his mouth and nose. Wordlessly, he handed masks to the Zivoniks. The control compartment was a fraction of its original size. Judging from the debris, there'd been three people inside when she'd impacted. Pilot and co-pilot, probably, maybe a company executive or an employee headed to or from that remote plant Alek had mentioned.

Aleksandr Zivonik spoke in a muted whisper through his mask. "Must've come down during one of the big storms or we'd have heard the crash from the house. Sound travels a long way out here. We can't be more than two, three kilometers from the house, tops. How long you figure it's been?"

"At a guess, given the state of the bodies, they've been dead at least a week. And there were some pretty bad storms last week, which could've forced them down. I had to fly through a couple of real humdingers and I was just skirting the edges."

How far could one frantic treecat run in a week's time, not pausing to eat or rest? Thoughts of Fisher brought his eyelids clenching down. The sound coming from the emaciated treecat got them open again. That sound was a feeble shadow of Fisher's familiar, comforting croon. The treecat huddled over what must have been the co-pilot, shaking and wheezing in a grief so sharp, Scott found himself blinking too rapidly and swallowing much too hard. The specter of death was always difficult to face, even for a physician who'd seen it strike many times before; witnessing this depth of grief from an alien creature for a lost human companion...

He turned aside, unable to hide the wetness in his eyes any other way.

A weight settled onto his shoulder and Fisher wrapped his tail around Scott's throat, crooning softly and rubbing his head against Scott's cheek. He clenched his fingers through his friend's thick fur and just stood there for a moment, trying to come to terms with powerful feelings which he knew from experience were no longer entirely his own. Aleksandr's voice reached him, speaking quietly into his wrist com.

"Twin Forks Tower, do you read?"

"Twin Forks, we read you, over."

"Aleksandr Zivonik, here. Doc MacDallan's with me. We, uh, just found a wrecked air car, looks like it's been missing a few days."

There was a brief pause, which Scott used to move closer to the grieving treecat. He hesitated, then stroked the thin 'cat gently. It quivered under his hand, but made no protest. Twin Forks Tower came back on.

"Cargo air car?"

"That's right."

"Yeah, we got a report on a missing cargo carrier about six days ago. Its crash beacon must've malfunctioned, because we haven't been able to trace it and the aerial surveys haven't been able to find it, either. I've got a fix on you. Good God, what were they doing out there? That's five hundred klicks off their flight plan. No wonder we couldn't find them."

"Well, they're found now. Looks like three bodies. Doc, you want to make the report?"

Scott cleared his throat, then keyed his own wrist com to the Twin Forks Tower's code. "Scott MacDallan, here."

"Wylie Bishop, Doc."

Scott had seen him once or twice for minor ailments. "We've got three confirmed casualties in the pilot's compartment. How many people were listed as missing?"

"Just the three. Conrad Warren, pilot, Arvin Erhardt, co-pilot, and Pol Rafferty, passenger. How'd you find that air car, Doc? According to the section maps, it must be three, maybe four kilometers from the Zivoniks' house, not what I'd call an easy stroll. Did the Zivoniks hear it come down?"

"No." He had to clear his throat. "I think the co-pilot must have been adopted by a treecat, because a half-starved treecat showed up at the Zivonik place today and led us back here."

"A *treecat*?" The shock in Wylie Bishop's voice was unmistakable.

"Yeah. My treecat, Fisher, insisted I hike out here, I didn't know why until we found the wreckage."

The com crackled sharply. "Good God. That xenology team is going to want every detail. Doc, I've got Mayor Sapristos on, patching him through."

"Scott?" The mayor of Twin Forks sounded weary. Nobody ever wanted a fatal air crash to strike their community and Sapristos was a good man who worked tirelessly to make Twin Forks and its outlying settlements safe, pleasant places in which to live, work, and raise a family. He took the deaths of anyone in his community very much to heart.

"Yes, Mayor?"

"Can you stand by at the wreck site? We've already got a recovery team airborne, headed your way. They'll be there in thirty minutes, at most."

"Roger, we'll stay, and we'd appreciate a lift back to the Zivonik place. I left my air car there and the Zivoniks don't want to be out here on foot after dark."

"Roger that, they'll lift you out, no problem."

"Thanks. Am I acting as official coroner for the crash?"

"Yes, you've got the job and thanks, Scott. I'd appreciate the help out there."

"Right. I'll begin the preliminary medical exams and investigation, although it's pretty obvious what the cause of death was."

"Copy that, and I'm sorry you had to be the one to find them."

"Yeah. Thanks. Just get that crash team out here, will you? It's going to be a long night."

"Roger that. The cavalry's on the way."

Their com units fell silent. Young Karl looked like a boy who needed to be violently ill and was holding himself under control by willpower alone. Scott sympathized. "Somebody should stand watch outside. With that hatch open, God knows what will be drawn by the scent. What *else*," he added, since it was clear that small scavengers had already found their way through the broken windows to take advantage of a macabre meal. "Take a spare rifle, too." He handed his to Karl.

"Yessir," the boy slurred out through his surgical mask. He took the rifle with a hand that was steady enough to suit, but exited hastily.

"What can I do?" Aleksandr asked heavily.

"Dig through the cargo and the storage bins, see if you can find a portable generator and some lights. This is going to take a while and the sun's going down. And call Irina, let her know what's happened."

The elder Zivonik nodded and started his search, keying his wrist com to call his waiting sister and wife. His voice, speaking softly, drifted back to Scott as Aleksandr broke the news to his family.

Scott tried to comfort the grieving treecat one last time and had to fight blurriness in his eyes when the 'cat clung to his hand, looking up with such a pleading expression he could hardly bear to meet the treecat's steady green gaze.

"I'm sorry," he whispered. "There's nothing I can do for him. I'm sorry."

Thin, three-fingered hands tightened briefly around his fingers. *"Bleek . . ."*

He crouched down, face-to-face with the treecat. "What?" he asked a little hopelessly, hating the language barrier that put such an uncrossable chasm between them. "Surely you understand there's nothing anyone can do? I can't help him. What is it you're trying to tell me?"

"Bleek!"

Scott listened hard with his emotions, with that sixth sense he'd inherited from generations of Scottish "sensitives," trying to make some sense of what he was feeling reflected through Fisher and perhaps even directly from this treecat. The chaotic emotions churning through him were far stronger now than they'd ever been with just Fisher alone. Overwhelming grief and loneliness . . . pain and exhaustion . . . and threading through it all like a trickle of hot, spilt blood, unending, anguished *rage*. He shut his eyes, trying to fathom the anger he was all but tasting, it was so strong. Why *anger*? Was this little treecat merely expressing the anger felt by many another victim of disaster, who'd lost a loved one in a senseless vehicle crash? Or was it something else, something deeper? More . . . sinister?

Scott blinked at the agitated treecat in sudden surprise. *Sinister*? Why had that particular word popped into his mind? The treecat was clutching tightly at his hand, clawtips just barely unsheathed, pressing into his skin. Scott stared into eyes the color of summer grass and wondered why he was feeling a dark suspicion that something about this seemingly ordinary crash was not quite right. *What* wasn't right, he couldn't begin to hazard a guess—and trying to pin down concrete reasons from the nebulous feelings received from a treecat was almost as difficult as trying to travel between star systems without Warshawski sails.

But suspicion lingered, a strong undercurrent of the anger reflected so powerfully by the treecats. Was the grieving 'cat suspicious of the circumstances of his friend's death? Or had the co-pilot been suspicious of something and the treecat was trying to pass along that feeling to Scott? According to the air car's markings, this was a BioNeering cargo vehicle. Scott didn't know very much about BioNeering, other than they'd set up business a couple of T-years back and had been expanding their business steadily, providing welcome jobs and cashflow for the Sphinxian export economy.

Other than that, he'd paid little attention to the company, having more than enough to keep him busy, what with his far-flung, madly pro-creative and fairly accident-prone patients, his occasional escapes into the wilds to go fishing, and—ever since that last, disastrous fishing expedition—learning everything he could get his hands on about Sphinxian treecats while recording his own daily, ever-wondrous discoveries. He hadn't had time to go fishing since and hadn't really missed it, not with his remarkable new friend to try and understand.

Huddled on the buckled floor plates of a blood-stained wreck, Scott gazed quietly into a heartbroken stray treecat's luminous green eyes and found himself vowing that he would get to the bottom of this mystery, whatever it took. If suspicion existed in this treecat's mind, then a careful investigation was warranted. If suspicion had existed in the human co-pilot's mind . . . then an even more cautious investigation was called for. People didn't carry around suspicions strong enough to leave a treecat in this pitiful state without good reason.

And if a reason existed, Scott MacDallan intended to unearth it.

In the sepulchral darkness beyond the blaze of artificial lights, they gathered, arriving silently to sit in the branches of the trees overlooking the place of disaster. The hunters and scouts of Walks in Moonlight Clan mourned, even as they listened to the voices of the two-legs who had finally discovered the flying machine which had come crashing down from the sky two hands of days before. The two-legs had come at last to this clearing of sorrow to reclaim their own. Walks in Moonlight Clan had come to learn the song of their grieving brother from Bright Heart Clan.

Within the ring of alert hunters and scouts, Clear Singer sat with her tail curled primly around her true-feet, ears cocked toward the alien voices, which she had never heard directly before. Memory singers did not leave a clan's central

nesting place without great cause, but True Stalker would not
leave the remains of his friend until the two-leg responsible
for that friend's death was punished—and for that to happen,
the other two-leg, who walked with Swift Striker of Laughing River Clan, must somehow be made to understand what
had happened.

It was beyond the hope of a starving, grief-stricken hunter
and a simple scout, even working together, to make a mind-
blind two-leg understand the evil done here. But if Clear Singer
added her own mind-voice, perhaps enough could be communicated to the mind-blind two-leg called "Scott" that the truth
would be discovered? Clear Singer could hope, for a grievous
wrong had been done and if she succeeded, that wrong might
at least be known, even though it could never be righted.

Clear Singer seethed with frustration, unsure of herself as she
had never been when questions of right and wrong among the
People were at issue. They knew so very little of the two-legs!
There were those among the People, some in her own Clan, who
had called for an immediate withdrawal from the two-legs, as too
dangerous to risk further association with, when word had spread
of the disaster in this clearing and its dreadful cause.

Yet retreat was not the wise course, Clear Singer could see
that as clearly as Sings Truly of Bright Water Clan had seen
it when the spring was still new and Climbs Quickly had first
bonded with a two-leg youngling. Yes, two-legs *could* be dangerous. The People had known that when the decision to reveal
themselves, to actively seek out more bonds with two-legs, had
been made and carried out. That decision had been the right
one, Clear Singer knew that in her heart, for the two-legs could
be tremendous allies, as well. Already the People had learned
things that had improved countless lives, in dozens—hundreds—
of clans.

And murder was not unknown, even among the People.

What Clear Singer did not know was how the two-legs
viewed the deliberate killing of their kind by one of their own
number. If Clear Singer accomplished the impossible, if she
somehow communicated with a mind-blind creature like the
two-leg Scott, if she somehow made him understand that murder
had been done in this tree-shattered clearing, what would the
two-legs do? A creature that would murder three of its own
companions could not be trusted to remain at large amongst
its own kind, nor could the People risk letting such a creature walk loose. A mind-sick two-leg who would destroy its
companions could never be trusted to refrain from committing murder against the People—and after what True Stalker

had seen and heard and had done to him, he had more than ample reason to fear for his very life.

If True Stalker went back with the two-legs, trying to bring the killer's actions to light—without the two-leg Scott understanding what True Stalker returned to—Clear Singer feared the grieving Bright Heart hunter would not survive another hand of days. But if he remained with Walks in Moonlight Clan or even returned to his own distant clan, the murder would never be known by any but the People. And that, Clear Singer could not permit. Not without at least trying. So she sent her call to the clearing, where the two who had summoned her to this place waited.

< *I am ready.* >
< *We will come.* >
It was now Clear Singer's turn to wait.

Swift Striker crooned softly, touching his true-hands to Scott's face to gather his friend's full attention. The mind glow he so loved focused all its glorious brightness on him.

"Fisher?"

He had learned, that day he'd first glimpsed the two-leg called Scott MacDallan, that his friend's mouth sound "Fisher" was the name his two-leg had given him, unable to hear Swift Striker's mind voice clearly enough to learn his true name. The name was so surprisingly close to his own name's meaning, he delighted in the sound of it from Scott's lips.

"What is it, Fisher?"

He pointed into the night, away from the downed air car, toward the place Walks in Moonlight Clan had gathered and now waited with their precious, irreplaceable senior memory singer. He knew the two-legs feared the night in open forest like this, with good reason, but Scott *had* to be made to understand. He pointed again. "Bleek?"

Along with that plaintive sound, Swift Striker put all the intense need he felt for Scott to come with him. At his side, True Stalker—whose grief was a knife-cut in Swift Striker's mind—added his own urgent summons, silently reinforcing Swift Striker's plea and even reaching out to grasp Scott's nearest hand in both True Stalker's own.

Scott twitched his face into the gesture of unhappiness. "You want me to come with you? Out there?"

The stubborn resistance Swift Striker had learned to recognize flared in his friend's mind glow. It was dangerous in the forest at night. Scott did not want to go anywhere near the trees at the edge of this ruined clearing.

"*Bleek!*" The grieving True Stalker ran to the shattered windows of the broken flying machine, bleeking his distress, came back and grasped Scott's hand again, dragging at it, tugging Scott's large, smooth fingers in the direction of the forest and the waiting Clear Singer. "Bleek! *Bleek!*"

True Stalker's reaction had startled Scott; water-blue eyes had widened. "What in the world's gotten into the two of you?"

At least, that was the emotional gist of the question. Swift Striker was still learning the two-leg language of mouth noises and although he had mastered many basic words, complex ideas and abstract concepts were laboriously difficult to translate. He knew that Clear Singer, waiting in the darkness, shared his frustration, with even greater reason. If a senior memory singer with the help of an entire Clan could not get across what True Stalker so desperately needed Scott to know, who among the People could?

"Bleek!" Swift Striker tried again, voicing his frustration the only way he could. "*Bleek!*" He, too, dragged at Scott's hand with one of his true-hands, while pointing urgently toward the waiting memory singer. If they could just get him outside, far enough from the other two-legs for him to realize other treecats were out there, *all* wanting him to come, Swift Striker knew Scott would risk any number of death fangs to try and understand what they were attempting to tell him. The love he felt for his two-leg friend that this was so was all the sharper for the darkness in True Stalker's mind, where a beloved mind glow would never be welcomed again.

The hunter's grief burned through Swift Striker's awareness, an agony none of the People could possibly have ignored, for True Stalker had sensed, despite the immense distance between them, that his friend Erhardt had *known* he and his companions were being murdered even as the flying machine fell, crippled, from the sky. And the two-leg responsible for that devastating crash had tried to kill True Stalker, attacking in his worst moment of pain and grief, with murder in her heart. His clan, already thrown into chaos by the two-legs' terrible, incomprehensible accident at their *research* place—an accident which was devastating his clan's home range—had packed their food stores and flint tools, their baskets, carry nets, and kittens with frantic haste, even while True Stalker fled for his life.

With a mind-sick two-leg attacking the People as well as her own kind, Bright Heart Clan's very survival demanded they immediately abandon their doubly-threatened central nesting place. Not only was their hunting range devastated, with many

of the animals they depended on dead, killed by the poisons
the dissolving trees emitted to keep any animals from spreading the two-legs' mysterious blight from damaged, dying trees
to undamaged, healthy ones, the clan's central nesting place
lay far too close to the two-leg habitation to risk leaving their
kittens and memory singers where this mind-sick, murderous
two-leg could all-too-easily find and strike at them.

And while the People had occasionally been forced to hunt
down and kill one of their own hunters or scouts who had
become murderously mind-sick, such as Bright Water Clan had
been forced to do when a High Crag Clan hunter had attacked
their scouts, trying to steal kittens for hideous purposes, Bright
Heart Clan could not trust the wisdom of doing the same to
a mind-sick *two-leg*. The newcomers were simply too powerful, too great an unknown to risk the entire future of the
People, even if their cause was a good one. Misunderstand-
ings between those who could not speak to one another were
far too great a risk to jeopardize the future of the entire People;
nor was there any guarantee that the two-legs *could* comprehend what had happened here, or comprehend it in time to
protect Bright Heart's kittens and females from their mind-
sick companion. So the Bright Heart Clan deserted their home
to find safety elsewhere and the grieving True Stalker, his entire
clan in flight, refugees in their own home range, had set out
to find his murdered friend—and any two-legs who might help
him prove that murder had been done.

He had found Swift Striker and Scott MacDallan.

Swift Striker, huddled now beside the remains of True
Stalker's murdered friend, tightened his true-hand around Scott's
finger and thumb, desperate to make his own friend understand. *"Bleek?"*

Scott regarded him for a long moment, his water-blue eyes
dark and troubled. The artificial lights which shed so brilliant
a blaze in the cramped space glinted on the fire-colored curls
of his head fur. Swift Striker had never seen a two-leg before
he'd found Scott, had never seen *any* creature with fur the
color of bright hearth fires. Scott's pale skin, lighter in color
than the cream in Swift Striker's own fur, was almost as
mottled as Swift Striker's pelt, not with fur, for most of him
was smooth and virtually furless, but with pale golden spots
and splotches, hundreds of them, as though little droplets of
sunlight had splashed across his skin and glowed now from
inside it.

Of all the two-legs Swift Striker had now seen, he thought
Scott MacDallan was by far the most strikingly decorated; that

his mind glow was as brilliant and unique as his appearance
only made Swift Striker love him the more. And he had tasted
his friend's determination to discover what had happened here,
knew that if Scott would only come with them, the chances
of his learning the truth would be far greater.

"Bleek?" he pleaded again.

"I ought to have my head examined," Scott MacDallan muttered.

But he was moving toward the shattered hatch and Swift
Striker could taste his decision to go at least a little ways with
them. Exultation sent his mind call soaring out to the waiting Clear Singer. < *We come!* >

True Stalker darted out through the window, while Swift
Striker chased after Scott and found his favorite place on his
friend's shoulder. The process of removing the two-legs who
had died inside the flying machine was finished and now two-
legs Swift Striker had never seen were moving all through the
machine, tinkering with bits and pieces of it and using tools
whose purposes Swift Striker could not begin to fathom. One
of these two-legs called out something to Scott.

"Doc, are you going to do an—?" Swift Striker could not
yet interpret some words, leading to frustrating gaps in two-
leg conversations.

"No, I'll—them later." Whatever it was, Swift Striker received
the impression of distaste for something unpleasant. "What
about you?" Scott called back.

"Almost done. Where are you going? The rescue car's that
way, not under the trees."

"I just wanted to check out something under the—" The
feeling Swift Striker got from that was "front of the flying
machine."

"Have you got a pistol?"

That word Swift Striker knew. Scott took either a *pistol* or
a *rifle* with him whenever he walked through a forested area
away from town or one of the far-flung houses they visited
so frequently. Swift Striker had seen him use the *pistol* once.
While not as devastating as the larger, longer weapon called
rifle, Scott's *pistol* had still killed a half-grown snow hunter
with only two thunderous barks from its long, thin tubular
end. The *rifle,* he knew from memory songs of those who had
witnessed them being used, could kill a death fang at full
charge, with only one such thunderous roar.

"Yes, I have my pistol, Garvey. I'm not a greenhorn newcomer to Sphinx, you know!"

The other two-leg laughed, although Swift Striker could taste the grimness behind that sound. All the two-legs who had come to this clearing were distressed by what they had found. Swift Striker knew that distress would increase sharply if they understood the reason they had found their companions dead here. At least, he knew Scott's distress would. The other two-legs, he wasn't quite so certain about. And that was one reason Walks in Moonlight Clan's memory singer waited for them in the trees. Swift Striker had learned a great deal about the two-legs, hoped he understood them sufficiently to judge how some of them would react, when they understood this wreck completely. But he had not learned enough. *Never enough.*

So he wrapped his tail around his friend's neck and crooned encouragingly as Scott picked his way cautiously through the debris of broken, jagged wood and torn metal at the base of the wreck. True Stalker waited for them at the edge of the forest, rising up on his true-feet to tug at Scott's hand.

"Bleek!"

Scott moved cautiously toward the looming trees, wariness sharp in his mind glow. His hand hovered near the handle of his weapon. When they reached the first thick trunks and spreading branches, he halted and would go no further. Swift Striker knew he would not leave the safe haven of the artificial lights, not without much greater incentive than they'd already given him.

< *He fears the darkness and the death fangs,* > Swift Striker called to the waiting Walks in Moonlight Clan. < *He will come no farther unless we show ourselves. If we give him reason enough to be curious, he will come farther. And two-legs know that a massed clan can kill a death fang with ease, for Climbs Quickly's youngling saw Bright Water Clan destroy the death fang that nearly killed her and Climbs Quickly.* >

Swift Striker listened intently to the response, hearing the hurried exchange of worried thoughts between clan hunters and the precious senior singer of Walks in Moonlight clan. A moment later, Clear Singer's mind voice, so much more powerful than any hunter's or scout's, answered clearly. < *We will show ourselves.* >

Like spirits of ancestors visiting in the night, the assembled Walks in Moonlight Clan materialized from the darkness, appearing on branches in a wide arc around Swift Striker and his beloved two-leg. Eyes gleaming in the harsh lights from the clearing, they showed themselves in a silent, welcoming mass.

"Good God!"

Treecats—*hundreds* of treecats—materialized out of thin air where moments before there had been only empty, shadowed picket wood branches. The fine hairs along Scott MacDallan's arms stood starkly upright. A wave of warmth, of welcome and encouragement, rolled over him with the power of a breaking thunderstorm. On his shoulder, Fisher said, "Bleek . . ."

—and pointed toward the darkness beneath the trees.

The treecats wanted him to go out there?

"But why?" he gasped, trying to understand why several hundred treecats would be concerning themselves over a simple air car crash. Surely they'd seen other crashes? This was hardly the first air car that had smashed into the Sphinxian forests during the past fifty T-years, killing all crew and passengers aboard.

Orrin Garvey's voice drifted to him from the back of the wreck. "Doc? You okay out there? Thought I heard you shout something."

"Yes, I'm fine. I was just startled by something I saw, that's all. I'm going to take a closer look down here."

"Don't take too long. We're just about set to pack up and head home."

"Right."

Scott wasn't sure why he didn't tell Garvey about the massed treecats gazing so intently down at him, but he was receiving the very strong impression that he was the only human welcome out here tonight. And that thought disturbed him far more than he liked to admit, coming as it did on top of his disquieted feelings about the wreck and the grieving treecat who'd brought him all the way out here to it. Humanity understood so very little about the tiny arboreals, any contact with "wild" treecats was unnerving, even after nearly a T-year spent in the constant company of a treecat recently converted into a city dweller. Coming face-to-face with what looked like upwards of two or three hundred wild treecats, *all* of them firmly putting themselves squarely in the middle of an ugly business, drew Scott's nerves taut against his bones with fear. That those same three hundred or so wild treecats were also focusing their uncanny attention squarely on *him* only made the situation scarier.

Scott MacDallan was no diplomat.

At the moment, however, he appeared to be the only human Sphinx's native inhabitants wanted to open diplomatic relations with. The treecats could've showed themselves at any time, to the Zivoniks, to Garvey or Vollney, or the pilot of the rescue car, but they hadn't. They'd waited, hidden in the darkness, until Fisher and the distraught stray had convinced *him* to follow them out into the trees.

Looks like I'm a diplomat, after all . . .

"Okay," he said quietly, addressing the hundreds of treecats who watched him so closely, "I know there won't be any hexapumas around, not with that many of you here. Although why you want *me . . .*" There wasn't much point in speculation. He'd find out shortly, for himself. Scott glanced over his shoulder toward the crash-investigation team finishing up their preliminary evaluation of the crash site, then stepped cautiously beneath the dark trees. He could feel the treecats' eyes following his progress as he left behind the safety and warm glow of lights in the clearing. Nervousness as well as fear prickled along his spine, but he trusted Fisher implicitly, for his companion had earned that trust multiple times over the course of their unlikely friendship.

At length, he spotted a faint glow beneath the trees and realized with a shock of surprise that a small fire burned just ahead. Old leaves and fallen deadwood crackled underfoot as Scott moved uncertainly through the darkness toward it. He caught the scent of woodsmoke, unmistakable in the still spring air. Then his eyes adjusted to the dim light and he made out small, furred shapes seated around the tiny campfire. Their positioning and some indefinable sense of emotion he was catching from Fisher told Scott this was a deeply formal gathering, thick with protocol. He swallowed sharply and wondered what to do. *I'm no xenologist! What if I blunder into this and mortally offend a highly placed treecat dignitary?* The xenologists hadn't even figured out how treecat familial and social organizations operated, never mind their political ones.

For a brief, blinding instant, Scott bitterly regretted his complete lack of camera or sound-recording equipment, despite the fact that his instinct to keep what he learned to himself was currently operating full tilt. Then Fisher jumped lightly to the ground and the half-starved treecat appeared from the darkness overhead, and Scott realized the council session—or whatever this might be—was already open for the main order of business. Fisher and the stray moved between ranks of large, clearly male treecats toward the fire, where they greeted a much smaller, slimmer treecat. Scott studied this one sharply, cursing the dim light. Ruddy firelight which flickered across this smaller 'cat suggested a darker, brownish tint to the coat, darker, certainly, than the grey markings in Fisher's coat. *Female?* Scott wondered. The other 'cats regarded her deferentially and Scott received an overwhelming sense of protectiveness toward her from the assembled treecats.

Maybe the treecats wanted him because Scott, alone of probably all humans on Sphinx, could sense their emotions so clearly? For the first time in his life, Scott's unwanted genetic heritage suddenly loomed as a major plus in his favor, rather than an embarrassing handicap to be hidden from friends, colleagues, and acquaintances at all cost. *If the treecats are communicating through telempathic means, maybe I'm not such a bad choice of ambassador, after all?* The thought encouraged him a little, even though he cringed at the idea of telling anyone what he was sensing at this council fire right now. *Better keep my mouth shut and figure this out on my own, rather than risk telling some off-world xenologist, "Yes, well, I sort of read the treecats' emotions, uh, like a psychic, you know . . ."*

No, that was definitely out. Whatever the treecats had to tell him out here, he was on his own when it came to pursuing it.

They were half-a-dozen paces from the low, crackling fire when Fisher turned and bounded back toward him. "Bleek?" He sat up on his rear-most legs, looking for the world like an oversized Terran prairie-dog. Fisher caught at Scott's fingers. "Bleek?" He was tugging Scott forward.

"Okay." Scott was willing to be led toward the tiny, crackling fire. The smaller, darker treecat's gaze was uncanny. Her eyes were also green, but a darker hue, more pine than grass. Scott towered over her. A remembered snatch of basic psychology prompted him to sit down, cross-legged, to face her, presenting a less intimidating presence to the tiny creature opposite the fire. "Hello."

She tipped her head to one side, studying him gravely. "Bleek."

A delicate voice, pure as silver bells. Scott smiled, scarcely aware that he did so. She was exquisite. "Why do you want to see me?" he asked slowly, without much hope of being understood, since it had taken Fisher a fair amount of time to learn as much human vocabulary as he knew. An instinct he'd learned to pay attention to when dealing with treecats told Scott this one had never seen a human before. At least, not a live one . . . An overwhelming aura of curiosity and surprise nibbled at his awareness, whether from her or from the assembled hundreds of treecats with her, he wasn't sure. Finding himself in the role of ambassador for his entire species weighed on Scott, made him concentrate doubly hard on every emotional impression he received. Whatever these treecats wanted, it was abundantly clear that the burden of figuring it out lay squarely on Scott's shoulders.

He gathered his resolve and waited.

Clear Singer felt a surge of hope as she studied Swift Striker's two-leg. He was, in truth, as mind-blind as she had known he would be, for she had learned all the memory songs of those who had gone among the two-legs and brought back the knowledge and taste of two-leg mind glows. But his mind glow was as strong as a roaring forest fire, compared with some of the two-leg mind glows in songs she had tasted and woven into her own. Swift Striker had chosen well, when he had crept through the forest the day he had first seen this two-leg.

< *This is the song of Swift Striker and his two-leg, whose name sounds like Scott MacDallan, in two-leg speech,* > she said to the assembled hunters and scouts of her clan. < *I sing it that you may taste the depth of courage and strength of purpose in this two-leg we seek help from, for this two-leg is the best hope the People have in this time of crisis.* > With the skill of long years and innate strength and sharpness of mind, Clear Singer spun the memory song for her waiting clan.

Sunlight fell in a dappled pattern through the trees, casting motes of brilliance and shadow across fast-rushing water beneath Swift Striker's perch. The soft spring air carried a tang of green things stirring to life, and from the forest floor rose the heady scent of wet, warming earth. The river was narrow here, where the island made it possible for long, horizontal branches to cross the gap and put down roots to form nodal trunks on the rocky island, itself. The river bridge thus created was one of many up and down this stretch of river, where it plunged and roared its way down out of the steep crags toward the valley far below.

Swift Striker loved this place, where rushing water foamed and swirled into deep, dark pools of mystery and lurking fish. He excelled at spotting them from above, at tracking them carefully, cautiously, waiting . . . then flash! He struck true, centimeter-long claws sinking into the wriggling, wet body an arm's length under the surface. Fur soaked and dripping, Swift Striker anchored himself with true-feet and tail and used true-hands and hand-feet to drag the heavy, struggling fish out of the water and up onto his branch, where he bit it neatly through the spine, killing it instantly. Nearly two-thirds as long as himself, Swift Striker's dripping prize would be a welcome addition to the cook fires tonight. Unwinding his carry net from his waist, he tied the fish securely and loaded it onto his back. His whiskers twitched unpleasantly as water soaked into his back fur, but the sweet, delicate flavor of baked fish tantalized his imagination with promised delights.

Fishing was easier, he chuckled to himself as he set off along the rough-barked branches toward Laughing River Clan's central nesting place, when it was done with large nets and many true-hands and hand-feet to do the hauling. But the dull work of dragging a netful of wriggling captives onto the shore could never compare with the delight of the flashing strike and the exhilaration of catching a canny old monster unawares and dragging it up onto a sturdy branch with one's bare claws. Swift Striker wasn't the only one of the People who felt that way, either; younglings approaching the age where they would first be taught the ways of the hunt begged him to show his secrets and even oldsters whose prime had long since passed smiled at the memory of their own long hours spent crouched above a deep pool, peering down into sunlit green depths, patiently waiting for just the right instant.

Sounding deep waters to tease out the riches hidden within was in his blood, a passion and a joy shared with a few, select others who understood in their hearts what it was that drew him again and again to the branches overhanging the deep pools and fissured holes in the rushing, whitewater river. It was this joy, a glow like a bright hearth fire on an ice-bitter winter day, that brought Swift Striker to an abrupt, quivering halt on a branch high above a roaring cascade of water, grass-green eyes dilating in shock as he tasted it from a completely unexpected direction. The mind glow beating against his awareness was as hot and powerful as a raging, forest-deep wildfire, crackling and alive and immense. He had never tasted anything like it—yet knew in an instant what it was, for the memory singers of his clan had repeated the memory songs of Bright Water Clan, of the impossible, awe-striking bond which had formed between a Bright Water scout and one of the two-leg strangers who had come from the skies.

Two-legs!

Swift Striker trembled with sheer delight as the power of the two-leg's mind glow and his own astonishment rolled through him. Then, shaking himself as though he'd fallen headlong into the water and dripped with waterlogged fur, Swift Striker crept slowly forward along his branch and peered cautiously down through the thick leaves into the dizzying drop of water and vegetation along the river's boulder-strewn banks. Two-legs had never come this deep into the mountains, had never been spotted anywhere near Laughing River Clan's home range. What were they doing here? Had they come to build nesting places of stone and not-wood, like those he'd seen in the memory songs received from other clans?

Poking his muzzle through an opening in the dark green leaves, Swift Striker scanned the rocky watercourse and spotted a bright flash of fiery color against the dark green foliage. Swift Striker stared, entranced, at the creature below. The two-leg was standing almost immobile in a pool of shadow where the great overhanging branches crossed the water to another small islet mid-stream, where another nodal trunk grew from stony soil to spread the great tree to the far bank. Quivers of excitement raced through Swift Striker, from the end of his sensitive nose to the tip of his bushy, prehensile tail, which twitched irresistibly now as he gazed for the first time at one of the newcomers to his world.

Unlike any of the two-legs in the memory songs his clan's memory singers had relayed, this one's head fur was as bright as a blazing fire, as full of unpredictable curls as a twisting vine. Like the two-legs Swift Striker had seen in the memory songs, its face was bare of fur, all smooth skin, pale, yet oddly speckled with a scattering of spots and splotches of golden hue, leaving the strange skin as mottled and subtle as the markings on Swift Striker's pelt.

Tall and angular, the two-leg seemed denuded of limbs, possessing only four, yet it possessed also an eerie, alien sort of beauty where it stood motionless on a boulder, peering intently into the deep water of a rocky pool, as delighted to be there and occupied by the challenge of capturing a prize fish as Swift Striker himself had been just minutes previously. The two-leg had no claws in its stubby fingers with which to secure a wriggling captive, and its true-feet were encased in heavy, cumbersome coverings that hid its feet from view. In fact, the two-leg's entire body was swathed in body coverings of enticingly strange stuff, differing colors and textures of it.

The two-leg held a long, slender rod of something that at first glance looked like wood, but upon closer inspection could not have been wood that grew from any plant Swift Striker had ever seen. The not-wood rod gleamed white, like winter ice, and sported odd, glinting bits and curlicues as silver as any fish's armor. A long, exceedingly thin, almost colorless cord trailed from it into the deep water of the pool. That cord was narrower than one of Swift Striker's claws. How had the two-legs braided such a thin cord? And what plant fiber had they used, to make it shimmer with almost no color at all?

As Swift Striker watched, entranced, the creature's hand—as speckled as its face—moved, touched something at the side of its pole, and the line blurred into motion, reeling back up to the tip of the quivering rod. A flick of the two-leg's wrist sent the line singing through the air again and a glinting, furry-looking thing at the end plopped into the deep water behind a boulder, its aim perfect despite the difficulty such a cast must have presented. Swift Striker didn't think he could have tossed a line from a pole into such a small pool without many hours of practice, not without striking the rocks, tangling it in the thick, overhead branches, or watching it skitter away down the rushing current where the river poured down between jutting grey rocks in a froth of angry white water.

Swift Striker settled comfortably on his branch, ignoring the steady drip of his own catch as it shed water into his fur, and waited, true-hands tucked under his chin, entranced by the two-leg below his perch. Cast after cast angled out above the roaring water and landed with sharp, quiet plopping sounds in the dark green depths. It occurred to him, after watching this curious ritual for several minutes, that the blurry thing on the end of the line looked and sounded like a fat, wriggling bug that had fallen into the water. The notion brought his ears pricking forward. He'd seen deep-dwelling fish rise from the gloomy depths to snap up such morsels when they plopped clumsily into the water. The idea that a fisher could trick his prey into mistaking a false bug for a real one caused his whiskers to tremble with intense interest.

Below, the line sang through the air again and the false bug popped into the still, deep water—which boiled abruptly as something enormous surged upward. A flare of intense excitement from the two-leg's mind glow caught Swift Striker with a shock of pleasure. His claws arched out, biting into the branch as though he'd sunk them deep into a struggling fish. Then the line was singing and the pole's tip bent nearly to the surface of the water. An enormous fish, bigger than Swift Striker, himself, surged up out of the depths, trapped somehow on the end of the line. His pulse raced. He found himself half-crouching along the branch, having surged to true-feet and hand-feet in his excitement. The monstrous fish lunged and fought like a maddened death fang at the end of the cord. Water sprayed in arching droplets as the enormous, glinting fish fought at the end of the two-leg's line. How could such a flimsy little cord hold the frantic weight of such a monster? The two-leg burst into motion, abandoning its shadowed perch on the enormous boulder. It splashed straight into the river, soaking its strange body coverings in an instant, fighting to keep the tip of its pole above the surface, slowly and inexorably reeling in the line and the struggling captive on the other end.

Feet slithering and sliding on the submerged boulders, the two-leg battled its prize and panted its visible delight. Its eyes glowed like sunlight on a deep blue lake, its golden-speckled skin flushed with reddish color that hadn't been there moments previously, when it had stood silently on the bank, waiting as Swift Striker, himself, knew so patiently how to wait. At last, after a battle that would have left Swift Striker exhausted, the deceptively fragile-looking line drew up short and the two-leg hauled the great fish up out of the water. Clear, unexpected sound rippled from the two-leg, bright and burbling, a strangely perfect accompaniment to the fierce glow of delight from its mind. The dripping fish was longer than the two-leg's arm, and the two-leg's arm was longer than Swift Striker, but the two-leg hoisted the fish with such ease it left Swift Striker gasping in surprise. It would have taken many of the clan's hunters to drag such a fish from the water; yet the two-leg held it one-handed, wading now back toward the shore and the boulder it had abandoned.

Strong as well as tall, he realized with a sense of wonder and discovery. The joy the two-leg felt to be wading through the swift current, its prize hanging from one hand, while the sun filtered down warmly through the trees and the rush of the river filled the air with music touched a chord deep inside his heart. *Not so different, then,* he sighed happily, beginning to understand how the Bright Water Clan's scout had been so drawn to the two-leg youngling it had somehow bonded with. His own clan had argued the merits of Bright Water Clan's decision that the two-legs should be studied directly, that those of the People who could, should try to establish such bonds as the now-crippled Climbs Quickly of Bright Water had done, to learn all that could be learned of these newcomers.

Swift Striker had felt a keen sense of excitement, listening to the Bright Water memory songs, had found his own heart pounding with the same terror and grim determination Climbs Quickly had felt, facing down a death fang alone, knowing he could not win, in a battle to save his two-leg youngling. Laughing River Clan had finally reached agreement that Bright Water Clan had been right to decide that the two-legs should be sought out and studied, particularly since the youngling two-leg had leaped, broken and injured as it was, to defend the fallen Bright Water Scout from the ravening death fang, as fierce in

protecting her friend as Swift Striker would have been in
protecting any member of Laughing River Clan.

But two-legs never came to the deep mountains where Laughing River Clan's central nesting place lay. They never even
passed overhead in their great flying machines that carried them
through the air with such astonishing speed, like the one that
had carried the broken, cruelly injured Climbs Quickly away
to be healed in the two-legs' nesting place. Swift Striker had
sorrowed that he would not be likely ever to meet a two-leg
or be given such a chance which Climbs Quickly and others
of the People had been given to bond with a two-leg, as the
People came cautiously out of a hiding that had lasted for so
many turnings of the seasons.

Yet here he was, clinging to a branch, enthralled by the wondrous brightness of this two-leg's mind glow, with no idea where
the two-leg had come from or how it had come to be so far
from the nearest two-leg nesting places, so close to him that
Swift Striker could hear as well as taste the laughter in its
voice and its bubbling, chaotic mind glow. The Bright Water
memory songs were accurate about two-leg minds, as well. His
delighted two-leg *was* mind-blind, his mind glow a churning
mass of emotions without any conscious thoughts forming from
them, as the People were so adept at doing, yet he glimpsed
a depth of intelligence in that mind glow, an intelligence that
tantalized and drew Swift Striker with a strength he did not
even want to resist. He found himself moving forward through
the branches, down and toward the riverbank, wanting nothing more than to peer into his two-leg's water-bright eyes and
touch its strange, hairless face and learn everything he could
possibly learn from the bewitching depths of this creature's
bright mind.

Swift Striker had nearly reached the boulder the two-leg was
wading back toward when it happened. The giant fish was still
struggling and flopping at the end of its line, ponderous and
heavy, and the two-leg was moving through a roaring swirl
of white water between rounded, massive boulders, watching
sharply for its uncertain footing in the foaming water. The
fish lunged just as the two-leg was placing a foot between
boulders, searching for an anchored footing. The two-leg was
jerked off balance. It uttered a short, sharp sound and started
to fall sideways. A scorching flare of surprise and pain swept
outward from its mind glow, blasting across Swift Striker where
he paused, rigid with abrupt alarm, on a swaying branch.

Then the two-leg fell heavily, the leg still planted in the swirling water twisting out from under it with a sharp shock of

pain through the ankle. It smashed down heavily, striking half-submerged boulders with its back and shoulders and head. Pain smashed across Swift Striker, left him momentarily blind with agony. The huge, armored fish, still lunging and fighting, crashed down across the two-leg's head and shoulders, crushing the two-leg's skull against unyielding rock. White-hot, blinding pain caught Swift Striker so hard he cried out with a sharp bleek of distress. Then darkness smashed down, erasing all but a thready trickle of that bright, powerful mind glow.

Swift Striker huddled frozen in place, deeply shocked. The great fish flopped away, lying trapped in the swirling water downstream. For just an instant longer, Swift Striker clung motionless to his branch, while the two-leg sprawled insanely across the boulders, half buried in the raging water. A dark stain leaked from its head, smearing the white water an ugly shade of red.

Then Swift Striker was moving, racing along the branches, flowing out above the angry river along the rough-barked wood that crossed like a bridge toward the distant island. The heavy fish strapped to his back hindered him. He tore impatiently at the knots of his carry net and freed it, dropping the fish with a negligent splash into the water, then swarmed down trailing branches that came within a few hand-spans of the two-leg's still form. A chill passed down Swift Striker's spine when he realized the two-leg had fallen with its face partially in the water, its nose and mouth lying just under the foaming surface. Another few moments of immersion and it would drown!

He used tail and true-feet to cling upside down from a branch just above the two-leg's head and tugged at its brightly curled head fur, lifting with all his strength. He managed to pull the furless face clear of the water and heard the shallow, ragged breaths it drew, but he couldn't possibly hold the two-leg's head like this for more than a few moments. Already the muscles along his arms and legs and back burned with the strain of holding up the heavy head. The carry net, still looped around his middle, flopped down his belly, hanging limp. The idea that flashed into his mind had him wrenching at the remaining knots with his hand-feet, freeing the net completely. He looped the net downward, snagging the two-leg's face in it, then strained and pulled and struggled to drag the carry loops up over the snagging branch from which he dangled.

The ropes slid over a sturdy fork in the rough-barked branch and held fast. The two-leg's face hung in the net, just clear of the water rushing past its oddly shaped nose, but it could

breathe now, safe as Swift Striker could make it until it woke
again. The pain in the two-leg's mind throbbed even with that
mind lost in unconsciousness. Swift Striker whimpered softly,
unable to erase that pain and needing to do just that, more
than he could recall ever having needed to do anything in his
life. Moving gingerly, still clinging upside down from the branch,
Swift Striker parted the silky, flame-colored head fur to peer
critically at a gash along the back which still bled. Angry
swelling already spread outward and the flesh was hotter there
than elsewhere. Another gash crossed the upper portion of the
two-leg's face above its eyes, where the huge fish had crashed
down against its head. The bruising here was even worse and
the bones felt wrong, as though the blow from the enormous,
armor-scaled fish had broken them. The blood leaking slowly
down the boulder from the great cuts alarmed Swift Striker.

He narrowed his eyes, recalling the memory song his clan's
memory singers had sung, of the two-leg youngling which had
halted Climbs Quickly's terrible bleeding where the death fang's
claws had torn the scout so cruelly. She had wrapped a cord
around the injury and tightened it down. But Swift Striker's
two-leg had not suffered injuries on a forelimb, which could
be tied off with cord, they bled from his head. Still, if he tied
something down tightly across the gashes, the bleeding might
stop. The two-leg's body coverings certainly provided sufficient
materials for such a wrapping.

Swift Striker shifted along the branch with his true-feet and
altered position cautiously, fumbling for his flint knife, then
tugged at a section of the covering over the two-leg's motionless arm. Sawing carefully, Swift Striker separated long strips
from the body covering, then moved gingerly, having to work
through the carry net he'd looped around the two-leg's face.
It was awkward work, but after a brief struggle, Swift Striker
succeeded in tying the strips down over both gashes. Blood,
dark red and terrifying, soaked into them, but the flow slowed
and gradually stopped. The two-leg remained unconscious, but
it was still alive.

Swift Striker stroked the smooth skin of the two-leg's cheek,
crooning anxiously. Touching the two-leg like this sent shocks
of strange pleasure through Swift Striker. Its head fur was
longer, silkier than his own, yet the face, so smooth and soft,
was not entirely hairless, he now realized. Tufts of fur grew
above its closed eyes, in an arching curve, and its jaw and
cheeks bore a fuzzy shadow of hair, as though the two-leg had
scraped its face against something so abrasive it had rubbed
all the hair off right down to the skin. The prickle of remaining

stubble was rough-smooth under his hands through the webbing of his carry net, the golden-mottled skin icy pale.

Swift Striker scented the wind, but could catch no trace of any danger, certainly not the stink of a death fang or the musky odor of a snow hunter. Death fangs, while not overly bright, knew better than to come this deep under the trees of a clan's home range, and snow hunters tended to keep to the high slopes and craggy peaks of the mountains. It ought to be safe enough to risk. Swift Striker let go with his tail and true-feet and landed softly on the boulder next to his stricken two-leg. He chittered softly in anxiety, able to do nothing else to help. Far too large and heavy to drag clear of the icy water, the two-leg would have to remain where it was until it regained consciousness.

Crooning anxiously, Swift Striker stroked the two-leg's bright, wet hair and waited.

Consciousness returned reluctantly, in patchy bits and pieces of confusion. Blinding pain through Scott's head dominated awareness for an uncertain stretch of time. Eventually other stimuli made themselves felt. Cold water rushed across portions of him, leaving him numb in several places and shivering all over. Deep-lying aches the length of his back told of injuries to muscle and soft tissue. His ankle throbbed inside his high-topped wading boot. Unyielding rock dug into his shoulder and ribs and thigh. An unfamiliar roaring in his ears gradually settled into the recognizable sound of rushing water. Memory, splintered and broken, stirred. He had been wading through a rocky stream, had lost his footing. He must be lying in the water, then, with rocks under him.

That made sense.

But something lay across his face, cutting into the skin like a web of ropes, and that *didn't* make sense. He stirred sluggishly, then bit back sour bile and a need to groan. For long moments, the only roaring he could hear was the pounding of blood in his ears as his whole head threatened to detach itself from his shoulders and go spinning away on the current like a child's balsa-wood raft. By the time his head had decided it would remain attached, after all, Scott knew he was in serious trouble. He was a medical doctor, after all, knew the signs and symptoms of shock and concussion as well as any other medical professional on Sphinx.

The fact that he lay sprawled in an icy mountain river, unable to move, while sporting all the classic textbook symptoms of head injury and physical shock, hundreds of kilometers

from the nearest hospital and several dozen meters from the
shelter of his air car, left Scott MacDallan cold with a fear
such as he had never known in his life. An aching, burning
crick in his neck prompted him to try, gingerly, to ease his
head into a slightly different position. He bit his lips and moved
his head fractionally, swallowing back a cry of pain, and realized
the sensation of webbing across his face was not an illusion.

Scott blinked slowly, wincing at the stab of light through
his skull when he opened his eyes, and made a discovery that
left him suspended between broken thoughts. His face lay
tangled in the mesh of a hand-knotted net of some kind, which
supported the weight of his head and left his nose mere mil-
limeters clear of the water. How in the world had he come
to be lying face down with his head in a net? Moving his arm
left Scott gulping down bile, but his arm did work, even though
the abused muscles in shoulders and neck shrieked their protest. He felt gingerly at his head, blinked stupidly as his fingers encountered rough knots and what felt like strips of cloth
around his forehead and down the back of his aching skull.
The netting was taut, looped, he discovered, over a low-hanging
tree limb. When he brought his hand down again, it came away
dark with blood.

At first, the low crooning sound didn't even register. He was
lying there, trying to decide when and how he'd managed to
tie bandages around his head during a state of concussed coma,
when he realized that his fear was rapidly ebbing away. That
was when the nearly subliminal sound that was sinking down
through the pain in his head, soothing him, somehow, registered.

He blinked with a tremendous effort and managed to look
up . . . and grass-green eyes peered anxiously right into his.

Scott came up out of the water with a convulsive yell. Then
sprawled across the boulder, vomiting helplessly while agony
lanced deep into his brain. He felt tiny, gentle hands touch
his head, his cheek and brow, knew instinctively that the
creature crouched beside him—whatever it was—not only meant
him no harm, it was trying to help. He didn't know *how* he
knew that; he just knew it, as surely as he knew he would
die out here if he didn't get out of this freezing water and
down the mountain and into the nearest available hospital. For
all of humanity's medical miracles, conquering diseases and
developing human cloning and other gene-manipulating technologies, even limited cybernetic enhancements, simple, stupid accident still accounted for an appalling number of deaths,
particularly on new colony worlds like Sphinx. Scott lay there

shuddering for long moments, huddled across the boulder, fighting the nausea in the pit of his belly, aware that he was quite probably going to be the next accidental death recorded in Sphinx's official records.

At length, gaining sufficient strength, he groped cautiously at the net still tangled across his face. He could feel other hands moving deftly, as well, working at the back of his head and above him. Then the net came loose and he was free. He blinked slowly and found a long, sinuous shape of mottled cream and grey fur busily winding the net around its middle, using its four upper-most limbs in a graceful fashion.

A treecat...!

As the shock of that sank dimly through his aching head, it occurred to Scott MacDallan that if the treecat hadn't wound that net around his face and looped it over that branch, he would have drowned long before regaining consciousness. His throat ran dry at the realization that this tiny animal had deliberately and quite cleverly saved his life. The treecat huddled down, crooning softly, and touched its face to Scott's, rubbing soft fur against his cheek in a gesture clearly meant to comfort and reassure. Wonder seeped through the fear and pain holding him prisoner. It gradually occurred to him that he needed to start thinking about a way to survive this predicament. And to do that, he had to get out of this icy water.

Scott inched his way awkwardly higher onto the boulder, trying to drag more of himself out of the river's freezing clutches, then clamped shut his jaws and explored his injuries more thoroughly, finding blood-soaked bandages of some kind which the treecat had clearly tied in place around the gashes in his head. When he probed the back of his skull, Scott groaned. But when he touched his brow, a bomb detonated behind his eyelids and icy panic came up with the vomit as he spewed helplessly into the river, fighting a pain in his head that he knew would kill him very soon if he didn't get help and get it fast.

Even if his skull wasn't broken, which it might be, with hairline fractures, the concussion alone was bad enough that he might not even be able to stand up, much less hike down the river to the distant bend where he'd parked his air car. He tried keying in the code for the Twin Forks emergency operations center on his wrist com, but nothing happened. The com unit was damaged, its circuitry broken from the fall against the boulders. He had a backup com unit in his backpack, but that was several meters away, across a rushing stretch of boulder-strewn river and up a sloping riverbank and back under the nearest spreading picket wood tree. Unless he could get his injured self out of this river and all the way up to that pack, he couldn't even call for help.

Black terror lapped at his awareness, rising out of a bottomless chasm in a flood far colder than the river he lay sprawled in. And straight through that terror, a sudden, unexpected warmth enfolded Scott, nudged him back from the edge of that terrifying black pit, drew him up out of panic and back to an awareness of the sunlit river and the touch of tiny, alien hands on his cheeks. He caught raggedly at the air and managed to open his eyelids into the harsh glare of sunlight. The treecat huddled down in front of him, crooning in distress. A moment later, it nestled right against him, pressing its warm body as close to his heart as it could hold itself. Three pairs of hands and feet gripped his shirt firmly, as if saying, *I'm not going to let you go*. The warmth and love rolling through him drew a broken sound from Scott. His panic and fear ebbed away with the wetness spilling down his face.

With a concussion and shock and blood loss to overcome and a broad stretch of treacherous ground to cover before he could even reach his communications gear, the odds against his survival had gone up immeasurably . . . but he wasn't quite alone.

Swift Striker huddled as close to his two-leg as he could press himself and sank deeper into the bonding trance. The two-leg's mind glow was similar enough to that of the People that he could, after a fashion, establish a bond, even though the two-leg clearly couldn't complete it. But he was able to drain away the ragged, cutting terror that rolled out of the two-leg's mind, aware of a not-quite-rightness that differed from the taste of his two-leg's mind-glow just before the disastrous fall against the rocks. Swift Striker had seen a youngling suffer damage to his head, once, when the youngling had mistimed a jump between branches. The disastrous fall hadn't been fatal, but the smashing blow of the youngling's head against the ground where he'd landed had left the youngling's mind glow crippled forever afterward. He'd been completely unable to form clear thoughts after that terrible fall. Less than half a season later, the youngling had quietly suicided.

The two-leg's terror and the broken taste of its mind glow reminded Swift Striker fearfully of that tragedy. He poured love and reassurance through the bond, determined to protect this wonderful, bright-haired creature, to get it safely back to its own kind. And he would stay with the two-leg, croon to it . . .

to *him*, he realized, sinking deeper into the trance . . . would keep him from the despair the mind-blind youngling had felt, if it were in Swift Striker's power to do so. The two-legs were used to being mind-blind, after all; perhaps Swift Striker's constant reassurances would help enough, whatever was actually wrong inside his head?

Determined to succeed, Swift Striker steadied the frantic chaos in his two-leg's mind glow, eased his fright, soothed and crooned and drew away the physical hurting and the sharp emotional pain, as best he could. The two-leg's pounding heartbeat gradually relaxed into a less frantic, only slightly irregular knocking and his breathing steadied down and his muscles turned from stone back to pliant flesh again. His two-leg was still afraid, but the blinding, jagged terror had gone.

Swift Striker rubbed his head against the two-leg's wet cheek and burbled softly, then pulled his head back and touched the two-leg's face with one true-hand. < *You must get out of this cold water,* > he thought firmly.

It was no use, of course. The two-leg was mind-blind and couldn't understand. But when Swift Striker pointed urgently toward the shore, his two-leg made some strange mouth noises that comprised two-leg language and stirred a little. The two-leg's emotional aura tasted now of faint, renewed hope and determination to try. A youngling of the People, so injured, would never have been able to accomplish what his two-leg must if he were to survive. Swift Striker scented the wind and listened hard for any hint of danger on the shore, then bleeked encouragement. Not even if Swift Striker summoned the entire Laughing River Clan, could he hope to carry his new friend to safety. His two-leg must save himself—with whatever feeble help Swift Striker could lend.

He feared it would not be enough.

The treecat blinked solemnly into Scott's eyes, still pointing toward shore, then made a soft sound. "Bleek?"

Scott reached up, hand wet and shaking and smeared red. He hesitated, then dunked his fingers into the freezing water to rinse off the blood. The treecat sat very still, permitting the touch of Scott's dripping hand and unsteady fingers. *Soft as dandelion down* . . . The treecat closed grass-green eyes as Scott stroked damp fur, then arched its long back and made a sound very like a buzzing purr. Through the blinding pain, the fear, and the freezing ache of numbing water where it rushed across his lower legs, dangling down from the boulder, Scott MacDallan smiled, enchanted.

The treecat sat up, peering into his eyes, then tilted its head and raised one arm, unmistakably pointing toward the bank once again. *Yeah, good idea,* Scott agreed muzzily. *Gotta get out of this freezing water.* Standing up was out of the question, however. Scott hunched himself into a semi-foetal position on his side, then eased his way gingerly over toward hands and knees. His head mushroomed and he gagged; but he made it onto knees and palms without vomiting. Scott knelt on the boulder, knees and feet in the rushing water, head low, trembling, and willed the nausea back. Water splashed up across his bare arm and he realized dimly that the strips of cloth around his head had been torn from his sleeve—or, rather, cut from it, given the sharp, straight lines and clean edges of those cuts. *Clever treecat, marv'lous treecat...*

He started to crawl toward the distant bank.

The slender, six-limbed creature hopped from boulder to boulder, dancing just ahead of him as he crawled. It bleeked in steady encouragement as Scott dragged himself from one rock to another, sometimes collapsing against sun-warmed stone to pant and rest. Whenever Scott paused, pulling himself half out of the water just long enough to catch his breath and gulp back the murderous nausea in his throat, occasionally immersed up to his armpits and thighs in rushing, cold water, he would look up to find the treecat just in front of him, sitting on the next boulder, waiting with an air of anxious worry.

If he stopped too long, the treecat bleeked urgently, a low, distressed sound, then hopped back to the boulder Scott clung to and touched one tiny hand to his face, urging him to motion again. When, some unknown stretch of time later, he collapsed across a rough-edged boulder, aware that he couldn't possibly go on, he was so exhausted, the treecat grew frantic.

"Bleek! *Bleek-bleek-bleek!*"

How many times that sound repeated, he wasn't sure, but the sharp cry finally penetrated the icy fog in his brain. Scott looked up slowly, shaking and cold with more than the freezing river swirling around him, and blinked up into uncanny, summer-grass eyes. The treecat's gaze bored into his own, visibly *willing* him to rouse himself from fatal stupor. The treecat grasped his face in both hands, the tiny fingers warm and supple, claws sheathed. The curiously firm gesture had the effect of a rousing slap. Scott felt some of the rising flood of hopelessness seep away.

He could almost sense, at the very edges of his awareness, the treecat's fright. Under other circumstances, Scott might have convinced himself he was hallucinating the treecat's fear as

a result of the head injury. But as he lay there, tasting his
companion's rising alarm, with one of its hands on his face
and its other hand pointing urgently toward the riverbank, Scott
found himself profoundly believing that his treecat was genuinely afraid for his life in the icy river.

That fear got Scott moving again. *You kept me from drowning, can't let you down now . . .* He slithered and splashed face-
first into the water again, half-crawling and half-floating to
the next rock, dragged sideways by the savage current and
fighting to keep his battered head above the surface. Had he
been alone, Scott knew he would've just lain there and died.

He'd been crawling for what felt like hours, promising himself
he could collapse at the very next boulder he reached, when
Scott realized the water was so shallow only his wrists and
knees remained immersed. With the infinite slowness of a
grinding glacier, he lifted his head, biting at his lips to hold
back the nausea. Sunlight shimmered in a painful haze across
a glare of rocks and clay which rose in front of him, dry and
baking hot in the sunlight.

He'd reached the riverbank.

A ghastly sound escaped him, defying translation; but he
was clawing and scrabbling at the rocks, digging in with fingers that sank into the soft clay, hauling and scraping himself upward, out of the river's deadly clutch. The rock was
hot and wonderful under his belly, driving away some of the
icy chill on his bones. Then the ground flattened out under
him and Scott collapsed forward onto a sun-warmed ledge above
the river, shaking violently. As exhaustion lapped at the edges
of his awareness, dragging him down toward oblivion, Scott's
last conscious sensation was the touch of tiny, three-fingered
hands against his cheek.

When, at last, the two-leg reached the rocky shore and
dragged himself, shaking and weak, onto the bank, Swift Striker
crooned approvingly and touched his wet face, trying to urge
him higher onto the bank, under the safety of the trees. But
the struggle with the icy river and the terrible injuries had
taken their toll; his two-leg collapsed utterly and slid into
unconsciousness, clearly exhausted beyond his ability to keep
going. His wonderful, smooth skin, mottled with those beautiful flecks of gold, was chilly to the touch. His two-leg needed
a fire to warm him.

Swift Striker swarmed up into the trees, searching for deadwood, using his true-hands and the flint knife and hand-axe
tied to his waist belt to break and hack pieces loose, then

dropped branches to the ground until he had a respectable pile. It wasn't enough to warm a creature the size of his two-leg for long, but it would help. Tail flicking in agitation, Swift Striker darted to the ground again and piled the rough branches to make what would be the largest fire he'd ever started. He used his knife to scrape bark and wood shavings for tinder, then set about striking his fire flint to shower sparks down into the dry bark and shavings.

He blew gently across the smouldering sparks and fed twigs into the flames—and grew aware of an intense, burningly curious gaze from his two-leg. Swift Striker looked up and found wide, water-blue eyes watching him, the surprise in his mind glow spilling over into delight as the bright fire crackled and licked at the larger branches. The exhausted two-leg made more mouth noises, which Swift Striker determined he would have to set about learning as quickly as possible, since the two-leg could never learn to speak the way the People did. Then the two-leg's mouth opened slightly in a curious gesture, the wide, strangely shaped lips lifting at the corners. The wonder in his mind glow told Swift Striker the odd grimace was an expression of pleasure.

He bleeked happily and fed more wood to the flames.

His two-leg stirred at length, looking around their immediate vicinity, then hunched forward on his side. His hand closed over a branch too large for Swift Striker to drag and pulled it closer to the fire. Swift Striker sat up on his haunches, surprised again by the two-leg's strength. He'd planned to use his hand-axe to chop the limb into more manageable chunks, but the two-leg dragged the whole thing with ease, injured as he was. The two-leg fumbled at a part of his body coverings which circled his hips, then pulled something loose, some sort of tool, by the look of it, although Swift Striker couldn't imagine what it might be for.

A vibrating hum startled him. Then *something* sprang into existence beyond the two-leg's hand, projecting out of the oddly shaped tool he held. Whatever it was, it sliced through the heavy branch as though passing through empty air. In seconds, a limb nearly as thick as Swift Striker's whole body and three times longer was reduced to kindling. Swift Striker's whiskers twitched and trembled in excitement. He wanted to look at the marvelous tool, yet feared that without knowing how to properly use it, he would do himself a grievous injury. His own flint knife felt clumsy and ridiculous by comparison. The People *must* learn more of the two-legs!

Once the cut-up branch was blazing brightly, the two-leg did something that caused the tool's hum to stop and replaced the marvelous knife-tool in some kind of holder at his hip. The fire crackled invitingly and the two-leg hunched closer to its blazing heat. He closed his eyes, huddling as close as he could get without igniting his curly red head fur, then lay still for long minutes. Swift Striker fed the fire with more of the big branch, running his true-hands over the perfectly smooth, flat edges, and wondered what other marvels the two-legs possessed. Slowly, the two-leg's dripping hair and skin dried in the warmth of the hot fire. His body coverings remained wet, but they had ceased to drip, now, and the front of his chest-covering was beginning to show dry in patches, as well.

When, eventually, the wood ran out and the fire began to die back, the two-leg stirred, opening his eyes once more. Fingers capable of such enormous power touched Swift Striker's fur, trembling and weak as a newborn kitten. Water spilled from the bright blue eyes and dripped down gold-speckled cheeks and his breaths shortened as his emotional distress deepened, coming in short, ragged gasps. The agony of fear and loneliness in his two-leg's mind was unbearable.

Swift Striker huddled close again, wrapping his tail around the two-leg's arm, stroking his head against the two-leg's cheek, focusing all his own energy on quieting the deep currents of fear and despair he could taste so strongly in the two-leg's broken mind. It seemed to help. His breaths deepened and water ceased to flow from his eyes. A few soft mouth noises came, gusting across Swift Striker's fur with his breath, then his two-leg struggled to sit up. Swift Striker crooned and pushed gently against his two-leg's shoulder, lending what little strength he could. His two-leg sat panting for a moment, then touched Swift Striker's fur and stroked gently down his back once again. He arched and purred ecstatically, reveling in the caress, so unlike anything he'd ever experienced.

His two-leg made low mouth noises, then pointed away under the trees, down river. The gesture was unmistakable. His two-leg wanted to go down the riverbank, for some unknown but imperative reason. The urgency Swift Striker felt from his mind glow was a bright furnace, impossible to ignore. There was something in that direction which his two-leg needed, desperately. And his two-leg was peering through the brush, as well, clearly hunting for something closer at hand. Swift Striker sat up on his rear-most limbs, looking—had he known—something like a Terran ferret with one pair too many feet and a head far more feline than weaselish. Swift Striker peered intently into the deep shadows beneath the trees and spotted what his two-leg must be searching for. A heavy-looking sack of some not-leather substance lay at the foot of a tree. A long, tube-like, not-wood rod, thicker than the pole he'd used for fishing, leaned against the tree trunk beside it.

Swift Striker had never seen one of the thunder-bark tools, but Song Crooner had sung the oldest of the memory songs, from Blue Mountain Dancing Clan and Fire Runs Fast Clan, which showed clear images of such tools being used to kill a charging death fang when the two-legs had first been sighted in the world. Clearly, this was what his two-leg searched for. Swift Striker bleeked excitedly and pointed toward the alien tools. The two-leg's lips quivered upward again and a wave of pleasure rolled across him, leaving Swift Striker burbling with happiness. His two-leg crawled toward the tools, moving with pained shakiness, and finally gained the tree where he'd left them. He ignored the long tube and dug into the not-leather sack, instead, bringing out another oddly shaped tool whose function Swift Striker could not fathom.

His two-leg made mouth noises at it, then fell silent. The tool sputtered strangely—*then two-leg voices came from inside it!* Swift Striker uttered a sharp sound of amazement and crept forward, staring. The tool spoke again, with a voice that was clearly a two-leg, yet Swift Striker knew that no two-leg could possibly fit inside that tiny little box, nor could he taste the mind glow or catch the scent of another two-leg anywhere nearby.

His own two-leg made the pleasure grimace at him, then made more mouth noises into the tool. But his two-leg's glow of pleasure was short-lived. Swift Striker felt a rising tide of worry from him as the tool spoke again and his two-leg listened in growing agitation. Then he peered toward the sky, clearly trying to see upward through the trees. Swift Striker could taste his frustration and sense of helplessness as he sat huddled at the base of the tree, listening to the bodiless voice from the tool. What could his two-leg want to see in the sky? Swift Striker scented the wind for clues. He could smell nothing out of the ordinary, although the wind was heavy with the scent of approaching rain.

—*Rain?*

"*Bleek!*"

Swift Striker swarmed up the tree trunk, racing through the tangle of branches until he clung to the thin twigs at the very canopy of the forest. Wind fingers ruffled through his fur as he peered up toward the distant mountain peaks. Dark storm clouds gathered on the mountain above them, thick with the promise of driving rain and lightning. Such storms were so common in the spring season, Swift Striker hadn't really paid much attention to the signs of the coming deluge. He didn't have far to travel to his clan's central nesting place, after all, and could easily outrun any storm to reach the snug, woven shelter waiting for him.

But his wounded two-leg could barely sit up, unaided.

The coming storm would slash down across them with unbridled fury. Nor was there any shelter his two-leg could reach that would protect him from the coming wind and rain and—if he tasted the scent of that wind right—hailstones, as well. Swift Striker had no idea how the two-leg had known the storm was coming, but clearly he had, or at least, the two-leg voice from the tool had known, for the voice had spoken and his own two-leg had tried to see the sky, worry suddenly thick in his mind glow. And he was right to worry, Swift Striker realized bleakly, watching the clouds boil down from the mountain peaks. There was no guessing how far away the nearest two-legs must be, so Swift Striker couldn't even begin to guess how soon others of his kind might be able to rescue him. It couldn't be soon enough, not even if they came in one of the flying tools like the one that had carried away the injured Climbs Quickly and his youngling—

Flying tools!

Of course! Swift Striker's two-leg *must* have used one to come this far from the nearest two-leg nesting places. That meant he must have left it somewhere close by. If his two-leg could reach it before the storm broke, it would provide shelter from the slashing hail storm on its way down the mountainside. From his vantage at the top of the trees, Swift Striker scanned the forest canopy, wondering where the two-leg might have left his machine. He knew what two-leg flying machines looked like, from the Bright Water Clan memory songs and those of clans which lived closer to two-leg habitations. And his two-leg had pointed down river, wanting to go that direction.

The wind was whipping through the treetops, swinging his perch in dizzy arcs, when Swift Striker finally spotted the clearing at the river's bend. Floods from melting snow had come roaring down the riverbed earlier in the season, smashing into that bend and gouging out whole trees. He had seen it happen before, other spring seasons, both here and along other twists of the river where it raged and tore its way down the mountainside. There was a flat, treeless stretch of ground there, more than large enough to hold a two-leg flying machine. And when the wind whipped the trees in just the right direction, Swift Striker saw a flash of alien, bright color, yellow as the

sun, shiny and strange, and quite large enough to be a curved
section of his two-leg's flying tool. Feeling a sense of triumph
the circumstances probably didn't warrant, Swift Striker
scrambled for safer footing in the lower branches, where the
rising wind didn't reach with quite so fierce a strength, and
raced for the ground and his injured friend.

" . . . no way we can get an air car up there in time, Scott,"
Gifford Bede's voice broke the bad news from Scott's backup
com-link unit. "That's a force-two thunderstorm brewing up
there. Even if we set out now, that storm would drive us back
to town inside thirty minutes. It's going to break over you in
about ten. Can you get to your air car?"

"Yeah, sure," he lied, knowing he couldn't possibly crawl
over terrain that rough in only ten minutes. It had taken him
more than twice that long just to crawl a few meters out of
the river. One glance at the chronometer in his backup com
unit told him more than thirty minutes had passed since he'd
landed that huge fish, so he'd been out cold for nearly *ten*
minutes with his face suspended in his little friend's net. If
he hadn't fallen with his arms and torso draped over a boulder, keeping much of his body mass out of the icy water,
hypothermia would've killed him, making it physically impossible for him to crawl to relative safety on the riverbank. And
now Scott had only ten minutes in which to drag his battered
self several dozen meters down a forested, boulder-strewn
riverbank to the safety of his air car before a force-two
Sphinxian thunderstorm burst over him.

The treecat listened to his exchange with Gifford Bede, then
uttered a curiously sharp, "Bleek!" and took off straight up
the tree trunk at top speed. It vanished into the branches, a
cream-and-grey blur streaking toward the treetops. A stab of
abandonment crushed through Scott, watching the treecat leave.
He leaned against the picket wood's rough-barked trunk and
bit his lower lip and wondered what the hell to do next. He
needed to fashion a walking stick of some kind, because he
needed to make better time than he could simply crawling all
the way to the air car from here, and he needed to wrap his
throbbing ankle to brace the sprain under his flexible boot,
and if he sat here much longer, that storm was going to come
howling down across him like a shrieking banshee and God
alone knew if he'd survive, exposed to the wind, the rain, and
the hail.

"Keep talking to me, Giff," Scott said in a choked voice. "I'm
all by myself out here."

"Roger. Hang on, Scott. Just get to your air car and you'll make it through fine. What's the rest of you look like?"

He explained the wrenched ankle and the need for a splint and walking stick.

"Okay, Scott, we'll talk you through this. You've got a vibro-knife with you, right?"

"Yes, I do. I . . ." He hesitated, looking across to the dying fire. "I used it to cut up a big limb the treecat hacked out of the picket wood I'm under."

The backup com unit crackled with silence for a long moment. "Come again, Scott? Did you say *treecat?*" He could hear the uncertainty in Giff's voice, even through the storm static which interfered with his com unit's signal to the orbital communications system it accessed. At this juncture, it had been only a couple of T-months since little Stephanie Harrington had first been adopted by a treecat and any human contact with the native sentients of Sphinx sent ripples of shock, excitement, and uncertainty through the planet's newest sentients.

"The treecat," he said slowly. "There's a treecat with me. Or there was. He just ran up the picket wood I'm leaning against and disappeared. He was with me out in the river when I woke up." Scott found it surprisingly difficult to say the words, because the implications, the depth of concern shown by one sentient race for another impacted him so deeply and closed up his throat. "He dragged a net around my head. Pulled my face up out of the water, looped the damned net over a tree limb. Kept me from drowning while I was unconscious. And when I dragged myself out of the river, he used some kind of stone tool to chop deadwood out of this big picket wood I'm under, then he started a fire going, I watched him use a flint to strike the sparks with."

"*Good God!*" Gifford Bede's disembodied voice echoed the same naked shock Scott still felt, having witnessed the astonishing things his little arboreal friend had done on his behalf. "You said the treecat's been with you since you woke up?"

"Yeah."

"And he wasn't there before you fell and struck your head?"

"No. At least, not where I could see him, because I've been looking for signs of treecats all day. When I woke up, I was sprawled across a boulder with my face hanging in a net. And he'd cut off part of my sleeve, wrapped compresses around the gashes in my skull. Kept me from bleeding to death, probably."

A rustle overhead drew Scott's attention. He gripped his backup com tighter and started to reach for his rifle. Then hope and a pleasure so intense it astonished him surged as a familiar cream-and-grey shape hurtled down through the branches. The treecat swarmed down the picket wood trunk and dropped lightly beside him. It rested one hand against his and lifted another to point urgently downriver.

"Bleek!"

"*Scott?*" The com crackled with wild static interference from the descending storm. "*What was that sound?*"

"It's the treecat," Scott whispered, awestruck. "He's come back. And he's pointing toward my air car. My God, I think he climbed the tree and *saw* it!"

"Well, if he's telling you to shag your butt out of there, you'd better pay attention. That storm is a mean monster and it's on collision course with your transponder. We're picking up high winds and big hailstones and more lightning than you'll ever want to meet up close and personal."

Given the amount of static shrieking through the com unit's pickup, that didn't come as a surprise. "Roger. I'll do my best, Giff."

"Okay. First, wrap up that ankle, splint it with anything you've got."

Scott rummaged through his haversack, pulling out plastiglass-filament tape and several sections of disassembled fishing rod, the spare he always carried. With his head swimming from the pain in his skull, Scott dragged his knee up until he could reach the throbbing ankle, then tried to hold the fishing-rod sections in place and wrap the plastiglass-filament tape around them. He quickly discovered he needed about four more hands than he currently possessed—and the only ones he did possess were shaking so violently, they were nearly useless. The treecat tipped his head to one side, ears pricked forward, studying the stiff pieces of fiberglass rod that kept toppling over, then bleeked softly.

With deft, three-fingered hands and strong, opposable thumbs, the treecat snatched up the disassembled sections and held them firmly against Scott's ankle, using all four of his upper limbs to hold them in place. Sudden salt stung Scott's eyelids. "Thanks, little buddy," he mumbled, pulling a length of tape loose and winding it around his ankle with shaking hands.

"What's the treecat doing?" Giff asked urgently. Scott knew Gifford Bede would be recording every second of their exchange, now that he knew treecats were involved—just in case Scott didn't make it back to give the xenologists a report.

"He's—"

Scott closed his mouth before he could say, *He's holding the pieces of my spare fishing rod against my ankle so I can tape them down.* Scott's sixth sense had just kicked in with as big a warning as he'd ever received from his hindbrain. That profoundly intelligent, life-saving bit of assistance, figured out in a flash of problem-solving intuition, so similar to the treecat's solution to prevent him from drowning, gave Scott a great deal of insight into treecat intelligence. *You might use flint tools, little friend, but there's nothing primitive about your level of sapience. Stephanie Harrington was right about that, and maybe there's a lot she's not saying, if half of what I'm picking up from you is accurate. The xenologists haven't got a clue, have they? This is data they haven't got, nothing like it, in fact. And maybe little Stephanie's got the right of it, keeping her mouth shut when those xenologists start poking at her. You're smart and you care—and how many of us humans would take advantage of the fact that your technology consists of stone knives and fire flints?* Well, if Scott got himself out of this mess, nobody would find out from *him* just how clever this treecat was. Better they erred on the side of caution, unsure what treecats could or couldn't do, than take advantage of them the way humanity had taken advantage of almost every other sentient aboriginal population they'd ever come across, just because they knew they could.

But that didn't stop Scott from wanting to learn everything he could about this particular treecat. A few well-informed, close-mouthed humans could do the treecats more political, sociological, and legal good than entire bureaus of well-meaning xenologists. Stephanie Harrington was only eleven. Scott MacDallan was a grown man and a respected professional in the far-flung community he served as physician. He could do a great deal, protecting this treecat and the hundreds of thousands, perhaps millions, of others. *If* he survived long enough to try. *God, how much more could I learn about you, what kinds of things could I accomplish, protecting you and your kind, if I had the chance?*

Scott wanted that chance, wanted it badly.

By the time he'd wrapped enough tape to stiffen his ankle, the blaze of late afternoon sunlight had vanished into an ominous, lowering darkness. Wind whistled and shrieked through the treetops and the smell of ozone and rain lay thick on the air.

"Gotta get downriver," he mumbled to himself. "*Have* to get to the air car."

"Scott?" Gifford Bede's voice was breaking up in the crackle coming from the comlink.

"Yeah?" He strained to hear through the interference.

"... tape around your ankle?"

"Yes, I've got it splinted."

"... stick ..."

"You're breaking up," Scott said, feeling tendrils of fear stir again as he glanced involuntarily skyward. "Say again?"

"... walking stick ..."

"Roger that, I'll try and cut a walking stick, Giff. Something sturdy enough to lean against and hobble across the broken ground between here and my air car."

"..."

It was no good. The storm's rising interference was too strong. Scott clipped the com unit to his belt, drew a deep breath and smiled at his anxious friend, who peered up at him through brilliant green eyes, then dragged himself slowly up the tree trunk. He fought dizziness and waves of sickness. "Don't let me fall, Jesus, don't let me fall and hit my head again." He made it up, leaning heavily against the tree trunk, then opened his eyes and peered upward.

The nearest branches were just within reach. Scott fumbled the vibro-knife off his belt clip and switched it on. The blade would cut through virtually anything known. It made short work of a section of branch as thick as Scott's wrist. The branch crashed down and Scott switched off the knife, hunkered his way cautiously back down again, then crawled along the length of the makeshift staff, lopping off side limbs and twigs.

The treecat shadowed him, peering curiously at the humming blade, but thankfully the treecat didn't offer to poke so much as a twitching whisker at it. "What must you think of this?" Scott asked, aware that the treecat wouldn't understand him, yet driven to communicate, somehow, with the creature who was so patently trying to keep him alive. He was also desperately trying to keep his own mind focused, battling not only the agony in his head, but a terrifying tendency to fog out and lose control of his wandering thoughts. With a force-two thunderstorm bearing down on them, Scott couldn't afford a foggy brain with thoughts as scattered as dandelion down on a gale-force wind. So he talked to the treecat as he crawled along the downed tree limb, lopping off branches and shaping his walking stick. "You know, little buddy, I can't just keep calling you 'creature,' can I? You've got a name, I'll wager, but what does it sound like in your language?" So far the only sounds he'd heard the treecat make were a curious, warbling sort of *bleek*, that buzzing purr, and a soft, reassuring croon.

As he worked with maddening slowness, Scott considered the problem.

"Any suggestions?" he asked his companion, who was busy solicitously dragging sharp-edged branches and twigs out of his way as he inched forward on hands and knees, to spare him cuts and splinters. "No? Well, you fished me out of that river, right enough. Maybe that's what I'll call you, little buddy. Fisher."

The treecat's reaction astonished him. It sat up on its hind-most set of legs, whistling sharply in visible excitement. Then it startled him by touching the disassembled fishing rod attached to his taped ankle, pointing to the river, and saying, "Bleek?"

Scott paused, momentarily oblivious to the onrushing storm, the agony behind his eyes. "Fisher?" he repeated. He touched the fiberglass sections of rod, pointed to the river, and made casting motions, said, "Fisher." Then he pointed to the treecat and said it again. "Fisher."

"*Bleek!*"

He found himself with an ecstatic treecat twining around his arm, head pressed strongly against his cheek, while the lithe, furred body purred like a well-tuned Terran housecat. Scott laughed shakily and petted the treecat with one unsteady hand. "I think that means you approve of the name? Is that what you're trying to tell me, Fisher?"

The treecat gave out a satisfied-sounding, warbling chirp, then pointed urgently to the sky. "Bleek!"

"Right." He'd let his thoughts scatter off the task at hand after all, distracted by the astonishing rapport the treecat was somehow building with him. A grim smile came and went as it occurred to Scott that what he was sensing might well be the same thing his grandmother had scared him witless with when Scott had been just a kid, when Granny MacChait had routinely anticipated things he said or needed, or when she'd known, from half a planet away without anyone calling her, that he'd been injured in an air car accident on his way to a nature preserve, simply showing up at his hospital room, or quietly giving out advice to neighbors who pointed to their heads and whispered behind her back about "that crazy old Scotswoman . . ."

The idea that he might have inherited the same curse—he'd never been able to think of it any other way, growing up—disturbed him deeply, even as he realized that he was "sensing" a great deal more from Fisher than anyone had reported picking up from the treecats who'd adopted them, even Stephanie Harrington—and that his ability to pick up so much emotional information from this treecat might prove to be of extreme value one day.

"Great, not only am I crawling around with a busted head and a bum ankle while a force-two thunderstorm howls down on me, now I find out I'm as psychic as Granny MacChait *and* I'm tuned in on a *treecat's* psychic aura." The notion— and his current predicament—were so absurd, he couldn't help it, he started to laugh. *I'm gonna die out here, if I don't shag my butt downriver, and I'm sitting here laughing like a maniac!*

Maybe it was just reaction hysteria?

"Bleek?" Fisher asked quizzically, peering worriedly up at him.

"Never mind, Fisher," Scott wheezed, wiping his wet face with shaking hands and wincing as thunder boomed above the forest canopy, which tossed in the rising wind with a sound like thousands of snakes hissing in rage. "Gotta get moving." Scott finished lopping off all the protruding limbs, then shut off the vibro-knife once more and slipped it back into its sheath. He dragged the thick pole across the rough ground, crawling backwards until he reached the tree trunk once again. Scott wanted to lean against it and shut his eyes and not move again until rescue came, but thunder echoed and boomed above the picket wood trees, closer every minute. The ominous darkness flared with lightning above the forest canopy. "Got to get moving, don't we, Fisher?"

Scott bit back a groan and struggled once again to his feet. He peered toward the river to get his bearings, strapped on haversack and rifle, then gripped the heavy wooden shaft he'd fashioned in both hands and shuffled forward a step, lean-ing his weight against it. He didn't fall, but his knees shook and his ankle screamed and the pain in his head blossomed like a bright fire flower at the heart of an incendiary bomb. He stood still for a moment, swaying and fighting down nausea which surged up his throat. Sweat stood out in beads along every millimeter of his skin. If he'd been smart enough to bring his medi-kit out here, instead of leaving it in the air car, he could've given himself something for the nausea, at least, which would've made hiking out of here a little easier, even if he didn't dare give himself a painkiller because of the head injury.

A low crooning reached him and Scott opened his eyes to find the treecat clinging to the picket wood trunk at eye level, staring at him with a worry that Scott could nearly taste. "Bleek?"

He swallowed down sour acid. "That way," he managed, pointing toward the bend in the river and his distant air car.

"Bleek!" The treecat pointed in the same direction, then

swarmed up the trunk to one of the straight, horizontal limbs that made the picket wood so unique.

Fisher could have outdistanced him in the blink of an eyelash, but he didn't. The treecat remained close above his head, crooning audibly as Scott lurched with agonizing slowness down the riverbank toward his air car. The wind picked up overhead and the snarl of thunder grew steadily closer. Lightning strobed through the lashing branches overhead, streaking from cloud to cloud. Before long, it would be snaking from cloud to ground—or the nearest convenient tree. Scott did not want to be under whatever tree served as a conduit for a river of raw electricity. Fear for the treecat's life sharpened his anxiety as he thought about lightning strikes in the picket woods overhead.

"Gotta make it to the air car." He chanted it half under his breath and struggled forward, leaning his whole shaky weight on the staff. With every step, his ankle throbbed and stabbed in protest, but that pain was nothing compared with the blinding agony in his head. The forest blurred around him, growing as faded and indistinct as his waning strength. Reality shrank, condensed to a fearful knot of pain inside his head and the need to shuffle forward another step and another after that, to crawl, awkward and shaky, over downed tree trunks, sharp outcroppings of rock, and jagged boulders tossed into his path by the roaring floodwaters of some past season. He gasped in the thick, storm-heavy air, trying to drag enough oxygen into his lungs to keep up his grueling, limping pace across the broken, rough terrain which skirted the riverbank.

When the rain struck, it did so with a shock. He halted a skid across suddenly slick leaves and mud, then stood huddled against the downpour, gasping and shaking and trying to regain sufficient strength to keep going. Rain pelted down, lashing at his back and head with ferocity only slightly eased by the trees between himself and the open sky. He was trying to get his bearings, having momentarily lost sight of the river through interposing underbrush, when he was half-blinded and deafened by a brilliant flash of lightning and a roar of thunder that beat against his whole body. Another blinding flash showed him a furry, bedraggled form on a branch just overhead. "Why don't you go home?" Scott shouted above the roar of rain and bruising thunder. "You're going to get struck by lightning if you stay up there!"

Between crashes of thunder, he heard a sharp sound from overhead, then gasped. The treecat jumped from the branch right onto his shoulder. Fisher's warmth was shocking against his drenched skin. The touch of tiny hands against his face, claws sheathed, left him awed. *"Bleek!"* There was sharp distress in that sound. Scott could feel the urgency of worry coming from the treecat, sensed somehow that Fisher would stay with him no matter what happened, just as Stephanie Harrington's treecat had charged a hexapuma rather than abandon her. He was face-to-face with a selfless honor that left him ashamed of three-quarters of his own species' history.

A warm, furred body pressed against the side of his head and the treecat leaned his face against Scott's cheek, oblivious to the blinding rain. Fisher was crooning into Scott's ear, touching his face, wrapping his tail gently around Scott's neck, all but shaking in his effort to let Scott know he wasn't alone in this terrifying disaster in the middle of a raging thunderstorm. Scott risked letting go of his crutch to lift one hand, touching the sentient creature riding his shoulder; he could feel as well as hear its contented purr as he stroked wet fur with unsteady fingers.

"Where did you come from?" Scott whispered. "Your people must live near here. I don't know why you're helping me, Fisher, but you can't know how glad I am that you are." Then, pondering the intense emotions he could feel pouring through him from the treecat, he reconsidered. "Then again, maybe you can."

"Bleek . . ." The sound was low, comforting. The treecat pointed through the downpour, in a direction that looked about right for the spot he'd parked his air car, what felt like a lifetime ago. "Bleek!" The treecat pointed emphatically; Scott could all but taste its rising urgency. So he started hobbling in that direction, still trying to get his bearings. If he'd thought he could find a cave closer, he would cheerfully have crawled into it; but the only place he was certain offered shelter was his air car, somewhere up ahead in that general direction. At least, he thought it was in that direction. When lightning strobed overhead, he finally caught a glimpse of the river, but he couldn't tell how far he'd come. The confusion of wind-lashed rain made it impossible to judge his position relative to where he'd fallen so disastrously, never mind to where he'd left the air car.

"Bleek!" The treecat pointed firmly ahead.

"Hope you know where we're going, Fisher." He kept slogging forward at a slow shuffle, uncertain of his footing in the mud and the thick layers of detritus on the forest floor. Fallen branches and deadwood and rain-slick rocks tripped him every few moments. Only his grip on the walking stick kept him from falling. The treecat stayed with him, a warmth on his shoulder and along his upper arm and a comforting presence that kept despair at bay. Whenever he paused, panting and hopelessly lost, the treecat pointed firmly through the lightning-slashed gloom and driving rain, clearly aware of where he wanted to go, even if Scott no longer was certain where they actually were going. He had no idea how long he'd been moving, hunched over against the stinging downpour, when he heard the first rattle of hail strike the trees like gunfire.

Then pain stung his back where a hailstone struck and Scott yelped, nearly losing his balance. He caught himself at the last moment, clinging to his staff, then stood shaking for a moment while hail smashed down through the canopy, striking the mud all around him. Scott was so wobbly, he wasn't even sure his knees would hold him for another step, and hail was falling all around him, smashing through the picket wood in a rain of destruction that showered broken twigs and branches to the forest floor.

"*Bleek!*" The treecat moved across his shoulders, arched his whole body protectively over Scott's head. One three-fingered hand appeared in his peripheral vision, pointing urgently ahead. Lightning flared wildly—

And Scott saw a break in the trees, saw the gleam of bright yellow paint on his air car. "*The car!* Fisher, oh, God, you wonderful, marvelous treecat!"

He slithered forward through the mud, gasping with effort, cringing every time hailstones cracked off branches overhead and splashed down past him. Almost there . . . another few meters, that was all . . . He came out from under cover of the trees and slipped in the sea of mud beyond. Scott yelled, aware that he couldn't stop the slide, knew he would fall, jarringly. He hit with his left shoulder, heard an animal squeal of pain . . . then discovered himself lying prone in the mud, with his head resting on a pile of wet, shivering fur. A faint sound of pain escaped the treecat. Scott whimpered, too, all but blinded by his own pain, but that sound of distress brought him to hands and knees, crouching over the treecat. Hailstones pelted down, striking his back, but he ignored the sharp, bruising sting and squinted down at the treecat.

A flare of lightning showed him the treecat under his shoulder, one of its middle limbs curled up tautly against Fisher's body. When he probed gently for damage, the treecat screamed. *Oh, God, that middle limb's gotta be broken. You could've jumped clear . . . why didn't you?*

Because if he had, Scott would've smashed his head against

the muddy, boulder-strewn ground and the treecat had known it, had sensed how much damage that would cause. Scott didn't need words to understand what the treecat had done. He fought a sting of salt in his eyes, blinked against it. He lifted the treecat in one arm, cradled it close, stricken by the mewling sound that escaped. Scott peered through the rain, spotted his air car less than two meters away. He crawled, one-armed, across the muddy ground, splashing through puddles and wincing at the jab of broken, splintered wood under his palm and his knees where the earlier flood had torn away the trees to form this clearing. It seemed like an eternity, but couldn't have been more than a few minutes, at most, when Scott finally fumbled his hand up the side of the air car, popped the latch, and crawled, shaking in every limb, into the dry shelter beyond.

He wanted to collapse right there on the floor.

Instead, he dragged the hatch shut, crawled forward, and switched on the power. Taking off in a storm like the one raging outside would have been out of the question under any other circumstances, but Scott needed medical help badly—and now, so did Fisher. And a storm like this one was liable to tear out whole trees and send them crashing downstream with flash flood waters cascading down the mountain canyon, potentially straight into his parked air car. He flipped switches, brought up the lights and powered up the air car's systems. Exhausted, sick with his own pain, Scott dragged himself and his injured companion up onto the mid-car seat cushions, then rummaged through the medical kit he carried everywhere he went—and had stupidly left behind. "Won't make that mistake ever again," he muttered aloud as he pulled out bandages and splints.

Scott bit his lips, knowing this would hurt the treecat, but that leg had to be splinted. He gently touched the treecat's injured limb. Fisher whimpered like a hurt child, but let him draw the leg out straight. It didn't feel broken, thank God, when he explored with cautious fingertips. He could feel inflammation and swelling, though, and stiffness, which suggested a bad sprain. He was no xeno-veterinarian, but he was a medical doctor and soft-tissue injuries were soft-tissue injuries, whether they occurred in a human, a bird, a horse, or a sentient treecat.

"I'm sorry, little buddy, didn't mean to hurt you like that. God, what a mess I've got us in. Hang on, Fisher, I'm going to get us out of this, okay?" Scott retrieved a moderate painkiller from his kit and injected his little friend, selecting one of the medications he'd read Richard Harrington had tested safely on his daughter's injured treecat. The treecat bleeked softly, a sound of mingled distress and thanks as the drug began to take effect. Scott tried to smile. "Yeah. That should feel a little better. Wish I could give myself some of that."

But Scott had to fly them out of here and painkillers did not mix well with head injuries *or* with flying through force-two thunderstorms. He wrapped the sprained middle limb in a cushioning plasti-foam bandage, then shifted Fisher and carefully strapped him into a protective webbing in the co-pilot's seat, which allowed him to remain suspended in a sort of sta-bilized sling that would reduce the jouncing they were going to get once this car was airborne. Scott then gave himself a badly needed antinausea medication and strapped himself into the pilot's chair. He tried to use the air car's com, but could raise nothing but static.

Worry gnawed at him, but he couldn't do anything about it right now and Gifford Bede had a fix on his transponder. He'd have to fly nap-of-the-earth to stay out of the worst of the sav-age winds, which meant the river was his best bet. Scott said a silent prayer, then powered up the engines and lifted off. His hands sweat on the controls and his head pounded to a savage rhythm of physical pain and gnawing fear, but he got the air car out over the open river and headed downstream. The cross-winds were a nightmare, even this low to the ground, and rain beat at the windows in a solid, leaden curtain; but his instruments showed him the terrain just below and ahead, and the anti-gravs kicked in automatically every few seconds, surging against sudden down-drafts that tried to swat them into the riverbed.

How long Scott hunched over the controls, fighting the wind and slewing them back and forth above the twisting, savage river as it snaked its way down out of the mountains, dip-ping and diving to avoid picket wood trees that grew out across the river's snaking bed to set down nodal trunks on islands mid-stream, he wasn't certain. Hail cracked and rattled off the canopy like machine-gun fire and lightning blinded him every few seconds, hissing and cracking so close, at times thunder vibrated through the car's airframe. But there finally came a moment when Scott realized the worst of the storm lay behind them. He'd gained on its leading edge and was now flying level over the valley floor.

Scott sent a heartfelt prayer of thanks winging its way and reached a shaking hand to the co-pilot's chair beside him, strok-ing Fisher's damp fur. Scott's caress earned a sleepy burble of pleasure from his injured friend and a burst of love and warmth through his mind.

"Hang in there, little buddy," Scott murmured softly. "It won't be long now."

He gained altitude, pushed the air car's speed to max, and laid in a course for home.

A low croon from several hundred voices jerked Scott back to the reality of a low, crackling fire and the massed presence of more treecats than he'd ever seen at one time. Across the fire, a slim, half-sized treecat with a mottled brown coat and pine-green eyes crooned softly, voice trailing into silence as she peered into Scott's eyes. Other voices died away as well, leaving only the sigh of wind high in the picket wood branches and the distant clang and echo of shouted human voices from the BioNeering cargo carrier's crash site. He blinked and felt a flush of embarrassment sting his cheeks. *Some ambassador I turn out to be, sitting here daydreaming about how Fisher saved my bacon, when this brown-coated treecat is clearly trying to tell me something important.* He sternly ordered himself to quit woolgathering, even though the sharpness of those memories, the ache of remembered fear and the shock and wonder of discovery were so immediate, gooseflesh still rippled across his arms and down his chest and back.

"I'm sorry," he said contritely to the female treecat.

"Bleek," she answered softly, her voice a splash of tinkling chimes in the breeze.

What happened next caught Scott totally off guard. The half-starved stray he'd rescued at the Zivonik farm touched Scott's knee with its hands—

—and reality swung dizzily, a blur of color and sound and sudden, wrenching anger. Faces swam briefly in his mind's eye and voices shouted in a sharp quarrel. Scott gasped, reeling under a sudden lash of fear and rage, literally tasting the urgency of someone's fury and steely determination to stop . . . *something.* He caught a flash of pictures in his mind, of a withered, sere picket wood forest, the trees denuded of leaves, bark peeling in shaggy, leprous strips, caught an overpowering sense of fear and despair and belly-twisting *rage . . .*

Then a single image hung in his mind: the twisted wreckage of a cargo transport air car and the broken, decaying corpse of co-pilot Arvin Erhardt, with a starvation-thin treecat huddled over his body, keening in an agony of grief and anger.

Scott sat trembling for long moments, gulping down air that tasted of woodsmoke and death, aware of a weight against his side where Fisher pressed against him, crooning gently. He blinked sweat from his eyes, focused slowly on the leaping, misshapen flames of the treecats' council fire, shivered in the sudden chill of the cool spring night. *How did* that *happen? And what in God's name are they trying to tell me?* Scott lifted a shaking hand to his face, wiped sweat from his cheeks and rubbed his eyes, trying to gather his composure again. *Maybe I wasn't woolgathering after all, just now, Jesus, how did she* do *that? Did she do that?* How else could he explain what had just happened to him?

Neither Fisher nor the stray had ever achieved anything remotely like what had just occurred, with crystalline flashes of sight and sound projected right into his mind's eye, pictures of places he'd never seen and voices he'd never heard, yet as clear as any memory he could call his own. The half-size treecat with the beguiling pine-green eyes was gazing intently up at him, the intelligence behind those eyes shaking Scott anew. *Christ, Granny MacChait, how did you ever live with this? Seeing and hearing what happened to other people, hundreds of kilometers away? People you didn't even know...?* He drew slow, calming breaths, felt the almost subliminal touch as Fisher—and perhaps many more treecats than Fisher—eased the sense of shock still pounding him.

When he looked up, Scott found the dark-furred female treecat crouched right next to him. She huddled beside the stray Scott had followed here, crooning gently to it. Grief poured from that treecat in almost visible waves, lashing against Scott's shaken sensibilities. He found himself stroking the thin back, murmuring softly to it, trying to ease its distress, too, and felt as well as heard a low hum of approval from the assembled 'cats. Pine-green eyes lifted, gazed into his.

Scott didn't know what to say, what to do. He cast back through the impressions he'd received, trying to make sense of what he'd seen and heard and felt. A violent quarrel between humans ... that much was clear. A quarrel that had involved primally sharp emotions and dark suspicions. That, at least, echoed the feeling he'd received from Fisher and the stray back at the wreck. A violent quarrel, laced with suspicion and a determination to stop ... *something* ... followed by a fatal air crash, spelled events far removed from "accident" in Scott's mind. Was *that* what the treecats were trying to tell him? That the crash hadn't been an accident? That it had been—his breath caught sharply—*murder?*

"Dear God," he whispered.

He knew, in a flash of intuition that might not be entirely his own, that he was right. But why? What had the victims in the cargo transport been trying to stop, that someone would have risked murdering three people to keep secret? This was far beyond the scope of a lover's quarrel grown lethal, far more serious than an angry brawl between drunken miners whooping it up in town on a Saturday night. This suggested deliberate, cold-blooded murder to hide something of profound importance to the killer, who had to be closely connected with whatever research was going on in that BioNeering plant. Worse, whatever that something was, it clearly involved *treecats,* a realization that shook him all over again.

Murder, industrial secrets, and treecats spelled a potential crisis of enormous proportions, with implications for the entire future of the Star Kingdom's relationship with its newfound, native sentient race. He saw again the flash of images he'd somehow picked up from these treecats, the barren, denuded picket wood trees, their naked and peeling branches stretching into the harsh sunlight like plague victims. He frowned slowly, playing it through again. Something had clearly killed this cluster of trees. Something so critical, people had been murdered for trying to report the reason.

"Bleek . . ." It was a piteous sound, half-pleading, half-hopeful. Scott looked down to find his thin little stray gazing steadily upward into Scott's eyes, waiting.

"Where?" Scott asked softly.

Like a compass needle swinging toward the magnetic poles, a directional "bump" appeared in Scott's brain, pointing inexorably toward the southwest. There wasn't much out that way, he pondered, reviewing his mental map of Sphinx's surface. A mining operation that was largely automated, a few farms . . . and BioNeering's experimental plant. That cargo transport was a BioNeering air car, the crash victims were all BioNeering employees. The familiar BioNeering corporate logo flashed into his mind's eye, the spreading picket wood tree with its nodal trunk formed from the double-spiral DNA helix. It took a moment for Scott to realize he wasn't visualizing it from the last place he'd seen that logo, the battered, scraped side of the downed transport. He was "seeing" it emblazoned on the side of a long, low building he knew very well he'd never laid eyes on. It came as a shock like icewater that the picket wood trees he could "see" nearby were all dead, their branches barren, their bark hanging in leprous strips . . .

Scott found himself on his feet without realizing he'd scrambled up. He was breathing hard, stomach clenched in sick knots. There'd been some kind of accident, a release of something that had devastated the picket wood system around that experimental plant. And whoever was in charge of that plant had resorted to murder, rather than have co-workers report the truth. How far must the damage run, by now? And what, in God's name, had they released? Had it even been accidental? Surely no fool would be insane enough to deliberately release an untested gengineered organism into the environment, in all violation of the Elysian Rule? The ecosystem of the entire planet of Elysian had collapsed, thanks to such ill-advised tampering.

Scott would not stand idly by and let that happen on Sphinx!

It occurred to him, as he stood there in the dim, flickering light from the treecats' fire, fists clenched, jaws aching, that the murdered trio in the clearing must have felt exactly the same way he did right now. Somewhere out there, a dark, diseased mind with blood on its soul waited for the return of Scott's crash team. That person had done murder once. They would kill again to protect themselves the moment he or anyone else started probing the dark secret behind this crash.

But he was going to find out who had killed these people and why, whatever it took. He *would* learn the truth. These treecats had done the impossible, trying to get their urgent message out to humanity. He didn't intend to fail them. Scott found himself staring into the pine-green eyes of a dark-furred treecat. She gazed up the long way into his eyes and something akin to fierce joy burst through Scott, coming, he realized with awe, from *her*. It echoed in waves all around him, from the hundreds of treecats gazing intently into his eyes.

"I don't know who," he said in a quiet, hard voice, speaking directly to the pine-green eyes of the female 'cat, "and I don't know how. But I will, by God, find out. However you did it, thank you for telling me."

He turned and stalked away through the smothering darkness, aware of rustlings in the branches overhead as the assembled treecats escorted him back to the bright lights at the edge of the crash clearing. He had to be careful, he knew that; with a situation as potentially volatile as this, treecats involving themselves in a spectacular triple murder in the human community, with God-only-knew what ramifications for the future of relations between the two species, he had to move with extreme circumspection until he had proof. He couldn't just blurt out his suspicions. Not only did he have to gather proof that would convince the Manticoran authorities, he had to present something concrete, rather than nebulous feelings received from treecats. And he certainly couldn't admit to having received the message through a psychic flash of intuitive suspicions and images obtained through *mindreading.* He'd be laughed straight off Sphinx. Or worse.

Even the most open-minded humans understood so little about their new neighbors, the idea of a treecat communicating such a thing as murder or a cover-up scheme to hide a major industrial accident—through clairvoyance, no less—would likely trigger everything from open skepticism to outright hostility to blatant panic. *He* knew he was right; but very few humans had spent anything close to a T-year coming to understand the nuances of the strange bond which existed between a human and the treecat which adopted him or her.

So he would have to proceed with extreme caution, nudging the crash team in the direction he wanted their investigation to go, gathering evidence on BioNeering's activities on his own in his official capacity as coroner for these fatalities. Thank God he'd had the foresight to ask Mayor Sapristos to make that official before he got started out here. But he couldn't even go to Sapristos until he had something concrete that didn't involve saying, "Well, sir, the treecats told me so" when everyone knew the treecats couldn't tell anyone anything, not directly, and he couldn't, *wouldn't,* risk telling the truth about his own personal, psychic secret.

Had it taken the combined empathic skills or telepathy or whatever they used, of that many treecats, massed for one single-minded effort, to get those few brief images and emotions across to him? Or had they realized there was something in his Scottish heritage that made him more receptive to whatever it was the treecats used to communicate? Treecats couldn't know the old Earth legends about the Scots and Irish being "fey," legends which still persisted, despite the complete lack of ability to measure such a thing, but they could certainly pick up human emotions and broadcast their own, at least to Scott.

The notion that the 'cats had somehow known that *only* Scott MacDallan would be able to understand their message left him more determined than ever to get to the bottom of this mystery—and to do it *without* jeopardizing the treecats' future by giving away too much information about them. At least, not before the humans on Sphinx could be convinced or coerced into establishing proper, civilized diplomatic relations that protected their little neighbors.

Whether or not the treecats *had* chosen him deliberately because of his genetic heritage, he couldn't be sure, and doubted that he or anyone else would ever know that particular truth; but he could certainly start finding answers to the questions posed by this crash. And he intended to begin with the air car itself, try to find out exactly what had caused that big cargo car to come down, not just assume it'd been downed by the storm. Just before he stepped out from beneath the last trees, he felt a familiar weight settle onto his shoulder and welcomed Fisher with a gentle hand. Then another weight dropped to his other shoulder and Scott found himself gazing into the brilliant grass-green eyes of his determined stray.

"Bleek!" It pointed toward the waiting crash team with stark emphasis.

"Oh, yes," Scott agreed softly. "We will, indeed!"

He broke cover into the clearing and rounded the bow of the misshapen wreck.

"Vollney! Keegan!"

The crash investigators appeared from two directions, one leaning out the open cargo hatch, the other jogging around the crumpled stern. "Doc?"

"There's something bothering me about this crash. I've flown through thunderstorms dozens of times, trying to get to patients who needed a doctor, flew through one with a concussion, once, to get my friend, Fisher, here, and myself to a hospital. I don't know exactly what we're looking for, but whatever it is, it caused this air car to go off course several hundred kilometers and crash without sending out a distress call or beacon signal. I can't believe an experienced pilot caught in a thunderstorm wouldn't com his position or turn on his emergency transponder, at the very least. What've you found so far? Was their equipment damaged by lightning strikes, maybe, that prevented them from calling for help?"

Nick Vollney and Marcus Keegan exchanged startled glances. Then Vollney said, "Uh, now you mention it, Doc, I haven't seen the kind of damage you'd expect from a lightning strike to their instrumentation. There's no characteristic popcorn denting from hailstones on the hull, either, although that's not definitive, since there are plenty of thunderstorms that don't produce low-atmosphere hail. But you've got something with the instruments, Doc, we've just been assuming the storm prevented them from calling out or setting their beacon, without really checking out thoroughly how or why. I'll get right on it."

Keegan added, "If it wasn't lightning, maybe a violent downdraft while they were at low level sent them into the canopy? But that'd mean their anti-gravs were malfunctioning and I didn't even check those." He frowned. "This may take a while."

Scott grimaced. "I may be tired, Marcus, but I'd rather know what caused this crash. Get on it, would you?"

"Right." The investigator crawled into the remains of the battered air car.

Scott was tired, so much so he'd have been happy to curl up on a picket wood limb, if it'd offered a quiet place to sleep. Instead, he rolled up his sleeves and dug out his surgical kit and mask, and got busy in the cargo hold of the rescue air car. He had three field autopsies to perform and the night wasn't getting any younger. The possibility that the killer had somehow drugged the victims was too great to ignore and might explain why they were so far off course and hadn't called in their difficulty. Unconscious or incoherent pilots wouldn't have been able to keep their car on course when the storm that must have masked the sounds of the crash from the Zivonik homestead had caught them somewhere between BioNeering's research facility and town.

Pine-green eyes burned in his memory as he set to work. At his side, a starvation thin treecat watched as Scott began the grisly work of cutting open the remains of the poor stray's murdered friend. A stab of rage tore through him. This time it was all his own. The treecats were counting on him to prove that what he gazed at right now was murder.

Scott did not intend to let them down.

Dawn was breaking over the Zivonik farmhouse when the air car settled in the broad sweep of grass beyond the kitchen garden. Scott reeled out, eyes bleary from lack of sleep, and stumbled beside Aleksandr Zivonik and his oldest boy toward the house. All Scott wanted was a mattress under him and a long, hot soak in gallons and gallons of steaming water. The Zivonik children, blinking sleepily, met them at the door. Irina Kisaevna appeared a moment later as they approached the door, looking gloriously tumbled from sleep and wholesome enough to drive away the stink of horror clinging to his very skin.

"How's Evelina?" Aleksandr asked, voice rough with exhaustion.

"Sleeping. So's Lev."

Aleksandr just nodded.

Irina kissed her brother's cheek and said, "Go on to bed. I'll see to Scott."

The big farmer made his apologies, then stumbled down the hall in the direction of his bedroom. Irina took Scott's arm and braved the stares of both treecats to kiss him, too, although not on the cheek. Irina tasted of home and warmth and sanity; Scott pulled her closer and just held her for a moment, not wanting to think about murders or autopsies or investigations yet to be made. Both treecats crooned anxiously where they rode his shoulders.

"You're exhausted, all of you, poor things," Irina said softly, pulling away to smile up into his eyes. "Come on, Scott, let me show you where there's a spare bed." She led him down a short hall to an open doorway. The bed was wide enough to accommodate three, without risk of colliding with elbows or knees; it was more than roomy enough for one exhausted doctor and two bleary-eyed treecats.

"Thanks, Irina." His own voice was hoarse with weariness. Scott stumbled into the darkened bedroom, groping his way out of his clothes and into bed, hardly registering the soft latch of the door as Irina closed it behind him. When he next opened his eyes, strong sunlight poured in through the windows and the smells of frying bacon and steaming coffee tickled his nostrils. According to the clock, he'd been asleep for five hours, not enough to catch up to himself, but better than none. He suspected it was the gnawing in his belly—and his little friends' bellies—that'd wakened him. Scott found a shower just off the bedroom and stood under it for a full quarter of an hour, just letting hot water sluice over him. He didn't want to remember the previous night, knew he couldn't run away from the grim responsibility waiting for him in this morning's blinding sunlight.

Today, he had to find a killer.

Someone—probably Irina, again—had laundered his filthy clothes while he slept. Scott greeted Fisher and the thin treecat, both of whom had curled up to sleep beside him, and reassured the stray with caresses and low murmurs, then dressed and headed for the Zivonik kitchen, accompanied by two ravenously hungry treecats. The oldest Zivonik girl was pouring coffee and the second-oldest boy was dishing up platters of eggs, bacon, and flapjacks. Irina, barefooted and wearing an apron, with stray tendrils of hair escaping the ribbon she'd used to tie it back with, was piling a stack of generously laden plates, bowls, coffee cups, and juice glasses onto an enormous tray, doubtless for her brother and sister-in-law. Bright smiles greeted him as he paused in the doorway.

"Good morning, Dr. MacDallan!"

"'Morning. Mind if I wrap myself around a plateful of that?"

"Help yourself," the tow-headed short-order cook grinned with a slight lisp. He was missing a front tooth. "And I shredded some more of that turkey carcass for the treecats."

"Thanks." Scott smiled. He dragged out a chair and plowed into the food as Irina carried the heavy tray out.

"Eat up, Scott. I'll just take this down to Alek and Evelina and be right back."

He nodded and smiled, mouth too full of fluffy flapjacks and crisp bacon to say anything. The treecats ate hungrily, as well, then bleeked in open delight when Stasya brought over a tray piled high with celery.

"I heard treecats like it." She smiled shyly.

Both 'cats were already chewing in ecstasy, shredding the celery into a sticky, wet mass.

"They do." Scott nodded. "God knows why. I never did."

The children giggled, tempting the treecats with more stringy, springy stalks. Irina returned and poured a cup of coffee for herself, then joined him at the table, blowing gently across the steaming liquid. "Will you be going back to town today?"

"I'll have to." He said. "Mind if I borrow your computer before I go? I want to check a few things on the net before I leave."

"Sure. I'll show you when you're done eating."

Scott was aware of her close scrutiny as he finished off seconds. Irina knew him well enough to realize something was up, something more out of the ordinary than weariness after an unpleasant business like last night's. Tiredness, she'd have expected, but Scott couldn't quite hide the tension gripping him as he struggled with the best way to attack the problem of acquiring the proof he needed. He tried to smile at her and she returned the gesture easily enough, but her eyes remained dark and concerned. But she didn't ask, which was one of the reasons Scott appreciated her company: she didn't pry. Maybe it was only that frontier folk minded their own business or maybe it was more a matter of Irina's innate respect for a person's privacy; even when she'd been at her most curious over Fisher's unexpected presence in Scott's life, she had never pushed for more information than Scott wanted to give her.

Whatever the reason, Scott appreciated it, now more than ever.

She set him up at the family's computer terminal and dropped a kiss on the top of his head, then left him to "go check on Evelina and the baby." Scott smiled and hooked into planetary data net. A short while later, Scott was pulling up aerial surveys and maps, delving into public records on BioNeering's corporate structure and export activities, and learning everything he could about the company's research facility southwest of the Zivonik farmstead. He was aware that he raced the sun if he hoped to fly from here to the site of the BioNeering plant, then make it back to town by nightfall. Scott did not want to be anywhere near that plant after dark.

When he checked the message queues on his home and business datanet accounts, wanting to be sure no professional emergencies had arisen demanding immediate attention—although any true emergency would've been automatically forwarded to his wrist-com—he found a message from the newly founded Xenology Institute, marked with the personal account code of Dr. Sanura Hobbard, chief xenologist of the team dispatched by the Star Kingdom of Manticore to study the treecats. Clearly, word about how they'd found the crash site had spread with lightning speed. That message was time-stamped less than ten minutes after he and Aleksandr Zivonik had called in the news the previous evening.

Scott frowned as he read the politely phrased request for a meeting to discuss "important behavioral developments with your treecat and Arvin Erhardt's, regarding the discovery of the crash site." He'd have to tell her something, he knew that much; but after a year in Fisher's company, his instincts about keeping quiet on the subject of treecat intelligence and other unique traits had been honed to razor keenness. He sent back a short reply that he'd contact her once he was back in his office. She wouldn't be happy; but he wasn't about to break what had, he suspected, become a code of silence amongst those who'd been adopted by treecats. Even little Stephanie Harrington had begun to get cagey when discussing the 'cats.

He did, however, set down a fair approximation of the full story in a coded file, which he started to route to his computer at home, so it could be retrieved if anything untoward happened to him. If anything went wrong out there, he wanted *someone* to know what had happened, so the murder investigation would still go forward. He was just about to press the "send" command when he paused, reconsidering the wisdom of sending it over the datanet, even in code. If anything *did* happen to him, he wanted to be sure the file was read by someone he could trust, someone who would actually believe him. That meant either someone who'd been adopted by a treecat—relatively few and far between, and Stephanie Harrington, the likeliest person to comprehend the full truth, was only a child—*or* someone who knew him well enough to believe the story even without direct experience with a treecat bond.

Scott routed the file to Irina Kisaevna's account, doubly pleased because he was able to do that right here, without sending the coded message through the planetary net where, it was conceivable, a person might be able to intercept a copy

and de-code it. There was a killer out there who would be
watching every move he made on the datanet during the next
few days, aware that he was acting as official coroner for the
crash. Transferring the file to Irina's account was simply a
matter of copying it straight into her private mail directory
on the family's computer. He put a header on it marked "to
be de-coded only in the event of Scott MacDallan's death" and
hoped like hell Irina would never have to read the blasted thing.

That unpleasant chore completed, he turned his attention
to the files he'd located on BioNeering, Inc. According to
BioNeering company records, at least those available on the
public net, the experimental research plant was operated by
a small staff headed by one Dr. Mariel Ubel. Ubel was listed
as chief research scientist for the plant, which was largely
automated, like the Copperwall Mine several hundred kilometers
away. Pol Rafferty was listed as her research assistant. Rafferty's
body was on its way back to Twin Forks for burial, in the
rescue 'car that had dropped him off at dawn. The only other
personnel employed at the plant were the other two crash
victims, who had pulled double duty as pilots for cargo transport
and mechanics for the facility's automated equipment.

The work Ubel's team had been doing was supposedly extrac-
tion of the chemical compound that allowed picket wood to
dissolve cellulose between healthy portions of a picket wood
system and any part of the community attacked by disease or
pest infestation. There were multiple, economically lucrative
uses for such a compound, and BioNeering was investigating
them, extracting the genetic material responsible for its secretion
from wood harvested at the plant, which served as Mariel Ubel's
primary research lab. She had been heading the effort to iso-
late the exact chemical compound and the genes that controlled
its diffusion by living picket wood systems under attack for
the past two T-years.

Mariel Ubel wasn't at the plant at the moment, according
to news posts on the net. She'd flown into Twin Forks with
the research facility's passenger air car to meet with company
officials, identify the remains of her colleagues, and recruit
replacements to keep the plant and its vital industrial research
operational. Since the facility was mostly automated, work in
progress could continue for a short period without direct human
oversight, allowing the scientist time to hire new staff in town.
That suited Scott perfectly. The fewer people around when he
arrived, the better.

The treecats' reaction to Mariel Ubel's photograph on the
computer screen confirmed Scott's dark suspicions: both cats

grew visibly agitated, bleeking in distress and anger at first sight of the strikingly beautiful blond-haired scientist's likeness. Fisher could never have seen Ubel in person; but the stray might well have known the woman first-hand and the anger radiating from both 'cats strongly suggested that the relationship had not been congenial. *No, it wouldn't have been, not if she's responsible for murdering his friend.*

What, Scott wondered, might the stray have been able to tell them, had he been capable of human speech? What had he witnessed in that BioNeering plant, between Mariel Ubel and Arvin Erhardt and the others? Mariel Ubel might well have gotten clean away with murder, if Scott hadn't stumbled across the stray and that crash site in the company of a couple of hundred treecats determined to get the truth across to *someone*. She might still get away with it, if he and the crash investigators couldn't locate proof that the crash had been anything other than tragic accident. BioNeering could be fined— stiffly—and possibly even have their business charter yanked for violation of the Elysian Rule, but putting Mariel Ubel out of business wasn't sufficient. Scott MacDallan wanted to prove the story the treecats had so painfully managed to convey to him, which meant he needed to get his hands on some solid evidence pointing to cold-blooded murder.

And the only place he could do that was at BioNeering's remote research plant.

Scott printed out the files on Mariel Ubel and her automated tree-processing facility and tucked them into his coverall pockets, then shoved back his chair. He'd seen enough for now. It was time to get this investigation airborne. He inquired after Evelina Zivonik and gave her and the newborn Lev a brief exam, reassuring the family that she and the baby were doing just fine, then said his goodbyes, thanked them for their hospitality, kissed Irina while the Zivonik children giggled, and took his leave. He left a copy of his flight plan with Irina as a safety precaution, giving her an alternative reason for going out there, so someone would at least know where he was going.

"I'm betting the stray comes from a treecat colony near there," he said quietly, "and now that his human friend is dead, I think he wants to go home. It's a long way for a treecat to go on foot, Irina, and I think that's why he's so thin and exhausted—he's already made that journey once, in this direction, just to reach his friend's body. I thought the least I could do is give him a lift home again."

"Of course, Scott."

Aleksandr, standing nearby, nodded and clasped Scott's hand

firmly. "You got a heart of gold, Doc." The big farmer, whose parents had emigrated directly from old Terra's Ukraine in the colony's first wave, making his family one of Sphinx's prestigious first shareholders, glanced at Fisher, who rode Scott's right shoulder, then at the stray, who'd taken up a perch on Scott's left. "Isn't hard to see why that treecat of yours adopted you. And you can bet I won't be forgetting this little stray anytime soon. Take care, Doc."

They shook hands, then Scott climbed into his air car and the treecats jumped down. They joined him in the cockpit as he powered up and checked systems. Scott made sure his rifle and pistol were fully loaded, then strapped the pistol on and clipped the rifle into its holder so it would be easily accessible, and made sure his medical kit was strapped down securely. He rigged the safety webbing for the treecats, a precaution he always put in place when flying with Fisher in the co-pilot's chair, and smiled when the stray and Fisher pressed their noses against the canopy to watch his takeoff. He waved to Irina, who blew a kiss, and to Aleksandr and the children, then lifted slowly above the farmhouse, with its sharply sloped, conical green roof, designed to shed the heavy weight of winter snow, and headed southwest.

The devastation wasn't as widespread from the air as it had seemed in the treecats' mental images, but it was enough to churn his stomach. The dispersal pattern was clearly wind-borne, fanning out from the research plant in a cone of blighted trees down wind. The initial cone of destruction was not the only area affected, either. Whatever had been released, it had spread outward, stretching away from the plant in a widening vee of wilted, peeling picket wood trees that stretched five kilometers or more to either side of the facility. A sharp line of demarcation existed beyond the damaged area, with withered trees on one side and healthy, vigorous picket wood systems beyond. The reason for this became clear as he hovered lower over the canopy.

There were gaps in the forest where wood had been dissolved away in the picket wood system's last-ditch defense mechanism, cutting off the stricken section of forest. Scott had seen photos of damaged picket wood stands with just such gaps, but never up close and never resulting from damage caused by a man-made agent. Whatever it was, it had apparently affected the wildlife, too, because Scott couldn't see any of Sphinx's multitude of native species moving through the blighted trees or on the forest floor near the gap in the canopy. The stillness of the forest was ominous; Scott wondered uneasily if the agent which had damaged the picket wood system had also proven lethal to the region's fauna. A glance at the painfully thin stray sitting on the co-pilot's couch beside Fisher caused Scott to clench his jaw muscles. If the local game had died or been driven out because their food supply had vanished, starvation could well stalk any treecat population in this region during the coming months.

His air car didn't have sophisticated recording equipment, but it was outfitted with a basic camera system he used to pinpoint likely fishing spots. He was recording every centimeter of this flyover, including the deep gouges in the blasted section of forest where five mechanical wood harvesters were busy literally chewing up the evidence of the disaster. The research plant's harvesters were designed to fell timber and grind it up and the remaining staff member down there had clearly set the harvesters on auto and left them running, determined to "harvest" all traces of the accidental—he hoped to God it'd been accidental, rather than deliberate—release of whatever they'd let loose down there. By the time Mariel Ubel returned with her new recruits, the work would be finished.

"She must've started harvesting the evidence the moment her colleagues took off to report the infraction," Scott muttered. "Six days of round-the-clock work, seven counting today. She almost got away with it, damn her."

If Scott hoped to obtain samples from the damaged trees, he had to grab them right now. He moved his air car out over the debris-strewn swath left by the harvesters and did a low-level flyover to film that, as well. Even if the release hadn't directly affected the fauna down there, with this big a disruption in the local biosystem, exacerbated by the massive scale of Mariel Ubel's clear-cutting operation, the animals that had lived in this stretch of forest would be long gone, looking for new feeding grounds and safer ranges away from those huge mechanical harvesters chewing up their old habitat. If the stray had come from a treecat colony based in the immediate vicinity of this research plant, those treecats were going to get mighty hungry, mighty soon, without any game to be caught or snared or however wild treecats hunted their prey. They were primarily a carnivorous species, given their dentition—and *whenever* herbivores vanished, carnivores went hungry.

"I am going to get inside that plant," Scott muttered, "and find out just what the hell Ubel's let loose out here."

The research plant wasn't a single building, Scott discovered as he moved his air car toward the sprawling facility. It was a series of structures connected by what would've been roofed walkways in other climes, but on Sphinx, with its harsh winters, took on the appearance of walled corridors from some medieval fortress, with sharply sloped roofs to shed snow. Several of the smaller structures were clearly living quarters for the facility's research staff. He spotted a greenhouse, several tool or machine sheds, and what looked very much like a small livestock barn with fenced paddocks attached to it. Several sleek horses lifted their heads from grazing and watched his cautious approach. The plant itself was an immense rectangular structure, large enough to store the expensive harvesters out of the elements during bad weather. A circular landing pad beside big bay doors marked the loading dock for the now-demolished cargo transport. A hangar nearby stood with its doors open, revealing two bays, one for the missing cargo carrier and one for the passenger air car Mariel Ubel had taken into town.

Then Scott's heart skipped a long, frantic beat.

That second bay wasn't empty.

"*Bleek!*" The treecats shrieked the warning simultaneously.

At the edge of that hangar bay, sunlight glinted on the muzzle of a high-powered rifle, aimed right at his air car. Scott yanked at the car's controls, shot them skyward even as he caught the blur of the weapon's discharge below his vulnerable belly. He rolled his lightweight craft in a sickening twist as the heavy rifle fired. The treecats slammed into the side of the airframe, shrieking in pain. *WHUMP!* The impact shook the whole air car. The control board lit like Christmas in Piccadilly. Smoke from fried electrical connections clouted his nostrils. The air car shimmied wildly midair, fighting the controls. They slewed sideways, yawed and pitched drunkenly. Scott swore savagely, flipping switches to backup systems, rerouting power, trying to gain altitude and distance from that open hangar bay.

WHUMP!

The second impact sent them spinning out of control. Scott struggled with the anti-grav generators, cut in emergency backup, fought the guidance system on manual, flying the *old*-fashioned way, without any on-board computers to assist him. The treecats were bleeking madly, their terror and fury rolling across him in waves as the air car spun first one direction, then bucked and staggered in another. The air car caromed straight toward the blighted forest on collision course. Scott keyed the com link, tried to broadcast even as he fought to gain altitude, heard only static. She was jamming his signal, making certain no distress call or warning went out.

The air car rose sluggishly, still pitching unpredictably as crippled systems labored to keep her airborne, but they weren't gaining altitude fast enough to avoid the trees. In a final, desperate measure, Scott cut the anti-gravs completely. They dropped like a stone, gliding in fast toward the shattered jackstraws of broken branches and shredded treetrunks below. Both treecats were frantic. *"Bleek!"*

Scott tried to pick out the smoothest, most level area of debris in the wicked minefield of protruding branches and punji stakes below. He switched in the faltering anti-gravs again, in an effort to hop over a tangle of lethal splinters the size of his torso, then wrenched at the controls. He cut the anti-gravs again and they hit belly first. The air car smashed down, bounced. The impact rocked Scott in his harness, snapped his head forward against the restraints. The safety webbing caught the treecats before they could impact against the dash.

They hit again, skidding sideways through sharp, protruding branches and woody debris. Metal shrieked, bent, tore. Scott snapped forward in his harness again, jounced his teeth together over a scream of pain as the airframe buckled and tore open at his side, shredded by a thick branch they skidded past, puncturing the car's skin like a can opener. They finally rocked to a halt, less than a meter from the closest standing trees. Scott blinked sweat out of his eyes and dragged in a lungful of smoky air. The control panels were sizzling, hissing. *Gotta get out, Ubel's going to be right on top of us...*

Scott fumbled with his harness, released the catches, crawled free. His arm was slashed where the skin of the airframe, peeled back by the branch they'd skidded past, had cut skin and muscle. It wasn't critically deep, but it was bleeding and hurt like hell. He crawled toward the co-pilot's seat, found the treecats untangling themselves from the safety webbing.

"Bleek!"

"You guys okay?" he asked hoarsely, trying to clear his vision enough to look for injuries.

"Bleek! *Bleek-bleek-bleek!*"

Get out fast! was the urgent message behind that verbal warning. Scott dug for his bulky medi-kit, slung it over one shoulder, grabbed his rifle where he'd clipped it to the dash, made sure his pistol was still strapped to his hip, then crawled toward the hatch. It was jammed. Scott gritted his teeth, unsheathed his vibro-knife, and *cut* their way out through the side of the dented airframe. He slithered out feet first and landed awkwardly in ankle-deep splinters and broken branches.

The treecats swarmed through the battered interior and

jumped down as well, flitting across the uppermost layer of shifting wood, on a direct course for the blighted trees. Scott followed as fast as he could jog through the treacherous piles of broken, splintered timber. The treecats gained the woodline and jumped for the nearest tree trunk. Scott followed gingerly and finally caught up, staggering forward into the clear, debris-free undergrowth of the dying forest. The treecats were chittering and broadcasting anger and fright. Scott tried his wrist com, but it was no use. Ubel was jamming this whole valley with something powerful enough to keep any transmission he might send from getting through.

He paused under the barren branches, listening hard as he gulped down air that stank of decaying wood and rotting leaves. The blighted trees were sere and brown, bark peeling off in loose, hanging strips. He tested the nearest low-hanging limbs, wondering if he might not be smarter to try climbing rather than running, which gave her a moving target, easier to spot than a stationary chameleon. But the branches were spongy and discolored and even the largest split under his weight.

Scott listened for any sound of approaching air car engines, but heard only the wind and the distant grinding roar of the harvesters at work. He set off at an oblique angle, heading for healthy forest. The crackle and crunch of deadwood under his boots advertised his location to any ears that might be listening, but he didn't have a whole lot of time to put distance between himself and the pursuit that was certain to follow. She couldn't afford to let any witnesses leave this blasted little valley alive.

Scott had almost reached the gap between the dead trees and the healthy forest beyond when he heard the sounds of a large animal crashing through the dead picket woods, headed his way. Alarm jerked through him, simultaneously with the sharp cries of warning from two keen-eyed treecats. Scott dragged at his pistol, cursing Mariel Ubel and his own carelessness in letting her shoot them down. *Maybe it's a hexapuma, scenting its first live game in a week? A hexapuma I could kill without too much trouble, but dammit, I don't have time!*

He gained the gap where the picket wood system had dissolved a twenty-meter-wide swath of open space around the damaged trees and lunged forward, frantic to gain the cover of thick trees beyond. He cast a wild glance back over one shoulder—

—and a horse burst out into the open from the ravaged forest, neighing sharply as its rider pulled up, placing herself between Scott and safety in the thick underbrush beyond. He skidded sideways, tried to cut and change directions, but she fired at the deadwood under his feet and the blast tripped him up. He went down hard, sprawling inelegantly amongst the rotting leaves and spongy branches on the former forest floor. He lay stunned for critical seconds while sweat prickled down his back and soaked into his shirt beneath his armpits.

Mariel Ubel was a superb horsewoman. She controlled her mount with knees alone, freeing her hands for the lethal rifle she now aimed dead-center at Scott's chest. The horse showed signs of a hard gallop, and Scott cursed himself for not having thought of this possibility. Of course she wouldn't have hunted him from the air; she knew as well as he did that spotting him under that thick green canopy would've been almost impossible, even with infrared sensing equipment, since bright light bouncing off sun-heated leaves in that dense a canopy would've confused any heat signature he might've given off—and infrared wasn't much use in broad daylight in any case. Much better to track him on the ground, where she could see and hear him.

He lay panting under Mariel Ubel's cold gaze for a long moment, aware that he couldn't possibly bring up the pistol in his hand fast enough to fire before she drilled him with that rifle. His own rifle hung down his back, where he'd slung it across his shoulder. Hard, ice-blue eyes flicked up and she met his gaze.

"Drop it."

Wind-blown blond hair framed a face that might have been beautiful, if she hadn't been about to cut him down in cold blood. She had the drop on him and they both knew it. "You can't possibly get away with this," he said, trying to talk his way into distracting her, hoping for just an instant's break in her concentration, which he could exploit to bring up his pistol and fire. His hand sweated on the plastic grip.

She laughed at him. "I already have."

"*Two* fatal crashes with you involved?" he came back. "And no storm to explain this one?"

She shrugged. "If I have to run, all I need is enough time to get off world and I can do that in less than an hour. Well before any air car from town can get all the way out here. They'd still be on their way when my ship went into impeller drive."

She must have been making escape arrangements from the moment she'd planned and executed her first murders. All she had to do was destroy the evidence of her violation of the Elysian Rule, close up shop quietly, resign her position, and be long gone before anyone had a chance to grow suspicious. Even if the murders were discovered, she'd get away clean.

"Mind telling me why?"

Pale brows arched. "Why?" Contempt dripped from her voice. "Because my career would have been destroyed, of course."

"I mean, what was it you released and why did you release it?"

Her mouth twisted in distaste. "One of Rafferty's creations. We were developing a test spray to use in controlled experiments, to see what effect our synthesized product would have. It wasn't my fault."

"Then it *was* you who released the stuff."

"It wasn't my fault!" she repeated sharply. "It could have happened to anyone! And if it hadn't been for those damned, meddlesome *treecats*, it wouldn't have happened at all! I told Erhardt to get rid of that thing!"

"Treecats?" Scott asked quietly. "How can the treecats be responsible for your accidental discharge of a deadly bio-agent?" He was achingly aware that Fisher and the stray were working their way toward Ubel through the branches that leaned out into the clearing, could taste their determination to stop her, could even taste the anger and revulsion they felt as they closed ground on her. The horse tossed its head restively and blew through distended nostrils, shaking its mane unhappily. A sharp command brought the animal to a standstill, but only for a moment. Its eyes rolled white as it sidled away from the stealthy approach of the treecats. Could the treecats be responsible for the horse's disquiet? Scott didn't know, wished he could count on it. Unfortunately, she was a good enough horsewoman, her concentration never faltered. She kept that damned rifle trained steadily on him the whole time.

"The treecats," she said bitingly, "are pernicious snoops and thieves! Arvin's damned pet broke into the lab while I was working alone one night, startled me in the middle of a critical transfer. The whole flask shattered, right into the exhaust vents! I tried to shoot the little bastard, but they're quick, damn them and it got away. My God, do you have any idea how much time and money and research went down the drain when that flask broke? I've got three separate biochemical firms bidding for the rights to my research, but with the fines Manticore is going to levy, I'll have to take it to *Mesa* if I want to make any damned profit at all, thanks to the stinking *treecats!*"

Mesa... Home of Manpower Unlimited, which provided cloned and bio-engineered human slave labor to corporate colonies looking for environmentally adaptive work forces they wouldn't have to pay for working in harrowing conditions. Any civilized star system shunned Mesan firms for the monstrosities they were. That Mariel Ubel was running straight for Mesa's bio-medical firms was not surprising; it merely confirmed the depths of her grasping, cold-blooded nature.

"What are the *Mesans* going to do with your discovery?" Scott bit out angrily. "Turn it into the next war's bio-weapon?"

"Enough talk! Drop that pistol."

She was going to kill him anyway. *I'll be damned if I just lie here and let her cut me in half without a fight!* He lifted his arm out to the side, as if complying with the order, letting the pistol dangle loosely in his hand. He couldn't possibly bring it up fast enough to hit *her*; but a horse made for a much larger—and lower—target.

"Going to shoot me here?" he asked. "Or herd me back to my wrecked air car first, so you don't have to drag the body?"

"Drop it!"

Now or never . . .

Scott wrenched the pistol around in his hand, saw Ubel's finger tighten down on the trigger of her rifle, knew he was going to die. A shrill, snarling scream of raw hate tore the air. A streak of cream-and-grey fur launched itself toward Mariel Ubel's horse, too far away, still, to reach *her*. Fisher landed on the horse's rear quarters, claws unsheathed and ripping into the animal's flesh the instant he landed. The horse reared with a sharp neigh. Scott rolled frantically sideways, even as Ubel ripped off her shot. The medical pack slung over his shoulder exploded. Heat seared his back as an animal scream of agony ripped from the horse. Scott rolled wildly to his feet, off-balance and staggering. Ubel clung to that damned saddle, leech-like, and swung the rifle around again before Fisher could reach her.

Scott dove, rolling in an effort to bring up his pistol. He could feel frantic terror and fury from the stray's mind as it raced through the trees, slower than Fisher because of the cruel deprivations it had suffered. Mariel Ubel's rifle tracked around. She aimed straight at Scott. He was still off-balance, still rolling, trying to bring the pistol up in time. Fisher flung himself toward her neck, claws bared, shrieking in fury, but he couldn't possibly knock that rifle aside from where he was. Scott fired wildly, knew he'd missed—

—and a starvation-thin treecat launched itself from the trees straight at the rifle's muzzle. The stray flung itself right down the bore, shrieking its hate and fury, directly between Scott and the rifle. The treecat's lunge knocked the tip of the muzzle slightly sideways, left it sprawled across the end of the muzzle just as the shot blasted loose. Psychic pain detonated behind Scott's eyelids just as he came to his feet, pistol still too low to do any good. The shot tore *through* the treecat and blasted into the deadwood at Scott's feet, just missing him. Scott stumbled, grey-faced and shaken. A broken ball of fur dropped to the ground from horse height. Scott was still moving, still bringing his own weapon up. He fired blind, aiming with trembling hands as the killer on horseback brought her rifle around again, seeking *his* life this time.

His shot struck her chest with brutal force at the same instant Fisher reached her throat. Mariel Ubel jerked in the saddle and screamed, a gurgling, ghastly sound. A look of shock crossed her face. Fisher's claws had ripped away half her throat in the time it had taken her to scream once. The rifle thudded to the ground from nerveless fingers. Then she crumpled down after it, landing with a hard thump. Her frantic mount reared and came down right on top of her, trampled her with flint-sharp hooves. A sickening crunch reached Scott. She didn't move again. Scott fell to his knees, panting and sick. Another treecat appeared in his blurred vision, dropped from the still-screaming, blood-ribboned horse. It bucked one last time and bolted into the trees. The second treecat huddled over the too-still shape on the ground.

Scott caught back an agonized sound and stumbled forward, half-blind, already knowing what he would find. The stray was dead, shot through the body with a weapon capable of dropping a hexapuma in its tracks. Fisher keened inconsolably, rocking back and forth above him. Scott gathered the broken body up, buried his face in the bloodied fur, grieving. The treecat had thrown himself deliberately between that rifle and Scott ... And it had *known* what a rifle could do. Had seen Scott's medical pack blown apart on his back, knew it was the same weapon that had downed their *air car*. And the stray had lunged straight into the shot's path, anyway, knocking the muzzle aside, saving Scott's life. Scott knelt on the broken ground, face buried in blood-streaked, dirt-matted fur, and cried.

You knew it would kill you, you knew ... Scott couldn't forgive himself for bringing the stray here, for causing it to choose in that hair-trigger instant of decision, felt the blame and the guilt so keenly, he would rather the shot had blasted through him. After everything the stray had done, achieving the impossible, communicating the truth that his human friend had been murdered, Scott had let Arvin Erhardt's killer destroy the stray's life.

And Scott had never even given him a name.

He huddled over the broken, nameless little treecat and grieved.

"It's never easy to lose a friend, is it?"

Scott looked up slowly from his chair to see Sanura Hobbard standing quietly in the doorway. He'd forgotten she was coming. Scott tightened his fingers briefly through Fisher's silky fur, needing the soft croon his friend gave him, then roused himself. "I'm sorry, Dr. Hobbard. Come in."

Fisher bleeked a soft greeting.

Her smile was hesitant, her dark eyes solemn. "Thank you, Dr. MacDallan, and thank you, too, Fisher."

That she included his friend in the greeting warmed a dull, cold ache deep inside. "Dr. Hobbard." He rose to his feet, shook her hand. "And no," he added, gesturing her to a chair, "it isn't easy."

"I'm sorry. We all are."

Scott tightened his jaw muscles briefly. "Thanks," he said in a low voice.

"We found a displaced group of treecats," she said quietly into the silence, "within a few kilometers of the plant. They were clearly trying to migrate away from the zone of devastation. We've already delivered the first emergency drops of food to them. A high percentage of the game animals in the blighted area were evidently killed by toxins emitted by the dissolving picket wood trees. Now that we know what's happened out there, we'll keep the affected treecats from starving until they can relocate to another range."

Scott nodded. His hunch had been right, then. That was good, he thought tiredly. It didn't balance the loss of the stray . . . but it helped. "I'm glad."

"I talked to Nicholas Vollney. They found what caused the crash."

Scott, lost in contemplation of the subtle shadings of grey and cream in Fisher's silky fur, looked up. "Oh?"

The xenologist nodded. "It was the air car's on-board computer. It had been tampered with, of course. Caused them to veer off course, shut down their beacon and communications gear, caused the anti-gravs to malfunction, then cut power entirely at a critical moment as they were losing altitude. That's how she did it. If you hadn't grown suspicious, it would never have been noticed." Sanura Hobbard hesitated, clearly needing to ask and equally clearly not wanting to cause him further pain; but she was, above all else, a professional xenologist.

Sensitivity to people's feelings had never stopped one, yet. "You know I have to ask. It's important, I don't have to tell you that, how important it is that we understand this. How did you know? Please, tell me."

Scott's mouth thinned and he shook his head. "There's nothing to tell, Dr. Hobbard. I've flown through a lot of thunderstorms. An experienced pilot would've set his beacon going, if nothing else. No mysteries, just plain old human intuition."

She leveled a cool, disappointed stare at him. "You're going to sit there and tell me there's *nothing to tell,* when a treecat travels five hundred kilometers to find his murdered friend's body, nearly killing himself in the process, locates the nearest humans he can find, drags them out to the crash site, and then throws himself between the killer's rifle and the human he's somehow convinced to investigate the suspicious crash? Dr. MacDallan, I wasn't born yesterday."

Scott pitied her. He really did. If he'd been in her position, he'd have wanted to throttle anyone holding back what she *knew* he wasn't telling her. But what the treecats had done was something the human colonists on Sphinx just weren't ready to hear, yet, not emotionally or psychologically or even politically. Stephanie Harrington was right to play the "I'm just a little kid, Dr. Hobbard," game with the xenologist. Until Scott was *sure* the Manticoran Star Kingdom or others like Mariel Ubel *couldn't* run roughshod over the treecats, Stephanie's was exactly the right game plan to play.

"I'm sorry, Dr. Hobbard," he said tiredly. "But there really isn't anything more to be said. The stray led us to the crash. I did the rest. And I still don't know why it jumped in front of that rifle . . ." The unsteadiness in his voice brought a flinch to the xenologist's eyes.

"I'm sorry, too," she said softly. She stood up, manner somewhat stiff, and said, "I hope you'll change your mind, Dr. MacDallan. You have my number."

"Yes. I do."

And they both knew he wouldn't be calling it.

She said good-bye somewhat awkwardly, then left. Scott sighed and stroked Fisher's fur. When he glanced up again, Irina Kisaevna was leaning against the door frame, just watching him. He tried to smile.

"I heard what she said," Irina told him quietly.

Scott just nodded.

"I didn't mean to eavesdrop, but I was coming to the office to check on you and the door was open . . ."

"It's all right."

She moved across the room, sat down beside him, took his hand in hers and just held it. He pressed her fingers in silent thanks. An odd expression touched her eyes as she sat there, quietly studying him. "You didn't tell her everything, did you? And no, I haven't read that file you left on my computer. But I know you, Scott, you didn't tell that woman everything. Not even close to it."

He tightened his hand gently through Fisher's fur once again. His friend crooned softly and touched his wrist with tiny, warm fingers, sharing the ache of a grief that pounded, dull and relentless, through him. His thoughts jumped back to a tiny campfire and the brilliant, pine-green eyes of a female treecat gazing up at him, the touch of a starvation-thin treecat's hands on his knee and the kaleidoscopic blur of images and sounds and emotional impressions that had swept through him from the stray's memory.

Irina, of all the humans on Sphinx, would understand—and keep the secret.

Speaking very quietly into a silence broken only by Fisher's soft, comforting croons, Scott MacDallan told her the story of the stray.

What Price Dreams?

David Weber

ONE

"Do you think we'll see any treecats?"

Adrienne Michelle Aoriana Elizabeth Winton, Crown Princess of the Star Kingdom of Manticore, sounded considerably younger than her twenty-one T-years as she looked out the window and asked the question over her shoulder.

Lieutenant Colonel Alvin Tudev smiled at her wistfulness and wondered if she even knew she'd revealed it. He suspected she did, and a part of him felt sadly flattered by the probability. It was not something she would have let anyone else hear, but the King's Own Regiment, supported by the Palace Guard Service, provided the royal family's bodyguards, and the lieutenant colonel had commanded the Heir's security force since she turned eleven. He knew she regarded him as a sort of favored uncle. It was a relationship he treasured, and not simply—or even primarily—because he was ambitious to rise to the very top of his chosen profession. Princess Adrienne was an easy person to love, he thought, and then felt his smile fade, for there was more than one reason she had allowed herself to feel so close to him. Her estrangement from her father had been carefully concealed by both the Palace staff and the Star Kingdom's news services, but nothing about any member of the House of Winton was a secret from Alvin Tudev.

Including the Heir's bitter loneliness.

"I don't know, Your Highness," he said after a moment.

"They say 'cats are pretty elusive. And the Forestry Service is enormously protective where they're concerned."

"I know." Adrienne sighed. "Daddy . . . discussed that with me last night. He doesn't much like the Forestry Service."

"I know." Tudev agreed. "But should you be confiding that to me, Your Highness?" he added in a gentler tone.

"What? The fact that fighting with each other is all Daddy and I still have in common? Or the fact that we'd fight *all* the time instead of just each time we happen to meet if he gave a big enough damn about me to bother?" Adrienne turned, and the wistfulness had vanished. The young woman who faced Tudev now looked much older than her years, not younger, and her brown eyes were filled with mingled sadness and bitter maturity. "It's not as if you don't know all about all of us already, Alvin. So if I can't discuss it with you, who *can* I discuss it with?"

"I don't know that you ought to be discussing it at all, Your Highness. I'm honored that you trust my discretion, but you shouldn't say things like that to *anyone*. Like it or not, you're the second most important political figure in the Star Kingdom . . . and you can't afford to be wrong about who you trust to respect your confidence."

"Because, of course, the public's perception of the tender relationship between the King and his beloved daughter must be maintained at all costs, mustn't it?" Adrienne said with such cold, quiet savagery that Tudev winced.

"Adrienne," he said after a moment, dropping the "Highnesses" he was usually careful to maintain, "I can't answer that." He smiled sadly. "I don't know the right answer . . . and even if I thought I did, it wouldn't be proper—or wise— for me to give it to you. I'm an Army officer, not a political advisor. My loyalty is to the Constitution, the Crown, and the Heir, in that order, and it's not my place to agree or disagree with all the decisions my duties make me privy to. And, unfortunately, my loyalty as the commander of your protection detail is to Crown Princess Adrienne, not just Adrienne the person. Which means it's *definitely* not my place to have an opinion on how the PR types should portray the relationship between you and His Majesty."

"I know." Adrienne turned back to the window, looking out across the palace grounds at the bulk of King Michael's Tower, and sighed heavily. "I'm sorry, Alvin. I shouldn't put you on the spot by asking you things like that. It's just—" She cut herself off, still gazing out the window, then drew a deep breath. "At any rate, I take it you're satisfied with the arrangements for the trip?"

"Yes, Your Highness." Tudev was relieved to return to a less excruciatingly private subject, though he was careful to keep his gratitude out of his voice. He watched the ramrod-straight back of his future Queen for a moment, then nodded to himself. Perhaps there was one thing he could do for this lonely young woman without intruding (officially, at least) into affairs which were no business of a serving officer.

"Ah, there is one point," he said, and Adrienne turned from the window once more at the odd note in his voice. "We still haven't resolved that small scheduling conflict," he told her.

"Scheduling conflict?"

"Don't you remember, Your Highness? The Yawata Crossing Chamber of Commerce wants you for a ribbon cutting for a new residential tower, but Twin Forks has put in a request for you to visit there and dedicate the new SFS admin wing on the same afternoon." Adrienne cocked a questioning eyebrow, and he frowned. "I'm sorry, Your Highness. Didn't Lady Haroun bring this up with you?"

"Refresh my memory, please, Colonel Tudev," she suggested, and he shrugged.

"I got copies of the original memos of request kicked down to me as your detail commander through Army channels, Your Highness. According to the header, Lady Haroun and Palace PR received copies at the same time. I assumed they would have informed you," he added blandly, "and as the CO of your protection detail, I thought I might save a little time by seeking clarification on the final decision directly from you. It's important that we know your schedule as far in advance as possible so that we can be certain all the necessary security measures are in place, you know."

"I see." Adrienne regarded him gravely, but her eyes began to twinkle. Nassouah Haroun, her appointments secretary, had most emphatically *not* mentioned the Twin Forks request when planning began for the state visit to Sphinx . . . and neither had anyone else. Which wasn't at all surprising, she thought, given her father's attitude towards the Sphinx Forestry Service and treecats in general. Like Nassouah, most of the Palace staff knew only too well how His Majesty would have reacted to the idea of his daughter going anywhere *near* the Forestry Service's planetary HQ, that hotbed of pro-'cat sympathy. In fact, Tudev was taking a considerable risk even mentioning the request. In fairness to her father (which was something Adrienne was aware that it had become increasingly hard for her to be), he hated the use of political power to reward sycophants or punish people who demonstrated independence. That made it unlikely he would demand Tudev's resignation . . . but it wasn't at all unlikely that he would have the lieutenant colonel removed from his present post if he discovered who'd mentioned Twin Forks to Adrienne. No doubt the request for Tudev's replacement would be carefully worded so as not to sound like an order to summarily squelch any further promotions, but it would certainly be seen as such by Tudev's superiors, however it was phrased. It was possible the Army would ignore the implications anyway; it was far more likely that he would be "encouraged" to take early retirement and end his career as a lieutenant colonel.

Then again, there's no particular reason anyone ever has to discover where the information came from—or how, at least, she told herself. One of her few prerogatives as Heir was the right to choose between conflicting events when scheduling official visits. It wasn't used very often simply because it was virtually unheard of for an Heir to know when conflicts arose. No one person could have kept up with all the requests that came in—that was why Adrienne had an appointments secretary and why Nassouah had the fifth largest staff in Mount Royal Palace—and the Princess seldom cared enough about her schedule to get actively involved in working it out. It was far easier to let Lady Haroun worry about the details and simply tell her where they were going when the time came.

But Elizabeth I had specifically granted her son Michael control over his own itineraries as her heir, and it had become an established tradition of the royal family. Not even her father could have denied that . . . not that she intended to mention this particular decision to him until it was too late for him to *try* to deny it. And Tudev had phrased his revelation carefully. She could testify under oath that he'd "let it slip" as a routine request. She knew him too well to think he would lie about it to his superiors if anyone asked him specifically how it had come out, but she also knew no one would ask him a thing if she'd already given her version of events. The word of the Crown Princess of Manticore was not questioned. If she said it had been a slip, then it had been a slip, and that was all there was to it unless her father himself demanded answers.

And he won't do that, she thought with a familiar ache of hurt and loss. *He would never, ever do anything that could raise questions about my actions. After all, I'm going to be Queen someday. It would never do to give anyone any cause to question the sacred honor of the House of Winton!*

She suppressed the pain and smiled at Tudev.

"Oh, yes. *That* conflict," she told him. "I was thinking we'd go to Twin Forks, Colonel. It's smaller and more intimate than Yawata Crossing. Besides, I was in Yawata just five months ago . . . and I believe Father will be there in about three months, as well."

"Very good, Your Highness. I'll add it to the Alpha List."

The Alpha List, as Adrienne knew, was the *real* itinerary for her visit to Sphinx. As a routine precaution, only Tudev and his immediate superior, Brigadier Hallowell, CO of the King's Own Regiment of the Royal Army, would have access to the Alpha List until just before she departed for Sphinx. Not even Lady Haroun would know exactly what was on it, and there were several lists of other potential sites for her visit. Full dress security arrangements would be made at every one of them, but most would be decoys. The practice had been adopted ten T-years ago, immediately after Adrienne's mother's death, as an additional security measure.

That thought brought its own fierce, eye-burning stab of anguish, but she let no sign of it show. She'd become quite skilled at hiding the hurt.

"Thank you, Colonel Tudev," she said, and smiled at him.

TWO

A silken blur of cream-and-gray fur scurried up the trunk of the tree humans called picket wood. It slowed as it reached the upper branches and became identifiable as a treecat . . . rather on the small side for a male. He was little more than a human meter in length from nose to prehensile tail-tip, and that same tail showed only six age bands. Since male cats threw out their first band at the end of their fourth Sphinxian year of life, then added another for each additional year, that made him nine planetary years—or just under forty-seven T-years—old. That was barely over the edge into young adulthood for a species which routinely lived five times that long, but he moved with an assurance at odds with his youth. Which was peculiar, for the tree he was climbing belonged to the most senior memory singer in all the world. Worse, he was not even of her clan . . . and while he hoped he was expected, he had *not* been invited.

He reached another branching intersection and found himself

face-to-face with another male, this one considerably bigger than
he, with the confident bearing of a veteran hunter. The older
'cat gave him a long, measuring look, but the youngster never
hesitated. He flicked his ears in a respectful enough saluta-
tion, yet he kept right on climbing at his slower, more deliberate pace, and the hunter let him pass.

So, the newcomer thought. Word of his coming had been
passed as Song Weaver had promised it would. That was something. Indeed, it was more than he'd truly allowed himself to
anticipate, for he had half-expected his clan's elders to pressure the young memory singer into "forgetting" her promise.
He twitched his whiskers in the equivalent of a human snort
at the thought and continued on his way, borne onward by
the sense of righteous indignation which had brought him across
half a continent for this meeting.

But then he reached the tree fork he sought, and he felt
himself slow abruptly. It was one thing to set out on even
the longest journey, confident in his own rectitude and calling. It was quite another, he suddenly discovered, to reach its
end and actually thrust himself into the presence of the most
respected living member of his own species.

He paused outside the large, comfortable nest tucked into the
uppermost reaches of the tallest tree at the very heart of the
Bright Water Clan's central nesting place, and somewhere deep
inside him a very young kitten discovered that it unaccountably
wanted to forget its own effrontery, turn around, and go home.
But it was only a brief pause. He had come too far to hesitate
now, and he shook himself, then advanced to the nest's entrance.
He stopped there once more and reached out with one true-hand
to strike respectfully at the hollow wooden tube hanging beside
the nest entrance. Generations of other claws had gouged the
tube, and countless impacts between it and the tree bole had worn
a deep depression through the picket wood's tough bark, but the
resonating musical note as it flew back against the tree was
sufficient for sharp ears to hear.

For an instant, the youngster thought the ears of the one
he sought must have lost their sharpness, for there was no
response at all. But then a mind voice spoke, and his own ears
went up in astonishment as it rolled through him.

< So, young Seeker of Dreams. You have arrived. I expected you
sooner. >

Seeker of Dreams—who had been called Tree Dancer until
his clan's senior memory singer derisively renamed him at his
last acrimonious appearance before the elders—sat very still,
tasting the serenity and amused, tolerant laughter of the mind

glow behind that incredibly rich and vibrant mind voice. All his young life, he had known that the memory singer called Sings Truly was the most powerful and skilled memory singer in the world. Indeed, she was one of the three or four most powerful in all the thousands of turnings of the People's memory. But that had been knowledge, not experience. Now the power and the beauty of her mind voice flowed through him, jewel-toned and clear as still water, yet edged with the immense power of every mind voice she had ever touched and reproduced as she sang the memory of the People into the web of time. They were all there, sounding like the chimes and cymbals of the two-legs in the timbre of her mind voice, and it took all the courage in him to find a reply at last.

< *Yes, Memory Singer,* > he said. < *I have come. I am sorry the journey took longer than you had expected. It was long, but I came with all speed.* >

< *Indeed you did.* > Sings Truly sent forth another surge of wry amusement. < *It was only that when Song Weaver warned me of your quest, I expected you to arrive in a flash of light and thunder, like one of the human's sky craft. At the very least I expected your fur to be somewhat singed by the speed of your passage!* >

Seeker of Dreams' ears twitched in acute embarrassment, and the fact that he knew Sings Truly could taste it—and that he could taste her increased amusement in reply—made things no better. But he also tasted her encouragement and genuine welcome.

< *If I had had a two-legs sky egg, I would have used it, Memory Singer,* > he admitted after another moment. < *But I had only my own feet and tail. Although I do believe I may have scorched my tail a bit swinging through that last stretch of straight wood beyond the mountains.* >

< *No doubt. Well, come in, kitten. You have come too far to be kept sitting outside my nest until it rains upon you.* >

< *My thanks, Memory Singer,* > he replied with all the sincerity her courtesy deserved, and uncoiled his sinuous body to enter the tightly woven nest.

Most of the People preferred snug nests, little more than twice their own bodies' length, for several reasons. For one thing, smaller nests were considerably warmer during the cold days. For another, adults were responsible for maintaining their own nests, and it was easier to see to the proper weaving of smaller roofs. Mated pairs regularly extended their nests, especially if they had kittens to rear, but they also returned to a smaller, more comfortable size as soon as possible.

But Sings Truly's nest was enormous, with room for at least a triple-hand of adults, and Seeker of Dreams blinked as his eyes adjusted to the dimness within and he realized someone had actually carried stones up the tree to build a sturdy hearth at its center. Such a luxury was unheard of, given the danger escaped fire represented to tree-dwelling creatures, but his surprise vanished as quickly as it had come. This was *Sings Truly's* nest, and if any of the People had ever earned such consideration, she had.

Then something rattled, and he turned his head and blinked in fresh surprise as Sings Truly pulled aside a curtain and stepped from behind it. The curtain was of some material he had never seen before, and he felt a flash of excitement as he realized it must be of two-leg weave. Or of two-leg *making*, at least, for it did not seem to be precisely woven at all. Rather it was all of one piece, with a soft and furry inner surface, which he felt intuitively certain was an even better insulator than the blankets and wall hangings the People wove from their own shed winter coats.

He had a brief glimpse of the much smaller, plain little chamber behind the curtain and realized it must be her own sleeping place, but that hardly registered at the moment. Not only did he have the curtain's odd material to ponder, but no other nest he had ever heard of had actually been partitioned inside, and the novelty took him aback. Yet it made a great deal of sense for a large nest when he thought about it. There was no real point building walls between People for that peculiar concept the two-legs called "privacy," for it was literally impossible for one of the People not to taste the mind glow of another at such close range, but the chamber walls and hanging curtain cut the nest up into smaller sections, each of which would be its own cell of warmth during the cold days.

< *So you approve of my curtain?* > Sings Truly cocked her head at him. < *Not all do. Indeed, some think it only one more sign my position has led me into pride.* > She bleeked a laugh. < *Most are careful not to say so, but their mind glows give them away.* >

< *Surely not!* > Seeker of Dreams protested.

< *I am not just a memory singer to Bright Water Clan, kitten,* > she told him in richly amused mind tones. < *I am also old Sings Truly, and I am aunt or cousin or honorary granny to every member of the clan. They have no intention of allowing me to forget that, and I think it is just as well. Besides—* > another bleeking laugh < *—I doubt I should know what to do with myself if someone did not disapprove of me!* >

< *Who would dare?* > Seeker of Dreams demanded, and then his whiskers twitched in fresh embarrassment as she laughed gently at his outraged ardor. Well, she was entitled to laugh at him, but that made his question no less valid. She was Sings Truly, the memory singer of memory singers and the one whose stunning vision had truly brought the People and the two-legs together!

< *You* are *a kitten,* > she told him at last, her mind voice gentle. Then she stepped fully into the central nest, and Seeker of Dreams felt a flash of shock as he saw her clearly at last. Her strong, beautiful mind voice and the mind glow that matched it were those of a young female in the prime of her life, but the memory singer he actually saw was shrunken with age. Her dappled brown pelt was so age-silvered it looked almost as gray as his own, and her left true-foot and hand-foot both dragged when she moved. Her whiskers were age-bent, she had lost her upper right canine, and now that he looked more closely, he could taste the constant, low-level pain of stiffened joints and aching sinews which had become an inescapable part of her life. It was so clear when he sought it that he was astonished he could have missed tasting it in the first place, but only until he realized he hadn't tasted it because *she* didn't. It was a fact of her life she could not deny, but she saw no reason she should dwell upon it, and her grass-green eyes glowed with a will to which the infirmities of an obviously failing body were merely an inconvenience.

< *So, young dream chaser,* > she said. < *As you say, you have come far to consult with me. What may this ancient singer of memories do for you?* >

< *I—* > he began, then paused, overcome once more by a sense of his own temerity. He was only a youth who had been granted his voice before the elders of Red Leaves Dancing Clan less than half a turning before, and as Song Mistress had pointed out, that scarcely qualified him to challenge the united decision of those same elders.

For just an instant, all he wanted to do was turn and go home, before he exposed his youthful lack of maturity and humiliated the rest of his clan by disputing the will of its elders. But then he remembered the songs of Climbs Quickly and the deeds of Sings Truly when first she became Bright Water Clan's senior singer, and his resolve stiffened. If anyone in the world would understand how one could be called to argue against restrictions, surely that person was Sings Truly!

< *I have come to seek your assistance, Memory Singer,* > he said with a dignity he found vaguely surprising.

< *My assistance,* > Sings Truly repeated, and her age-blunted whiskers quivered with bittersweet memory. < *There was another scout of the People who asked my assistance,* > she told Seeker of Dreams. < *I gave it . . . and he almost died of the giving. Indeed, he did die of it in the end. Would you have me repeat that gift?* >

< *I would,* > Seeker of Dreams replied, and this time there was no question or self-doubt in him. He looked into her eyes, letting her taste his sincerity, and she sighed.

< *Your elders are right, Seeker of Dreams,* > she told him at last. < *You* are *too young. Go home. Wait. Live longer before you race to meet the dark.* >

< *I cannot,* > he replied simply. < *I have heeded the songs, Memory Singer, and I taste the two-leg mind glow in them, like fire in a night of snow and bitter wind. It haunts my dreams, and I yearn to taste it more clearly—to take it for my own and give myself to it. And I wish to know more of the two-legs' worlds, and their tools, and all their marvels. It is a hunger and a need within me, and I cannot reject it or turn from it.* >

< *And if you feed that hunger, you will die,* > she said softly, and flicked her tail in interruption when he would have responded. < *Oh, not immediately, little brother. But the humans— and that is what they call themselves; not "two-legs"—are shorter-lived than we, and those who bond to them . . .* > Her mind voice trailed off, and he tasted a complex alloy of grief, guilt, and loss in her mind glow.

< *I did not realize how short-lived they are when Climbs Quickly bonded to Death Fang's Bane,* > she admitted after a moment, and her mind voice was so soft he wondered if she had ever admitted it to anyone before. < *She was so young, no more than a kitten of her kind. I never dreamed she would live so short a time! Yet even though she lived a long life for the humans, Seeker of Dreams, it was for less than eighteen turnings, and when she died, Climbs Quickly chose to go into the dark with her.* > The memory singer looked straight at her young visitor, and her eyes were very bright but soft. < *A part of my heart died with him, little brother. He was my youngest brother, of our parents' final litter, and I loved him—perhaps too much, for I have never truly known if I supported him because reason told me it was correct, or because love left me no choice. But this I do know, youngling; he should not have gone so soon, not for another full eighteen turnings of his own. Yet if you achieve that which you wish, you will perish even younger than he, for he was three full turnings older than you when they bonded, and few among the humans have mind glows so strong and stable—and at so young an age—as Death Fang's Bane's. You*

*will not find another so young, and if you bond to an adult, one
whose life is half spent when first you meet, then what awaits you
when your human dies?* >

< *I do not know, Memory Singer,* > Seeker of Dreams said, and
dipped his ears with grave formality. < *Perhaps, I, too, will go
into the dark with my two-l—with my "human." But perhaps I
will not, too. It is customary for one of the People to follow his or
her mate into the dark, yet it does not always happen. Sometimes
there are things undone—things one knows one's mate would wish
one to complete, or kittens to raise, or another whose mind glow
fills the hole in your soul. Sometimes there are not, and no one
can know which will happen in his life until it is upon him. Yet
that does not keep us from seeking the ones among the People with
whose mind glows we must bond. Why then should we allow it to
stop us from seeking out the ones among the humans whose mind
glows call out to us in our dreams?* >

< *You are so like Climbs Quickly.* > Sings Truly sighed. < *He
had no reason even to worry about the possibility, for none of us
guessed such a thing might be accomplished, yet he had that same
certainty . . . and stubbornness. You do realize why your elders seek
to prevent this, do you not?* >

< *Of course I do, Memory Singer. Am I a mere kitten, unable
to taste what truly fans their anger with me? They love me. They
do not wish to see me bond to a human and "throw my turnings
away." As you, they fear I will bond to an adult, one with only
three or four turnings left to it, and so they would have me wait
until my own turnings and those of the one I might bond to would
be better matched and I would "sacrifice" less of my life. But I have
tasted the mind glows of others who have taken that advice and
never gone among the humans at all. Rather they find mates in
the passing of time, and that is good, for it is not right for one of
the People to be unbonded and alone. Yet there is also that sadness in them, that knowledge of the path not followed and the dream
not sought. Life is choice, Memory Singer, and any choice—even
the taking of a mate, and the life bonding, and the kittens who
grow strong in the warmth of their parents' mind glow—may breed
sorrow. Indeed, the same choice may bring great happiness yet also
great pain. I am young, but I have seen and tasted it in the lives
of others. Yet the life in question is mine, and it is only fitting
that I bear responsibility for the decisions which weave it. I respect
my elders, and their love warms me, yet have they the right to
forbid me to protect me from myself? Is that not alien to the ways
of the People?* >

< *It is,* > she affirmed sadly.

< *Then the right to choose is mine, and however much I respect*

my elders, and however much I understand that they act out of love, it is I who must decide. Yet I would not simply defy them, and that was why I sought you. You are Sings Truly, she who first recognized the value of our bondings with the humans. And you are also the most senior memory singer of all the People of all the world. I do not ask you to attempt to overrule or command my elders. That would be wrong, even if they chose, because of who you are and all you have done, to obey you. But I ask that you support me in this. That you tell them what you have told me—that it is my right and my decision to make. >

The aged memory singer gazed at the young scout before her, tasting his sincerity. More than that, she tasted the call of which he spoke, the yearning. She saw it seldom among the People, yet each time it appeared, she felt the pain anew, for each time it reminded her of Climbs Quickly. She had come to realize, over the long Sphinxian years, that there had always been something different—special—about her brother. His mind voice had been stronger than that of almost any other male she had ever met, and he had always been independent-minded and strong-willed . . . and most skilled at tasting mind glows. He would have made some female a wonderful mate, and yet there would always have been that something different deep within him. He would not have known what it was, or what to do with it, but he would always have known it was there, like a thorn buried in the pad of a hand-foot. The unused capacity and ability would have been like that, somewhere deep down inside, and he would never have been fully happy or content, for his full talents would never have been tested or used.

Except with Death Fang's Bane. There, with that alien, two-legged creature not even of his world, those talents *had* been used, and her brother had soared on wings of glory. She had told Seeker of Dreams that Climbs Quickly's life had been cut short by his bond, and so it had, but oh, how *brightly* he had burned before the dark!

And she had seen that same talent again and again since he bonded to the human youngling Bright Water Clan had named Death Fang's Bane. It was rare, yet now that the People knew what to look for, Sings Truly believed it had always been there in some of them. It was simply that no one had ever recognized it because there had been no two-legs to summon the possibilities forth. But as the songs of Climbs Quickly's epic battle against the Death Fang and his bonding to the human who had fought it with him winged around the world, more and more of the People had come to the Bright Water range with that same something. They had recognized its taste within themselves from the memory songs of Climbs Quickly, and they had hungered to fill the void within them as he had, with the glorious power of the mind-blind humans' mind glow. Not so very many of them, out of all the numbers of all the People, perhaps . . . but more than even Sings Truly had expected when she first spoke out to defend the value to the People of such bondings.

And too many of them went into the dark too soon, she thought sadly. *So glorious and bright the human mind glow. . . . Is it because they live such short lives? Does their soul consume itself, pouring out in that brilliant furnace? All of the People who have ever tasted it know its power, yet those who embrace it— Are they the most fortunate among us, or the most cursed? And I, who first defended Climbs Quickly, what responsibility do I bear for all of those People who have bound their lives to the humans and seen so many turnings pass unspent from their true-hands?*

She gazed at Seeker of Dreams, tasting his respect for her, his admiration. There was no question in *his* mind glow. But he was young, and certainty was the possession of youth, while Sings Truly was old. She had lived long, even for one of the People, yet soon it would be her time to journey into the dark. She thought about it more often of late, wondering if she would meet Climbs Quickly again beyond the darkness, and if Death Fang's Bane would be with him. She hoped so, for both of their sakes.

And because she hoped that, she could not reject Seeker of Dreams' plea.

< *Your elders have renamed you truly,* > she said after a long, still moment. < *But recall that even the most skilled hunter may find himself the hunted.* >

< *I will not forget it, Memory Singer,* > he promised, and for the first time, there was no sting to the name he had been given. Not when Sings Truly used it in such a mind voice. His head rose, and he met her eyes steadily until she flicked her ears in approval.

< *You understand that even now the humans do not know how clever we truly are?* > she asked him.

< *I do,* > he assured her.

< *Actually, I have always suspected that Death Fang's Bane guessed very early that we sought to conceal our full cleverness,* > Sings Truly mused. < *Certainly Darkness Foe, the human called Scott MacDallan, in their speech, did. And so did Death Fang's Bane, although she had far less proof of it than Darkness Foe did. She was frighteningly clever herself, you know, with a mind glow*

like a crown fire, and she loved Climbs Quickly deeply. I have believed for turnings that she realized what we sought to hide and actually helped us to do so. >

< *I have not heard that in any of the memory songs,* > Seeker of Dreams said.

< *Because I never put it into one of them,* > she told him tartly. < *I was never certain—you know we can taste only their mind glows; we cannot hear their thoughts, although we have learned to know the meaning of a great many of the mouth noises they make. Such as the fact that they call themselves "humans" and not two-legs. But if Death Fang's Bane understood what we sought to do and why, she was clever enough—and loved Climbs Quickly enough—never to ask him.* >

< *With all respect, Memory Singer, I am not certain I under-stand why we* continue *to conceal our full cleverness from the humans. After all, we have not hidden it from* all *of them. What of Darkness Foe? He, at least,* knew *how clever we are. Did he not hear the memory song of Clear Singer? All of us have heard the memory songs of Swift Striker and True Stalker and Darkness Foe and their battle against the human evil doer who destroyed Bright Heart Clan's range and slew True Stalker's two-l—human.* >

< *You speak truth, youngling,* > Sings Truly conceded. < *Yet for all his courage and love for Swift Striker—and grief for True Stalker's death—Darkness Foe was not like other humans. Some of them are . . . less mind-blind than others, and Darkness Foe was more sensitive than any others we have met, even Death Fang's Bane or the clan which sprang from her. But recall even so that making him hear—if, in fact, he* did *hear—took the full voice of Clear Singer, a memory singer of great skill and strength, and the support of three hands of hands of hands of hunters and scouts of Walks in Moonlight Clan. Yet with all that strength supporting her, not even Clear Singer or Strikes Quickly was ever certain how much of the song he truly heard. When Clear Singer sang the song of his bonding with Strikes Quickly, his mind glow changed as the song was woven, yet she herself told me tht she did not know how much came from her song and how much from memories of his own which she but evoked. There was no way she could know, for even in the song, she could not hear his thoughts.* >

< *That is true,* > Seeker of Dreams admitted, flicking his ears as he acknowledged her correction. < *Yet it is also true that since the days of Death Fang's Bane and Darkness Foe we have bonded with them for six hands of turnings, and they have done much for us. Their own elders have ordered that we and our ranges be pro-tected from the evil doers among them, like she who slew True Stalker and his human, and they have taught us many things we*

would never have known without them. Surely we need fear them no longer! >

< *You might be right,* > Sings Truly replied. < *But once the shell of that nut is cracked, the People will never be able to put the kernel back inside it. And never forget, Seeker of Dreams, that like the People, humans are hunters. And like the People, there are good and bad among them. We have observed that the good out-number the bad, and that the rules made by their elders—their "kings" and "queens," as they call them—have been mostly good ones. But many of those rules are strange and confusing to us, for they deal with concepts and possibilities we do not understand. And never forget, youngling, that the reason those rules are required is to prevent the bad among them from doing wicked things, or that the power of their tools and all the many devices they possess and the things they know make them more dangerous to the People than any death fang. Even those who would never hurt one of the People on purpose could easily do so by accident.*

< *All of that is true, and reason enough for caution, but con-sider also this. Even among the People, a clan is wary of those who may pose a threat to it. There have been fights between clans over ranges and nesting places. We are not proud of it, but we know it happens, even as we know there are occasions when one of the People deliberately kills another out of hatred or anger or greed—even love . . . and especially out of fear. The same is true among humans, but so long as they do not think we are as clever as they, they will not see us as a threat. Indeed, their elders see us all as younglings, to be protected and nurtured, and we encourage them in that. Perhaps we cannot taste their thoughts, nor they ours, not even the ones like Darkness Foe or Death Fang's Bane, yet the bond is there, and though they may not taste as we taste, still something within them seems to sense us, whether they know or not, when we turn all our will and skill to reaching them.*

< *And this one thing all of the People who have bonded with humans do, Seeker of Dreams: they ask their humans to keep our secret. We do not seek to compel or to deceive into doing as we wish, for it would be an evil thing to whisper orders into the ear of one who trusts us in a voice he does not know even exists. We but ask, as Climbs Quickly asked Death Fang's Bane and as Swift Striker asked Dark-ness Foe, and we do not know if they hear us even in their dreams, yet so far all have kept our secret. And so their elders continue to debate our cleverness, and to protect us, and do not see us as a threat. But those things could change, and I would not have us risk that change until we have built sufficient bonds as bridges between us that the humans know we are no threat and will never be one.* >

< *But has not that day already come?* >

< *As I say, I do not know the answer to that question, but my heart says no, Seeker of Dreams. There are so few among the People who can and will bond to the humans, and humans live such short lives. I know of no more than five triple-hands of hands of People who are presently bonded to humans. That is not many against all the numbers of humans on this world . . . and so far,* all *of the People to bond have done so here, on this world. Less than a single hand of us have been to any of the other worlds the humans own, and there are so* many *humans. Those of the People who have bonded tell tales of world upon world, hands of hands of hands of them. And of all those worlds, our humans claim only three. We do not understand how their clans and those of all those other worlds meet and communicate, or how they resolve differences, but we know there is much contact between their worlds . . . and that not all humans regard us as* our *humans do.*

< *No, Seeker of Dreams. There is too much we do not yet know or understand. Bright Water's elders were wrong to oppose Climbs Quickly's bond with Death Fang's Bane, yet there was also wisdom in their caution. We have begun the task of building our bridge to the humans, and the work goes well, if slowly. Yet the bridge remains fragile still, and will for many more turnings. Let us not race out onto the branch only to discover it will not yet bear our weight, kitten. Do you agree, or—* > a devilish gleam of humor flickered in her mind glow < *—must I . . . convince you to see this as I see it?* >

< *Ah, no, Memory Singer,* > Seeker of Dreams said very carefully.

< *Good. In that case, let us consider instead how best to convince your elders to agree gracefully to that which you desire.* >

THREE

Princess Adrienne sat with her feet tucked up under her in the armchair in her suite aboard HMS *King Roger I* while she gazed sightlessly out the armorplast view port. The suite's dimmed lights made the star-spangled view still more glorious, yet she scarcely even noticed it as her mind drifted through channels which had become far too well worn.

She'd always disliked the names tradition insisted upon hanging on each new royal yacht. This one, for example. It sounded . . . arrogant to name a ship after her own great-great-great-grandfather. Of course, the choice hadn't been made by the royal family—the Navy had picked the name when the Admiralty built the *Roger* as its predecessor's replacement— and no one *else* seemed to object. But she couldn't help it.

Maybe it's just because he was King, and Daddy is King, and I don't want to be Queen, but they're going to make me. I ought to just let them crown me, then abdicate. That'd fix them all!

She toyed with the notion, visualizing the consternation. The fact that she was an only child and that her widower father had steadfastly refused to remarry had always made the political establishment nervous about the succession. It wasn't as if she didn't have a dozen cousins in varying degrees who could step into the breach, but the Star Kingdom's population had developed an almost frightening veneration for the House of Winton . . . and she was the last member of the family's senior branch.

Of course, I've read great-great-grandmother's personal journals, she thought. *That has to make a difference in how much veneration I feel for the monarchy. I wonder how many people realize the Crown was supposed to be mostly a figurehead? A puppet for the House of Lords? Well, they got more than they figured on with Grandma Beth!*

She grinned, but then the grin faded as she remembered what her ancestress' successful Constitution building had dumped on her own plate. Damn it! She was sure there were thousands of people simply *dying* to be King or Queen! Why couldn't she just pick one of them and pass the job to someone who actually wanted it?

She sighed and picked a bit of fluff off her bathrobe. She held it up on her opened palm, then puffed a breath of air at it and watched it sail off into the unknown. She lost sight of it almost instantly in the dimly lit cabin, and a sudden spasm of hurt lashed her as it brought back another day when a ten-year-old Adrienne had watched her mother's ship depart HMS *Hephaestus* for Gryphon. She'd been supposed to accompany the Queen Consort, but something had come up. Some minor detail which had derailed her own schedule. And so she'd simply accompanied her mother up to the space station to wave goodbye and then watched the yacht—that one had been named *Queen Elizabeth I*—until it vanished into the immensity of space, just as the bit of fluff had vanished.

And like the bit of fluff, she had never seen it—or her mother—again.

She bit her lip hard, as much in anger for letting memory ambush her as in anguish at reliving it, and forced it down, down into the deep places in her mind. It subsided sullenly,

like a hungry neoshark, sinking back into the shadows but
never truly gone. She felt it there, circling at the core of her,
waiting for another opportunity to erupt from the depths and
rend her afresh. And it would attack again. She knew it would.

She drew a deep breath and shoved her hands into the pockets of her robe, and then, slowly, she forced herself to relax
and draw happier memories to the surface. Memories of her
mother before her death . . . of her father before her mother's
death.

A great many people had been astonished when Crown
Prince Roger wedded Solange Chabala. Not by the fact that
she wasn't a noblewoman, for the Constitution specifically
required the Heir to marry a commoner, but rather because
she was so . . . well, *plain*. With all the Crown's subjects to
choose from, surely Prince Roger (who possessed the Winton
handsomeness in full measure) could have picked someone who
stood more than a hundred and fifty-one centimeters and had
a face that was more than merely . . . comfortable looking.
Oh, in the proper lighting little Princess Solange could pass
for pretty, but she'd been undeniably plump, and she'd never
managed to cultivate the air of boredom which was any proper
aristocrat's birthright. Instead, she'd *bustled*, and she'd smiled
incessantly, and she'd always been *doing* something, and somehow, without anyone's realizing it was happening, she had
gathered the entire Star Kingdom to her heart and it had
discovered that, without quite knowing how, it had learned
to love her.

As Adrienne had. And her father. Indeed, King Roger had
adored his Queen, and she had exercised a profound impact
upon him. In his youth, Prince Roger had been the darling
of the Liberals and the despair of his parents, for he'd been
strongly attracted to the assertion that monarchies were obsolete.
That argument had been around almost since the beginning
of the Star Kingdom, of course, but in the last thirty or forty
T-years the Liberal 'faxes had begun pointing to the growing
Republic of Haven and its daughter colonies as the way of the
future. Not even the discovery of the Manticore Wormhole
Junction forty-five T-years before Adrienne's birth seemed likely
to allow the Star Kingdom to close the vast gap in wealth and
power between it and the Republic, and "the dead hand of
monarchy" had been a favorite Liberal explanation for why
that was so. For herself, Adrienne had been impressed by the
fact that none of the Liberal Party's aristocratic members had
ever been heard to comment on "the dead hand of the *nobility*" or to offer up their own privilege and wealth upon the

altar of economic equality, universal suffrage, and democracy. But Roger had found much of the Liberal platform very appealing, although he hadn't quite known what to do about the Liberal notion that the monarchy, as the first, most fundamental barrier to the implementation of their sweeping changes, must be removed.

Until Princess Solange arrived, that was. Even now, with all the hurt and all the pain since, Adrienne had to smile whenever she thought of how her mother's impact had shaken Manticoran political circles. She was energetic, kind, caring, cheerful . . . and implacable as a Sphinx glacier. Her Gryphon yeoman background had gifted her with a sturdy sense of independence, a fundamental distrust of aristocrats who kept talking about how much they wanted to "help the common man," and a deep sense of trust in the monarchy. It never occurred to her that the Crown might be anything but the commoners' natural ally against the wealth and power of the aristocracy—whether that aristocracy described itself as Liberal, Conservative, or Reactionary—and she went through Mount Royal Palace like a hurricane of fresh air.

Those had been the good years, Adrienne thought now. The years when her mother and father had been a team. When first Princess and then Queen Consort Solange had convinced her husband to stop dabbling with theories of social engineering and get down to the pragmatic task of making the monarchy work to produce the things he'd longed to give his subjects. Adrienne could still remember childhood nights, sitting at the dinner table with her parents while she listened to them stripping the bones out of one problem after another, analyzing them, coming up with strategies. She'd been too young to understand what they were trying to accomplish, but she'd felt their energy and vibrancy, the gusto with which they tackled the job, and she'd known even then that it had been *both* her parents. That her father was the strategist and the planner, but that her mother was the power plant that drove the machine and the warm, caring heart which had become her husband's moral compass.

And then, just before Adrienne's eleventh birthday, *Queen Elizabeth*'s inertial compensator had failed under power.

She had been pulling close to four hundred gravities when it happened. There had been no survivors, and the derelict ship, manned only by the dead, had attained a velocity of over .9 *c* before anyone could intercept it. *Queen Elizabeth* had been traveling at that speed when she struck a tiny lump of matter—later estimates were that it was probably no more than a couple of cubic meters in volume. Her over-stressed particle shielding had already failed, not that it would have done much good at her final velocity even if it had functioned perfectly. The explosion had been visible to the naked eye throughout most of the Manticore Binary System, if one knew where to look.

Roger II had known where to look. He'd stood on a balcony of Mount Royal Palace and watched the searing flash of his wife's funeral pyre without so much as a single tear . . . and he had never wept for her since.

But the man who had come back inside from that balcony never smiled, never raised his voice in anger or laughter, either. He might as well have been a machine, and all that mattered to the machine was the power of the greater machine he ran. All of the tactics he and Queen Solange had worked out were at his fingertips, and he used them ruthlessly, yet the heart had been cut out of him with his wife. He remained scrupulously fair and puritanically honest, but there was no laughter, no joy. No room for humanity, because humanity hurt. It was better to be the machine running the machine, to lose himself utterly in providing his subjects with efficient government, however cold and unfeeling, than to risk feeling anything ever again.

And the one creature the machine had feared most in all the universe was a small, slender child who had just lost her mother. For that child could have *made* him feel again, could have dragged him back to face his agony, and so he'd used the press of his duties, and the formality of palace etiquette, and the need for tutors to teach her all the things she had to know, as excuses to hide from her. He'd pushed her away, fought to crush her into some sort of mold that would squash out the perfect automated successor for a machine which had once been a man. She was his heir, his replacement part, and that was all he dared let her ever be, lest she, too, die and wound him all over again.

She hadn't understood, of course. All she'd known was that when she'd needed her father most, he had deserted her. And because she was her mother's child, and because she'd loved him so much, she had reasoned that the fault must be hers and not his. That she must have done something to drive him away.

That logic had almost destroyed her—*would* have destroyed her but for the fact that she *was* Queen Solange's daughter. Her mother had been loving, but she had been equally and unflinchingly honest, and she had imbued her daughter with both those qualities. It took almost two T-years for Adrienne to realize what had actually happened—to recognize that her father had shut her out because of the damage he'd taken from her mother's death, not because of anything she had done. And in at least one sense, she'd realized it too late. Not too late to save herself, but too late to forgive her father.

She understood—now—what he'd done. She even understood why, and that his present cold, uncaring persona sprang out of how deeply he'd once allowed himself to love. But she also understood that countless other people had lost beloved wives or husbands or children and managed, somehow, to remain more than reasonably functional pieces of machinery. And she understood her father's selfishness, his inability to look beyond *his* hurt and *his* loss and *his* pain to the daughter he still had or to realize that his actions had deprived her of her father, as well as her mother.

He'd been a coward. He hadn't loved her enough to be there for her. That was what she could not forgive him for. A part of her kept insisting she was wrong to be so harsh. Some people were stronger than others, and he'd pushed her aside out of pain, not cruelty. But it didn't matter, and she wondered sometimes how much of the anger and the fury she felt for him was her way of sublimating her own anguish at her mother's death, as if she could somehow subtly blame him for *all* her pain if she only tried hard enough.

Now she sighed and closed her eyes wearily.

Someday Daddy and I are simply going to have to reconcile, for the Kingdom's sake, if nothing else! I just wish I knew how we can possibly do it. And I suppose that if I'm going to be honest, this little excursion to Twin Forks isn't going to help matters.

She grimaced again. For the last ten T-years, her father's one ambition had been to make the Crown truly supreme, and he'd devoted all his formidable ability and obsessive energy to that task. Adrienne had no doubt that Roger II would go down in history as second only to Elizabeth I among the builders of the Manticoran monarchy, and she knew many traditional power groups were dismayed by how his reforms had pruned and chopped away at their ability to influence policy. Several had attempted to resist their systematic emasculation, but none had been able to defy the avalanche named Roger II.

Except one. The Sphinx Forestry Service had one tremendous advantage over every other independently-minded bureau upon which Roger had directed the force of his will: a direct Constitutional commission. The Ninth Amendment specifically recognized the treecats as the native sentient species of Sphinx, guaranteed their corporate title to over a third of the planet's land area in perpetuity, and expressly required the Forestry Service to act as the 'cats' legal guardians, advocates, and representatives. The Crown had the right to name the head of the Service, but only with the advice and consent of the House of Lords, and the Lords had long since realized how the wind set in Mount Royal Palace. They'd begun to fight back against the reduction of their own prerogatives with every weapon at their disposal, including a stubborn refusal to consent in the appointment of a suitably obedient SFS chief who would run the Service the way Roger wanted it run.

That alone would have been enough to focus his cold, unforgiving ire on the Service, but he also found it an intolerable insult that a full third of Sphinx—all of which had originally been Crown land—had been placed forever beyond his reach. To make things worse, much of that land held vast, untouched mineral deposits. The ability to confer those lands on allies in the Lords—or in the House of Commons—would have been an enormously potent weapon, and the man who had become totally committed to the supremacy of the Crown hated the 'cats for depriving him of it.

Which is foolish, Adrienne thought. *No, be honest—it's downright stupid! He's still got most of the Unicorn Belt and all the Gorgon Belt over in Manticore-B, and that doesn't even mention the better part of thirty-seven moons, or the Crown lands he still does have on Sphinx. Plus Gryphon and even Manticore! For that matter, most people would prefer an asteroid grant, because it's so much cheaper to work asteroids than an old-fashioned, dirtside mine. But I don't suppose anyone ever said obsessions have to make sense, and Daddy has more than enough of those to go around.*

She sighed sadly and pushed up out of her chair. *King Roger* was due to depart for Sphinx in six hours, and she needed to get some sleep before their arrival. Besides, sitting here and rehashing all the things which had gone wrong in her life in the last ten T-years was pointless—and so was indulging herself in an orgy of "poor little princess" misery. Her mother had always told her the universe was the way the universe was, and that all anyone could do was deal with it as she found it.

Of course, Mom was always figuring out ways to suck the universe into doing what she wanted . . . and she usually found one when she needed it, too. She smiled wearily and stepped into her sleeping cabin and unbelted her robe. *I wonder what she'd think of my subterfuge with my itinerary? She'd probably be pissed at me for using it as a way to tick Daddy off, but maybe not. One thing I know for certain: she'd be pissed as* hell *at him for the way he's acted since her death, so maybe she wouldn't be so mad at me after all.*

I hope not, anyway.

Crown Princess Adrienne slipped into bed, waved the lights out, and settled down into her pillows, and deep inside her, where she could scarcely hear them any more, the tears of a lonely little girl fell into the silence.

FOUR

"I don't like it."

"You *never* like it, Henry. That's why I work with you."

"Huh?" Henry Thoreau's face wrinkled in puzzlement, an expression which made him look even more like one of the genetically enhanced buffalo being experimentally introduced to Gryphon. He stood a full two meters in height, with a broad, meaty face remarkable for its extreme plainness, whereas Jean-Marc Krogman was a small, sleek whippet of a man. Krogman was also the more intelligent of the two, but that very intelligence prevented him from underestimating Thoreau. The bigger man was no genius, but neither was he stupid . . . and he *was* pragmatic, with good instincts, and very, very good at what he did.

"You never like it," Krogman repeated now, "whatever the job. But that's good. It's what keeps you on your toes and makes you so good at spotting potential problems before they bite us on the ass."

"Oh." Thoreau rubbed his nose while he considered that, then shrugged. "So fine. That means you should listen to me. And I'm telling you that this one is too high profile. We try to pull it off, and we'd better plan on migrating to some neobarb colony no one ever heard of and staying there for good, 'cause there sure as hell ain't gonna be a hole deep enough to hide in here! And I don't know about you, Jean-Marc, but I kinda like it here. 'Specially compared to someplace like Old Earth or Beowulf," he added pointedly.

"As do I," Krogman agreed. "Nor do I have any intention of leaving. But in this instance, I think the prominence of the mark makes you unduly nervous. And it would be . . . unwise to change our minds this late in the game. Our client would take a dim view of that, you know." He cocked a quizzical eyebrow at Thoreau, and after a moment the big man nodded glumly. "Besides, the pieces are all in position, and our weapon has been thoroughly prepped, if I say so myself. No, Henry. It doesn't matter how high profile the job is when the work is properly planned and executed. We can get to her and get away clean. After all," he smiled thinly, "it's been done before."

"Ha! I've heard the rumors, too, and that's all they are. No way in hell that was a hit!"

"Oh?" Krogman cocked his head, and his eyes glinted. "You think not? Then tell me this—how many *other* inertial compensators have failed in the last ten T-years?"

"Huh?" Thoreau rubbed his nose again, then shrugged irritably. "How the hell should I know?"

"A fair question," Krogman conceded. "The numbers are scarcely a matter of general interest, and some research would be required to discover them. But unlike you, I've looked into it—a matter of professional curiosity, you understand—and the answer is none. Not a single compensator has failed aboard a single Manticoran vessel since the *Queen Elizabeth*'s. Don't you find it just a little odd that the *only* ship to suffer complete and catastrophic compensator failure in all that time also happened to be the single most carefully maintained vessel in the entire Star Kingdom?"

"I guess it does sound funny, put that way," Thoreau admitted after a moment.

"Indeed it does," Krogman said with another smile, "and I wonder how it was managed? Of course, whoever pulled it off was also far luckier than anyone has any right to plan for. He couldn't possibly have counted on having the ship blow itself—and any evidence—the hell up. But I'll guarantee you that anyone who could get to the royal yacht's compensator would have set up a defense in depth that would have held even if someone had managed to intercept the ship and bring it back intact."

"That's a pretty big supposition," Thoreau pointed out.

"Maybe. On the other hand, I've got a strong suspicion that the people who hired us were behind that hit as well. And that they're connected pretty damned high up at Court, too." Thoreau raised an eyebrow, and the smaller man shrugged. "It's exactly the same MO, Henry. Rather than attack the King directly—and maybe start someone looking for high-placed conspirators who might profit equally directly from his demise—they go after targets that attack him only obliquely. Hmm. . . ."

He leaned back in his chair, thinking hard while summer Sphinx sunlight spilled over the street-side cafe.

"I wonder," he murmured at last. "Do they only want to cripple him? To derail this passion of his for making the Crown supreme? Or will they go for him directly later?"

"If they want him diverted, then they weren't as smart as they thought the first time around—assuming what happened to the *Queen Elizabeth* really was a hit—now were they?" Thoreau snorted. "Sure, they got the Queen, but he's only been an even bigger pain in the ass for anybody else who wants a slice of the pie since she died."

"To the contrary, Henry. They were smart enough; they just hadn't counted on how much it would hurt him, and they got a bad case of overkill." Thoreau frowned, and Krogman shrugged. "Think about it. If someone did sabotage the ship to cripple the King, they succeeded. They simply didn't cripple him in the way they'd anticipated. Instead of abandoning government while he tried to put his private life back together, he totally buried himself in his work to avoid the wreckage of his private life. Given how much he and his wife both loved their daughter, I would've made the same call and expected him to bury himself in the *kid*, instead."

"And you would've been wrong," Thoreau said with a certain satisfaction, and Krogman grinned. His towering partner seldom got a chance to point out errors on his part, especially in matters psychological, and Thoreau enjoyed the rare opportunities to gloat. Not that Thoreau was foolish enough to *want* Krogman to make mistakes, which was one reason Krogman was amused rather than irritated by the big man's gloating.

"I would've been wrong," he conceded. "But I don't think he'll be able to just keep going if he loses the kid now. Oh, no. If anything happens to the Heir, everything he's been avoiding since his wife's death will jump up and go straight for his throat, Henry. I'm as sure of that as I am that we're sitting here right now. But is that what they want, or will they go after him directly while he and his security people are still reeling?"

"If they do, then they can damned well find someone else for the job!" Thoreau said bluntly. "And that goes for you, too, Jean-Marc! I've done some risky things with you, but I am *not* going after the frigging King of frigging Manticore!"

"No one's asking you to," Krogman soothed. "But it *would* make sense, wouldn't it? I mean, if they wanted to manipulate the succession." His eyes took on a faraway expression, and he pursed his lips. "Everyone thinks what happened to

Queen Elizabeth was an accident," he mused. "Well, everyone but the PGS and the King's Own, at least, and even they probably lean that way. And if things work right, everyone'll think what happens to the Heir is the work of a lone madman. Security for the King will tighten up, sure, but I wonder if anyone else has considered how removing his wife prevented him from producing any other heirs while removing his daughter will eliminate the only heir he has. Which means that if they eliminate *him*, why, the direct line of Winton will go— *pouf!*"

He snapped his fingers, and Thoreau twitched uncomfortably. He looked around the cafe quickly, suddenly nervous about listening ears. But it was early, they sat alone in a sea of empty tables still awaiting the normal lunch rush, and neither of them had been foolish enough to raise his voice. Besides, he'd swept for bugs himself, and neither he nor Krogman had any sort of criminal record to attract official attention. Or not, at least, here in the Star Kingdom and under the names of Thoreau and Krogman.

None of which made him any happier about Krogman's speculations. The possibility that someone might have managed to sneak a bug in on them despite his best efforts was bad enough, but his partner's musings were frightening. People in their line of work became dangerous when they knew too much . . . and their employers became dangerous to *them* when those employers only *thought* they knew too much. Besides, he'd heard that same note from Krogman before, and it usually indicated that the other man was mentally prospecting for fresh opportunities. Which was a good thing, most of the time, but would be a decidedly *bad* thing if it got them any deeper into some kind of plot aimed at toppling the monarchy outright.

"Yeah, well, maybe you're right about all that, Jean-Marc," he said, "and maybe you aren't. But what *we've* got to worry about is the operation we signed on for, and I'd feel a hell of a lot better if we already had her real itinerary."

"All we can do is all we can do," Krogman replied with a philosophical shrug. "We told them they'd have to provide us with the intel to get our boy into position, and they agreed. So if they don't get us the word this time, then we wait for the next time she comes out where we can get at her. Either that, or they find themselves another team."

"I don't much like *that* thought, either," Thoreau muttered, and Krogman quirked an eyebrow. "The thought of their finding another team," the big man amplified. "I mean, what if they've already lined up somebody to pop *us* right after we pop her? Kinda tie up the loose ends real quick, just in case?"

"A thought," Krogman murmured, and there was a gleam of respect in his eyes as he regarded his partner. In point of fact, Krogman had already considered that possibility, but the fact that Thoreau had also pondered it gave it additional point.

Of course, that's always a part of the game, isn't it? And our "clients" know that we know that they know that we know it. So if I were the people we're working for, and if I were as smart as I've been giving them credit for being, would I also be smart enough to know that people like me always cover our asses? Or would I be smart enough to figure out a way to pop me and get away with it no matter how *thoroughly I've covered my ass?*

He smiled dreamily at the thought.

"Here! Take it and get the hell out of my life!" the uniformed woman hissed, and threw the data chip viciously at the elegantly groomed man. They stood between towering banks of Terran rhododendron in Mount Royal Palace's Grand Garden, atop the hill overlooking the city of Landing, and Manticore-A hung on the western horizon. The cool breezes of evening sighed in the glossy green leaves, and the shadows were dense enough to blur their features, but the insignia of a commander in the Royal Manticoran Navy glittered on the woman's collar.

"Now, now, Anna!" The elegant man caught the chip with negligent grace. "That's no way to talk to someone who's paid you so well for your services."

"Paid? You call it *paid?*" The commander sounded strangled, and her fisted hand quivered at her side. "I never took a goddamned *cent* from you!"

"Ah? Well, I suppose not," the elegant man agreed. "But there are other commodities than money, aren't there, Anna? Like silence. Yes," he mused, "silence can be quite valuable, can't it? Especially when it keeps someone like you in the service of the Crown rather than buried on a prison asteroid somewhere. Or possibly just buried, if the court-martial happened to feel particularly vindictive. Normal bribes and contractor kickbacks are one thing, after all, but when substitution of substandard materials leads to the deaths of—what was it? *Sixty* of your fellow Navy personnel? Well—"

He clicked his tongue and shrugged, and the woman physically twitched with the rage boiling through her. But he was right, damn him! All he had to do was drop a hint in the right ear, and her career, her freedom, and quite possibly her life would be over.

But the smartass bastard's overlooked the flip side of the coin, she thought savagely. *Sure, he can wreck my life. But I can do the same for* him, *too, and if I turn King's Evidence to nail a* damned duke *for treason, they just might let me walk, too!*

The thought helped steady her, and she drew a deep, hissing breath.

"You've got your information," she said flatly, "and I hope it doesn't do you a damned bit of good. *I* sure couldn't break the encrypt."

"Just as long as it's the right file." The elegant man's voice was no longer lazy, and the woman felt a sudden flicker of fear at its sudden coldness.

"It's the one you asked for—that's all I can tell you," she said. "That's all *anybody* could tell you about a Blue File without the encrypt key."

The elegant man seemed to consider that, then nodded slowly, and she relaxed a bit at the evidence that he meant to be at least a little reasonable. Blue Files were the most closely held of all military data. Their encryption programs were the best in the Star Kingdom, and their file designations were randomly generated strings of letters and numbers to avoid names which might offer any possible clue as to their contents. All the commander knew was that this particular file had been designated as "A1108G7Q23," and that she had pulled it out of the files of the King's Own Regiment. And, frankly, that was all she *wanted* to know about it.

"Then I suppose I'll just have to find myself a key," the elegant man said, and smiled. "You wouldn't happen to know where I could find one, would you, Anna?"

"No, I wouldn't," she said shortly.

"A pity. Ah, well. Thank you ever so much for your assistance. If I should need any other small favors, I'll be in touch."

He raised one hand and twiddled its fingers in a dismissive, shooing gesture, and she clenched her jaw. But she also made herself turn obediently and leave.

Let the prick enjoy himself for now, she told herself venomously. *I'm just about ready to put the blocks to his ass.*

She smiled thinly into the gathering evening gloom at the thought. It was risky, and she'd implicated herself hopelessly if anyone else ever found it, but the file she'd put together on all her "patron's" demands over the years was just about thick enough.

Another few months, she thought, nodding a brusque salute

to the sentry outside Mount Royal's Lion Gate, and turned to her left, stalking down the pedestrian mall with a long, angry stride.

Just a few more demands like tonight, and it'll be enough to take to Justice and barter for a pass on the bribery charges. Hell, I'll even settle for five-to-ten in a cell if it lets me take the son-of-a-bitch down with me!

Commander Anna Marquette, senior military aide to the Second Lord of the Manticoran Admiralty, never noticed the dark-haired woman behind her. There was no reason she should have, for the stranger had mastered the art of unobtrusiveness. It was, in fact, her stock in trade, and she moved through the sparse, evening foot traffic as if she wore a cloak of invisibility, making no more impression than the breeze itself on anyone who saw her—or, rather, *didn't* quite see her—as she drifted along behind Marquette.

As a matter of fact, the commander mused as she made the familiar turn to cut through Eminger Park, *maybe I shouldn't wait even another month. I don't know what the damned file he wanted was all about, but it* was *a Blue File. That means* someone *sure as hell thought whatever's in it was important enough to bury deep, and if that's true, then—*

The unobtrusive woman touched a button in her pocket, activating the contact lens in her left eye. An illuminated display which only she could see appeared to float before her, and she felt a glow of satisfaction as she carefully checked its icons. The closest thermal signature was fifteen meters in front of the target, and there was no one behind them for at least eighty meters. That was more than enough for her purposes, and she smiled slightly. The target's habit of taking the same route from the Palace back to Admiralty House every single time had made planning ever so much simpler.

Her left hand made a peculiar little twisting gesture, and a small gray tube, cross section thinner than a drinking straw, slid into her hand as she took three larger strides and closed the distance to the commander. One more stride to her left, and her right shoulder jostled Marquette ever so lightly as she stepped past her. The officer's head snapped around, eyebrows rising in surprise at the sudden contact, for she'd never suspected that anyone was behind her.

Perfect, the unobtrusive woman thought.

"Oh, I'm so sorry!" she apologized, and her left hand came up. Marquette didn't see it until the last instant, and even then, no warning bells rang until the gray tube hissed and sent an invisible burst of precisely designed nanotech biochines straight up her nostrils. She heard the sound, then, and her eyes began to widen in shock, but she never felt a thing . . . until the terrible, utterly incapacitating agony as the tiny machines created what all but the very closest of autopsies would insist was a natural cerebral hemorrhage.

The unobtrusive woman didn't even pause as the commander went down in a boneless heap. There was no need. Her nannies had already done their jobs; now they were busy dissolving into odds and ends of "blood protein" that would pass any scientific examination. They would even have the right genetic markers, because the biolab which had built them had been provided with tissue samples from the target's BuMed records to use for building blocks.

Confident in the quality of her own work, the assassin neither shortened nor lengthened her stride. She simply walked away, like any other stroller in the park, without even a smile to betray her satisfaction with a job well done.

"You're certain you got all of it?" the elegant man asked.

"Positive, My Lord," the man in the Palace Guard Service uniform assured him. "The hard copy was exactly where we thought it would be, and I vacuumed every bit of it out of her electronic system, as well. It's gone. Or, at least, if it still exists anywhere, no one else will ever be able to find it if *I* can't."

The elegant man frowned ever so slightly at that, for he hated qualifiers. On the other hand, his minion had a habit of succeeding at even the most difficult tasks. He also had the reach and the avenues of information, both official and private, to make good on his boast. And truth to tell, it was better to work with people forthright enough to make qualifying admissions rather than promise more than they could truly deliver.

The PGS man only stood there, gazing calmly at his employer, as if he knew precisely what thoughts were flowing through this mind, and the elegant man smiled.

"Excellent. I won't forget this," he promised, and walked away with a nod.

FIVE

< *See over there? To the right?* >

Seeker of Dreams looked in the indicated direction as he and Leaf Stalker paused in the fork of a tree. The Bright Water hunter had volunteered to escort Seeker of Dreams to the gathering place of the humans who watched over the People, and Seeker of Dreams appreciated his kindness. The other's mind glow told him they were kindred souls, but though Leaf Stalker felt a sort of wistful envy of his quest, the hunter did not share it. He knew more of humans than many of the People, and he spoke often with the People who had bonded with them, yet he lacked that need, that urgent hunger to seek out the human mind glow, which drove Seeker of Dreams.

And he is wise not to seek the bond without it, Seeker of Dreams thought, and it was his turn to feel a wistful envy, for Sings Truly was correct. Only one driven by a need he could neither master nor resist would choose the path he had, for he *was* young. It was almost certain that the dream he sought would send him to his death before half his allotted turnings were sped, and he felt a sharp flicker of sorrow for all the other things he would never see and experience. As Leaf Stalker did not share his own quest, so Seeker of Dreams would not share the slow, sweet turnings—the mate and kittens, the snow times, and mud times, and green, drowsy times—that the hunter would know.

< *Do you see it?* > Leaf Stalker asked again, and Seeker of Dreams looked more carefully, then flicked his ears in assent. They were too distant to make out many details, but a straight, sharp edge of green, darker than the leaves about them, stood out against a bright patch of sky, and something about it prodded at his memory. Not of anything he had ever seen with his eyes, but of something from the memory songs. . . .

< *It is the roof of the central nest of Death Fang's Bane's Clan's range,* > Leaf Stalker told him almost reverently.

< *Truly?* >

< *Truly. I come here often—sometimes I have spent full days watching over them.* > The hunter sighed, and flicked his tail in perplexity. < *Yet there remain so many things I do not understand at all, or understand only a little, as a kitten might. Even those who have bonded find much about the two-legs—the humans—impossible to comprehend. They embrace many concepts so strange to us that not even those who have learned the meanings of their mouth sounds can explain them to us. They try, and with each turning we creep a little closer to the quarry of knowledge, yet I often think we will never truly understand the two-legs. Perhaps—* > the hunter turned his head to gaze directly at Seeker of Dreams < *—you will prove my fear unfounded. I hope you may, Seeker of Dreams.* >

< *I will certainly try, Leaf Stalker,* > Seeker of Dreams promised almost humbly, and Leaf Stalker bleeked a quiet laugh.

*< Only taste our mind glows, little brother! Here we cling, like two
decrepit old elders peering into the future! Come! I will race you to
the river, and we will let the future see to itself. After all— >* the
hunter was already streaking down the picket wood branch, but
his laughing mind voice carried clearly *< —the future always
does! >*

"I *still* don't like it," Henry Thoreau muttered, but this time
he was careful to keep his voice so low not even Krogman
could have heard it—had he been there. Which he wasn't. The
big man snorted at the thought, for it was far too late to be
worrying over what he liked or disliked. An ancient proverb
about burning bridges flickered through his brain, but he paid
it scant heed. He had no attention to spare from his present
occupation.

No one looking at him would have guessed his nerves were
twisted cable tight as he sat on the public bench and scanned
a hardcopy newsfax. The remains of a simple but tasty lunch
from a vendor at the corner lay on the table before him, along
with a tall glass of lemonade, and he casually checked his watch
as he turned a 'fax page.

The shady park adjacent to the Sphinx Forestry Service's
HQ was a pleasant place for a leisurely lunch, but it was
unusually well occupied today, for news of Crown Princess
Adrienne's visit had been released to the public four hours
ago. Many of Twin Forks' citizens had opted to take a long
lunch break, and people from outlying freeholds had begun
arriving over an hour ago. City work crews were supervising
a small fleet of remotes as the bustling mechanisms rapidly
assembled bleachers from which the Star Kingdom's subjects
could gain an even better view of their future monarch and
hear the address her speech writers had undoubtedly prepared
for her, but for now the park just outside the SFS's perimeter fence was attracting most of the waiting bodies.

Thoreau allowed himself a mental grimace, though no sign
of it touched his face, and wondered whether he was more
reassured or worried that their client had, indeed, managed
to get them the Princess' accurate itinerary. On the one hand,
the information had been invaluable. On the other, the fact
that their employer had the reach to get his hands on data
that closely held spoke ominous volumes about his capabilities in general. After all, if someone who could put this all
together decided to get rid of any liabilities—

Stop that! he told himself sharply. *Jean-Marc's made the
arrangements, just like he always does. If anything happens to us,*

the shit will hit the fan big time when his insurance policy dumps into the public data net.

Sure it would. Of course, Thoreau suspected he and Krogman would take little personal satisfaction from the repercussions of their joint demise, but that wasn't exactly the point. And in the meantime, he had a job to do.

On the surface of it, it was a simple and rather pointless task, particularly for one with his skills in the efficient application of violence. But well-honed as those skills were, he would not need them today, for he had a single, unique qualification for his present task: anonymity. Despite a checkered past in certain other jurisdictions and under other names, his record was squeaky clean in the Star Kingdom of Manticore. That—and the bright red handkerchief in his breast pocket—was all he had . . . and, thanks to the skills Krogman brought to their partnership, it was all he needed to assassinate the Heir.

"Welcome to SFS, Your Highness." The tall, red-haired man in the green and brown uniform of the Sphinx Forestry Service bowed as Adrienne stepped from the air car. His beret bore the Star Kingdom's rampant Manticore, but the patch on the right shoulder of his tunic showed the silhouette of a treecat, and the single golden star of a lieutenant general on his collar marked him as General William MacClintock, the SFS's commanding officer and current head of the Forestry Service Board.

Adrienne held out her hand and smiled the smile she'd been trained to produce since childhood, but it was harder than usual as the six-limbed, prick-eared, cream-and-gray creature on MacClintock's shoulder gazed at her with bright, curious green eyes. She gripped the general's hand firmly, but even though she knew it was rude, her eyes were on the fascinating, graceful treecat, and she heard a soft chuckle from the SFS's CO.

She'd seen video of treecats, of course, but it wasn't the same at all, for the imagery simply couldn't have prepared her for the reality's alert gaze or the crackling sense of intelligence it seemed to project straight into her brain.

The 'cat measured perhaps a meter and a half from the tip of its sharp muzzle to the end of the silky tail that hung down MacClintock's back. Although the long, lean body looked bulkier than it actually was thanks to its luxurious coat of fur, she could see why some people described its species as a six-limbed first-cousin of an Old Terran weasel or ferret. But that description had never really seemed accurate to her before, and now that she'd actually seen a 'cat with her own eyes, it seemed even less so. Oh, there was more than a touch of the weasel in that sinuous body, but it actually reminded her more strongly of images she'd seen of an Old Earth creature called a lemur . . . aside, of course, from the undeniably "feline" head and ears.

The impressions cascaded through her, and then the 'cat flipped its ears and bleeked politely at her, and General MacClintock chuckled even more loudly.

"I think Dunatis just welcomed you as well, Your Highness," he said, and Adrienne pulled her attention from the 'cat to raise an eyebrow at him.

" 'Dunatis'?" she repeated.

"The Celtic god of mountains, Your Highness." MacClintock shrugged with a smile. "Given that his clan makes its home up in the Copperwalls, it seemed appropriate. Although if I'd known him better when we met, I think I might have settled on a god with a lower sense of humor. Or maybe a taste for arranging minor catastrophes!"

"I see." Adrienne smiled back. "I've read quite a bit about treecats, and I rather got the impression most of them have senses of humor. I think that's one of the things that makes them most fascinating to me—the way we seem to agree on what's funny, I mean."

MacClintock gave her a rather sharp look, then glanced at Lieutenant Colonel Tudev, but Tudev only smiled blandly. He'd warned the general that the Heir didn't share the King's resentment for all things treecat, but he hadn't indicated that the Princess had gone so far as to do genuine research about them.

"Actually, Your Highness, we're cautious about generalizing from our friends," the general said after the briefest of pauses, "because we can never be certain how typical they are of their species. It's tempting to assume they're a representative cross section of all treecats, but the low absolute number who adopt human friends argues against that."

"Because if they were truly representative we'd see a higher number of adoptions," Adrienne agreed with a nod. "I know. I was struck by the logic of that when I read Jason Harrington's work on them."

"*You*'ve read Jason's monograph?" Surprise betrayed MacClintock into the untactful question, and he colored brightly. "I'm sorry, Your Highness. I only meant I was surprised it had come to your attention. It hasn't had a very broad circulation."

"I know, and I've wondered why that was."

"Well," MacClintock grinned, "I shouldn't say it, Your

Highness, but I suspect it's because he isn't a very good writer. Not as good as his great-grandmother was, anyway."

"From what I've heard, very few people were as good as Dame Stephanie at just about *anything*," Adrienne said dryly, and MacClintock nodded.

"I believe you could call that an accurate statement, Your Highness. A most determined lady, Stephanie Harrington. Are you a student of her accomplishments?"

"Not as much as I might like to be," Adrienne admitted. "But for someone as influential as she was, she seems to've spent a great deal of effort avoiding publicity."

"That's true, Your Highness. I rather wish someone would do a good scholarly biography of her. That *Trailblazer of Dreams* thing by Simmons was a piece of popularized garba— Ah, I mean it was poorly researched and largely fictionalized," he corrected himself hastily, "and it's downright bad history. Despite the SFS's best efforts, people are already beginning to forget what a monumental role she played in Sphinx's history— or that of the entire Star Kingdom, for that matter. Unfortunately, that was apparently the way she wanted it, and the Harrington family has steadfastly refused to release her private papers. Until they do, it's unlikely anyone will be able to do a job much better than Simmons'. Which is a pity."

"It is, indeed," Adrienne agreed, and looked up as Tudev checked his chrono and cleared his throat. She grinned at her chief bodyguard's studiously maintained non-expression, then smiled at MacClintock.

"I'm afraid that's Colonel Tudev's polite way of reminding me I have a schedule to keep, General," she said with a charming air of apology. "I'm not especially looking forward to the speech—which will be my third of the day—but I *am* looking forward to my tour of your new wing. Would you be kind enough to lead the way?"

"I would be honored," MacClintock assured her, and swept another, deeper bow before he turned to do just that.

SIX

< *So this is the great meeting place,* > Seeker of Dreams mused, and Leaf Stalker flipped his ears in agreement. They perched on the high, chalet-style roof of the brand new main administration block of the Forestry Service's HQ. A dozen more

People perched with them, and Seeker of Dreams felt the
welcome of their mind glows as they recognized the need which
had brought him here. More than that, he felt their deep
satisfaction with the bonds that same need had drawn *them*
to establish.

< *It is,* > Leaf Stalker agreed, and turned to one of the others
on the roof. < *Greetings, Parsifal,* > he said. < *What are the
humans so excited about?* >

Seeker of Dreams looked more closely at the one Leaf Stalker
had called "Parsifal." The peculiar name had an odd taste in
the Bright Water hunter's mind voice, and Seeker of Dreams
felt a little thrill of excitement he knew was foolish as he
realized that was because it had been intended as one of the
two-le— As one of the *human's* mouth sounds. *"Words,"* they
called them, he reminded himself, trying to fit his mind voice
around the sound and wondering how any creature could
possibly make such strange noises as the humans did. But the
name was more than a mere oddity, for it was the human
custom to give new names to their friends after bonding. That
was no doubt inevitable, for if the People could never make
the sounds humans made, humans were equally incapable of
tasting the names by which People called one another. Yet the
acceptance of such human names was also of deep significance,
for each was the formal acknowledgment of a person's acceptance of a bond which only death could dissolve.

< *They are much excited, are they not?* > the one called Parsifal
agreed in a soft mind voice rich with tolerant amusement and
affection. < *My human has been carrying on almost since first
light. She is one of the Guardians' hunters,* > he added for Seeker
of Dream's benefit. < *Her special duty is to watch for evil doers
and prevent them from acting against the law of the humans, or
to hunt them down and punish them afterward if they do so anyway, and she is very good at it,* > he said with a certain pride.
< *I believe that was the reason they summoned her so early.* >

< *There is an evil doer here?* > Seeker of Dreams asked in
surprise, and Parsifal bleeked a laugh.

< *There may be,* > the older hunter said, < *but that is not
the reason for their excitement. Look there. Do you see the big black
air car with the armed humans standing watch about it?* > Seeker
of Dreams recognized the human term—or one of the *many*
(and often bewildering) human terms—for a flying egg and
flirted his tail in agreement as he looked at the vehicle. < *The
one they call a "princess" came in that, and my human was summoned to be one of those who help to protect her.* >

< *"Princess"?* > Seeker of Dreams repeated carefully.

< *It is a title of respect, like Chief Clan Elder, or Memory Singer,* > Parsifal explained. < *We—* > his mental wave took in the others on the roof with him < *—have been trying to understand it more completely, for there are odd things about it. For one, our humans regard this "princess" with great respect and treat her in all ways like the most senior of elders, yet she is little more than a well grown youngling. We have not been able to decide how one so young could be so important, yet there is no question that it is so. Also, Sylvester—* > he nodded to one of the others, an older hunter sitting near the end of the roof line < *—was close enough to taste her mind glow, and the taste of authority was strong in it. It was a very powerful mind glow,* > Parsifal added in a mind voice of profound respect, < *yet there is much pain in it for one so young.* >

"And this is the new boardroom," Lieutenant General MacClintock said as he opened the double doors and stepped aside to usher Adrienne through them before him.

She nodded and stepped into the large, richly carpeted room, and her entourage followed. It wasn't a very numerous entourage, as such things went. Since they were indoors and under cover, the bulk of Alvin Tudev's protection detail was actually outside the building, watching the perimeter. Only Tudev himself and four handpicked sergeants in plain clothes accompanied her. Well, them and Nassouah Haroun, two PR flacks, Lieutenant General MacClintock, three other senior Forestry Service officers, the new admin wing's chief engineer, and a two-person HD news team. And, of course, two treecats: MacClintock's Dunatis, and Colonel Marcy Alcerro's Musashi.

"We're quite proud of it," MacClintock went on, following her into the room's cool, quiet spaciousness. "We needed the space, but to be perfectly honest, we took the opportunity to provide ourselves with, um, *comfortable* quarters while we were at it."

"So I see," Adrienne agreed with a smile, surveying the chamber appreciatively. Then her eyes narrowed as she saw the life-size portrait hanging above the room's massive conference table. She walked across the carpet, trailed by her escort, and gazed raptly at the painting.

It was a spectacular work, executed in the neo-oils style. Its custom-engineered photo-reactive compounds had been blended with a master's hand, trained and stimulated to grow into exactly the image the artist had sought and then frozen forever under a coat of stabilizer at just the right instant. With the proper computer support, the same technology could have created a visual image with the precise accuracy of a hologram coupled with the solidity and "texture" no light sculpture could ever match. But this portrait had not been produced by a computer. It wasn't that perfect. What it *was*, she thought with a sense of awe, was a masterpiece—an *interpretive* masterpiece whose very imperfections were part of its magnificence, the proof it had been created by a human hand and mind and eye, and not by the uncaring perfection of electronics.

"That's an Akimoto, isn't it?" she asked quietly, and the SFS CO gave her another sharp look. She'd impressed him several times already with the breadth of her interests, and he supposed he should be getting used to it by now, but he wasn't.

"Yes. Yes, it is," he agreed. "But we didn't commission it, Your Highness," he added hastily. "Ms. Akimoto presented it to us as a gift."

It was Adrienne's turn to look at the lieutenant general in surprise. She knew why he'd offered the explanation. An original neo-oil by Tsukie Akimoto would have cost almost as much as the Forestry Service's entire new administration center.

"She presented it as a *gift?*" she repeated.

"Yes, Your Highness. She chose the subject, executed the work, and presented it to us with the single stipulation that it be displayed in our board's meeting chambers."

"But . . . why?" Adrienne asked, eyes back on the stunning portrait.

The woman in it was well past middle age. She had bright eyes and a mouth which looked like it smiled easily, yet she also radiated an aura of almost frightening energy and focused purpose. She was of slightly less than average height, with thick white hair, and she wore the green and brown of the SFS with a brigadier's two golden planets on her collar. She also wore the gold-bordered blue-and-white ribbon of the Order of Merit, and a cream-and-gray treecat sat proudly on her shoulder. The 'cat was larger than many, and badly scarred. The tip of its right ear was missing; the plushy fur on the right side of its face bore a pattern of white streaks, tracing the scars beneath; and its right foreleg had been amputated just below the shoulder. It sat on its person's right shoulder, its tail hanging down her back while its remaining true-hand rested on her head, and the artist had captured the love in both of her subjects' eyes with haunting fidelity.

"Because she wished to, Your Highness," MacClintock said quietly. "Perhaps you weren't aware that Ms. Akimoto was adopted by a 'cat herself some years ago?"

"What?" Adrienne looked at him, then shook her head. "No, I wasn't. I knew she was a Sphinxian, of course, but I don't believe her adoption could have been widely publicized without my hearing something about it."

"It wasn't—widely publicized, I mean," MacClintock told her. "Ms. Akimoto has always been something of a recluse. She seldom leaves her family freehold—they were First Shareholders, you know—and she hasn't been off-planet at all since her adoption." He smiled faintly. "Very few of us would consider taking our friends off-world without a very pressing reason, I'm afraid. Not that I don't suspect the little devils would love to go! But perhaps you've noticed we tend to be a little on the protective side?"

Adrienne nodded feelingly, and his smile became a grin.

"Well, they probably don't need *quite* as much protection as we insist they do, Your Highness. Physically, they're extremely tough, with the weaponry to look after themselves in most threat situations. Dunatis?"

The 'cat on his shoulder obligingly raised a long-fingered true-hand and spread it, unsheathing the four centimeter-long scimitars which armed it. He held them up for her to see, then bleeked cheerfully, and the ivory claws vanished as he retracted them.

"The problem," MacClintock went on more seriously, "is that they *aren't* well equipped to look after themselves in situations where the threat is neither immediate nor physical. The specific legal rights granted to them by the Constitution are fully enforced here on Sphinx. *Off* Sphinx, however, matters are much less clear."

"You're talking about the Treecat Rights Bill," Adrienne said flatly, and he nodded. His expression had become rather more wary as he heard her utterly uninflected tone, but he didn't back off.

"That's precisely what I was leading up to, Your Highness," he admitted. "We at SFS believe the Ninth Amendment was clearly intended to recognize the 'cats as sentient beings—with minor child legal status—on all three of the Star Kingdom's worlds. As I'm sure you're aware, however, certain political and economic interests have taken the position that our inability to measure their actual sentience with 'demonstrable, replicable precision' means their sapience is no more than a legal fiction. Moreover, they argue that since the Ninth Amendment refers specifically to their status on *Sphinx*, it doesn't apply to their status on Manticore or Gryphon. It's nonsense, of course. Unfortunately, no one thought to test that aspect of the amendment—or its original supporting legislation—for over thirty T-years after ratification. The question simply didn't arise prior to then, even on the rare occasions when one of the 'cats went off-world. But then in 107 A.L., the Richtman Corporation tried to move in, and—"

"I remember, General," Adrienne said, cutting him off even more flatly than before, and Dunatis shifted on his shoulder as he sensed the Heir's emotions.

The Richtman Corporation had been a Manticoran front for Manpower Unlimited of Mesa. No one had known it at the time, for Richtman had hidden its connections to the Mesa System with care. And for good reason, given the vast bulk of humanity's attitude towards Manpower and its huge cloning and bio-engineering operations. Just over six hundred and fifty T-years had passed since Old Earth's "Final War" unleashed all the horrors of unrestricted genetic and biological modifications. The war had officially "ended" in 943 P.D. . . . but humanity had been well into the fifteenth century of the Diaspora before Old Earth truly recovered from its carnage, and most of humankind had learned a hideous lesson from the near-total destruction of its mother world.

The Mesa System had not. For all intents and purposes, Manpower Unlimited owned the star system outright, and if Beowulf's eugenicists were better trained and more skilled, Mesa's had far more . . . scope for their talents, for Mesa rejected the Beowulf Code's ban on casual manipulation of the human genotype. Manpower Unlimited cheerfully produced cloned slave labor, genetically-engineered "indentured servants," and even more deadly versions of the Final War's "super soldiers." Humanity being what it was, there were always buyers (clandestine ones, at least), and since Manpower was already a moral pariah, its directors saw no reason to retain any scruples whatsoever.

None of which would have mattered to the Star Kingdom if not for the fact that the treecats were empaths.

A few of the wilder, more speculative xenobiologists maintained that they were also telepaths, but that was a much more problematical claim, and no one had ever been able to produce any scientific evidence to support it. Their empathy, however, had been demonstrated too conclusively for any reputable scientist to dispute, and that was what made them of interest to Manpower Unlimited. Despite millennia of testing, no one had ever demonstrated anything like reliable, quantifiable, reproducible ESP in humans, or in any of the other handful of sentient species humanity had encountered. Until the treecats.

The mere possibility that the 'cats *might* be telepaths had sufficed to send Mesan agents creeping into the Star Kingdom to acquire samples. Empathy might have been enough by itself, but the economic implications of discovering how telepathy worked and how to genegineer it into humans were incalculable for something like Manpower Unlimited. Its operators had wanted test subjects and tissue donors, and no one could have had any illusions as to what would have happened to those subjects.

As far as anyone knew, none of the clandestine Mesan efforts had succeeded. Empaths were elusive quarry, and the Forestry Service had made protecting the 'cats against trappers its number one priority from the outset. But the potential prize had been great enough for Manpower to invest what was later determined to have been upwards of eight hundred million Manticoran dollars to create the Richtman Corporation for the purpose of lobbying to legalize the "humane, nonlethal capture" of treecats "for purposes of beneficial scientific examination and export to interstellar zoological institutes."

In addition to whatever had been spent creating the Richtman facade, an unknown (but undoubtedly enormous) investment had also flowed into various political hands through both registered lobbyists and also some very *sub rosa* channels indeed. It had been a massive effort, and while Manpower had never seen the hoped for return on its money, the Ninth Amendment and its enabling legislation had not emerged unscathed. Efforts to "amend" the legislation so as to emasculate it had failed, but the Richtman legal experts had launched a flank attack by pointing out that the Ninth Amendment was predicated on the definition of treecats as "sapient." Where, they demanded, was the proof of that sapience? After all, how intelligent did a creature which could sense the emotions of any possible testers have to be to *counterfeit* sapience?

The best testing techniques available had been brought to bear, by treecat partisans and their opponents alike, and the most anyone could honestly say was that results were inconclusive. Rather wildly so, in fact. Some tests insisted the 'cats were as intelligent as humans themselves; others insisted they were actually somewhat less intelligent than Old Earth's pre-genegineered dolphins had been. Oddly enough, they appeared to test better at problem-solving when no human testers were present, which seemed to stand the "empaths counterfeiting sentience" argument on its head. It was almost as if the 'cats had decided not to cooperate in certain instances, or even to deliberately prejudice the results, which was ridiculous, of course. But ridiculous or not, the salient point was that everyone was forced to agree the tests were inconsistent, and the anti-amendment forces insisted that inconsistent was simply another way of saying "valueless."

The 'cats' relatively small size was also pounced upon by Richtman's lawyers, who pointed out that no other known sentient species had such a low body mass, and no one could deny that 'cat brains were much smaller than human ones. Their supporters might argue that the enlarged nodes of nervous tissue found at each pelvis functioned as secondary brains of some sort, but that, too, had never been scientifically demonstrated.

Xenobiologists from all over explored space had been attracted to the Star Kingdom as the dispute heated up. The 'cats were only the twelfth nonhuman sentient species ever discovered (assuming they *were* sentient), and that was enough to bring scores of scientists flocking in to examine them. Unfortunately, the 'cats didn't appear to want to be examined, and "wild" 'cats tended to disappear whenever a new team of scientists set up shop in their neck of the picket woods. 'Cats who had adopted humans were more readily available . . . but they were also more readily *protected*. Besides, those who doubted their intelligence argued that 'cats who had adopted weren't suitable test subjects. After all, if they *were* telepaths as well as empaths, how could anyone know he was actually testing the 'cat and not simply the efficiency of its link to its human partner?

A certain percentage of out-system scientists had grown steadily more angry at the dearth of test subjects. They seemed to feel the Forestry Service ought to have netted "wild" 'cats and dragged them in for study purposes, if that was the only way to get them. The SFS certainly shouldn't have been *protecting* the elusive little creatures! It was probable that most of the scientists of that opinion had been completely legitimate, but at least some had been imported by Mesan interests to help muddy the water . . . and all of them had been doomed to disappointment when it came to changing the SFS's mind.

The result had been a blistering debate about what the treecats truly were, and the Gryphon planetary government (after some extraordinary infusions of secret "campaign contributions") had actually passed a planetary referendum calling upon the Crown to revoke their sapient status. The Constitution provided for referenda from the planetary parliaments as a grass-roots avenue for offering amendments, and the Gryphon act had been intended as the opening shot in such an effort. It had failed, but not without lending the debate a life of its own, exclusive of Richtman's efforts. For one thing, unscrupulous speculators had scented additional, potentially enormous profits. If the Ninth Amendment could be repealed and the 'cats stripped of their status as sentients, their claim to any of Sphinx's surface would also be overturned. Precisely what would happen to all that land—whether it would revert to the status of Crown land or be up for grabs by anyone with ready cash—was unclear, but if those same anyones with the ready cash could just take a hand in drafting the language that repealed the amendment. . . .

The battle had dragged out for years. Every vote indicated that a clear majority of Sphinxians were staunchly opposed to repeal, supported by a much thinner majority of those living on Manticore. Gryphon had consistently voted *for* repeal, but Gryphon was a special case where vote "managing" was a thriving industry run by the relatively small handful of powerful nobles who had secured a stranglehold upon its local economy. (Which, in no small part, helped explain why Queen Consort Solange, like most of Gryphon's yeomen freeholders, had seen the Crown and its central authority as their only real ally against the local aristocracy's depredations.)

In the end, an enterprising newsie, with the help of allies within the SFS, had managed to burrow through the maze of interlocking corporate identities behind the Richtman Corporation and discover the Mesan involvement, and the entire effort had come crashing down. But by that time the exact status of the 'cats had been thrown into considerable confusion, and the argument that the Ninth Amendment had been intended to protect them solely on Sphinx—which Adrienne, like MacClintock, considered not only bizarre but totally specious— had gained a toehold among certain mainstream legal scholars. The fact that the Star Kingdom had been in existence for barely a hundred and thirty T-years when the debate began hadn't helped. The original Constitution had already been extensively modified and reinterpreted (very creatively indeed, in some cases) as the Crown, the Lords, and the Commons worked out the *real* balance of power. Indeed, one reason the Ninth Amendment had taken so long to ratify in the first place had been that the document it was intended to modify had been in such a state of flux.

By now, almost fifty T-years later, the anti-'cat forces were in full retreat. Only the financial interests which wanted to get their claws into the lands reserved for the 'cats were still pushing the argument, and the Treecat Rights Bill had been

introduced in the House of Commons by an unusual alliance
of Liberals and Conservatives in an effort to put the entire
matter to rest. Personally, Adrienne considered the bill unnecessary. Whatever its critics might claim, the Ninth Amendment's
language was clear, specific, and certainly not ambiguous. It
had taken the tortuously creative efforts of entire battalions
of skilled legal sophists to find a way to misinterpret it, and
even then ninety percent of the Star Kingdom's constitutional
experts had rejected the argument as bogus. So what was *needed*,
she thought grimly, was simply for the Crown to enforce the
Ninth Amendment the way its framers had always intended.

Which was the reason for her flat tone and MacClintock's
mix of deference, defensiveness, and obstinacy, because the
Crown—in the person of King Roger II, who had come to hate
the 'cats for reasons of his own—flatly refused to enforce it.
In fact, his Solicitor General had actually been heard to say
that perhaps the Gryphon interpretation might have a bit more
merit than most constitutional scholars believed. Needless to
say, that same Crown had also marshaled its efforts—and quite
successfully—to stop the Treecat Rights Bill dead in the House
of Lords. And even if it somehow eventually passed both
Houses, it was extremely unlikely King Roger would even
consider signing it into law . . . and even less likely that its
supporters could ever muster the three-quarters majority
required to override a royal veto.

"It *is* a pity Dame Stephanie wasn't alive to lead the defense
of the amendment," Adrienne said after a long, tense moment,
her tone an obvious bid to defuse the tension and shift the
subject. "I doubt its attackers would have fared very well against
her."

"I don't imagine they would have either, Your Highness,"
MacClintock agreed, accepting the change. The two of them
turned to gaze at the portrait once more, and the lieutenant
general smiled. "She and Lionheart would have turned them
into hamburger; they'd certainly done it to tougher opposition
than that!"

"Then the story about the hexapuma is true?"

"Yes, Your Highness. A lot of the details are uncertain—
it's one of those things about which I wish the Harrington
family would turn loose whatever documentation they have—
but it happened."

"Unbelievable," Adrienne murmured, and MacClintock
snorted.

"My advice is to not apply that word to anything you ever
hear about Stephanie Harrington, Your Highness. Or not

without checking it out very thoroughly ahead of time. She was the youngest person ever to discover an alien sentient species. She is also the *only* human ever to face a hexapuma armed only with a vibroblade belt knife and survive. She joined the Forestry Service—which, I regret to say, was no great shakes at the time; we were still a privately-funded, only semiofficial body—when she was just seventeen T-years old and almost single handedly reorganized it into a Crown agency which, by the end of her life, had become what I fondly believe to be one of the finest eco-management organizations in this sector of the galaxy. Not to mention, of course, being the first person ever adopted by a 'cat, for which *I,* at least, can only be grateful."

"She deserved more than an Order of Merit," Adrienne said, but he shook his head.

"What she may have deserved and what she *wanted* weren't the same thing, Your Highness. Several accounts insist she was offered a peerage when the Ninth Amendment passed. I don't know about that—the Harringtons may—but it's a matter of public record that she declined the Order of the Star Kingdom because, unlike the Order of Merit, the knighthood it conferred would have been hereditary, not simply a life title."

"She declined a peerage?" Adrienne blinked, and the lieutenant general shrugged.

"That's the tradition, and it would match what we know of her. Her family are yeomen, and proud of it. In fact, she was an only child who retained her maiden name when she married expressly because she was determined there would be a 'Harrington of Harrington' but *not* a nobleman living on the Harrington freehold after her. *And* she found time to produce six children to be sure of that, despite everything else she was involved with! And two of them were adopted by 'cats, too. As a matter of fact, I believe the Harringtons have a higher percentage of adoptions than any other family on Sphinx."

"I still say she deserved more than the Order of Merit," Adrienne declared, then smiled. "On the other hand, I rather doubt that *I* would have pressed the point or argued with such a, ah, *formidable* person about it!"

"Which indicates great wisdom on your part, Your Highness," MacClintock told her. The two of them gazed at the portrait of Stephanie Harrington and her 'cat for several more moments in a silence which had once more become companionable. Then MacClintock cleared his throat and waved gracefully at the boardroom's door.

"And now, Your Highness, I believe that speech you didn't
want to give is waiting for you."

SEVEN

Henry Thoreau sat on the bench with an unworried expression and reread his newsfax for the third time. No one looking at him would have thought he had a care in the universe,
but looking tranquil at need was one of his several talents,
and at this particular moment, it was one he needed badly.

He let his eye drift across his chrono as he turned a 'fax
page—again—and his carefully concealed disgust ratcheted up
another notch. The target and her entourage were over twenty
minutes behind schedule.

He allowed himself a mental grumble that never touched
his face and commanded himself not to pay any attention whatsoever to the blank-faced young man sitting to his left. The
younger man appeared to be reading a book. Actually, he was
only hitting the advance button at regular intervals while he
stared unseeingly at the display, and Thoreau hoped he wouldn't
run out of pages before the target reemerged into the open.
Having some sharp-eyed security type notice that there was
someone sitting there staring at a blank book viewer would
not do wonderful things for his and Krogman's plan.

His nostrils flared slightly at the thought of his partner. He
knew why Krogman couldn't execute the hit himself, but that
didn't keep him from feeling increasingly grumpy about his
own exposure as the delay dragged on. Krogman was the one
who'd crafted their weapon, and Thoreau found himself wishing
Krogman could have pulled the damned trigger himself, as well.
Except, of course, that Krogman couldn't possibly risk being
physically present when the attack went down. His record might
be clean in the Star Kingdom, but he *was* a registered psych
adjuster.

Unlike many star nations, the Star Kingdom had ruled involuntary psych adjustment of anyone for any reason strictly
illegal. The Star Kingdom wasn't alone in refusing to use it
as a punitive sentence, but many other worlds allowed for the
involuntary adjustment of individuals deemed dangerous to
themselves or society. The people who allowed it viewed it—
officially, at least—as equivalent to the old "not guilty by reason
of insanity" plea. The Manticoran view, however, was that

psych adjustment didn't *cure* anything; it simply crammed in an additional set of compulsions which forced the adjusted individual to *act* as if he had been cured. That was all very soothing to society, no doubt, and might well prevent an "adjusted" serial killer from killing again, but Manticorans considered that it was both simpler and more ethical—and moral— to shoot someone than it was to lock him up for life in a prison inside his own skull. Besides, even in jurisdictions which routinely employed it, there were those who argued that psych adjustment tended to make mental health professionals lazy. Why bother to fix a problem when one could simply use a hardwired patch to make sure it didn't bother anyone . . . except, of course, for the person who still had it?

And then there were the regimes that just *loved* adjustment. It was too expensive for use on a mass scale—mostly because of the time involved; the materials cost was ludicrously low— but it could be extremely effective when employed against strategic targets like key leaders of opposition groups. Nor had the military implications passed unnoticed. Though the Deneb Accords forbade adjustment of captured enemy personnel, everyone knew it would happen anyway if someone thought he could get away with it. The development of drugs and techniques to resist it had been on the list of every major military for centuries, and, for the most part, they'd succeeded in producing workable defenses. They weren't perfect, and they could usually be broken by old-fashioned sensory deprivation or systematic abuse. They also required periodic updating as adjustment techniques were improved to defeat them, but at least they managed to prevent adjusters from turning the pre-space nightmare of the mass brainwashing of troops into a reality.

But like any other form of technology, it was extremely difficult to simply shove adjustment back into its bottle. Personally, Thoreau couldn't imagine availing himself of the service. Have an irresistible compulsion—even one he'd selected himself— implanted in *his* brain? No, thank you very much. He believed he'd pass. Yet there were those who did just that, for reasons ranging from a desire to be addiction-proofed to people who wanted to lose weight to those who feared compulsions in the dark crannies of their souls would drive them into criminal acts. The Star Kingdom might reject imposing adjustment on anyone, but it would not stand in the way of someone who voluntarily sought it, and a small, highly regulated and closely supervised psych adjustment industry existed for the sole purpose of providing the service to those who wanted it.

Which was why Krogman couldn't have even the remotest connection, including that of simple proximity, with the young man with the book viewer. Deafening klaxons would sound in the brain of the most imbecilic security officer in the known universe if a known adjuster was anywhere near a "lone mad-man assassin" who just happened to murder the Crown Princess of Manticore.

Just having Krogman register with Manticoran immigration as a psych adjuster upon their arrival in the Star Kingdom had carried an uncomfortable degree of risk. But it had been necessary. While Krogman would never be so stupid as to select a patient of his own—or one he'd ever officially seen in *any* capacity—he had to have access to the patient files and facilities he needed. The best way to acquire that was to hide in plain sight by setting himself up as a licensed adjuster with a small but comfortable practice, and the original Jean-Marc Krogman had been a well trained and competent adjuster back in the Solarian League. So had the current Jean-Marc Krogman (although he had maintained a much lower profile, given the clientele he served), and since the original Krogman no longer required his identity, the man who now wore it had appro-priated it without fuss or bother. After all, he and "Henry Thoreau" were the only two people who knew the real Krogman was dead.

With such a comfortable, outwardly legitimate identity, the current Krogman had found it child's play to set up an effec-tive cover, and The Organization—which Thoreau thought was one of the less imaginative names the local organized under-world could have assigned itself—was delighted to have an adjuster of its very own. Crime lords always needed one odd job of adjustment or another, and they paid lucratively for Krogman's services. On the other hand, not even The Orga-nization knew about the freelance jobs Krogman and Thoreau occasionally undertook. Which was just as well. After all, one or two Organization kingpins had fallen afoul of imaginative underlings able to visualize the advantages of having one of the underling's rivals suddenly, and for no apparent reason, gun down their mutual boss (thus creating a vacancy at the top) before dying in a hail of gunfire from the bodyguards of the late, lamented boss in question.

Of course, both The Organization and law enforcement were well aware of how adjustment could be misused, which was another reason the law took such a dim view of the profes-sion. Officers of the King's justice routinely considered the possibility of adjustment any time a killer "just snapped," and it was relatively simple for a trained psychiatrist to recognize the signs of adjustment in a subject. But that was why people like Krogman commanded such astronomical fees, for the true mastery of their art lay in subtlety, careful recruitment, anonymity, and misdirection.

Every policeman knew adjustment was a possible explanation for almost any murder, but good adjusters of a criminal bent were rare, and *all* adjusters were carefully regulated. Because of that, actual cases of adjusted murderers were far less common than bad mystery writers liked to suggest. As a result, investigators tended to look for more everyday motives first, so whenever possible, Krogman picked as his weapon someone who *had* another motive. When someone murdered someone else whom they had always hated, the police looked at the history of killer and victim and found their motivation there rather than seeking more esoteric and unlikely causations.

In addition, Krogman preferred to program his weapons for kamikaze attacks. Of course, he didn't want them to look deliberately suicidal—that was another thing that started nasty, suspicious police thinking in terms of adjustment—but it was relatively simple to program someone to make a mistake with lethal consequences if bodyguards were involved. Lovers' murder-suicides were another technique of which he was rather fond, because police saw so many they were effectively routine. Only when he had no other option did he rely on a weapon with no personal motive for the attack, and then he invariably saw to it that the killer did not survive his victim.

But the true key to his success was that he always remembered the best way to avoid detection was to set things up in the first place so no one had any reason to suspect the killer had been *commanded* to kill, and his current weapon was a masterpiece. This hit had first been commissioned over a T-year before, and for the last ten T-months, the young, friendless drifter he'd selected as his tool had systematically created all the proper back trail of a fatally obsessive personality. His inexpensive rooms had been converted into a veritable shrine to Crown Princess Adrienne. Guided by Krogman's "adjustments," he'd begun with occasional, rambling journal entries and progressed steadily to the point of mad obsession with the Princess. The sheer length of time over which he had collected and created his hoard of pictures, hardcopy and electronic clippings, and diaries would surely convince any but the most paranoid and indefatigable of investigators that it was genuine, the product of a deranged mind working in isolation.

That was Krogman's primary line of defense, and he expected it to hold. If it failed, however, his second line of defense was anonymity. No one had ever seen him and the drifter together, and he had taken excruciating pains to insure that there was nothing at all to connect him in any way, however indirectly, to his tool.

And, of course, he had made absolutely certain that the young man in question would not survive his victim.

But all of that explained why the only choice to launch the attack was Thoreau. Someone had to do it, if only because of the ancient K.I.S.S. principle. Human minds were complex mechanisms. Given the proper circumstances, they could defeat even the most deep reaching and thorough adjustment, and the more complex the adjustment, the more opportunity for the adjusted individual's mind to find a chink in the programming and wiggle through it. That meant complicated trigger commands increased the risk of failure exponentially, and they could afford no slip ups on this operation. So the trigger had been kept as simple as possible: an innocent visual cue no investigator studying security camera imagery later could possibly associate with the attack.

In this case, a red handkerchief in a breast pocket, combined with a man reading a newsfax and drinking lemonade, and a sneeze.

Now if only the target would get her ass out here so that Thoreau could launch the weapon and be done with it.

EIGHT

< *May we get a closer view of this "princess"?* > Seeker of Dreams asked Parsifal. The older cat looked at him and cocked one ear.

< *You are ambitious, youngling,* > he observed. < *And hasty, perhaps. You have not yet tasted the pain in her mind glow.* >

< *Perhaps I am ambitious, yet I do not think so. I have no reason to think she is the one I seek. But you yourself spoke of the power of her mind glow, and even if she is not one to whom I might bond, I hunger to taste it for myself. And as for her pain,* > Seeker of Dreams flicked the end of his tail with a trace of sadness, < *it is not uncommon among the People for the strongest mind glows to be forged in sorrow and loss,* > he pointed out.

< *Truth,* > Parsifal agreed after a moment. He straightened

and stretched, yawning mightily, and Seeker of Dreams felt his mind voice reach out to another. Seeker of Dreams could not taste the conversation—not unusual when one did not know the far end of a focused link—but he sensed the flow of information. Then Parsifal nodded, his mind glow radiating satisfaction, and peered down over the building's wide roof.

< *There,* > he said. < *The humans strengthened the "gutters"— those troughs at the roof edge which catch water—so People might perch upon them, and Musashi tells me the princess will be coming through that door to reach the place prepared for speaking. We have just enough time to move there before they arrive. Come!* >

"Thank you for showing me your new building, General," Adrienne said as they walked toward the exit side-by-side.

"You're more welcome than I can say, Your Highness," MacClintock replied. "And the thanks cut both ways, you know. An expression of royal interest, well—"

He shrugged, and Adrienne nodded with another, familiar stab of hurt. She was grateful he'd been too tactful to complete the sentence, but she knew what he'd meant. And much as she'd enjoyed her visit, she felt ominously certain her father would recognize the same impact. There would be no fights, no screaming fits. He wouldn't even lecture her. He knew she disagreed with his attitude towards the treecats, and so he would recognize her trip to Twin Forks for what it had been. But he wouldn't even acknowledge her small act of rebellion. He would simply allow for it in his next set of calculations, and he would give her one of those chill, impersonal looks—the sort that said "Wait and see how *you* like it when you're Queen"—and then he would ignore the episode completely.

Was that the real reason I came? she wondered unhappily. *Because I wanted to anger him enough to get some reaction out of him? Am I still that desperate for some sign he even cares? And is it really possible I could be so stupid as to think I could get one?*

She swallowed the thought and smiled brightly as Mac-Clintock opened the door.

Seeker of Dreams crouched on the gutter, and the massed background blaze of human mind glows washed out from the crowd outside the building. It had been there from the beginning, of course, but Seeker of Dreams had buttressed himself against it without even realizing he was doing so. It had been the empathic equivalent of squinting against a blinding glare, but now he opened his "eyes" wide, sending his empathy out to quest for the mind glow Parsifal had told him of, and the sheer energy rising up behind him was almost terrifying.

Somehow I had not expected there to be so much difference between the memory songs and the reality, he thought, half-dazed by the excitement and anticipation flowing from so many mind glows. *I should have. All the songs agree that human mind glows are more powerful than any of the People's, yet how could even the greatest memory singer recreate such raw power?*

He shook his head, hunching forward as if into a high wind, and slowly forced the seething tumult out of the front of his own mind. He pulled his own personality free of it and reached out once more, searching for the "princess," and suddenly his ears twitched and his tail kinked straight up behind him.

Not possible, he thought. *This is* not *possible! No one, human or of the People, can radiate such a mind glow! Surely its power would consume any in whom it burned!*

Yet even as he thought that, he knew better, for he felt the reality walking down the hall towards him. *Such power,* he thought in awe. *Such clarity and strength!* He tasted the mind glow's compassion, its sense of order and responsibility, of dedication. And he tasted the love its owner carried like a welcoming fire, waiting to warm and comfort any who called upon it.

And he tasted pain. Terrible, aching pain—an emptiness that cried out to be filled. He did not understand the source of that pain, for how could one possessed of so much power to love be crushed by rejection and abandonment? Where were the human elders, their memory singers and mind healers? How could any species allow one of its own to suffer so hideously when all she longed to do was to love and be loved in return?

For just one instant, as he hovered on the brink of Adrienne Winton's loneliness and broken love, Seeker of Dreams shuddered before the horrid suspicion that the memory singers had been wrong—that humans were all mad. Surely it was the only answer for the sharp-edged agony he tasted amid the jewel-like splendor of that mind glow's other facets! But then he remembered. Humans were mind-blind. They could not taste as he tasted, and so, perhaps, they did not even suspect how dreadfully wounded their "princess" was. It even made sense, in a way, for the other things he tasted within that mind glow included pride, a sense of duty, a refusal to whimper or plead or beg, and an iron-boned determination to never, ever show weakness.

His heart went out to her—this princess he had never so much as seen—and he made a small, soft sound, almost a whimper, as he recognized his fate. He felt himself reaching for that bright splendor, even knowing he must embrace the darkness, as well, and a corner of his own mind wailed for him to run. To flee and hide, as he would have fled a death fang itself. But there was no escape. The mind glow had captured him. He tasted Parsifal's half-shocked, half-unsurprised mind glow—and pity—beside him as he reached out to the human furnace, yet the other 'cat was distant and far away, almost trivial beside the human walking obliviously towards him.

Is that the true secret of their mind glow's power? The loneliness? The fact that they cannot *hear one another or taste one another's inner hearts, however much they long to? Such a terrible, terrible price, if it is . . . and yet such glory it produces! And how very much love they have to give.* He shook himself once more, awed by the raw courage it must take to feel so much love when no human could taste his beloved's love in return. *They know so much, are so clever, have so many tools and marvels, and yet I pity them,* he thought wonderingly. *But they are magnificent in their loneliness, in the isolation each carries with him even in the midst of all his fellows.*

Then the door opened.

Alvin Tudev saw the Princess stop dead. She didn't simply stop walking forward; she froze, with the sudden, absolute shock of someone who had just taken a bullet.

For a moment, that was precisely what he thought had happened, and a spasm of horror rocked through him. He hurled himself forward without conscious thought, bulldozing through the plainclothes sergeants of his own detail to reach her, and he was only dimly aware of startled shouts as he hurled other human beings aside. He was already gathering his muscles to leap on her, smothering her in his arms and slamming her to the ground while he offered his own body as protection against follow up shots, when she broke her momentary stasis. Her head snapped around, and Tudev just had time to throw his own weight to one side before he plowed into her from behind.

He grunted with anguish as his solidly muscled bulk drove shoulder-first into the old-fashioned brick wall of the SFS's new admin building. For a moment, he was certain he'd broken at least his collar bone, but that scarcely mattered. Indeed, he hardly felt it through a flood of relief almost more terrible than his original horror as he realized his Princess was unharmed.

But if she was unhurt, then why stop so suddenly? And why was she—?

The answer presented itself before his mind finished forming its second question. A small, sleek body dropped from the gutter with a high, ringing "*Bleeeeeek!*" of joy, and Adrienne's arms opened to receive it. The treecat fell into her embrace with a grace that seemed inevitable, and a triumphant chorus of other treecat voices joined the newcomer's paean of exultation. Adrienne's arms closed about the 'cat, hugging it to her, her brown eyes blazing with a joy and raw, loving welcome that hit the lieutenant colonel like a fist, and the 'cat clung to her in return, rubbing his cheek ecstatically against her own.

Oh ... my ... God, Tudev thought with an odd, distant sort of calm. *His Majesty isn't going to be at* all *pleased about this!*

Adrienne Winton stared into the brilliant green eyes, and an incredible wave of love and welcome poured from her. She'd studied all the information on treecats she could get her hands on, but none of it had prepared her for this moment. The descriptions of what it meant to be adopted had always struck her as maddeningly vague, incomplete, confusing. It had sometimes seemed as if all those fortunate souls were involved in some conspiracy to keep the rest of the human race from knowing what it felt like.

Now she knew better. They hadn't explained it because they *couldn't*. It was like smelling a color or trying to weigh diamonds with a spectrograph. There simply were no words for the sensation she felt at that moment, yet her brain stubbornly insisted on trying to find some way to process the information.

The treecat was an empath. She knew that, just as she knew that at this very moment, the lithe little creature could feel her own emotions and the brilliant welcome blazing in her soul, and she longed desperately for the ability to feel *his* emotions, in return. But she couldn't. Unlike him, she was only human, with the limited perceptions of a human brain. And yet . . . and yet there *was* something. . . . She couldn't pin it down, couldn't drag it out to look at it or analyze it. She couldn't even have proved she wasn't imagining whatever it was, and yet she was certain she was not. And whatever it was, it sank down into the dark and lonely depths of her spirit like cleansing lightning, bringing warmth and life to the shadows where she had been alone for far too long.

✧　　✧　　✧

Seeker of Dreams stared into the human's round-pupilled brown eyes and tasted her confusion, puzzlement . . . and joy. He truly had not intended to bond to her when he reached out for her mind glow, yet now he had, and at last he fully understood that which had driven him to seek this moment. That yearning, that need and unused ability which had been part of him for so long, had flared bright and fierce in the instant he touched her mind glow. He had actually *felt* the sharp, reverberating "Snap!" as the two of them socketed into place, each filling the hole in the other's soul. He did not know if he had been meant from birth for *this* human, or if another of the People might have filled the wound gaping at her heart, and it did not matter. What mattered was that he had found her, and in the moment of finding, they had come together. He could already feel the increased power of his own mind voice, the sharper, stronger reach of his ability to taste other mind glows. It was as if his person had become a warm, brilliant sun, beaming power and strength into him, making him more than he had ever dreamed of being.

Yet even as he crooned his loving welcome and rubbed his cheek joyously against hers, he also tasted the tragedy of their bond. He was like a tiny world, circling the sun of her mind glow as the humans said the People's world circled *its* sun. Like the world, he had life and purpose of his own, yet also like the world, he could no longer be whole and complete without his sun. In that sense, the two had become one . . . yet his human would never taste what he was tasting, never know the depth of his love as he could know hers. He felt oddly certain that she had already tasted more than most humans ever did—that, like some of Death Fang's Bane's younglings, she was more sensitive, more alive to the bond than other humans—but her experience would never be even a shadow of his own.

And he also knew Sings Truly had been correct. This was a young human, but not nearly so young as Death Fang's Bane had been. Perhaps she would live another fifteen turnings, which would be a long life indeed for a human, but then she would die, and Seeker of Dreams would have lived only twenty-four turnings of his allotted forty-eight.

He did not think she realized that. Not yet, at any rate, for he felt no sorrow, no grief for him, and he knew he would whenever she finally realized their bond was almost certain to cost him half his normal span. And it would *be* a tragedy, he thought, to go into the dark so young. But it would also

be right, for he would cling to her glorious mind glow wherever it went, into light or into dark or into nothingness at
all, and be content.

"Your Highness?"

Adrienne tore her eyes from the treecat as MacClintock's
gentle voice invaded their reverie. She blinked at him, trying
to refocus on something beyond the 'cat in her arms, and he
smiled.

"Forgive me for intruding, Your Highness, but you've been
standing there for just over five minutes," he said apologeti-
cally.

Dunatis sat on his shoulder, crooning down at Adrienne and
her 'cat—*her* 'cat! she thought in exultant wonder—and beyond
them she saw Colonel Alcerro and Musashi. Both older 'cats
crooned as if to vibrate the bones right out of their bodies,
and as she stared at them, she realized she was hearing the
same sound from dozens of other sources. She raised her head,
gazing up at the treecats lined up along the admin building's
eaves, and the same soft, welcoming music washed down over
her from all of them.

"Five minutes, General?" she asked at last, turning back to
MacClintock.

"Almost six, actually." His right hand fluttered for a moment,
as if he wanted to grip her shoulder—an act which etiquette
made totally out of the question—and his eyes smiled at her.
"The average is around thirteen, I believe. Left to my own
devices, I wouldn't bother either of you until you were both
ready to come up, but—" He waved the hovering right hand,
and she blinked again as she followed it to the rest of her
entourage.

Lieutenant Colonel Tudev stood watching with no expression at all. No, that wasn't quite correct. He was favoring one
shoulder, and there were pain lines around his mouth, as if
he'd injured himself somehow when she wasn't looking. For
a moment she thought those lines were of disapproval for what
had happened, but then she saw the wry resignation in his
eyes, and a sense of apprehension surged through her.

Oh my God, Daddy is going to kill *me for this! Bad enough I
came to Twin Forks without telling him, but this—!*

One look at Nassouah Haroun's face more than confirmed
her thoughts. Lady Haroun's expression was one of unmiti-
gated horror, as if she were certain His Majesty would feel
his daughter's appointments secretary should somehow have
prevented this disaster from occurring, and the palace PR types

looked equally horrified. In fact, they looked so stunned Adrienne felt the corners of her mouth twitch. She closed her eyes and clamped her jaws against the totally inappropriate laughter suddenly fighting to break free, and somehow she managed to stop almost all of it. The one spurt which did escape, she transformed into an almost convincing cough, but forty seconds passed before she trusted herself to open her eyes and look at them once more without completely losing it.

Oh, my. This is all going to be quite . . . difficult, isn't it, little friend? she thought, gazing down at the adoring treecat in her arms. *I'll bet you never even guessed what a frying pan you were leaping into, did you?*

The 'cat only sang his buzzing purr to her and reached out to pat her cheek with a gentle true-hand, and she smiled brilliantly and lifted him so she could bury her face in the soft, creamy fur of his belly. She held him that way for several seconds, then lowered him once more and turned back to MacClintock. Unlike his uniform tunic, the shoulder of her light jacket was unreinforced fabric, totally unsuited to treecat claws, so she cradled her new companion in her arms as she smiled at the SFS CO once more.

"I quite understand why you can't simply let us work through this at our own pace, General," she told him. "Besides, it would be impolite of me. There are people waiting for my speech out there, so I suppose we'd better get to it."

"Of course, Your Highness. Ah, just one thing first, though." She quirked an eyebrow at him, and he smiled diffidently. "I was just wondering if you've thought of a name for him, Your Highness?"

"Already?" Adrienne's other eyebrow rose to join the first one.

"Well, it seems to work in two basic ways, Your Highness," MacClintock explained. "Either a name comes to an adoptee almost immediately—as it did to Colonel Alcerro here—or else he tends to spend quite some time thinking about it to get it just right. I was merely wondering which it would be in your case?"

"I see." She considered for a moment, then shrugged. "I think you'll have to put me into the second category, Colonel. It's going to take me a while to think of a name anywhere near the one this wonderful fellow deserves."

"Good," MacClintock said, and grinned at her look of surprise. "I fell into the second category myself, Your Highness. That's one reason I asked. I just wanted to assure you that not having a name jump up and bite you immediately doesn't indicate that anything is wrong with you or your bond." He reached out and touched the 'cat in her arms gently, running his fingers down its spine, and smiled as it arched in pleasure. Then he looked back at Adrienne again.

"And now, Your Highness, I'm afraid we really ought to get on with that speech of yours."

NINE

Finally!

Henry Thoreau couldn't suppress his grunt of satisfaction as the cheering began. Princess Adrienne was over an hour late, but she was on her way at last.

His vantage point in the park gave him an excellent view of the speaker's platform, but he couldn't see much else. That was deliberate—staying back a little helped him blend anonymously into the crowd—but it also meant he hadn't been able to see whatever had occasioned the last delay. All he knew was that the Heir's entourage had stopped abruptly, stayed that way for ten minutes or so, and then started moving once more.

Well, it doesn't really matter what kind of glitch their schedule hit, he told himself as the leading edge of the Princess' attendants entered his field of view at last. *What matters is that she's on her way now.*

He drew the red handkerchief from his breast pocket.

Seeker of Dreams rode in his person's arms, and the noise of the humans beat over him like a great, rushing wind. He had never imagined so many mouth sounds being made all at one time, yet the mind voices of Parsifal and others assured him humans often made such noises. He found that hard to believe, but Musashi sent him an image of thousands of humans seated around a large green field while two smaller groups of humans ran back and forth, kicking a white sphere. Musashi was no memory singer, but his image carried the concentration and hint of excitement his person had felt as she watched the sphere move up and down the field, and then one of the humans on the grass hit the ball with his head, not his foot. It sailed right through the hands of another human and plopped into an upright net, and at least half those thousands of watching humans surged to their feet with a deep, roaring sound of wild approval.

Seeker of Dreams had no idea what the humans had been up to in Musashi's images. It felt almost like the competition as two teams of junior hunters or scouts raced one another through the branches searching for the senior scouts seeking to evade them. But that was different—a serious test to determine which were ready to assume more demanding, responsible duties—and only those involved paid it much heed. Such competitions were the business of those being tested, yet the humans had gathered in huge numbers to watch *others* compete, and seemed wildly excited about the outcome.

Best leave that ground runner for a later hunt, he told himself. *Besides, it is not the same as this excitement, anyway. This excitement is focused on my person, and through her, upon me, as well.*

The sheer power of it lashed at him, making him taut and uneasy, yet there was an odd euphoria in it, as well. It was all but impossible to separate individual mind glows from one another in the midst of such tumult, but he tasted the welcome, the excitement, the sense of deference. In a strange way, it tasted much like his own feelings for Sings Truly. Or perhaps that was too strong. Perhaps it actually tasted more like his feelings for Leaper of High Branches, his own clan's chief elder. He did not understand how such intensity of emotion could focus on one so young as his person. If they had been able, as he, to taste the glory of her mind glow, perhaps he might have understood, but they were mind-blind, and she was far too young to be an elder in anyone's clan.

He looked up at her, and she looked down quickly, as if she had felt his eyes. Her mouth moved in the expression—the "smile"—he had been told humans used to show pleasure to their mind-blind fellows, and the deep warmth of her mind glow echoed the expression. He bleeked up at her, reaching high to pat her cheek once more, then turned his attention outward. It was difficult to separate himself from her mind glow, but he badly wanted to understand why all these others felt such respect and veneration for her.

He sent his empathy questing outward once more, and fresh surprise at the manner in which his range and sensitivity had increased washed over him. He could actually reach out into that vast crowd and taste the mind glows of individual humans he could scarcely even see, despite all the background energy and passion. It was difficult to tune that background down enough to taste clearly, but it *ought* to have been completely impossible, and he reveled in his newfound abilities.

There was an older female human, her mind glow blazing

with welcome. And there behind her was another female, this one less delighted to see his person—not from any personal animosity, but because of something else, some human thing Seeker of Dreams did not understand but which appeared to involve decisions and the making of rules—but still excited and focused. And there—

Seeker of Dreams stiffened as he sensed the dark, twisted knot of *wrongness* pushing through the crowd towards his person. It was terrifying, like finding one's self trapped on the ground as a death fang closed in, and he gave a high, warning squeal of alarm. He jerked up, head questing, eyes searching for the one he had tasted, and then he saw him—a male human, little older than his own human, who thrust his way through the crowd while his own burning stare locked to Seeker of Dreams' human. And something was wrong, wrong, *wrong!* Seeker of Dreams tasted the deadness, the emptiness within his mind glow, and that was terrifying enough. But there was worse. For even as the empty human forced his way towards Seeker of Dream's human, some tiny part of him cried out, screaming for help, as if his innermost self were trapped in a bog of quicksand. That tiny part wailed in terror, fighting desperately against whatever pulled him forward, yet it could not resist the compulsion, and the taste of the human's despair was almost worse than Seeker of Dream's sudden realization that the other meant to *slay* his person!

He reared up in her arms, baring his fangs, and those around his human faltered and fell back from the rippling snarl of his war cry. Some cried out in alarm, and one or two of her protectors reached for the weapons they carried, but they lacked his empathy. They could not taste what he tasted, and so they turned towards *him*, guided by their physical senses alone, unaware of the danger coming closer with every instant.

But others *could* sense what he sensed, and he heard the sudden, high-pitched snarls of at least a dozen People. Dunatis and Musashi, Parsifal and Leaf Hunter and others whose names he had never learned reached out to him, tasting what he tasted, sensing the darkness through him, and he heard more human cries of shock and confusion as a wave of cream-and-gray fur exploded from the roof of the new admin wing.

Sixteen treecats launched outward in prodigious leaps that carried them clear of the crowd and into the trees of the landscaped grounds. They flashed through the branches, converging on Seeker of Dreams and his human and the darkness that threatened them, and consternation and confusion came with them. Not one human being had the least idea of what they were doing, or why, and there was no time for anyone to figure it out.

Alvin Tudev heard the 'cat's sudden, rippling snarl. He'd never heard anything like it, but he recognized its meaning with the instant intuition of instinct. His own head came up, searching for whatever threat the 'cat had detected, but he saw nothing. Only the path to the speaker's platform, and the rows of spectators behind the barricades holding them back.

But some of those spectators were beginning to react to the treecat's snarling fury. They recoiled, shrinking away from him, and heads were turning as a flood of additional 'cats flashed through the trees towards them. They had no idea what was happening, but they would have been more than human not to be alarmed, and alarm pushed them back. They couldn't move far—they were too tightly packed for that—but their common instinct seemed to be to avoid crowding the Heir.

All but one. Tudev didn't think about it, for there was no time to think. There was only time to see and react, and he did. He saw the one person who bucked the movement of the crowd, kicking and shoving to get *closer* to Princess Adrienne, and trained instinct shrieked a warning even louder than the 'cat's snarls.

Seeker of Dreams sprang from his human's arms. She tried to prevent him, and he felt her surge of confused fear—not for herself, but for him—as her arms tightened. But she was an instant too late, and he arrowed through the air like a vengeful demon. A gray-haired male human flung up his arms, covering his head with a strangled cry as Seeker of Dreams landed on his shoulders, but he didn't even pause. He only ricocheted onward like a rebounding ball, on a course that took him straight towards the empty one.

Tudev saw the young man's hand slide inside his jacket, saw the Heir's treecat slashing through the crowd like a missile, heard the other 'cats' passage through the trees like a gray hurricane. The rest of his detail was still looking in the wrong direction, drawn towards the only threat they could identify: the 'cats' movement. Only Tudev realized, however imperfectly, what was actually happening, and there was no time to explain it to anyone else.

"*Gun!*" he screamed, and for the second time that day, he flung himself at Princess Adrienne's back.

This time he didn't turn aside at the last moment.

✦   ✦   ✦

< *Alive, Seeker of Dreams!* > The mind voice shouted in the back of Seeker of Dreams' brain. < *The humans must have him alive!* >

It was Parsifal. Mind voices were fast and certain, much quicker to give and receive information than the humans' mouth sounds, yet even so there was too little time for Parsifal to explain what he meant . . . and Seeker of Dreams did not *want* to understand. His human had been threatened. All he cared about was the need to end the threat, quickly and forever, and he bared his claws as he bounced from the last innocent human and launched himself straight into the face of the empty one.

< *Do not kill him!* > Parsifal screamed, and now Musashi and Dunatis added their mind voices. Seeker of Dreams hissed defiance, but their command beat in upon him.

The empty human's hand rose, and Seeker of Dreams diverted his attack in the last fraction of an instant. He hit that hand and its arm with all six sets of claws, and the empty one screamed as centimeter-long knives of bone sank deep. Needle-sharp fangs slashed the back of his hand, slicing muscle and tendons, and his fingers sprang open involuntarily. The pistol fell free, bouncing as it hit the ground, and he shook his arm in frantic horror as Seeker of Dreams clawed and bit and tore.

The programming burned into his brain commanded his left hand to press the button in his pocket—the one which would detonate the three kilos of explosive he wore like a breast plate. If he'd gotten close enough, that would have been his weapon to assassinate the Heir; since he had been intercepted, it was the precaution which should have killed him and half a dozen others—possibly including the Heir, even now—and so insured no one would ever realize he'd been adjusted for his role.

But powerful though it was, that programming had never counted on eight kilos of enraged, scimitar-clawed treecat. The pain and shock were too much to be ignored, and his left fist beat frantically at the monster ripping his right arm to pieces. It was raw instinct, inescapable as breathing, preempting the commands another had locked him into obeying, and it delayed him just long enough.

Two more treecats hit him, and he screamed in agony as the extra weight took him to the ground. The newcomers went for his left arm as Seeker of Dreams had gone for his right, and he writhed and fought madly as the hissing, snarling confusion of gray fur and bone-white claws enveloped him. He had no way to know the last thing they wanted was to kill him. All he knew was that a tornado had crashed over him, and there was no time for him to do anything except try frantically to protect his face and eyes.

Adrienne clutched desperately at the treecat, but he squirmed out of her arms like an Old Earth eel, then flung himself away from her, still trailing that terrible, rippling war cry. She reached out futilely, instinctively starting after him. She was completely focused on *him*, unaware of anything else . . . and completely unprepared when eighty-four kilos of hard muscle and bone slammed into her from behind.

Her neck whiplashed as Lieutenant Colonel Tudev brought her crashing to the ground. He had no time to be gentle; he hit her like a rugby player charging for the goal, and her universe went dark as her head hit the ground.

Seeker of Dreams felt his human's mind glow go out, and a wail of grief and terror escaped him. He turned from the empty human, streaked and splashed with his target's blood, and the other humans—those few who had not already gotten as far away as they could—fell over one another in frantic efforts to clear his path. He shot back towards her, wailing his fear, and behind him two SFS rangers, a Twin Forks city policeman, and two members of the Heir's security team flung themselves upon the young man the 'cats had brought down.

Seeker of Dreams scarcely noticed. He flashed across the ground towards his person, and then skidded to a halt. Another human was just rolling off her back—the big, heavily built human for whom his human had radiated such affection and trust—while she lay very still on the ground. Blood seeped from one temple, darkening her tightly-curled hair and streaking her dark skin, and something deep inside Seeker of Dreams twisted even tighter at the sight. But he could also sense her mind glow once more. It was weaker, dimmer and slower, yet it was there, and he felt a great shudder of relief go through him as he realized she was only stunned.

"Sorry, little guy," Tudev muttered. The wailing 'cat had exploded back out of the confusion like a blood-soaked ghost, closing in on Adrienne like a homing missile. The lieutenant colonel had already realized he'd knocked the Heir out when he tackled her, and he hoped to hell that was *all* he'd done. Still, a concussion was better than a bullet would have been, and he'd had no way to know how efficiently the new 'cat and the Forestry Service rangers' 'cats would neutralize the threat.

The treecat didn't even look up. It only crouched on all six limbs, pressing its nose beseechingly against the Heir's face. Its eerie wail had faded, but Tudev could hear the small creature's frantic, buzzing purr even through the confusion of shouts and screams and other panic sounds. He looked down at the 'cat, still more than a little groggy himself, then knelt beside it. The shoulder he'd hurt before hurt even worse now, and it refused to move when he ordered it to, so he used his other hand to stroke the 'cat gently.

"She's going to be all right," he told Seeker of Dreams. "You saved her, and she's going to be all right."

Henry Thoreau was much too far away to see what had happened, but he knew it hadn't been what was *supposed* to happen. There'd been shouts and screams in plenty but no explosion, and he felt a sudden, dark shudder of fear. The lack of an explosion *might* mean some alert bodyguard had recognized the threat, gotten his weapon out, and killed the programmed assassin, but it was far more likely something had gone wrong and they'd taken the young man alive. And if they'd managed to do that and handed him over to a psychiatrist, the fact that he'd been adjusted would be glaringly obvious, and then—

Thoreau swallowed hard. He had to get out of here. Even if they had the kid alive, they'd need time to figure out he'd been adjusted . . . and by whom. Or they ought to. But he couldn't be sure of that, and he and Krogman had to get off-planet *now*.

Fortunately, the panicked reaction of the crowd should cover his escape. Some people, predictably, were fighting to get closer to whatever had happened, drawn to the excitement like moths to a flame, regardless of danger. But a much greater number wanted to get *away* from a situation of which they grasped only fragments, and Thoreau let himself merge into the stream of humanity funneling towards the park gates.

The treecats called Dunatis and Parsifal looked at one another as the human scouts and hunters converged on the one Seeker of Dreams, Musashi, and Leaf Hunter had brought down. Other treecats gathered around them in the trees, and Parsifal tasted the fury washing about their mind glows. The bright, jagged need to attack flickered within all of them, yet they had themselves under control, and he turned back to Dunatis.

< *This is not right,* > he said flatly. < *Seeker of Dreams was right. This one—* > his tail flipped towards the bloodied young

man being handcuffed below them < —*is empty. I have never
tasted the like in any human, yet there is something. . . . There!* >
The human writhed madly, screaming a wordless protest
against the alien commands buried within his mind. He fought
frantically to obey them even as the tiny, independent core
of him which survived wailed in the bottomless terror his
mind-blind human captors could not understand. < *Did you
taste it?* >

< *I did,* > Dunatis replied grimly, and several other mind
voices agreed. < *This is evil, brothers.* > Lieutenant General
MacClintock's companion looked out over the surging sea of
humans, and his tail flicked with fury. < *This was done to him.
I do not know how, but it must have been the work of some human
evil doer.* > The other 'cats nodded. All of them had bonded
to Forestry Service personnel, and all had been forced to
confront the division between law abiding people and crimi-
nals. < *I have never heard of its like, but there is much we still
do not understand about the tools and knowledge of the humans.
No doubt they will know how this could be accomplished. Yet they
are occupied now with surprise and confusion. It will be some time
before they think clearly, and they are mind-blind, unable to taste
what hides behind their fellow humans' eyes.* >

< *But we are not mind-blind,* > Parsifal said, and Dunatis
flicked his ears.

< *Spread out, brothers,* > he commanded. < *It may be that the
evil doer responsible for this thing is nowhere near, that he had
no need or desire to witness the working of his plans. But it is also
possible he is near at hand. Seek him, and if you find him, summon us. Perhaps—* > there was grim, vengeful anticipation in
Dunatis' mind voice < —*we can . . . delay his steps until our
humans arrive to ask him how his day has been.* >

Thoreau wanted to use his size and strength to plow an
escape route through the crowds, but he dared not. He had
to blend, vanish into the protective confusion, and so he let
the press of people carry him towards the gates. They were
moving slower than he would have liked, but at least they were
moving, and—

A high, sibilant hiss from above jerked his head up. Grass-
green eyes blazed down at him from a branch two meters above
his head, and the hiss became a low, rumbling snarl as his
gaze met those eyes. He swallowed in sudden terror and started
to turn away, only to freeze as another hiss came from the
tree behind him. Another 'cat hissed at him, and then there
was another—*and another!*

Henry Thoreau stood paralyzed as fourteen silken-coated arboreals glared down at him, lashing their tails while ivory claws kneaded in and out of the tree bark. There was nothing cute or cuddly about them, and he felt the bright, angry intelligence behind their unflinching eyes as they pinned him with their green glare.

They know, he thought. *The little bastards* know *I had something to do with what just went down! But how?* How *could they know? Unless—*

And then he had it. They were empaths, and his emotions might as well have been screaming his guilt at the tops of his lungs, as far as they were concerned. But they were the only ones who knew. If he got away, there would be no way they could pass that information on to anyone else.

All he had to do was get away.

He swallowed again, then began to back slowly away.

He'd gotten perhaps three meters when a needle-fanged tide of treecats came flooding out of the trees.

TEN

Adrienne Michelle Aoriana Elizabeth Winton opened her eyes slowly. Her head hurt, her face hurt, her *back* hurt, and her right eye refused to focus properly. *Aside from that,* she thought woozily, *there's not a thing wrong with me. Now if I could only remember* why *I hurt. . . .*

She stared up at the ceiling, trying to get her thoughts herded up and moving in a single direction. It was a difficult task, but then something shifted on the pillow, right beside her left ear. Silky softness stirred, just brushing the surface of her skin, and she gasped in sudden memory. Her head snapped over, and the bright green eyes of the treecat looked back at her while a soft, buzzing purr welcomed her awakening.

She stared at the 'cat, and her thoughts were still slow and confused. But she wasn't too confused to recall that moment when the 'cat dropped into her arms, and she reached out for him once more. Pain lanced through her skull with the movement, but the 'cat flowed into her embrace, hugging her neck with his strong, wiry forearms while he rubbed his head ever so gently against her cheek.

"I see you're awake," a familiar voice said, and she looked past the 'cat as Alvin Tudev, one arm in a sling, appeared in the door of what she now realized was a hospital room. "Good," the lieutenant colonel went on. "It's been a while."

"How—" She cleared her throat. "How long is 'a while,' and what happened?"

"A while is several hours," he replied. "And what happened is a bit complicated. As far as your headache is concerned, I'm afraid that's my fault. I hit you a bit harder than I meant to."

"*You* hit me?" she repeated carefully, and he nodded.

"One of the things bodyguards do when there may be bullets flying around, Your Highness. There wasn't time to ask politely, or I would have." He smiled, and she realized his half-joking tone was a reaction to his relief that she was all right. "As to *why* I hit you, you can thank your little friend." Adrienne raised an eyebrow, and he shrugged. "He and his buddies have just demonstrated a very good reason for a monarch or his heir to be accompanied by treecats everywhere they go," he said in a much more serious tone.

"An assassin," she said. The word came out in a half-whisper and her eyes darkened as she realized what Tudev was leading up to, and he nodded.

"An assassin," he confirmed. "But the 'cats sensed him before he got into range, and they all went straight for him. Your friend got to him first, but the others were only seconds behind. They not only took him down, they managed to hold him— alive—until us mere two-foots could figure out what was going on and close in on him. And that," he added grimly, "wasn't as easy as you might think, because the poor bas—" He stopped and cleared his throat. "The assassin was wired up with enough explosives to send himself into orbit without counter-grav," he continued, "and he would've done it, too."

"That's crazy," she said.

"No, Your Highness," he said even more grimly. "It was supposed to *look* crazy." Adrienne looked at him in confusion, and he sighed. "We're still just getting started, Your Highness, but it's already clear your intended assassin was psych-adjusted for the job. It's going to take weeks to even begin finding all the triggers and compulsions, but it seems pretty evident that one of his compulsions was to blow himself up—and take you with him, if possible—in order to keep us from realizing he'd been programmed."

"Oh my God," Adrienne whispered, and Tudev nodded.

"I think He—and the 'cats—had an awful lot to do with the fact that you're still alive, Your Highness. More than that, the 'cats may have caught us a break on cracking this entire plot wide open."

"What do you mean? And *what* plot?"

"To take your second question first, this had to be an inside job in at least one respect. The killers were here waiting for you, in position, before your visit was announced. That means somebody gave them a copy of the Alpha List, because Twin Forks was only *on* the Alpha List; it never appeared on any of the decoy lists. And that means somebody was able to extract a Blue File and decrypt it, which takes a very highly placed source, and *that* implies a far wider reaching plot than anyone in my line of work likes to think about. Still, given your father's success in concentrating authority in the Crown, I can see where he could have aroused the, um . . . *forceful* opposition of some powerful people."

He paused, and Adrienne nodded with a shiver.

"As for cracking the plot, however," Tudev went on with a wolfish smile, "we believe we've got the man who actually triggered the assassin's attack in custody, and we owe *that* to the 'cats, too. He was two-thirds of the way out of the park when ten or fifteen of the 'cats zeroed in on him. The Forest Service types' best guess is that they were able to pick up his emotional reaction to the failure of the attack and use that to target him. Apparently," the lieutenant colonel's smile turned even more lupine, "he panicked and tried to run, and the 'cats swarmed him. They didn't actually hurt him much—aside from a *lot* of scratches, some pretty deep—but they absolutely shredded his clothing, and his confidence went with it. By the time the first Twin Forks cops got there, he was curled up in a knot in a corner of the fence screaming for someone to rescue him. He practically *begged* them to listen to his confession if they'd just keep the 'cats away from him. And he did confess, too."

"But—" Adrienne paused, thinking as hard as her aching head allowed, then shrugged. "Will that hold up? Can't an attorney argue that it was coerced?"

"Ah, but it wasn't coerced by an officer of the *court*, Your Highness. In fact, the cops were scrupulous about informing him of all his rights, and they never threatened him in any way. It was the 'cats he was afraid of, not them, and the 'cats have no official standing . . . except that of minor children." He shrugged. "I don't see any problems. Particularly not," he added in icy tones, "in a case like this one."

Adrienne looked at him, wondering if he even realized how utterly implacable he sounded. But then his expression changed, and he cleared his throat once more.

"Ah, there is one more thing, Your Highness," he said with

an edge of discomfort. "I was, of course, required to inform His Majesty of everything that occurred." Adrienne nodded, her face expressionless iron, and he went on. "I commed the first report to him immediately after the incident, because I wanted to be certain he got it from us rather than the newsies. Since then, I've sent several follow-up reports on all that's happened."

"I see," Adrienne said.

"Yes, Ma'am." Tudev checked his chrono and drew a deep breath. "Forty-seven minutes ago, we received a transmission in the royal family's encryption, Your Highness. It was addressed to you. I've had the com techs set it up on your terminal here, but we require your voice print to release the encrypt."

"I see," Adrienne said again. Then she nodded to him. "Very well, Colonel. Thank you—for everything, including my life— but I would appreciate it if you could leave me alone for the next little while." She smiled wanly. "I've got some mail to listen to."

"Of course, Your Highness," Tudev murmured, and withdrew. There were some things, he thought, no bodyguard could protect a person from.

Seeker of Dreams had followed the subtle flow and change in the taste of his person's mind glow as she and the one called Tudev spoke. He liked Tudev—liked the taste of his mind glow and his fierce protectiveness. But he'd also tasted Tudev's unhappiness over whatever he had just told her . . . and the bitter hurt which had flared through her when she heard it. It was not anything Tudev had done; Seeker of Dreams knew that. But it *was* whatever had caused the great sorrow which every one of the People had tasted in her mind glow, and he tensed inwardly as she gathered her courage.

He reached out to his link to her and felt it there between them. It was unlike the bond he might have established with another of the People, for her end of it was anchored in a strange blankness, an almost-awareness which hovered just below recognition. She knew it was there, he thought; she simply could not perceive it, could not reach out and complete the weaving another of the People would have accomplished.

Yet he felt and tasted so *much* even through the unfinished weaving, and if she could not reach out to him, still he could reach *in* to her. And so he extended himself into their linkage, cautiously, testing each step as he took it, until he could

156 WORLDS OF HONOR

lay his mental touch upon the grief at her heart. And then, as he would have with another of the People, he drew that grief to him.

He tasted her surprise, her sudden suspicion that he was somehow soothing her, and his buzzing purr deepened. She sat up in bed, and he flowed into her lap and curled there, tucking his nose against her, smelling the strange-not-strange scent of her, and his grip upon her sorrow tightened. It was *her* sorrow, not his, and so it did not bite upon him as it did upon her. He was distressed that she felt it, but it could not hurt him, and he spread himself across its jagged edges. She was mind-blind. He could have reached in through their link, had he so chosen, and taken her sorrow from her so completely she would feel none of it ever again, and she could not have stopped him. But that was against the most ancient traditions of the People. Deeply though he was tempted, he would not do it, for what would begin as an act of love could well become something else with the passing of time. Even the most well meaning person could do incalculable damage if ever he decided what pain, what sorrow, he would take from another, for he could always find sound reasons to take one more pain, one more unhappiness . . . until the one he loved and had tried to help became like the empty human who had sought his person's life. Pain and sorrow were terrible burdens, to be shared with those who loved one and healed when healing was possible. Yet as he himself had told Parsifal, even among the People, the most powerful mind glows and the strongest People were often bred of sorrow and the need to face it.

Adrienne looked down at the 'cat, her eyes huge. The subtle touch deep within her was more sensed than felt—a presence which revealed itself only in the absence of her pain. No, she thought, not *absence*. The treecat had not taken her pain from her; he had simply . . . moved between it and her. As Alvin Tudev had placed his body between her body and harm, so the 'cat had somehow placed his love between her and her sorrow. It was still there, and it still hurt dreadfully, but she no longer faced it alone, and that made all the difference in the universe.

"Thank you," she whispered, bending to press a kiss between his ears, and his purr buzzed still louder as he leaned his weight against her. For one more moment she allowed herself to luxuriate in his love, but she had her own responsibilities, and she refused to put off that which she must do.

She drew a deep breath and reached out to the com terminal.

It wasn't a standard hospital unit, and her mouth crooked in a half-bitter grin. The special high security com systems followed her wherever she went . . . even here, in a hospital room. Had a tech slipped in and connected it while she lay unconscious? Probably not, she decided. Among the many details her security detachment always worried about whenever she traveled was which hospital she would be taken to in case of emergency. If they worried about things like that, then they probably also saw to it that the hospital they chose would have the proper communications equipment if she happened to need it.

She pushed the thought aside and pressed the acceptance key beside the blinking light of a waiting message. A soft tone sounded, and she cleared her throat.

"Message release authorization," she said slowly and distinctly. "Adrienne Michelle Aoriana Elizabeth, Alpha Seven, Hotel Three, Lima."

A moment passed while the computers considered her voice and the authorization code for this trip, and then the screen lit with her father's face.

He looks dreadful, she thought. His eyes were swollen, and the lines in his face looked etched and burned with acid as he stared into the pickup. He said nothing at all for several seconds, then inhaled sharply and began, abruptly, to speak.

"I know why you went to Twin Forks, Adrienne," he said, and she sat very still, for his voice was different. It was flat, harsh, its edges eroded and ragged—a far cry from the toneless, uninvolved, and perpetually, lethally reasonable voice she'd come to dread. "I knew you were going before you ever left Manticore, and it made me furious—just as you meant it to— but I didn't say anything. And because I didn't, I almost lost you."

His flat voice wavered suddenly with the last four words, and he stopped and clamped his jaw, nostrils flaring while his cheek muscles clenched. Adrienne stared at the display, stunned, for she had not heard that much emotion from him in the entire ten years since Queen Solange's death.

"I know I've hurt you, Adrienne," he said finally, his voice flat once more, but hoarse. "I even know how and why. I'm not an idiot, however idiotically I've acted. But knowing wasn't enough. It should have been."

He sounded almost as if he were rambling, but each little burst of words came out in a staccato rhythm, focused into laser sharpness despite his harrowed tone.

"It should have been enough. It *would* have been enough,

if I hadn't been so afraid. But I thought— No, that's wrong. I didn't really *think* at all, but I *thought* I had. And it seemed safer to be cold, to push you away, to—" He paused and cleared his throat once more. "I don't have to tell you all the stupid things I did," he resumed after a moment. "God knows that if I know what they were, *you* know even better. And I know I have no right even to hope you might understand why I did it . . . or forgive me for it. That's why I won't ask you to."

"But—" He stopped again and drew a long, shuddering breath, and his swollen eyes gleamed suspiciously. "But I almost lost you today," he said hoarsely. "Perhaps I already have, and I won't blame you if that's true, but today I almost lost you forever, like . . . like I lost your mother. And I realized that if I *had* lost you, if you'd . . . died today, then any chance I might ever have had to tell you how sorry I am, or to tell you how much I love you, or to even *try* to repair some of the hurt and harm I've done would have died with you. And I can't have that, Adrienne. Maybe that's the ultimate cowardice—that I'm too terrified to lose you with the coldness still between us to keep that safe, uncaring coldness there. I don't know. I only know that when Colonel Tudev's first message came in, I—"

He broke off, face working, and covered his eyes with his hands. His shoulders shook, and Adrienne heard the treecat in her lap crooning to her as tears spangled her own burning vision.

"I'm sorry, baby," he told her in a shaking voice. "God, that sounds so *stupid*—so useless and tiny after all I've done, but I can't— They're the only words—" He sucked in a deep, wracking breath. "I don't know another way to say it," he said finally. "I won't blame you if you don't forgive me. I made my choices, my decisions. They were wrong. They were stupid. They were cowardly. But I made them, and they hurt you horribly, and if you hate me for that, I earned it, and I know it. But this much I promise you. It may take something as horrible and terrifying as today to get through to me, but I *can* learn, Adrienne, and whether you can forgive me or not, I will never shut you out again. Perhaps we can never be like we were before your mother died. If not, the fault is mine, and I accept that. But now I *know* how stupid I've been. I can't turn away, pretend I don't know. So at the very least, I will treat you as a monarch ought to treat his heir— as someone to be consulted and involved, whose opinion counts and who has the right to demand explanations of me. I would like . . . like very much—" his voice cracked again

"—to do better than that, as well. I would like to learn to act like a father once more, but I know that's not something I can demand of you or order you to let me be. It's a position I'll have to try to earn again. I may not succeed, but I intend to try, and—" he managed a shaky smile while tears trickled down his face "—one thing I've learned to do is try really hard when I want something badly."

"I know you have, Daddy," she whispered through her own tears as he paused once more, and her hands caressed the treecat in her lap. She'd waited so many hopeless, pain-filled years to hear those words. Now she had . . . and he was right. In her dreams, she'd seen them coming back together, their scars magically healed—seen him once more as her adored father, and seen her as his beloved daughter. But he'd hurt her too badly for that. The wounds went too deep, and that innocent perfection had been lost to both of them forever. They had become worse than strangers to one another; they'd become sources of pain, of hurt and loneliness, and that could be neither forgotten nor forgiven in a moment, whatever she wanted. Indeed, she didn't know if it could ever be forgiven at all.

But I do know that if we don't try, we can never even hope to fix it, she thought, feeling her tears splash her hands where they rested on the treecat's silken fur. *And at least he's come this far, reached out this much to me after so long. I can't just rush home and tell him all is forgiven, that it's all water under the bridge. But I can go home and let him try, and I can try, and maybe we can patch something together between us once again, if only for the sake of Mother's memory.*

"On another matter," her father's voice said from the com, and she blinked, then rubbed at her eyes with one hand, "I understand I also have to change my opinion of treecats." He managed a more natural looking smile, and there was a ghost of true humor in his voice. "Colonel Tudev has kept me up to date, so I know one of them has adopted you. And I also know he and his friends are the reason you're still alive. Which means, of course, that I owe them and all their relatives a debt I can never hope to pay.

"But just because I can't pay it, doesn't mean I don't have to try, so as soon as I finish recording this message, I'll be sitting down with the Prime Minister to discuss the withdrawal of the Crown's opposition to the Treecat Rights Bill. The Sphinx Forestry Service will be getting a somewhat larger budget over the next few months, as well, and I would be very grateful if you would ask General MacClintock if he would be so good as to accompany you back to Manticore so that he and I can discuss how best to clarify—and enforce—the treecats' legal status as quickly as possible.

"In addition," his recorded image looked straight into the pickup, meeting his daughter's gaze levelly, "I would ask you and your new friend to come home to Mount Royal Palace. I understand from Colonel Tudev that the 'cats have rather conclusively demonstrated their ability to sense the hostile intent of would-be assassins. I find that an excellent reason to encourage my daughter to consort with them, and I intend to ask the SFS to reassign a few of their enforcement personnel to the PGS. More to the point," his mouth tightened, and grim pleasure flickered in his eyes, "I agree with Colonel Tudev. This had to have been arranged with the help of a high-level leak and, probably, with some high-level conspirators, as well. And that being the case, I am looking forward with considerable anticipation to introducing as many 'cats as possible to the people here at Court who might have profited from your demise. I know it won't be admissible in a court of law, but if we know where to look, I feel quite confident that men and women like Colonel Tudev will be able to find the evidence we require. Or at least," his smile was cold, "to keep the guilty parties far too busy running for their lives to try any more plots . . . or ever enjoy themselves or their lives again."

Adrienne felt her own mouth quirking as she visualized the scene as her 'cat and a dozen or so others suddenly found themselves with the free run of Mount Royal Palace. Whoever had tried to kill her was undoubtedly well enough connected to realize why they were there, and for the first time in far too many years, she found herself in complete and total agreement with her father.

For several seconds she smiled at the com while her father smiled out of it, but then his smile faded and his voice softened.

"But that's for the future, Adrienne. For now, just be well. Come home to me. However foolishly I've acted, I love you, and I want the opportunity to prove that to you once more. Please."

He stopped speaking and gazed out of the display for a moment longer, and then the message ended, and Adrienne leaned back against her pillows and hugged Seeker of Dreams to her breasts while fresh tears misted her vision. He twisted in her arms, wiggling until he could nestle his blunt, triangular jaw down into the angle of her collar bone, and the deep, buzzing strength of his purr burned into her flesh and sinew.

It was all his doing, she realized wonderingly. He'd dropped into her life like a whirlwind, and he was the only reason she was still alive. He and his friends were the only reason anyone even knew there'd been a plot to be discovered, not simply some lone, deranged assassin, and they were the ones who were most likely to discover who the plotters were. And if the miracle she'd prayed for occurred—if somehow she and her father were able to piece back together even a shadow of the warmth and love they once had known—that, too, would be possible only because of the 'cat in her arms.

"I haven't even named you," she whispered into one tufted ear, and the ear twitched. The 'cat raised his head just enough to look into her eyes, and she smiled tremulously. "I guess I really am one of the slowpokes Colonel MacClintock was talking about," she told him, "but you'll have to be patient with me. It has to be the right name for all you've accomplished this afternoon . . . and somehow I don't think you'd like 'Miracle Worker' very much when you learned what it meant!"

Seeker of Dreams gazed into his human's eyes and tasted the fragile bubble of amusement deep within her. He did not yet understand what had passed between her and her father, but there would be time for that, and now that he knew the source of her hurt, he could help her—and her father—deal with it. He knew he could do that much, and he looked forward to it. But just now, what he most savored was the humor and the joy within her, and the way the sorrow and the release of long held pain made both of them brighter despite their fragility.

He felt the turnings he might have known fall away from him, cast aside without regret as his empathy nestled close to the brightness and the beauty of his person. He would never know what those lost turnings might have brought to him . . . yet if he had not chosen, had not bonded, he would never have known even a fraction of the joy and awareness and love that were his now. It was a fair trade, he decided, and reached up to touch her face with one true-hand.

Adrienne Winton looked into her 'cat's bright green eyes, and ever so dimly she sensed the depths of his thoughts, the solemnity of his contemplations. There was something painfully profound about the moment, a sense of decisions made and prices paid, and for one more moment her breath caught in her throat as a poignancy she did not truly understand swept over her.

But then the 'cat she had yet to name reached out a true-hand. He touched her face, then leaned closer, until the very tip of his nose brushed hers. His whiskers quivered as their eyes held to one another, so close her own tried to cross. She held her breath, waiting for some deep, meaningful signal from him . . . and then he drew back and nipped her sharply on the nose.

"*Owwww!*" Her hand shot up to cover her nose, but the cat had already sprung away from her. He landed on the head of her bed and clung there, head-down, with both true-feet and one hand-foot, flirting his tail daintily while he bleeked laughter at her. She could almost hear his mental "Gotcha!" and she laughed back at him as she felt her spirit soar.

Seeker of Dreams felt his person's joy rising like sap in mud time, felt the scaly mental scabs cracking ever so slightly about the wounds deep within her, and bleeked another laugh at her. He remembered what Sings Truly had said, of how even the best hunter could suddenly find himself the hunted, and he knew she had been right. He had come hunting his dream; now he had found it, and it had captured him, and in the fullness of time, it would slay him.

But if not that, then something else would slay me in time, he thought. *And though the choice was mine, the joy will be a thing we both share. Perhaps our time will be short, but oh, how we shall blaze against the night! The memory singers of the People will sing our song so long as there are People, and she and I will go on as one forever!*

He gazed down at her for one more brief, endless moment, and then he released his grip on the head of the bed and pounced upon her, growling and capturing her hand and arm like a kitten, and the happy music of laughter, human and treecat alike, burned like a beacon against the darkness.

Queen's Gambit

Jane Lindskold

Coming out of a perfect double spiral flip high over the blue sands of the Indigo Salt Flats, Roger glanced over to see what Angelique thought of his performance. Gracefully poised on her own grav ski, dark hair whipping behind her in the wind, his wife and queen raised her hand in salute before executing the maneuver herself.

Her time was a trifle slower, but her control even better. Roger chuckled to himself. The judges—if there had been any—would have given the round to her.

"Ready for a quad, Angel?" he asked her over their com link.

"Why not?" she replied, her laughter rich. "I can't recall when the conditions have been so perfect."

"You go first," he answered.

"So you can study my technique?" She laughed again. "As Your Majesty commands."

Her quadruple spiral flip ended with a little flirt that could almost have been counted as another half turn.

King Roger III of Manticore hand signaled his appreciation for her technique, then checked his readouts. If he was to win this round in their private competition, he needed every advantage to be taken from the slight wind and the thermal updrafts.

When he judged conditions to be as close to ideal as possible, he glided up into the first spiral. Perfect!

The second went as smoothly, the third without a hitch. He was moving into the fourth, concentrating on gaining the

velocity to imitate Angelique's flourish at the end, when he
felt the ski jump under his feet.

He was far too experienced in the vagaries of the grav ski
to believe that he had imagined the sensation. Temptation to
ride the jolts out arose—although he had never competed
publicly, he knew that he was among the best grav skiers in
the Star Kingdom. But he also knew too well that his kingdom would be thrust into turmoil if anything happened to him.

Almost as swiftly as temptation rose and was rejected, his
left hand was reaching for the tab that would release him from
the grav ski and onto the stand-by grav pack. Another jolt,
this one a buck that must be visible from the ground, shook
his hand from the tab.

Over the com Angelique said, "I'm closing to help, Roger."

"I'm holding, love," he responded, continuing to fumble for
the release.

Then impossibly, the grav ski failed completely. The velocity he had brought into his last spiral now turned against him,
ripping his hands away from the release tab.

Below him the salt sands glittered bright, hard, and utterly
unforgiving. He died with the sound of his wife's scream in
his ears and the sensation of a distant heart breaking from
grief.

Elizabeth III, Queen of Manticore, stood with her fiancé,
Justin Zyrr, in the small ante-chamber into which they had
retreated after viewing the holo-video of Roger III's death.

After the first play through thirteen year-old Prince Michael
had bolted from the room, sobbing wildly. His relationship with
his father had been affectionate enough, but recently acrimony
over Roger's insistence that the boy enter the Navy had colored their meetings. Now those disagreements would never be
resolved.

Normally, Justin would have worried about the boy, but he had
no attention to spare from the tall, slim young woman who stood
like a statue carved of mahogany, her features eloquently display-
ing her grief. Physically, they were not much alike.

She was dark of skin, hair, and eyes. Blond and blue-eyed,
he was day to her night—a fact that the news services had
happily seized upon and turned into iconography. At twenty-
eight, he was the elder by a decade, taller, broad of shoulder
and chest, but with a long, lean build. His posture was vaguely
military, a remnant of his single term in the Army.

Gradually, Elizabeth's expression changed, resolution sculpting
the grief into something firm and purposeful.

"I just don't believe it was an accident," she said, her first words since they had entered the room.

Justin gathered her into his arms, felt some relief as she relaxed within his embrace. It would have been almost too much if she had rejected the small comfort he could give her.

"Accidents do happen . . ." he began.

"I know they do," Elizabeth interrupted, "even to members of the House of Winton. Edward the First died in a boating accident. His sister succeeded him. Her name was Elizabeth, just like mine."

Her laughter held a ragged, almost hysterical note.

"Maybe it's bad luck to have an heir named Elizabeth," she continued. "Make a note of that, would you, my dear?"

Her treecat, Ariel, who had been sitting on a tabletop observing the conversation, gave a reproving "bleek." The Queen glanced at the 'cat, then pulled back within the circle of Justin's arms to look up at him.

Her eyes, dark brown behind velvety black lashes, were wet with the tears she would not shed in public—not when her bravery was needed to reassure both her little brother and her many subjects.

There had been little enough time for tears in the scant hours since King Roger's death. Directly following the verification that the King's accident had been fatal, she had been summoned from her Introductory Manticoran History class at the University and taken to a small student lounge. There, amid much-used furniture and vending machines, she had learned of her father's death, taken the Monarch's Oath, and accepted the loyalty oaths of the Speakers of both Houses of Parliament.

From the student lounge she had been whisked into a press conference where—pushing away the prepared statement—she had spoken of the King eloquently and from her heart.

Roger III had been a popular monarch; his sudden death hit his people hard. As the first monarch to receive the pro-long treatments, his people's unspoken expectation had been that he would rule for decades to come, his wisdom guiding the Star Kingdom of Manticore into the increasingly complex politics of its fifth century.

"Ariel seems to think I'm being too rough on you," Elizabeth said, softly, through her tears. "I'm sorry, Justin."

"Apology accepted," he said. "You've been through too much recently. I don't expect you not to snap."

"But I do," she said firmly. "I am the Queen. I'm afraid I'm not permitted to snap. Not even at my fiancé—perhaps *especially* not at my fiancé. You shouldn't be the whipping boy for the rest of the Star Kingdom."

Justin laughed. "I'd like to say something gracious like: 'Yet if your Majesty needs me as her whipping boy, I would be pleased to serve her in that fashion.' Honesty forces me to admit that I wouldn't like that role very much."

"But will you serve me?" Elizabeth asked seriously.

"Either you personally or as my Queen," he replied promptly.

He might not be as empathic as a treecat, but he could sense that Elizabeth's mood had shifted. When she pulled from his arms, it was not in rejection, but because she needed to pace. Sitting in a chair near Ariel's table, he watched her slim form cross and recross the room, waiting while she composed her thoughts.

"Justin, I don't believe my father's death was an accident." She paused, held up a hand for silence. "Most of us prefer to think otherwise, but assassination hasn't been a stranger to the House of Winton. Remember, there was an attempt on Queen Adrienne's life while she was still Heir, and William the First was actually assassinated by a psychotic."

"But by a *psychotic*," Justin protested. "Your father died in a grav skiing accident. We both saw the tapes. Grav units can go bad. Not often, but it does happen."

Elizabeth began pacing again. "Maybe so, but aside from the fact that my father's security guards always carefully inspected any vehicle he used, I have another reason to believe his 'accident' was anything but an accident."

"What reason?"

"I gave him a brand new ski for his birthday. When I went into his suite to chat with him before he and Mother left for this jaunt, he made a point of mentioning that he was taking my gift with him. I even saw that his valet had laid the gear out to be packed."

"Yes?"

"Now, I only saw the accident on holo-video," Elizabeth said slowly, "but I'm almost certain the ski he was wearing in that accident was not the one I gave him."

"He could have changed his mind," Justin protested. "His security staff might not have passed the ski for use. Or you might not have seen clearly when you were watching the holo. The speeds involved were rather fast."

Justin forbore from adding that her eyes had been misty as she watched the replay of her father's last moments.

"I know all that," Elizabeth answered regally, "but I still have my doubts. That's why I asked you if you'd serve me. I need you to investigate my father's last hours. If he wore a different ski, I want to know why. If he didn't, I want to know if the one he wore was properly inspected. I want to know everything."

There was no trace of tears in the dark eyes now. She was every inch a queen. Even if Justin hadn't loved her, he would have been commanded by her royal aura. When he nodded his assent, she took both his hands in hers.

"Thank you, Justin. I can't do this myself. I'm going to have too many eyes on me, too many issues to face. I can't even trust my own security staff. If the ski was somehow tampered with, one of them may have had a hand in it. You, I can trust."

"Always."

Elizabeth smiled at him, glanced over to where Ariel was purring rather smugly. "I know."

"Shall I leave now?" he said, pretending to take offense at her reliance on the treecat's opinion.

"Stay a bit." Elizabeth sighed. "I expect that soon enough someone is going to come along wanting to discuss the politics of the succession."

Justin pulled Elizabeth into his lap. Ariel, deciding that this was a good thing, piled into Elizabeth's lap and began purring noisily, kneading with his true-hands.

"Politics?" Justin said. "What politics? You're Queen. Michael will be your heir. Right?"

"Only to a point." Elizabeth rubbed her hands over her eyes. "By Manticoran law, I must have a regent until I'm twenty-one T-years. Since I'm past my sixteenth birthday, they can't foist just anyone on me. I nominate my regent; Parliament confirms or rejects my choice. We do this until we're both happy. I suspect it could be an ugly time."

She sat in thoughtful silence for a moment, then, twisting in his lap to face him, she twinkled.

"Then there will be the question of our marriage."

Justin felt a sudden, cold fear that somehow Elizabeth would be taken from him. They had been engaged with King Roger and Queen Angelique's full approval since soon after Elizabeth's seventeenth birthday. Could Parliament force Elizabeth to break the engagement, choose another spouse?

"Question?" he squeaked.

This time Ariel's reproving bleek was for both of them—Justin for doubting Elizabeth, and Elizabeth for her choice of a joke. The treecat rose and patted Justin on the side of his face, his other true-hand resting on Elizabeth's shoulder.

"I shouldn't tease," Elizabeth admitted ruefully. "Justin, no one can make me break my engagement with you. I don't even expect it to be questioned. However, the line of succession has just grown shorter by one. Originally, we planned to marry after I turned twenty-one, right?"

"Right," he answered, his voice back to normal.

"Now I expect there will be some pressure for us to marry sooner."

"I don't have a problem with that."

"Nor I, particularly," she said, "but there will be those who do. Some will think a proper mourning period should be observed. Others will worry that the distractions of a wedding, a husband, pressure to produce an heir, will distract me from my duties as Queen."

"So they'll want you to wait."

"Exactly. After all, there are the cadet branches of the House. My Aunt Caitrin and her children can carry on if something happens both to me and to Michael before I have children of my own. . . ."

Her voice trailed off. Small and forlorn, she leaned her head back against his shoulder, tears trailing down her face.

"Justin, I don't want to think about it!"

"Then don't," Justin suggested, "for right now. Don't think about anything at all."

When he hugged her, he wasn't at all certain that the purring was coming only from the treecat.

A tentative rap at the door to the antechamber interrupted their cuddling. Elizabeth rose from Justin's lap, brushed a hand over her hair, and spoke in a calm, level voice:

"Come."

The door opened and a member of the uniformed Palace Guard Service entered and saluted.

"Your Majesty, Crown Prince Michael wonders if you would grant him a moment of your time."

Justin raised an eyebrow. Already things were changing. Yesterday . . . this morning even, the guard would have simply smiled, given minimal warning, and let Michael charge in. Today . . . now . . . until new protocols were established, Elizabeth must be treated with all the deference and protection due to her august rank.

Not seeming to notice the change in procedure, Elizabeth nodded. "Thank you, Taki. Ask him to come in."

Crown Prince Michael, Heir to the House of Winton, was widely acknowledged as a handsome boy. Despite the beginning growth spurts that were adding inches to his height, he seemed to be escaping the weedy stage of adolescence. Even at thirteen, he resembled his athletic father.

At this moment, however, not even his own mother would have called him handsome. His eyes were red and his brown skin grubby with tear streaks. He looked at his sister.

"Do I have to bow or something now?"

"Did you to Dad?" she asked calmly.

"Only on court occasions."

"Well then, what do you think?" Elizabeth said reasonably. "Don't be pig-headed, Mikey."

The Prince winced at the nickname, which recently he had decided he'd out-grown. Since "Mike" was already taken by one of their cousins, he'd started insisting on "Michael."

Elizabeth knew her brother perfectly well and grinned. "You don't need to remind me what to call *you*, Michael."

Justin rose from his chair.

"I think you two need some time alone." He kissed Elizabeth lightly on one cheek and patted Michael on the shoulder. "I'll be in my quarters if you need me. Otherwise, I'll see you at dinner."

The soon-to-be Prince Consort left without further pause. Michael watched the tall, blond man go.

"He's nice," he said, almost grudgingly. "Are you still going to marry him?"

Elizabeth looked surprised. "Of course. No one could stop me. Why do you ask?"

Michael walked to the table, patted Ariel, and flung himself onto the chair Justin had just vacated. Wrapping his arms around the back, his chin pillowed on the headrest, he looked vastly uncomfortable. Only years of watching him choose similarly contorted poses reassured his sister that he was not purposefully tormenting himself.

"I guess," he said, finally answering her question, "I wondered because Dad liked him so much. I thought he might have pushed him at you."

"Like he was pushing you into the Navy?" Elizabeth asked, easily following her brother's train of thought.

"Yeah."

"No, marrying Justin was all my idea. From the time I first met him, I realized he was special. Fortunately, Mom and Dad agreed. All they asked was that I finish college and reach my majority before we married."

Michael swiveled the seat of the chair and looked up at her.

"Are you going to have to go back to the University now that you're Queen?"

Elizabeth squarely met brown eyes so like her father's that her heart caught in her chest and her own eyes were hot with sudden tears.

"Don't you really mean 'Am I going to have to go back to military school now that I'm Crown Prince?' "

"Yeah."

Elizabeth shrugged. "That's up to Mom, isn't it? I'm certain I'll be consulted, as will the new Regent's Council, but I'd guess that Mom's word will win out. Crown Prince or not, you're still her son and the Navy is a very acceptable profession for a prince. If you want to do something else, you should start by talking with her."

Michael didn't so much get up from his seat, as erupt, leaving the chair rocking on its heavy base. Fists clenched, eyes suddenly streaming tears, he faced an adversary neither of them could see.

"I . . . I don't *know* what I want!"

He bent his head, too proud in his young manhood to ask for the hug he so obviously wanted. Elizabeth embraced him.

"Oh, Mikey, Mikey. . . ."

This time the Prince didn't correct her, just gripped his arms around her waist and bawled into the shelter of her body.

"Beth . . . Beth . . . We . . ." He sniffed, brought the words out more clearly. "We fought before he went away. Dad wasn't happy with my quarter report—said that I wouldn't get into the Academy with those grades, Prince or not. I told him I didn't care. . . ."

Sobbing engulfed him. Elizabeth squeezed her little brother, wishing she could radiate comfort to him as Ariel did to her. The treecat caught her distress at the boy's unhappiness.

Elizabeth might be Ariel's human, but he was fond of her brother. Jumping from the table, the 'cat set his true-hands against Michael's leg and purred loudly.

Eventually, Michael's tears stopped. Releasing him, Elizabeth wiped away tears of her own.

"I . . . I'm going to miss Dad, Beth," the boy managed. "How can you be so brave? Aren't you scared about being Queen?"

"Yes," she admitted, "but I have you and Ariel and Justin and Mom and lots of other people to help me. I only wish I didn't need to be Queen quite yet. I wish Dad . . ."

A sob rose hot and thick in her throat. She felt Ariel's soothing mental caress, although the 'cat's true-hands still rested against Michael's leg. With the 'cat's support, she managed to choke back the sob.

"I wish things were different. I wish that we could follow the plan we designed—college first, then some on-the-job training. Now I don't have a choice."

"And I still do." Michael looked at her, the beginnings of a mature resolve forming beneath the tear streaks. "Thanks, Beth. You've been a lot of help."

"Good." She reached out and squeezed his shoulder. "There's still time before dinner. Let's go upstairs. The next week is going to be filled with the coronation, the viewing and the funeral, along with all sorts of public receptions. This may be our last chance for a bit of peace."

"After you, Your Majesty," Michael said, with a deep bow and a flourish of his hand.

The Queen giggled and, scooping up Ariel, preceded the Crown Prince from the room.

In the Crown Chancery of Mount Royal Palace a very exclusive council met. They numbered five: Queen Mother Angelique, the Duke of Cromarty, Duchess Caitrin Winton-Henke, Dame Eliska Paderweski, and Lord Jacob Wundt.

One was wife, another sister to the late King; the remaining three had been his close associates, both professionally and personally. Only one thing could have drawn them together at a time when each longed only for privacy to mourn, to compose thoughts and lives torn asunder by the King's sudden death: their loyalty to the King and his ideals . . . and to the abstraction that was the Star Kingdom of Manticore.

That did not mean their sorrow didn't show. It sat at the table with them like a sixth member of their party, one they did not mention but whose presence they all felt. And King Roger, though his body even now was being autopsied and prepared for public viewing, made an almost tangible seventh.

"Coffee, Allen?" Dame Eliska pushed the carafe across the table's polished wooden surface.

The Duke, slim and elegant, his hair showing silver that had not been there when he began his tenure as Prime Minister, shook his head. "I don't dare. My stomach is roiling."

"Tsk, tsk, Allen," the Queen Mother said, her teasing tone almost convincing. "Prime Ministers should never admit to possessing either upset stomachs or nerves."

"I'll remember that," Cromarty promised. "Still, I haven't been Prime Minister very long. Given current events and the inevitable challenges my majority is going to face, I almost wish another party would take over."

"Pshaw," was the Queen Mother's only response.

"You've been Prime Minister longer than poor Elizabeth has been Queen," reminded Lord Wundt. "Poor, poor child. What a terrible burden she must bear."

"My 'poor, poor child,'" Angelique said almost tartly, "is now your reigning Queen. Such comments forget the dignity of her office."

Jacob Wundt had been the Lord Chamberlain for the House of Winton since the middle of Samantha II's reign. Whip-thin, tall, and balding, he had seen Samantha succeeded by Roger and now would see Roger succeeded by Elizabeth. It was his quiet, sincere desire that he not see the throne change hands yet again.

His position, privy to the workings of the Royal Family yet not one of it, granted him patience with the Queen Mother.

"Of course, Your Majesty," he said softly. "I stand corrected."

It was Caitrin Winton-Henke who looked sharply at her sister-in-law.

"Angelique! Your grief is no excuse to forget yourself. Jacob said nothing more than what each of us is already thinking."

Angelique Winton would not have accepted a reprimand from anyone else, but Roger's beloved sister had always been friend and confidante to the impoverished commoner who had found herself elevated to Queen.

"Jacob," she said, turning to face the Lord Chamberlain, "I apologize."

Knowing the Queen's pride and temper (a temper Elizabeth had inherited in full) better than most, Wundt accepted her apology with a smile.

"We're all weary, Your Majesty, and likely to be more so before the next several days have passed."

"And Elizabeth will be the most weary of all," Winton-Henke added. "Thank goodness she has Ariel to support her."

Eliska Paderweski cleared her throat. "And if *we* are to support her to the best of our abilities we must get on to the business at hand."

Dame Eliska's first ambition had been to serve as a Manticoran Marine but, on medical leave following injuries received during an action against a Silesian pirate base, she had discovered a talent for handling people and paperwork. This, coupled with the ferocity of her Marine training, had made her an ideal member of the Palace administration. Over time, she had risen to serve Roger in the coveted role of Chief of Staff.

"I don't wish to sound callous," Paderweski continued, "but I've already received numerous requests for interviews with Queen Elizabeth. I refuse to push her, but an official statement from the Palace would be helpful. Until a formal Council of Regents is appointed, this group must make a few temporary policy decisions."

"And," Cromarty added, "when Parliament convenes its special session tomorrow morning before the formal Coronation, I should have some idea of what the royal pleasure will be."

Duchess Caitrin Winton-Henke lifted a hand for attention. "Why hasn't Elizabeth been asked to join us?"

"I wanted to give her some time to recover from viewing the holo of the accident." The Queen Mother's voice broke on the last word. "She watched it three times and, despite Ariel's support, she was very upset. I thought it would be easier for her if she had an opportunity to rest."

"Perhaps." Caitrin Winton-Henke tilted her head in a mannerism that recalled her brother. "I'm not certain I would care to have my fate discussed without my presence."

"Discussed only," Cromarty reminded her. "We can't decide anything for her. As difficult as it may be for us to accept, the college girl of yesterday is our Queen today. We can advise, but we cannot do a jot more."

Silence filled the small room, broken only by Queen Mother Angelique reaching to refill her coffee cup.

"Then shall we proceed?" Dame Eliska said briskly. "As I see it, we have three issues in front of us: the choice of a Regent, the selection of the Regency Council, and Elizabeth's marriage."

Cromarty nodded. "If we could begin with the Regent, that would be helpful. The Regency Council, most probably, will be formed from those candidates we select."

Dame Eliska activated a note pad. "An obvious candidate is Queen Angelique; another is Duchess Winton-Henke."

No one protested her nominations. Angelique had been married to King Roger for almost thirty years, for twenty-five of which he had been King. Her astute knowledge of politics was respected within the Palace. Although, in the interest of presenting Roger as a strong, decisive monarch, she usually refrained from public statements of policy, those times that she had chosen to speak had left no one in doubt about her understanding of the important issues.

Caitrin Winton-Henke had retired somewhat from palace life after her brother had provided first Elizabeth, then Michael to separate her from the likelihood of inheriting the throne, but Samantha II had not permitted her second child to grow up in blithe ignorance of political realities. Even though she had been Crown Princess comparatively briefly, Duchess Winton-Henke took seriously the responsibilities that went with being a member of the peerage, and her husband made most of his own decisions in consultation with her.

Her title of "Duchess" might be only a life title, a reminder (along with the Winton name that she added to her husband's when she married the Earl of Gold Peak) that she was sister to the King and one that she would not pass onto her children, but those who knew her considered her a perfect example of what a duchess could be.

"Earl Gold Peak's Centrist leanings—and thus those of Duchess Winton-Henke—are widely known," Cromarty noted. "Some may protest that a Centrist Prime Minister and a Centrist Regent would deprive the Opposition of a fair opportunity to influence policy. The Queen, of course, is above mere party lines."

"True," Dame Eliska agreed. "Do you have any other suggestions?"

Cromarty toyed with his empty coffee cup. "Perhaps a member of the Crown Loyalists would do. They regularly ally themselves with the Centrists, but they're not precisely of our ranks. Their respect for the Monarchy is absolute and should make Elizabeth's dealings with her Regent easier."

"Good point," Angelique said. "Any off-the-cuff suggestions?"

"Howell, Ayre, and Dugatkin all suggest themselves," Cromarty said promptly. "Even if one of them isn't selected as Regent, I think a place on the Regency council for at least one of them would be wise."

"Remember," Caitrin reminded them all, "Elizabeth is past sixteen. She must make the nomination. I suggest we present her with this slate and let her make the final decision."

"I second that motion," Jacob Wundt said. "Elizabeth is certain to have ideas of her own. We would be foolish to waste time refining our choices further."

Dame Eliska drew a line under her list and started a new page with the heading "Marriage."

"And the Queen's marriage?" she asked.

"I suggest," the Queen Mother said, "that I issue a personal statement reaffirming my support for Elizabeth's choice in her fiancé. I cannot believe that Elizabeth will *not* want to marry Justin."

"True," Wundt said. "He was with her at the holo viewing earlier today."

"Timing for the marriage could be an issue," Paderweski warned. "Too quickly and she may be seen as callous. Too slowly and concern about the succession will be inevitable."

"Elizabeth's coronation is tomorrow," Wundt said. "That and the King's funeral will feed the public desire for ceremony for a time. Perhaps asking her to delay her marriage until a politically sensitive moment would be wise."

"It very well might sway the Commons," Cromarty admitted. "After Elizabeth's engagement, support for a few of King Roger's less popular policies rose there. I'm not certain a wedding would help much in the Lords beyond the Crown Royalists."

Dame Eliska drummed against the table with her stylus. "It's hard to say. I can have my staff conduct some discreet opinion polls."

"Good idea," Caitrin said. "On such a personal issue, I would prefer to present Elizabeth with more than our own conjectures."

Nods rippled around the table.

Paderweski scribbled a note, then said, "If we could take a few minutes for a distasteful subject before we adjourn, I would like to discuss protocol and arrangements for the funeral. It's been almost twenty-six T-years since the Kingdom dealt with a monarch's funeral. We're going to need to politely brief many of those who will be attending."

"I," said Queen Angelique, "have attended at least one. If I might beg to be excused?"

She pushed her chair back from the table and unshed tears glittered in her dark eyes.

"Your Majesty," Wundt said promptly, rising as well.

As one, the group rose, and Caitrin Winton-Henke looked after the retreating widow, remembering the society gossip nickname from many years before.

"Poor little beggar maid," she whispered.

In another conference room, in another part of the same city, another very exclusive council was meeting. As with the council in Mount Royal Palace, several of the members would be recognized as public figures; unlike the royal council, it was the most heartfelt wish of these councilors that their meeting never become a matter of record.

Willis Kemeny, Ninth Earl of Howell, was perhaps the most nervous of the lot. A husky man whose chocolate brown skin suggested a crossover with the House of Winton some time in the past, he was a highly placed member of the Crown

Loyalist party. His name was one of those bruited about as a possible successor when old LeBrun retired as Party head.

If pushed, trim, fashionable Lady Paula Gwinner, Baroness Gwinner of Stallman, would call herself a Liberal, yet a perusal of her voting record would reveal expedience rather than allegiance to a particular political philosophy. The youngest person present—a mere twenty-eight T-years—she defended her erratic votes as a reflection of her zeal in studying each issue. Most critics when caught beneath the glare of her golden-brown eyes chose to agree rather than argue.

Neither Marvin Seltman nor Jean Marrou were members of the House of Lords, but they each had held seats in the Commons for many terms. Their attention to the issues that would influence their constituents had made them popular and fairly secure. Marrou was even developing a following outside of her own district.

The last member of the group, Major Padraic Dover, was the only one who did not hold a seat in Parliament, yet in many ways he was the one most privy to the inner workings of the Palace. A native of Gryphon, he served in the Bordeaux Battalion of the King's Own Regiment. For the last eight years, he'd served as a liasion between the regiment and the PGS.

It was Dover who raised his wine glass in an ironic toast.

"The King is dead! Long live the Queen." His voice dropped in tones equal parts menace and triumph. "*Our* Queen."

The fierce emotion in his voice could not escape his allies. Earl Howell frowned slightly.

"Elizabeth is not yet 'ours,'" he reprimanded primly. "True, King Roger has been dispensed with, but we have yet to complete the maneuvers that will enable us to adequately influence the young Queen."

Marvin Seltman, short, dour, ambitious, and embittered by the status quo, nodded agreement.

"But with the King dead," he said, "the field is much more open. Are those of you in the Lords ready to deal with the issue of the Regency?"

Howell and Gwinner nodded.

"We've instigated a whispering campaign in the Commons," Seltman continued. "It's difficult. Our house has always supported the monarchy strongly, but we're not really looking to undermine the monarchy—simply to suggest that a Regent who is too close kin to Queen Elizabeth won't be in a position to objectively direct her actions."

"Good," Howell said. "I've been doing the same in the Lords. The Crown Loyalist's unstinting support of the monarchy stands me in good stead there. After the special session tomorrow, I'll have a better idea of what's being planned."

"Cromarty," Padraic Dover added, "is at Mount Royal today. I doubt that the visit is purely social."

"Certainly not," Howell sniffed. "Cromarty's Centrists may have been effective toadies to his Late Majesty, but he wasn't of their social circle."

"Duchess Winton-Henke is also at Mount Royal," Dover said. "Her husband and children are due this evening."

"Winton-Henke is a likely candidate for Regent," Howell said. "If you should hear anything that can be used to undermine her . . ."

"Of course I'll pass it on," Dover said. "However, I'm more interested in learning what you're doing regarding Justin Zyrr."

"We're doing everything in our power to delay the wedding," Jean Marrou spoke for the first time.

She was a naturally quiet woman, blind from birth. Her optical nerves would not respond to regeneration therapy simply because there had never been anything to regenerate. The reason for her blindness was uncertain, but she believed, as her parents had, that her mother's exposure to a strain of Artemesian measles brought in by a Solarian League trading ship had caused the damage.

Although the Star Kingdom had long traded actively with other systems, Jean Marrou's upbringing had made her fiercely isolationist. King Roger's policies of trade and expansion made certain—as far as she could tell—that quarantine procedures would be inadequate and that other innocents would be exposed to diseases like that which had ruined her eyes.

Lovely, fair, and terrifyingly intelligent, she had responded to Marvin Seltman's gentle probes with a ferocity that had surprised him. Only her iron self-control made certain that she would not expose the plot in one of the rare evangelical fits that broke her normal composure.

What Seltman did not know, what would have terrified him if he had, was that among the equipment she habitually carried was a small computer with a visual scanner. This fed her a steady stream of information on who was present at a given gathering. It also indicated small details like who was in converse with whom. Unknowns were flagged and filed as such. Routinely, she analyzed this data and drew the conclusions that had made her a brilliant political strategist.

Marrou continued, "However, whether we delay the wedding or not will have no effect on Zyrr's position unless you can follow through with your promise to discredit him in

Elizabeth's judgement. You'll also need to bring yourself to her attention in a positive fashion."

Dover nodded sharply. "I know all that. I've also known Beth since she was a girl. I'm certain I can win her over. It's just a matter of getting that interloper Zyrr out of the way."

"And then," Seltman said, spinning his wineglass between his fingers, "with one of us as Regent and another as the Queen's spouse, we'll be in the perfect position to steer the monarchy to our own ends!"

After the meeting adjourned, Marvin Seltman and Paula Gwinner departed in the same vehicle. The other members of the cabal had assumed they were having an affair—a belief they encouraged through small gestures and occasional indiscreet comments. The real reason for their closeness was coolly political.

"Your stocks have just paid a dividend," Seltman said, passing Gwinner a small portfolio.

She opened it and smiled at what it contained. Paula Gwinner had been born to a title, but the title had not come with much in the way of property. That hadn't mattered to her when she was small, but she still recalled the smarting shame she'd felt as an adolescent when she first realized that some of their social peers sniggered at her father's shabby evening clothes or her mother's increasingly out-of-fashion formal wear.

After her own disastrous debut, she had resolved that when she inherited the title, she would somehow acquire wealth as well. Careful investment of her small inheritance had been a beginning. Gradually, she had learned to hear the note in a person's voice that meant a bribe was being offered. After some study, she learned what to accept and what not to accept. Her fortune grew and, when immediate need was satisfied, she learned to crave power as well.

Marvin Seltman had first approached her in the guise of a member of the Commons courting a member of the Lords. Only after he was certain of her ambition did he take her into his confidence. Now they both served a power other than the Star Kingdom of Manticore.

"Then the news of King Roger's death has arrived in the People's Republic," she said, tucking the portfolio away.

"It has reached my contact," Seltman said, "and our next payment will come when an acceptable Regent has been announced."

"It's so nice to know Haven is as ambitious as Roger feared."

Gwinner smiled as she spoke. "I only wish I were as certain of our Manticoran allies. Howell may dislike Roger's expansionism, but his Crown Loyalist training will be clamoring to the forefront in the next several days."

Seltman shrugged. "They were the best I could find. Howell's loyalty to Manticore is unquestioned and unquestionable—his prominence in the Crown Loyalists makes it so. Happily for us, he can stretch his definition of the Crown to exclude a monarch whose extra-System politics seem to threaten the status quo in Manticore."

"I wonder," Gwinner said, "if Roger ever realized how unpopular his decision to annex Basilisk would be?"

"I'm certain he realized it would have its opponents," Seltman said, "but he trusted that the aura of royal authority would help him to make his decision work—and so it has for twenty years."

"Eighteen," Gwinner corrected, "and a good thing, too. The Crown Princess was born the same year Basilisk was annexed."

"Ah, yes, the 'Duchess of Basilisk,'" Seltman sneered. "Good King Roger's way of making certain everyone knew he planned to stick to his guns."

"If Elizabeth were much older," Gwinner reminded him, "we wouldn't have the same opportunity to influence her. I only hope we haven't waited too long as it is."

"She's a college freshman," Seltman waved a dismissive hand. "Right now she's casting about for an anchor. We will provide her with one—two if we're lucky."

"Do you really think Dover will be able to discredit her fiancé and win her hand?"

Seltman shrugged. "I hope so, but it hardly matters. We needed an ally within the Palace Guard. I had despaired of finding anyone corruptible until my spies brought me word of Dover's words on the announcement of Elizabeth's engagement."

"He really had fancied her for himself?" Gwinner asked, shaking her head.

"Why shouldn't he?" Seltman replied. "The Constitution's requirement that the monarch must marry a commoner raises fantasies with every new heir. Dover's ambitions weren't totally unreasonable, and he'd plotted a career path that would take him into Elizabeth's orbit. From what he says, she even took a liking to him when she was younger."

"Apparently she outgrew those fancies," Gwinner said. "It must have infuriated Dover when she accepted a man who, superficially, isn't all that different from our Padraic."

"I agree," Seltman nodded. "Like Dover, Justin Zyrr is from Gryphon and has a military background, but unlike our good Dover, he left the Army and went into research and development."

"And met the Princess when she was on a school trip," Gwinner laughed. "Love among the test-tubes."

"Pedestrian, perhaps," Seltman said, "but her relationship with Zyrr is a fact of her life and therefore must be an element in our planning. If Dover succeeds even partially, Elizabeth loses another reliable support of her young life."

"Tell me," Gwinner said, "for all the talk in today's meeting about the need to 'discredit' Justin Zyrr, you don't expect Dover to do any such thing, do you?"

"No," said Marvin Seltman. "What I expect is that Dover will kill him."

The day after Roger III's death began with the formal coronation of Queen Elizabeth III. Following the ceremony, Justin Zyrr departed Mount Royal Palace for the Indigo Salt Flats where the King had met his death. He left openly, taking his own private air car, nor did he have a bodyguard. Only after he and Elizabeth were wed would he be followed everywhere he went.

When he arrived at his destination, he was startled to see his radar display becoming crowded with large quantities of private vehicle traffic. The PGS had never been happy that King Roger chose to practice a sport that so exposed him to danger, but at least the Indigo Salt Flats were isolated, many kilometers from any dwelling, a quality which had provided a readily sealed security perimeter. Moreover, Roger had purchased the lands with funds from his privy purse, assuring that the Flats would remain private and undeveloped.

Justin had visited the Flats a few times to ski with the King. During those visits, he had been captivated by the deep violet-blue sands rising and falling in glittering dunes. Walking on them with the King, Justin had made believe that they strolled on the surface of a deep, mysterious ocean.

He felt tears welling and dashed a single burning trace away with the back of his hand, angry at his lack of composure. If Elizabeth could be brave . . .

The beeping of the air car's com unit came as a relief. A dry, almost mechanical, voice stated:

"Vehicle, please be notified that you are approaching private lands."

"Acknowledged. Is this a private channel?"

"It is."

"I'm Justin Zyrr, Queen Elizabeth's fiancé. She asked me to come here."

There was no change of inflection in the official voice: "Climb into a holding pattern while we confirm your identity."

A stream of coordinates followed and Justin obeyed. Several minutes later, the com unit came alive again.

"You are cleared to proceed. Stop at the check station for further confirmation."

"Acknowledged."

Justin homed his vehicle in on the beacon that now signaled him from deeper within the Flats. He noted the line of grav tanks marking a perimeter. Most of those trying to cross that armed line were newsies. The rest of the visitors seemed content to stop to one side of the line. A regular stream of people were going back and forth between . . .

He amplified the range on his air car's cameras.

People, young and old, men, women, and children, were filing between their parked vehicles and a makeshift shrine at the edge of the Indigo Salt Flats. The shrine itself was nothing more than a flat outcropping of rock, but it was heaped with small offerings: flowers, pictures, folded notes, personal mementos. He recognized a reproduction of the group portrait taken on his and Elizabeth's engagement, a withered tenth anniversary coronation wreath, a ceramic replica of King Roger's treecat, Monroe.

Respecting the Royal Family's grief, the people of Manticore were making an impromptu pilgrimage to the last place on the planet where their king had walked alive. No doubt when Roger was buried his tomb would become the focus for the outpouring of their sorrow, but for now his subjects journeyed to the place of his death.

Tears flooded back, hot and unrelenting, and this time, Justin let them fall, trusting the autopilot to bring him in. He wished Elizabeth were there—and even more that Roger were. Somehow, it seemed too much that the King would miss this last spontaneous tribute to his twenty-five years of rulership, to his life of service.

Justin banished his tears when his air car came in on the tidy landing strip that had been constructed for King Roger's convenience. A small cluster of buildings sprouted off to one side: guard house, private chalet, hangars. Each was built to withstand an attack on the sovereign or his guests; each, in the end had been helpless to prevent the death that had come to the King in their shadow.

As Justin stepped down from his air car, the door to the guard house opened and a man walked out to meet him. Like all members of the Royal Family's regular security detachment, he was an Army officer in the scarlet facings of the King's— no, the *Queen's*—Own Regiment. A tall man, with the well-muscled look of a heavy-worlder and the shoulder flash of the Copperwalls Battalion, he walked with a slight limp.

"Justin Zyrr?"

"Yes."

"I'm Captain Adderson." The captain spoke with the clipped accent of the Ice Gia Settlement on Sphinx. "If you'll come inside, I'll complete your ID check."

"Of course."

Justin hastened to follow Adderson into the cool shadows of the guardhouse. The captain smiled and indicated a seat near his desk.. Glancing around, Justin noted that scanners that would have done a battleship proud were activated, their data translated into a holotank that, even as Adderson turned to his new task, he monitored with part of his attention.

"I saw you this morning at the coronation, Mr. Zyrr."

"Were you there?"

"No, I've been assigned to the Salt Flats Detail since my leg was broken—I don't regenerate, and the docs couldn't fix it perfectly. Most of the time the post is little more than an honorable semi-retirement, but I've been needed here today. The pilgrims have been showing up since an hour after the King's death was made public."

Adderson pressed Justin's hand to a print scanner, pricked a blood sample, and then directed him to look into a optical scanner. His tone as he continued was a trace defensive.

"Some of the Detail thought of the visitors as ghouls and I suppose some were just that—especially the newsies. Most respect the perimeter, though. They just come to weep and pray. That's why I think of them as pilgrims."

Justin nodded. "That was exactly my thought when I saw them. What did the newsies think they'd find here?"

Adderson shrugged. "I don't rightly know. The King's body has been taken away, the wreckage cleared. All that was completed within an hour of his death."

His voice softened as he spoke, so that the last words were all but inaudible.

"Were you on duty yesterday?" Justin asked.

Pretending to be busy transferring the scanner results to the personnel files gave Adderson a moment to collect himself. When he spoke again, his tones were almost normal.

"I was," he said. "And I saw what happened right in there."

Adderson gestured toward the holotank with his head. Behind him the computer pinged its acknowledgment that Justin's record agreed with the data he had just supplied.

Justin took a deep breath. He could move on now, but if Elizabeth's guess was correct and not simply the out-welling of grief, Adderson could be a valuable resource—or a potential enemy.

"Could you tell me what you recall of the King's last day— the little, personal details?"

Adderson looked suspicious. "You're not looking to sell this to the newsies, are you?"

"No, I'm not." Justin kept his instinctive resentment from his voice. "I'm asking so that I can tell Queen Elizabeth. She's just lost her father, her mother is brokenhearted, and her little brother . . ."

"Poor Prince Michael," Adderson said. "So young to have so much sorrow."

"Exactly," Justin said. "I wanted to be able to give Beth a verbal portrait of her father's last day. Something for her to hold onto during these next few days when it will be too easy to only remember him laid out for his funeral. Was he cheerful?"

Adderson nodded. "Laughing and teasing the Queen, making plans for their competition. They'd been practicing fancy maneuvers. She was nearly as good as him—better at some things."

Justin nodded, remembering the holo of the King and Queen gracefully gliding, looping through the air side by side. For a moment he entertained the terrible suspicion that Queen Angelique might have plotted to kill her husband, but he dismissed it as soon as it had formed.

"So they agreed to ski separately," Justin prompted.

"That's right," Adderson continued. "The Detail techs checked their equipment, and the King had a bit of a row with them when they refused to pass the ski he'd brought with him."

"Oh?" Justin felt his pulse quicken.

"Yes, it was a new model," Adderson said, "and they didn't like the power reading on the molycirc connecting the ski and the belt unit. The King didn't want to hear what they told him, said he couldn't believe it was malfunctioning. I think it was a new set."

Justin refrained from mentioning that the grav ski had been a gift from the new Queen. If that ever became common knowledge, Elizabeth's own honor might be in question.

"But he listened to the techs' advice?" Justin asked.

"That's right, in the end he did. He had other equipment stored here, from other jaunts, and he ended up using an older set." Adderson frowned. "For all the good it did him."

Determined to distract the captain before he could think too far into the implications of the King's accident, Justin rose.

"Has the computer cleared my identity?"

"It has indeed," Adderson said. "Unless you've altered your hand prints, eye prints, blood, and genotype, you are indeed Justin Zyrr. Do you want to tour the grounds?"

"If I might," Justin said.

"Of course you might," Adderson said. "You're as close to the Queen's husband as you might be, and this is her family's land. The records show that you've been here before."

"Yes."

"Then you know the basic rules." Adderson chuckled and quoted: "'Wear a hat and dark glasses to protect you from the sun's glare, don't eat the salt, and carry water along if you expect to be out more than a short time.'"

"I have everything I need in my air car."

"Then take your walk. I'll keep a weather eye on you from here." Adderson paused as if considering, then he continued, "And you may meet another man walking about out there. He's a scrawny fellow with a fringe of white hair—pre-prolong. I didn't ask and he didn't say, but I believe he may be with the Security Ministry. The computer accepted his clearance faster even than it did your own."

"Thank you for warning me," Justin said. "I'd have been startled to meet someone out there unaware. I'll check in with you before I leave."

"Thank you, Mr. Zyrr."

Justin gathered hat, glasses, and a belt flask of water. Then he crunched down the sandy blue slope to the flats over which the King and Queen had skied just the day before.

He didn't really have much idea what Beth expected him to find. Popular wisdom still held that a criminal would be drawn to the scene of the crime, but, even if that were true, the assassin would be mingling now with the throng of pilgrims, perhaps gloating, feeding on their grief, or perhaps feeling remorse, an urge to confess . . .

No, that would be too easy. Adderson's recollection that the King's ski had indeed been changed for another set—a set that could have been sabotaged in advance—did lend some credence to Beth's theories, but then it had been the difference between the skis that had led her to become suspicious in the first place.

To pursue that too closely would be merely to confirm circular logic. He needed something more.

Trudging across the blue salt sand, he wasn't at all certain he would find anything, but for Beth he would continue to look.

Using what landmarks he remembered from the holo, Justin located the general area where King Roger must have crashed. Here the glittering blue crystal sand was gouged and torn, not only from the King's fall, but from the emergency vehicles and personnel who had rushed out to him.

Hunkering down, Justin shifted some of the salt through his gloved fingers, knowing even as he did so that the effort was futile. Perhaps he should go to the morgue where the King's body was being prepared for the viewing, but what could he learn there? He was no pathologist, no forensics specialist. He was just a research engineer!

Footsteps crunching across the sand brought him from his revery. Rising and turning in one graceful motion, he faced the newcomer.

"Justin Zyrr?"

The man who extended his hand in a friendly manner was small and wiry, his features shadowed beneath the brim of a wide straw hat. Justin's general impression was of twinkling grey eyes set amid deep lines and a great floppy mustache. He took the proffered hand and shook it firmly.

"I am Justin Zyrr."

"Captain Adderson told me I might find you out here." The man's voice seemed too deep to come from such a slim chest. "I decided to make 'might' a certainty."

He paused to wipe sweat off his forehead with the back of his hand.

"I'm Daniel Chou."

"With the Security Ministry, Captain Adderson implied."

Chou grinned. "Captain Adderson must have liked you. I don't suppose I'm violating any rules by confirming your guess. After all, you will be the Prince Consort—and, more importantly, Queen Elizabeth trusts you."

Oddly, Justin felt himself coloring. There was something about the little man's brash manner that made him feel like a boy at his grandfather's knee. Given the changes of the last twenty-four hours, the feeling was not at all unpleasant.

"Shall we hoof it back to the landing strip?" Chou said. "Or do you need to do more looking about?"

Justin glared at the blue salt as if it was deliberately trying to hide the truth from him.

"I'm not certain there's anything to look for," he said.

Chou nodded. "Not here, although we had to look. We may have more luck inspecting the remains of the grav ski."

"Why should we do that?" Justin asked, reluctant to take anyone into his confidence without Elizabeth's express permission.

"For evidence," Chou answered. His grey eyes had stopped twinkling. "Evidence to prove King Roger was murdered. Certainly you don't believe his death was an accident, do you?"

Everyone rose and bowed as Queen Elizabeth III entered the council chamber. Tellingly, to a long-time political observer like Duke Cromarty, she accepted the monarch's homage as her due. The fact that she'd been Crown Princess all of her life might explain part of that calm demeanor, but the Prime Minister thought there was something more here.

She might be a girl of eighteen, but she was savvy enough to know that those who had raised her might find it difficult to recall that she was their ruler now. By accepting the homage as offered, she was reminding them all who made the final decisions.

After the Queen had greeted them, Dame Eliska brought the informal regent's council around to business.

"This morning's coronation went well. My polls, formal and informal, show that support for the Queen is high in both houses of Parliament. The sooner the matters of Regent and Regency Council are resolved, the more likely they are to be resolved easily and in the Queen's best interest."

Elizabeth nodded. "I have reviewed your recommendations for Regent and I think they are all sound." Even her voice was different, Cromarty thought. She spoke with a deliberate precision, an air of maturity which was new to her yet far too natural, too . . . inevitable, to be feigned. "Duke Cromarty, do you have anything to add?" she asked, and he cleared his throat.

"Yes, actually, I do. Apparently, there's some resistance to the idea of having either your mother or your aunt serve as Regent."

The Queen Mother started. "I protest! There is a long tradition of—"

Elizabeth interrupted her mother with a gentle hand to her arm.

"I need to hear what the Prime Minister has to say," she said in that same, new voice. "Allen, I am intrigued by your use of the words 'mother' and 'aunt' to describe two of the candidates for Regent. Normally, you observe protocol to a fault. Is there a reason?"

The Prime Minister nodded. "Yes, I chose those words because they reflect precisely the scuttlebutt I've heard. The concern being expressed is that someone as close kin to the Queen as the Queen Mother or Duchess Winton-Henke might not be in a position to advise but might try to rule in your stead."

"Bluntly put," Elizabeth said, "the concern is that I will be dominated by my mother or my aunt."

"Yes, Your Majesty."

"A pity," Elizabeth mused. "I had just about made up my mind that Aunt Caitrin would be an ideal Regent. No offense, Mother, but I *do* think it would be difficult for us to distance ourselves from our established roles."

The Queen Mother looked hurt for a moment, but then she smiled.

"I agree. It might indeed be hard for me to stop thinking as your mother—and as Roger's wife. You don't need a Regent who might be inclined to say 'But your father would have done it this way.'"

Elizabeth squeezed her mother's hand. "Thank you for understanding. I have reviewed this council's other suggestions and, while I have nothing personal against any of the Crown Loyalist candidates you indicated, I would prefer to have Aunt Caitrin. Your Grace, do you think the Henke holdings can spare you?"

Caitrin Winton-Henke nodded. "They can. The Earl of Gold Peak is quite able to discharge his responsibilities without me."

"Very good."

Elizabeth thoughtfully stroked Ariel for a moment before continuing.

"I haven't forgotten the concern Duke Cromarty reported." Her smile became impish. "I believe the only way to defuse it is to nominate a candidate who would be unacceptable to Parliament for some reason. When the fuss over the first candidate has died down and Parliament has been reluctantly forced to reject my suggestion, then I can nominate Aunt Caitrin. If Dame Eliska is correct, the general desire of Parliament is to support me. Rejecting a second Regent—especially one so well-trained for the job—would go against that general impulse."

A moment of silence fell while the council digested both the plan and the new Queen's willingness to indulge in political manipulation. Duke Cromarty raised a hand.

"Yes, Your Grace?"

"That is very clever, Your Majesty, but what if Parliament confirms your first candidate?"

"There's a simple way to handle that possibility," Elizabeth answered. "I make certain that whomever I nominate is someone who can function in the role—and someone who will be willing to step down for Aunt Caitrin after a bit of time has passed."

"You would need to trust that person a great deal," Duke Cromarty warned. "I expect you have someone in mind."

The Queen nodded, a hint of a grin twitching the corners of her mouth.

"I do indeed." She gestured across the table. "My Lord Chamberlain, Lord Wundt."

"Your Majesty!" Jacob Wundt exclaimed. "I am not fit for the role of Regent!"

Elizabeth smiled at the thin old man.

"You are more fit than many," she said. "As Lord Chamberlain you served and advised both my father and my grandmother. You are a valued asset to the House of Winton. Moreover, I can convincingly speak both of my trust in you and in your irreproachable loyalty to the Kingdom."

"But—!"

The Lord Chamberlain's new protest was cut short by Dame Eliska. She looked up from the figures she had been entering into her computer pad and her smile was broad.

"I believe that Queen Elizabeth's choice will function just as she hopes. I've done some preliminary demographic analysis and the Lord Chamberlain should be rejected, but only after sufficient debate that Duchess Winton-Henke would be confirmed easily."

"And," Duke Cromarty said, "if Lord Wundt is confirmed, he would be a sound Regent. After some months of service, he could claim that his advanced years make him unable to continue. If we wait to make that announcement until some minor crisis requires that the Queen have a Regent in place quickly, then Duchess Winton-Henke should be confirmed without protest."

The Lord Chamberlain's mouth was opening and shutting, but no noise was coming forth.

"Without some gambit like this," Duke Cromarty continued, "I'm uncertain that either the Queen Mother or the Duchess would be confirmed as Regent. I'm at a loss to explain this sudden surge of anti-nepotism—anyone who knows the Lords knows that nepotism is the way of the aristocracy—but it is present."

Elizabeth stroked Ariel, her own features schooled to polite neutrality, but the 'cat's loud purr gave away his own satisfaction.

"Then this is how we will proceed," she said. "As for the Regent's Council, I would like to nominate those here present, the Prime Minister, the Majority Leader for the Commons, and at least one of the Crown Loyalists you suggested earlier."

Paderweski made a note. "When you say the Majority Leader for the Commons, you mean whoever holds that position rather than Rosanna Wilson?"

"Yes. I don't plan for the Regent's Council to meet over-frequently," the Queen replied. "Therefore, the added duties should not be onerous."

"And," Caitrin Winton-Henke said, "since the Regency Council will already have the Prime Minister, we don't need another noble to balance the representative from the Commons, yet we can keep the suggestion that this is a private cabal to a minimum."

Queen Elizabeth arched her eyebrows. "And why shouldn't it be a cabal? This is a monarchy, after all. My father was no figurehead, and I certainly don't intend to be one."

A soft chuckle fluttered around the council table. Elizabeth joined in, then continued.

"I realize that I may not have made myself clear," she said. "I would like Duke Cromarty to serve on the Regent's Council whether or not he is serving as Prime Minister."

Allen Summervale came from an ancient line of Manticoran aristocracy, otherwise he might very well have given some indication of how very pleased he was by this sign of the Queen's favor.

"Thank you, Your Majesty," he said, bowing slightly. "I will endeavor to serve you well."

Dame Eliska changed something on her note pad. "So I should indicate that the Prime Minister will be expected to serve on the Regent's Council."

"Yes."

"Very good," Paderweski smiled. "Perhaps their Graces could make some discrete inquiries—check with LeBrun—to see which of the Crown Loyalists would be best for the post."

Cromarty and Winton-Henke both nodded.

"I'm willing to bet that Howell will be their choice," the duchess said. "He's been rising steadily within the party."

"We shall see," Elizabeth said. "Now, are we ready to adjourn? Any more business for now?"

Heads shook around the table.

"Very well. We all have far too much to do. I'm certain that I'll see some of you at the viewing this evening." She gestured for them all to remain seated when she rose. "Until then."

Ariel in her arms, the Queen departed the council chamber. When the door slid closed behind her, Jacob Wundt spoke softly, reverently:

"Long live the Queen!"

"Amen to that," Cromarty affirmed. "Amen to that."

Once Justin's air car was aloft, Chou chose to elaborate on his earlier comment.

"We always investigate the death of a monarch, even when, as with Queen Samantha, the cause of death is apparent and easy to confirm."

"She died from heart failure, didn't she?" Justin asked.

"Everyone dies from heart failure," Chou said with an odd, wry grin. "In Queen Samantha's case, the immediate cause of her heart's failure was deterioration of her circulatory system beyond the point that regeneration therapy could effectively repair the damage. However, even that is too specific. She died of old age, which is not a bad way to go."

Justin nodded, thinking how the concept of old age was changing with the advent of the prolong therapies. The man seated in the passenger seat would probably die of old age some time early into his first century. If Justin died from the same cause, he would be closer to three hundred years old.

Did those born just the wrong side of the prolong acceptance barrier resent those who were young enough to accept the treatment or did they rejoice that their children's lives would be extended?

Certainly the dangers of prolong went far beyond the overpopulation that was often cited as the greatest implication of the extended life span. Commoner born, Justin tended to look at the aristocracy from the outside. The idea of some of the more hidebound members of this most-privileged class being able to extend their influence for centuries made him shudder. And what would their children do while they waited to assume their inheritance?

King Roger had seen that Manticoran society faced death by stagnation, which was one he had pushed for Prince Michael to enter the Navy despite the boy's hesitancy. Would other aristocratic parents be so farsighted? Silently, Justin resolved that his and Elizabeth's children would not be trapped by their parents' longevity.

Daniel Chou interrupted his revery.

"What are you thinking about?"

"Change," Justin said honestly, "and how with King Roger's death Beth could very well be Queen for centuries to come. It's strange to realize that between her youth and prolong she could reign for nearly as long as the entire Star Kingdom has been in existence."

"A slight exaggeration," Chou said, "but not by much. That's one of the reasons she would make such a valuable pawn."

"Pawn?" Thinking of his strong-willed, assertive fiancée, Justin chuckled. "Not Beth!"

"Perhaps not," Chou agreed, "but you forget that most of the Kingdom doesn't know our new Queen as well as you do. The news media's polite forbearance regarding the monarch's private life has meant that although the Heir was often in the public eye, those occasions were official, not private."

"I see what you mean," Justin said, "and I begin to understand what you're leading up to."

"If we are to assume murder," Chou said, "then we must look for motive. True, the King had made enemies, but his death does not strike me as a crime of passion."

"If it was murder," Justin cautioned.

"For the sake of discussion, let us assume it was." The impish grin on Chou's weathered features made it seem as if he was suggesting a party game.

"Very well," Justin said, less comfortable with the idea.

"King Roger III was well-loved, but his decisions were not always popular. Correct?"

"Correct—especially in the area of foreign policy."

"Now, what if you didn't approve of King Roger's policies? How would you feel about his continued reign? Remember, he was our first monarch to receive prolong."

"I would be terrified," Justin admitted, getting into the spirit of the game. "With prolong, King Roger would be in a position to continue those policies for at least another two hundred years."

"And he would most certainly strongly influence his heir," Chou said. "Therefore, King Roger must be eliminated."

"You're so cold!" Justin protested.

"Only practical and paranoid. They're required traits for my job."

"Go on, then."

"Obviously, if eliminating the King is to do any good, it must be done within a narrow window of time."

Chou paused, inviting Justin to pick up the thread.

"Elizabeth," Justin spoke slowly, "must be young enough to

need a Regent, but not so young that the Regent would effectively rule in her stead."

"Precisely!" Chou applauded. "And she must need that Regent for some years, enough years that her views on policy could be influenced and that influence expected to last."

"When you look at the situation that way," Justin said, appalled yet excited, "King Roger's death becomes not a random accident or a spur of the moment assassination, but the result of a carefully developed course of action. Still, I'm not certain we aren't being too paranoid."

"Very well," Chou said. "Let us look at this from a slightly different angle. When would you say would be the earliest time that conditions would have gained our hypothetical conspirators what they wanted?"

Justin thought for a moment, weighing the various elements.

"Perhaps when Elizabeth was sixteen. Before that she would have been too easily dismissed as a child."

"Did anything happen to the royal family when Elizabeth was around sixteen?"

"I'm not sure," Justin mused. "I didn't meet her until that very year. I'd never been much interested in the royal family, to be honest. That's why we hit it off so well. Beth was on a tour of the research lab where I work and wandered into a restricted area. I was giving her hell when her bodyguard hurried in. When he addressed her as 'Your Highness' I suddenly realized why this pretty girl seemed so familiar."

Justin felt his face grow hot at the memory and he chuckled.

"She wrote me the prettiest apology letter. It crossed in the mails with *my* apology. Beth thought that the coincidence was so funny that she screened me."

"I imagine you were surprised." Chou laughed.

"Was I ever!" Justin agreed. "We talked for over an hour, just like old friends. Her father was ill and she really needed a friend."

"Think about what you just said," Chou prompted.

"She needed a friend?" Justin answered, puzzled.

"Right before that."

"Her father was ill." The implications hit Justin all at once. "King Roger was ill—very ill! Not many people knew that, but Beth told me. I guess she knew I wouldn't let the news out to the media."

"And you didn't."

"But the King recovered!"

"From a viral infection." Chou was no longer laughing. "The Star Kingdom of Manticore takes its good health for granted.

Most infectious diseases were conquered centuries ago. We were never as isolated as many colonies. Mutated diseases like those that ravaged Artemis and Raiden never were a problem for us—especially since we did not let up on the strict quarantine and decontamination procedures from our expedition days."

"We had our own Plague," Justin reminded him, fearing that the old man had made such an art of paranoia that he saw conspiracy where there was none.

"Check your history books," Chou said. "The Manticoran Plague most likely evolved from a small family of viruses the original survey team missed—or that evolved during the six centuries between the initial survey and the arrival of the colonists. Whatever the case, Manticore is not prone to sudden, unexplained viral infections—and I find one that strikes the King alone particularly suspect."

"Maybe so," Justin said. "I suppose you have copies of the medical records on his illness."

"I do, and you're welcome to review them."

"I will, but before I trouble Elizabeth with these theories of murder and conspiracy, I want to take a look at that grav ski."

"Are you saying that the Queen does not share the suspicions that brought you to the Indigo Salt Flats?"

Justin hesitated. "She suspects her father was killed. I don't know what else she suspects. Beth . . . has a temper. I don't want to tell her something that might affect her judgement."

"Yet, if we do find proof of murder, she will need to be told."

"I know. Let's just wait until then. Tonight the wake begins. In two days she must officiate at her father's funeral. That's enough."

"As long as I know that you won't try to keep me from doing my job, I'm willing to wait." Chou grinned, impish once more. "I would have anyhow."

Justin shook his head in disbelief. One moment coolly paranoid, spinning theories that encompassed not only murder but grand treason, the next like a creature from a child's pretend, Daniel Chou was not an easy man to understand. Fortunately, he was an easy man to trust.

After departing the council, Elizabeth made her way through the convolutions of Mount Royal Palace until she came to her father's private office. Motioning to her guard to remain outside, she pressed the call button, thereby warning the occupant that she was there.

If one member of the family had been more deeply hurt by her father's death than even the Queen, it was her father's treecat, Monroe. The 'cat had been in the chalet at the moment of Roger's death and his eerie keening had forewarned the security staff that the accident had been fatal.

Monroe had returned to Mount Royal with King Roger's body, but, unlike a human in a similar circumstance, he had shown no desire to sit with the body. Perhaps his carnivore's direct view of the universe accepted more immediately that a body without a spirit was just so much dead meat. Perhaps he could not bear to see his best friend's form still, cold, and bereft of his animating spirit.

Since his return to Mount Royal, Monroe had hunched, keening and ragged, on his perch in the King's office. Not even Ariel had been able to coax him to eat, but Elizabeth visited whenever she could. Treecat experts, mostly members of the Sphinx Forestry Service, had warned her that Monroe could do any number of things at this point.

Most 'cats who lost their humans (a frequent occurrence pre-prolong, as a 'cat's natural life-span was around two hundred years) suicided. That had always been the great tragedy of the human-treecat bond, yet the 'cats had always made it clear that they accepted the price they paid to adopt their human companions. Now, of course, prolong promised to reverse the age differential, and no one was certain how that would affect relations between the two species.

Normally, in a case where the 'cat did not suicide, it simply returned to Sphinx and rejoined its clan, although in very rare cases, a "widowed" 'cat would adopt another human. So far, Monroe had not indicated any desire to return to Sphinx, and his palpable grief made Elizabeth fear that she would return to her father's office to find the 'cat dead.

She slid open the office door to find Monroe sitting alone. Several members of her father's staff had offered to keep watch with Monroe, but the 'cat had become agitated, as if proximity to another's grief heightened his own.

Ariel bleeked a welcome and leapt from Elizabeth's arms to sit by Monroe. Sitting back on his true-feet, Ariel used his true-hands to groom the other 'cat. Monroe didn't move, but Elizabeth imagined hopefully that his green-gold eyes brightened in response.

"Want something to eat, Monroe?" she asked, extending a piece of celery, fresh from the crisper.

Monroe didn't even as much as curl his whiskers. Ariel grabbed the dainty from Elizabeth's hand and began chomping on it himself, bleeking and chirping what could only be encouragement.

Deciding that her interference could not help, Elizabeth sat in her father's chair and studied the clutter on his desk. Its very disorder vividly reminded her that he had only planned to be away for a day or two.

"Dad . . ." she whispered. "I wish . . ."

Her soliloquy was interrupted by the beep of her pocket com. She took it out and glanced at it, and the caller ID told her that Michael was looking for her.

"Yes, Michael?"

"Our cousins are here—Mike and Calvin. Can we come up?"

"You know where I am?"

"I asked Dover. You're in Dad's office again."

"That's right. Sure, bring them up. Did Uncle Anson come, too?"

"He's with Aunt Caitrin and Mom."

"Then come up. We have some time before the viewing."

Switching off the intercom, Elizabeth swiveled her father's chair so that she could look out the window. Below she could just see the edges of the Blue Hall where preparations were being made for her father's final public duty.

"'Viewing.' It sounds so cold," she mused aloud.

She hadn't expected any response so when a furious snarl greeted her words she leapt up and turned. On his perch, Monroe had risen on all six feet, arched his back, and was hissing at the group clustered in the doorway.

"I guess we should have knocked," Michael managed to say, his eyes wide.

"Don't worry," Elizabeth said, motioning them into the room. "Monroe hasn't been himself since Dad died."

Her words were comforting, but she did not dismiss the 'cat's response lightly. Ariel reinforced her own impression that Monroe had been reacting to something—or someone—specific.

Who or what? Certainly the 'cat had not been responding to any of the small group now clustered in the office. The Henke cousins had been in and out of the Palace all of Elizabeth's life. It couldn't have been Mike or Cal that Monroe had spat at.

Who though? Not for the first time, Elizabeth wished that her ability to communicate with Ariel extended beyond their empathic bond. Ariel certainly knew more than he could tell, but they were trapped by an unbreachable language barrier.

Even if Monroe had caught a stray thought or emotion from someone passing by, there had been the usual corridor traffic in addition to the guards escorting Michael and the Henkes, far too many people in the area to make guessing easy.

Impulse passed, Monroe was now slouched in his earlier apathy.

Shaking her head, Elizabeth filed the mystery for later consideration and turned her attention to her cousins. Both were darker skinned than Michael or Beth and both wore their curly hair close-cropped, but there was no doubt which of the two was the girl.

Michelle Henke—firmly established as "Mike," much to Prince Michael's disgruntlement—possessed definite femininity that not even the uniform of a Navy lieutenant could disguise. Her brother, Calvin, had taken his degree on Manticore and was already firmly in place as the Earl of Gold Peak's right-hand man.

Mike was the first to bridge the silence. She crossed to Elizabeth and embraced her. The Queen was touched to realize that despite her own deep and very real grief, Mike's dominant emotion was concern for her.

"I can't say how sorry I am about Uncle Roger, Beth." Mike shrugged. "There just aren't words."

"No, there aren't," Calvin agreed. "How are you holding up, Beth?"

"They've kept me so busy I haven't really had time to accept that he won't be coming back," Elizabeth answered honestly.

"I wish they'd keep me that busy," Michael said forlornly. "I've had too much time to think. Mike, what can you tell me about the Navy?"

"That's a big question, Michael. What is it you want to know?"

"I guess I want to know whether I should . . ." He choked back a sob. "Should I . . ."

"Join like your dad wanted you to?"

Crown Prince Michael nodded.

Lord Calvin Henke dropped into a chair.

"Maybe you should think about it from the other point of view, Mikey," he said. "What would you do if you don't join the Navy? There aren't many jobs out there for heirs apparent—even if all they're in line for is an earldom, like me. And unlike me, you can't depend on inheriting the title."

"Depend on?" Michael looked puzzled.

"Unless I die first," Calvin clarified, "I will someday inherit my father's title and responsibilities. In your case, as soon as Beth and Justin start churning out more Wintons you get shoved back a step or two in the succession. You have a lot more freedom than Beth or I do. What do you want to do with it?"

Michael frowned. "I never really thought of it that way. Dad was so careful to tell me how important a duty I had. The way you put it, I'm just so many spare parts."

Mike Henke laughed, a rich contralto that warmed the room. "Welcome to the club, cousin. I, for one, want to stay spare parts. Cal can be Earl. I'm going to be an Admiral. How about you?"

When the thirteen year-old didn't answer, Calvin picked up the discussion.

"Honestly, Michael, you could get away without doing much of anything. There's always a demand for royals to officiate at ceremonies. Or you could get into politics. One of the advantages of being a Winton is you have a seat in the Lords waiting for you. As long as you don't break too openly with Beth, you could have a vigorous career. The Crown Loyalists would just drool if you were at their meetings. Then there's the ambitious younger set. You could join them."

Michael's eyes widened. "I don't want to make a career of meetings! Dad always made Beth and me go to some of the open sessions of Parliament. I've never been so bored!"

"Think about it," Calvin said, refusing to relent. "There is power there, power and influence. Not all of it would be because your sister is the Queen."

Beth hid her smile in Ariel's fur as Mike took over where her brother had left off. King Roger should have let the Henkes double-team Mikey years ago!

"In the Navy," Mike said, "the question of privilege is less important. Oh, sure, there are those who rise due to family connections—I'm not going to even pretend otherwise. But after a point the jerks get bumped out on half-pay and the better officers rise to the plum commands. There's also prize money to consider. I have an inheritance coming to me and a good allowance, but I love the idea of making my own fortune."

This last caught Michael's attention. Neither Queen Angelique nor King Roger had believed that their children should be spoiled. He was still young enough that the idea of a fortune of his own, for which he would not have to answer to anyone, was quite enticing. Still, he hesitated.

"I'd hate to be one of those who fail," he said, "one of those who end up out of half-pay. What if I flunk out? My grades haven't been the best lately."

"You won't know unless you try," Mike said practically. "My

Academy roommate was a dunce at math. Her astrogation was more intuitive than logical, but since she had promise in other areas, her instructors worked with her, and she graduated near the top of our class anyway. You're a prince of the House of Winton. They're going to have real incentive to work with you."

The intercom chimed, warning them that they would be expected at dinner within the quarter hour.

"Can we talk more about this?" Michael asked. He glanced at his father's desk as if he expected to see him sitting there. "I want to do the right thing—and not just try to make Dad happy."

"You bet," Mike draped a hand around his shoulder. "Would Your Royal Highness care to escort the Honorable Michelle to dinner?"

Michael laughed and took her arm with grace.

"In the absence of your fiancé," Calvin said, offering his arm to Elizabeth, "may I escort Your Majesty?"

The playful fashion in which he used her new title reassured Elizabeth that her cousins were determined to treat her with respect—and not to let her get too far above herself. Happily, she lightly stroked Monroe good-bye, gathered Ariel, and accepted Calvin's arm.

When the door opened, Monroe raised his head as if listening for something. His head remained raised, his ears perked, long after the door had closed behind them.

"When do you need to be anywhere?" Daniel Chou asked Justin.

"I need to be at the Palace for the viewing later tonight. I bowed out of a dinner invitation though," Justin said. "The Henkes—King Roger's sister's family—are coming in."

"Don't you like them?"

"I do, quite a bit, but I thought that the families might relax more if I wasn't present. They need the space to weep and, even if I am special to Elizabeth, to most of them I'm still something of a stranger."

Chou smiled. "I can see why Elizabeth chose you. You have an innate sense of protocol—very useful."

"I think," Justin said with complete honesty, "that she chose me because I met her and liked her without realizing that she was the Heir. In fairy tales, the commoner is always discovered to be a princess in disguise. Having been a princess all her life, I think that Beth found being taken for just anyone a relief."

"And soon you will be a prince," Chou said.

"By marriage." Justin turned to look at the old man. "I never wanted to be part of the aristocracy. They have too many responsibilities. Now, in order to marry the woman I love, I need to take on those responsibilities. Strange, isn't it?"

"One of life's little ironies," Chou agreed. "Since you aren't expected anywhere for a few hours, let's go look at the grav ski and then—if you don't mind—get some dinner. My treat. You can drop me off on your way to the Palace."

Justin nodded. "That sounds good."

They parked Justin's air car in a sheltered space near a small, nondescript, grey, rectangular building mingled in with other similar buildings. The place was not ugly; rooftop gardens spilled flowers down the walls. However, it did not register in the imagination.

"This place is constructed to be forgotten," Justin commented.

"That it is," Chou agreed. "A good thing. Come inside."

Justin got an indication of Chou's importance within whatever hierarchy he belonged to when his ID admitted them past checkpoint after checkpoint without need for query or confirmation. At last, Chou unlocked a door as plain and nondescript as the building itself.

"Here we are," he said. "All the materials from the crash were brought here. I've done some preliminary inspections, but I must admit that I haven't found anything significant. That's why I went back to the Indigo Salt Flats, to see if something might have been missed."

"Did you find anything?"

"No."

They inspected the shattered gear in companionable silence. Justin's area of expertise was tangential to grav technologies, but he had used grav units in the past, was familiar in theory with what made the compact device counter gravity. After a long, careful inspection he glanced at Chou.

"Anything?"

"Nothing."

An idea, faint and insubstantial as an evening shadow came to Justin as he stood studying pieces of the broken ski.

"Adderson said that the King had planned to use a different ski set."

"He said something about that to me, too."

"Do you know what happened to it?"

"It was brought back here. It's in that case over in the corner."

With a glance for permission, Justin picked up the case and swung it onto the counter.

"Can we run a diagnostic on this?"

"Sure."

Chou did not chatter, merely handed Justin the instruments he needed. Only after Justin had run the check three times did Chou finally speak.

"Very, very interesting."

"Yes."

"There's nothing at all wrong with this ski set."

Justin set down the diagnostic scanner. "I didn't think there would be. Beth gave it to her father for his birthday. New sets are rather carefully checked—especially when they're being sold to the Crown Princess."

"So that means that whoever directed the King away from using this set is in on the conspiracy," Chou said. "Or so we can hope. I'll do some checking on who was on duty that day, see if Adderson remembers specifics."

"Would there be security videos?" Justin asked hopefully.

"Not in the chalet. That was the Royal Family's private area. Now, what do you want for dinner?"

"I don't know if I have much of a stomach for eating right now," Justin answered. "I don't think I really believed that someone murdered the King until this moment."

"We don't have much evidence," Chou cautioned. "What we have is closer to the negative space in a sculpture—something that helps define what is there but is nothing in itself. A good defense council would laugh us right out of courts."

"What do we do next?"

"Dinner." Chou leaned and patted him on one arm. "You'll want it later. We'll plan while we eat."

Justin nodded. "Let's go then. I'll let you to pick a place where we won't attract attention."

"I know just the place," Chou promised.

"Some super spy hangout?" Justin tried to joke, but his voice sounded flat even to him.

"Something like that," Chou said. "I was thinking of my apartment. I'm not a bad cook."

"Let's go, then."

They put away both the pieces of the shattered grav ski and the undamaged ski before they left.

"We haven't found much," Chou said, looking into the room as he dimmed the light and closed the door. "But it's a beginning."

In a suite in a private hotel so committed to discretion that few people even knew it existed, Marvin Seltman and Jean

Marrou watched the news service coverage of the first night of King Roger's wake.

"Look at them!" Seltman almost snarled. "Most of them actively opposed the King, many of them probably raised a private toast when the word of his death came, but to see them weeping you would assume they'd lost their dearest friend."

Jean Marrou turned her blind face toward the news screen. A small implant beneath one ear let her tune into special detailed commentary. The narration told her which august personages were paying their last respects to King Roger III of Manticore.

Tonight was reserved for the cream of the peerage. The new Queen and her family were present to greet them and accept their condolences. Tomorrow the lesser nobles and important commoners would be admitted—including the elected members of the House of Commons.

"I wonder if the Queen will be present when we attend tomorrow's viewing?" she said.

"Don't tell me you can't wait to meet her!" Seltman snapped.

"I have already met her," Marrou said. "She seemed like a nice child. No, I was not anticipating meeting a celebrity. I was wondering about her treecat."

"Her *treecat*?" Seltman spoke the word as if he could not believe that he had heard aright.

"Yes, studies show that they have a marked telempathic sense. No doubt it's strongest with those humans they bond with, but I understand that they can 'read' others as well."

"And?"

"And I was wondering if Queen Elizabeth's 'cat might be able to read us—what we've done."

"They're telempaths, not telepaths," Seltman corrected. "They read vague emotions, not thoughts. Any treecat attending the viewing is going to be so overwhelmed by strong emotions that any inadvertent hostility we let leak out will be part of the flood."

"I hope so."

"In any case," Seltman continued. "I feel no hostility at all towards our little Queen. I feel nothing but a great deal of affection. If our plan works, she is going to be our ticket to advancement."

"And to protecting the Kingdom from adverse out-system influence," Marrou said woodenly.

"Exactly, Jean, exactly," Seltman soothed. "The others should be here soon. I wonder what rumors they will have picked up? The Queen's nominee for Regent is going to be announced tomorrow, but Paderweski's savvy. She's going to have permitted some strategic leaks so that the Palace will have responses planned."

Marrou touched the implant. "We should know fairly soon. Earl Howell just departed. Paula should be on her way."

"She wasn't high enough ranking for tonight's little gathering," Seltman said, "but she was going to visit with some of the ambitious young turks. They'll have an entirely different line than Howell's."

They fell into silence then. To be completely honest, neither particularly liked the other. Jean Marrou found Marvin Seltman ambitious and coarse. Seltman distrusted Marrou as a fanatic whose dreams would ultimately come to ruin. Still, for now each believed that the other was useful.

Earl Howell arrived first, Lady Gwinner a few moments after. Padraic Dover, like all members of the Queen's Own, was standing a "voluntary" extended watch.

As he took his seat in one of the overstuffed leather chairs, Howell looked haggard. Seltman, deferential as always (although privately he found the older man's lack of backbone disturbing), poured him a snifter of Gryphon cognac. By contrast, Gwinner was bubbling with suppressed energy. Seltman embraced her, sniffing lightly for traces of intoxicants. If she had been indiscreet . . . but he found nothing and decided that her effervescence was purely enthusiasm for a project going well.

"Earl Howell," Seltman said after all were settled with drinks and a plate of delicacies had been in everyone's reach, "perhaps you could tell us about the viewing."

He wanted to scream "Did you learn anything!" but knew the Crown Loyalist needed to be handled with extreme delicacy.

"The King's body was laid out very tastefully," Howell began, as if by dealing with inconsequential matters he could work his way toward the difficult material. "And his widow and children were in attendance. They seemed quite distraught, but the Queen Mother spoke kindly to me and the young Queen offered her hand, saying that my loyalty to the Crown had come to her attention and she would remember it."

Howell's voice broke.

"How sweet of the little Duchess of Basilisk," Gwinner said, only a touch of acid in her voice. "Or now that her father is gone, will she be assuming the title of *Princess* of Basilisk that *he* took?"

At another time, her approach might have been heavy-handed,

but this time it was perfect. Howell stiffened, sipped his cognac, and much of the exhaustion dropped from his features to be replaced by something rather like hope.

"Perhaps we will not need to concern ourselves for much longer with the question of what titles go with that improperly annexed system," he said. "LeBrun told me this evening, confidentially . . ."

He paused until everyone had nodded.

" . . . that the Queen in seriously considering a member of our Party for her Regent's council and that, if he were asked . . ."

"Which he will be," Gwinner interrupted.

Howell raised a chiding eyebrow, " . . . that I will be his first choice."

"Congratulations," Seltman said. "This also means that you would be considered as a candidate for Regent as well. Do you have any idea who the Queen will be nominating tomorrow?"

Blind Jean Marrou raised a hand for attention. "May I hazard a guess?"

Seltman was taken aback. Marrou had been with him all evening and had admitted when they met that she had no idea who the candidate would be. Had she been holding out on him? However, her almost uncanny talent for political analysis was one of the reasons he had recruited her. It might be amusing to learn what she would say.

He glanced at the others, saw some reflection of his thoughts in their expressions, and grinned.

"Certainly, Jean. Who do you believe will be nominated as Regent?"

"Normally, I would not hazard a guess based only on listening to news commentary," she began, clearly enjoying the moment, "but tonight I had the distinct impression that the Lord Chamberlain, Lord Jacob Wundt, is her choice."

Both Howell and Seltman gasped. Gwinner shook her head, laughing.

"Incredible, Jean! That's exactly what I heard from my sources. How did you know?"

"Listening to the description of the Queen's party tonight," Marrou said smugly, "I noticed that she frequently called the Lord Chamberlain to her side."

"But this was a social/political function," Howell protested, "that is his usual role. How could you tell that anything had changed?"

"The frequency, the proximity, the fact that he also spent time speaking with Cromarty. As you know, Wundt is closer to being a Crown Loyalist than anything else. His new friendliness with the Prime Minister seemed to indicate that Cromarty now finds him useful."

Seltman nodded. "Interesting. Padraic's reports confirm that Wundt has been part of the informal council meetings that have been held today. I had assumed his presence was because he could provide information on the inner workings of Palace protocol. However, My Lord, did you hear anything that would confirm this?"

Howell had stopped gaping like a fish, but he continued to study Marrou as if her talents were akin to sorcery. Marrou did not help to settle him by appearing to feel his gaze and turning her blind eyes on him.

"Yes," Howell managed. "LeBrun did say something of the sort. He also said that he expected the party to be somewhat torn on confirmation. Our platform usually is complete support for the Crown and, as you've noted, Wundt is by personal inclination one of our own, but his age and the fact that he has not actively participated in debate on the issues make him a poor choice as Regent."

Seltman rubbed his hands briskly together. "If even the Crown Loyalists have second thoughts, than some of the other factions must be truly torn. When is the vote for confirmation to be held?"

"The question will open for debate tomorrow at ten," Howell said. "Protocol demands that it not be called to the vote until reasonable discussion is held. However, the need to put in place both a Regent and a Regency council suggests that no one will choose to filibuster."

"I second that," Gwinner said. "Since Wundt has never firmly allied himself with any one party, no group will see a benefit from delaying the vote. My guess is that we will have a vote by midday tomorrow."

Marrou nodded. "I suspect the pacing in Commons will be similar. Our general support for the Crown will not extend to rubber-stamping the Regent. A few well-made speeches . . ."

"Can we expect one from you?" Seltman asked. "I am somewhat less popular."

"That's true," Marrou agreed. "Your personal ambitions are too well-known. While they frequently garner you respect, since no one thinks you would promote an issue you haven't carefully researched, I think too much interest in the Regent would seem suspicious."

Seltman stared at her, trying to decide if he had just been insulted. He decided that he had, but that it was not worth comment.

"I shall hold my tongue then," he said. "You will speak. Earl Howell will certainly be expected to speak, since he is a rising hope within his party. Paula?"

Gwinner nibbled a piece of cheese before answering. "Let me get a feeling for the mood of the House. Given my youth and my position as a second-generation prolong recipient, I don't wish to speak out against an older candidate. It could cause something of a backlash. If I can find an angle that is not age or party related, either I'll speak or I'll put the idea into one of my more ambitious colleague's minds."

"Who do you have in mind?" Howell asked.

"Sheridan Wallace hates anything that promotes established privilege," Gwinner replied, "but he's smart enough to say so tactfully. I can use him."

"Who do you think will be the Queen's second choice?" Seltman asked. He was amused to see that everyone looked at Jean Marrou. Knowing she could not see this, he prompted, "Jean?"

"I can't say based on what I heard tonight," she said honestly. "I will have a better idea after I attend tomorrow's viewing, especially if I can schedule my timing to match the Queen's attendance."

"She won't be there all day tomorrow?" Gwinner asked.

"No," Marrou said. "The newscast noted that this would be unduly exhausting. Instead, various members of the royal family will be attending in shifts. I believe that the Henkes will be taking on some of this duty."

"They were all present tonight," Howell noted. "Lord Calvin Henke and Justin Zyrr both stayed close to the Queen. The Honorable Michelle shadowed the young Crown Prince."

"The House of Winton and its offshoots have always been clannish," Seltman said. "Although I don't have Jean's gift for analysis, I still suspect that the Queen's next candidate will be a family member. Paula, I suggest that you begin to lay groundwork for why this would be unacceptable."

"I'll do what I can," she promised. "Certainly, Earl Howell can't. It would look too much like self-interest."

Jean Marrou stood, balancing herself lightly against the back of her chair. "If we are finished with tonight's discussion, I believe I will make my way to my hotel. If I'm too late screening my husband, he'll screen and wonder why I'm still out."

"You could screen from here," Seltman offered.

"No, I would be more comfortable among my own things." She smiled. "Besides, if I am to attend the viewing during the Queen's vigil, I need to rise early to make some inquiries."

"Good night then," Seltman said.

The earl, with the instinctive social courtesy of his rank, rose and walked her to the door.

Deep in her own thoughts as she left the hotel, Jean Marrou switched off the small computer unit that regularly scanned her environment and reported on those present. Even if she had not been distracted, it is doubtful that she would have taken note of the security guard who held the door for her or bothered to run a cross-check to learn that she had encountered the man before at the estate of the Earl of North Hollow.

As predicted by many, Lord Jacob Wundt was not confirmed as Regent for young Queen Elizabeth. After heated debate, a vote was taken and Parliament sent its regretful refusal.

"We'll wait until tomorrow to name Aunt Caitrin as our next choice," Elizabeth said to Dame Eliska and the Queen Mother. "That will give ample opportunity for the pundits and politicos to guess."

"Should I put out any hints?" Paderweski asked.

"No," Elizabeth said decisively. "I think not. Simply state that I regret the result of Parliament's vote and will be reviewing their objections to Lord Wundt before selecting my next nominee."

"Acid, Beth," Queen Angelique commented. "Your father would be proud."

"Thanks," Elizabeth grinned. "Now, I believe I have a few hours in my schedule to spend with Justin. If you would excuse me?"

"Of course, Your Majesty," Dame Eliska said, concealing a slight smile.

"Have fun, dear," Queen Angelique added. "And give Justin my love."

Ariel romping beside her, Elizabeth hurried off to her suite in King Michael's Tower. Justin, his handsome features somber, was waiting. After they had embraced, Elizabeth sat him down firmly and planted herself in his lap.

"Tell me, Justin," she said. "I don't need to be as sensitive as Ariel to know that you have found something out—and that you don't like what you've learned."

Taking a deep breath, Justin said, "I have every reason to believe that you were correct in believing that the King was assassinated."

As concisely as if he were presenting an experiment report, Justin told her of his visit to the Indigo Salt Flats, of his meeting with Daniel Chou, and, finally, of their conclusions. When he finished, Elizabeth's eyes shone with tears.

"I knew," she whispered, "but I so wanted to be wrong."

"You might as well have been for all the evidence we found," Justin said flatly. "Chou is right. Negative evidence won't hold up in court. We need something more."

"Chou is checking the records for who was at the Flats that day?" Elizabeth queried.

"That's right."

"Then we can't despair until we know what he learned. Justin, you must be my ears and eyes in this. With the Regency confirmation and the wake, I cannot spare attention."

She squared her shoulders. "Until we know beyond a shadow of a doubt that this is the Kingdom's business, I must apply myself to ongoing problems."

"Problems?"

"Nothing that I can't handle with Cromarty and Mother's advice, but the existing business of the Star Kingdom didn't stop simply because the King died. Already there are those who are trying to use this period of transition to their advantage."

"That's hardly fair!"

"No it isn't, but my Parliament is filled with canny politicians. I may not agree with their tactics, but I'm rather like a starship captain who takes battle damage in a skirmish and then finds an enemy squadron bearing down. There simply isn't time to complain about fairness."

Justin nodded agreement and chuckled. "It still isn't fair."

"True," Elizabeth squeezed his hand, "but it could be worse."

"How?"

"I could be facing this without you."

Chou wasn't very hopeful when he met Justin late that morning.

"I've checked," he said, "and I have the names of everyone on duty on the chalet on the day of the King's death and for a week before. No one on the list has the least blemish on record, not that I expected to find any."

"No," Justin agreed. "Anyone on report would have been put on duty elsewhere. The Star Kingdom doesn't take risks with its monarchs."

"And," Chou continued remorselessly, "I've run mock-ups based on the available data and there are numerous ways the accident could have been caused. The most likely is a small receiver set mounted on the ski and controlled by remote."

"Wouldn't that have been found during the diagnostic?"

"It would if it was set in the ski's own works," Chou said, "but if it was placed in a strap or within a bit of decoration . . ."

"Or if the person doing the diagnostic chose to overlook it," Justin added. "Did you find out who dissuaded the King from using the ski set that Beth gave him?"

Chou nodded. "It was a member of the King's Guard named Padraic Dover. He's a native of Gryphon and has an impeccable record."

"I've met him," Justin said. "He's been on the Palace staff since Beth was eight or ten. That doesn't make him a likely suspect."

"No," Chou agreed, "but that's exactly what we need to look for—an unlikely suspect. There is no one who is likely."

The two men sat in silent meditation, Chou stroking his drooping mustache, Zyrr frowning and chewing on his inner lip.

"I suppose I'd better speak with Dover," Chou said at last. "Do you want to attend?"

"Why don't I speak with him?" Justin suggested. "If you call on him he's going to know that something is up. Even if he's innocent, a casual mention of the interview could start rumors."

"The PGS questioning a member of the Queen's Own," Chou mused. "Yes, it might raise questions. You can talk to him more casually. But I'd like to be present—concealed—if possible."

"We can work something out. Can you get into my suite at the Palace without being noticed?"

Chou merely smiled.

"Then before I leave here I'll try to set up an appointment with Dover so you know when to meet us."

Twenty minutes later, Zyrr had made the appointment for later that same day. Returning to the Mount Royal complex, he was accosted by Michelle Henke.

"Hi, Mike."

"Justin! You're the very man I was hoping to find."

Zyrr doubted that the Honorable Michelle had found him by accident. Already, the confident young woman left little to chance.

"What can I do for you?"

"It's Monroe. He's becoming increasingly despondent. We're worried that he's going to suicide. He won't tolerate anyone but immediate family near him, so we've been taking turns sitting with him, but right now everyone is scheduled elsewhere. Michael and I are set to be at the viewing next; Calvin is out meeting with some of the young turks, trying to sway their vote for one of Beth's projects, Mom is—"

"I get the picture. Do you need me to take care of Monroe?"

"Would you? Michael's with him now."

"Do you think Monroe would come to my suite? Someone is coming to meet me there."

Mike tilted her head thoughtfully. "I don't see why not. A change of setting might be good for him. If he fusses, you can have your appointment redirected to Uncle Roger's office."

Justin glanced at his chronometer. "I'll run over and relieve Michael one way or another."

"You're a prince!" Mike gave him a quick peck on the cheek.

"Not yet," he smiled.

Laughing, the Honorable Michelle hurried off to don her uniform for the viewing.

Mike, Justin mused as he walked over to King Roger's office, couldn't fail to make an impression on young Michael. He'd be willing to bet that the Crown Prince was being not so subtly indoctrinated in the virtues of a Navy career.

When the guard at the door signalled Prince Michael that Justin had arrived, Justin was admitted with indecent haste.

Michael must have taken the initiative to have his valet bring his formal wear to the office so that he could dress while he waited, for he stood by his father's desk, nearly attired in his court finery.

"Justin!"

"You're the second person in ten minutes to greet me with such delight," Justin said wryly. "I suppose I should be honored. Mike has filled me in and I'm here to spell you with Monroe."

"Thanks, Justin." Michael gestured to where the treecat lay limp and bedraggled on his perch. "He's quit eating, only drinks a little water. Beth says she thinks the only thing keeping him from quitting is knowing that we're worried about him."

"So we want to stay close." Justin completely agreed.

He walked over to the limp 'cat and stroked him, suppressing his shock when he felt how sharply the 'cat's backbone stood out beneath the fluffy camouflage of his coat. The cat's eyes were closed and not even a hint of green flickered when Justin tried to tickle him under his chin.

"Are you even certain that he's conscious?" he said, shocked.

"No," Michael said wearily. He seemed years older than the boy who had burst into tears at the memory of his argument with his father. "The vet said that Monroe isn't conscious much of the time, but that he can probably still feel our concern."

The Crown Prince extended his arm. "Can you help me with my cufflinks, Jus? These are Dad's. They're harder to snap tight than my old ones."

"No problem."

Justin fastened the cufflinks and straightened the lace front of the boy's dress shirt. When King Roger I had become the first monarch of the Kingdom of Manticore, he had commissioned an artist to design court dress. His only dictums had been that the new attire would be comfortable, elegant, and equally suited for male or female wear.

The artist had done his work brilliantly, Justin thought as he helped Michael into his jacket. The tail coat worn over tailored trousers had been borrowed from ancient England. The ruffled shirt with its lace cuffs had been taken from a slightly earlier time. There was no hat to create awkward clutter, and the footwear consisted of low-heeled boots that looked elegant while permitting the wearer to stand comfortably for hours.

By tradition, each noble house had its garb tailored in colors corresponding to those of its family's crest—in the case of the Wintons dusky blue trimmed with silver, although the Queen wore the red and gold of the Star Kingdom of Manticore. Awards, marriage alliances, and the like were indicated by slim bands at the cuffs. Since tradition also dictated that the fabrics be sumptuous brocades, a gathering of the nobility was awe inspiring indeed.

Commoners wore clothing of similar cut, but avoided both brocades and color combinations that directly mimicked an aristocrat's heraldry. However, Members of Parliament were encouraged to allude to the district they represented in the colors they elected to wear.

On the few occasions in his pre-Elizabeth life where a uniform would not serve, Justin had opted for rather generic colors. Since his official engagement, however, he wore a combination of Gryphon's bronze and dark brown with bands in the Winton colors at his cuffs. Idly, he thought that before he dismissed his valet, he had better make certain his clothing was ready for tonight.

When Michael had left, Justin crossed to Monroe.

"Come on, fellow. Time for a change of venue."

The treecat didn't budge from his perch. However, when Justin picked him up he came away with only a token grasping of his claws.

"You need some fresh air, Monroe," Justin said firmly, aware that even weakened, Monroe could do him serious harm. "Don't fuss."

Monroe didn't and, although they attracted some attention as Justin carried the 'cat through the back ways to his suite, they arrived without incident.

Settling Monroe on a heap of pillows at one corner of his sofa, Justin conferred with his valet about the condition of his formal wear, then dismissed the man until he should call for him.

When Monroe rejected his bribes of celery and he failed to locate Chou, Justin settled down, feeling slightly disgruntled, to wait for his appointment with Padraic Dover.

For Padraic Dover the time since King Roger's death had been an exercise in frustration. The first stage of the plan had gone so smoothly that he had naively believed the second would as well, but he couldn't even get near the Queen, much less find time to charm her.

Part of this was his own duty roster. His seniority proved to be a bane, granting him special honors such as standing watch over the King's body. If Queen Elizabeth was not in a meeting, making a public statement, or keeping vigil with her father's body, she was closeted with family members. Once, briefly, their paths had overlapped during the viewing, but although she'd greeted him, there had hardly been opportunity for conversation.

And finding Justin Zyrr had been as difficult. From one of his associates, he learned that Zyrr had visited the Indigo Salt Flats and wandered about for a while. Otherwise, he had been in and out of Mount Royal on such an irregular schedule that Dover had not been able to cross his path.

Therefore, Padraic had been astonished when he received a polite letter from Zyrr asking if Dover would call on him early that evening. For a moment, Dover had panicked. What if Zyrr *knew*?

Then he'd reassured himself. How could Zyrr know anything? They had been careful. The receiver had disintegrated on impact as planned; Dover had destroyed the transmitter himself. As panic ebbed, Dover realized that a golden opportunity had been given to him. He would be alone with Zyrr— at Zyrr's own request.

As he inspected his uniform before the meeting, Dover constructed his cover story. He would stick to the truth for openers. Zyrr had summoned him to his apartment, then he had asked Dover to participate in some perversity.

Running his tongue over his lips, Dover toyed with his options. He could say that Zyrr asked him to acquire the services of one of the more notorious courtesans. Or he could say that Zyrr had propositioned him. Padraic smiled cruelly as he considered how he would feign reluctance to discuss the encounter, then reveal Zyrr's unspeakable wishes.

Of course, at some point during the encounter as reported by Padraic Dover, Zyrr would have become violent. Dover would have been forced to defend himself—for once he was glad that Zyrr was such a big man; it would make his own use of deadly force understandable.

Elizabeth was a sweet, compassionate girl. Surely she could be manipulated to take pity on a shocked and horrified member of her own Guard. At this point, Dover's thoughts slid into pure, improbable fantasy. He was imagining Elizabeth's tearful but romantic marriage proposal when his chronometer chimed, reminding him that his destiny was only moments from beginning.

Pressing the call buzzer, he was somewhat surprised when Zyrr answered the door himself. One of the holes in his plan had been what to do about Zyrr's valet. He had resolved somewhat reluctantly (for double murder weakened his story of indignant outrage) that the man must also die.

"Major Dover," Zyrr nodded greeting, motioned Dover into the apartment.

Dover followed with alacrity, sizing up both his opponent and the sparsely furnished living quarters. Not even the smallest noise betrayed the presence of another person and he began to hope that they were indeed alone.

"I've taken the liberty of dismissing my valet so that we can talk in private." Zyrr looked unwontedly serious. "I must ask you to swear by our shared birth world that nothing we discuss goes beyond this room."

"I so swear," Dover replied promptly, wondering if his guesses could have been correct and Zyrr required something illicit of him.

His initial plan had been to kill Zyrr immediately and then fill the remaining time with setting the stage for the "seduction." Now curiosity got the better of him. He permitted Zyrr to motion him to a chair and watched attentively as the Queen's fiancé took his own seat on the sofa next to a battered, rather ugly cream and grey throw pillow.

"I would like to speak with you about certain events on the day of King Roger's death," Zyrr began.

Dover felt a surge of terror, but kept his expression neutral.

"I understand that you were on duty at the chalet when the King was getting ready to go out skiing." Zyrr paused long enough for Padraic to manage a stiff nod. "Captain Adderson, who was also on duty that day, recalls that you ran the diagnostic on the ski set the King had brought with him."

Dover's thoughts raced in circles as he tried to reconcile the content of this interview with his glorious fantasies of only moments before. What had Seltman told him to say if questioned? The words had been drilled into him before the accident, they must be there . . .

He heard his own voice, sounding flat and wooden: "Yes, I ran the diagnostic. According to the read-out, the grav ski set was unreliable."

Although it might be considered a breech of protocol, he rose to his feet. He could not kill Zyrr from across the room. The death blow must be dealt hand-to-hand, otherwise his tale of an over-strong reaction to a physical advance would not stick.

Blithely unaware of his own danger, Zyrr continued:

"I ran a diagnostic on that very ski set myself," he said, "and found nothing at all wrong with it. In fact, it was newly purchased equipment, fresh from the factory."

Padraic's wooden voice answered, his mind intent on crossing the few remaining steps: "I only did my duty, Sir. According to the read-out the diagnostic tool gave me, the grav unit was malfunctioning."

"Perhaps your diagnostic tool was in error," Zyrr said, sounding almost relieved. "Please relax, Major. I mean you no harm."

But I mean you harm, Dover thought, and, moving as if to return to his chair, he chopped his hand down in a killing blow.

It never reached his target. In a sudden fury of spitting, hissing grey-and-cream fur, the ragged throw pillow resolved itself into the attacking form of a thin, but still deadly treecat.

"Monroe!" Zyrr shouted, lunging to his feet, uncertain whether to go after Dover or the 'cat.

Dover tried to take advantage of Zyrr's indecision to bring his blow home. The treecat had clawed his chest, but its prolonged fast and general despondency had so weakened it that what should have been a deadly assault failed to do more than tear the heavy, anti-ballistic weave fabric of his uniform.

Undecided no longer, Zyrr dodged Dover's blow, but his evasion brought him up against the edge of the sofa. He fell backward.

With one hand, Dover grabbed at the treecat, ripping its hold from his tunic front. With his other hand, he fumbled for the pulser at his belt. Shooting Zyrr would be harder to explain, but the apartment was soundproofed and he was certain that he could be convincing, especially with the marks of the treecat's assault on his uniform.

He should not have been able to miss at such close range, but Zyrr kicked the low coffee table out so that it hit Dover in the shins. The shot went wild, plowing a bloody gash across the top of Zyrr's right shoulder.

Stumbling back a few steps, Dover was reaiming when Monroe lunged at him again. The treecat chose to forsake the dramatic leap in favor of sinking his teeth into the soft area behind Dover's left knee.

Dover screamed and kicked, trying to batter the six-legged fiend loose and only seeming to anchor the 'cat more deeply. He felt blood running down his leg into his boot, then a dull pain as Zyrr came to his knees and knocked the pulser from his grasp.

"Surrender, Padraic Dover," a calm voice demanded.

Still trying to dislodge Monroe, he saw that a skinny old man with drooping mustaches had entered the room, a pulser in one hand. Dover's bowels weakened as he recognized one of the senior members of the PGS, the comic little man that everyone in the Service knew to fear and respect.

In the face of Daniel Chou's unforgiving gaze, the fight went out of him. Dover dropped his hands.

"Padraic Dover," Chou repeated coldly, "I place you under arrest for attempted murder of Justin Zyrr, the murder of King Roger III, and the crime of grand treason."

There was a moment of pure silence and stillness during which even Monroe's muffled growling ceased. Dover felt the fangs and claws leave his leg. Slowly, he raised his hands.

"I . . ." he began.

Then there was a surge of grey and cream and before he could lower his hands, Monroe flung himself from the fallen coffee table into Dover's unprotected face.

Padraic Dover's world became a wreckage of red. Blood washed down his face, blinding him; something was wrong with his throat. He couldn't breath. Horrified, he recognized the ragged, burbling noise as his own breathing and felt the blood flowing down his windpipe, choking him.

There was shouting around him, words about a med team. Someone was pulling the furious treecat away. It all seemed curiously distant, though. From the one eye that was not washed over with blood, Padraic saw the ceiling light fixture and realized that he was lying on his back. Odd. He hadn't remembered falling.

A voice, powerful, insistent, demanding answers, was questioning him, asking about the King's death, if he'd had any allies in his crime. He realized that he could choke out a few words if he tried.

"Tell me!" Chou was saying.

"Why should I?" Dover managed to gasp.

And then, pleased with himself, he died.

Later that evening, Jean Marrou went to pay her respects to the King and tried to puzzle through the subtleties of mood and human interaction. Her implant whispered information from which she wove a tapestry of who was in favor with whom, who was rising in influence, who was falling although unaware of the slide from grace.

This was a familiar game to her, one she played without needing to divert much of her conscious attention to it. Her interest was in the young Queen and those gathered around her. The new nominee for Regent would be a member of the Queen's family. All the signs pointed to that, although the speculation that eddied around her proved that others were not as adept at reading those signs.

Her satisfaction faded the longer she observed the royal group. Something was wrong, of that she was certain. Justin Zyrr hovered closer to the Queen than was his wont—over three centimeters closer on average than he had during the previous evening's vigil.

The Queen's treecat was edgy and alert—again, more so than it had been the previous night. Her computer reported that it restlessly scanned the crowd, as if searching for someone. At that moment, Marrou resolved not to join the line of those slowly filing by the casket, for it would take her too close to Queen and 'cat.

Catching something of the tension of those she observed, Jean Marrou remained only long enough to be seen, to trade platitudes with various colleagues, and then to plead exhaustion and retire. No one would think oddly of that. She had learned long ago that her blindness made people pity her and assume a fragility she did not possess.

Leaving the viewing, Marrou proceeded by a circuitous route to the rendezvous where she was to meet her co-conspirators. She would be early, but she could have a drink, compose her nerves, and review her records to find support for her growing conviction that the next candidate for Regent would be the Duchess Caitrin Winton-Henke.

Upon arriving at the hotel, she opened the door locks with

a series of old-fashioned keys. Computer locks, while more complex and more secure, also kept records. Eschewing the grav lift, she walked up the stairs, still working on composing her thoughts. A small corner of her mind was debating whether to order a small meal rather than a drink as she put her key into the final lock.

As she pushed the door open, she became aware of voices in conversation. Eavesdropping had been a profitable pastime ever since she was small and discovered that adults tended to forget that a blind child was not necessarily deaf. Softly closing the door behind her, she waited in the entryway, her naturally acute hearing augmented by one of the units in her computer.

Even as her implant informed her that the people conversing were Marvin Seltman and Paula Gwinner, she recognized their voices. She quashed a small impulse to retreat and re-enter with more noise when she realized that what she was hearing was not lovers' banter but something much more interesting.

"Dover didn't show up for our rendezvous today," Seltman was saying. "I made some inquiries, and I believe he may be in disgrace. He may even be dead."

"Lucky for us," Gwinner said.

The clinking of ice in a glass made Jean Marrou smile slightly. Whenever she was nervous, Gwinner toyed with something. Her voice remained cool.

"I suppose that means that we can give up on our hope that he would succeed in replacing Zyrr."

"True," Seltman said, "but then that was never any more than a long-shot. Dover has fulfilled his purpose in our plans. Perhaps it's best for us that he was put out of the way before he could realize how futile his hopes were and decide to betray us."

Something about his inflection on the plural pronouns made Marrou's skin crawl. Seltman continued:

"Our allies wouldn't care to have the plot exposed. Rather than rendering the Queen vulnerable, knowledge that King Roger was assassinated would solidify support behind her—especially in the Commons. Normal folk love anything that makes them pity royalty for their lot."

Paula laughed. "True. No one assassinates bus drivers or factory workers. If Dover is truly out of the way, we are safer. Neither of the others will speak—they have too much to risk."

"I hope so," Seltman said. "Earl Howell is invaluable now—especially if he gets a place on the Regent's council. I worry more about how Jean would react if she ever realized our friends' part in King Roger's illness a few years ago. . . ."

"How could she?" Gwinner scoffed.

"There's something witchy about the way she plays with data patterns," Seltman replied. "I wouldn't underestimate her, not for a minute."

"Do we really need her?"

Marrou held her breath, waiting for the answer.

"Yes," Seltman said slowly, "especially at the start. Her popularity in the Commons makes her an ideal person to promote some of the policies that will create a favorable atmosphere for takeover."

Gwinner's ice clinked. "She's fairly Progressive in her point of view—we'd do better with a Liberal. Progressives have the sense to realize Haven is a threat."

Marrou, standing still as a shadow despite an urge to turn and run, bit into her lip to keep from gasping aloud. Suddenly, those cryptic pronouns were making terrible sense.

"We are creating an atmosphere," Seltman reminded Gwinner, "which will help slow the Manticoran military build-up. A Progressive can do that as well as a Liberal. Remember, Jean rather desperately wants our system to remain a private little archipelago in the cosmos. That impulse will fuel her eloquence in our cause."

Poised to run, Jean Marrou realized how foolish that would be. If she didn't show for the meeting, then the others would become suspicious. She must make an entrance, stay, talk calmly about issues, and only then, when she was safe, consider what action to take next.

Could she confide in Howell? Hardly. He would panic and do something foolish that would get them both killed. Nor did she feel up to blackmailing the two Havenite sympathizers— even if her own loyalty to the Star Kingdom would have permitted her to do such a thing.

Chewing the inside of her lip, she reached behind her. Opening the door, she let it fall shut behind her.

"Anyone here?" she called.

Earl Howell had not been happy with Marrou's prediction that Duchess Winton-Henke would be named Regent, yet he no more doubted her than a primitive would have questioned a shaman. His dreams had been full of himself as Regent, directing the young Queen, becoming her favorite, his influence extending for centuries. A place on the Regency Council was not large enough for such dreams.

He had kept the three of them late, discussing options, tactics, plans to stop this nomination as well. Marrou had planned and plotted with the rest, aware that her safety rested on her being needed.

Then, when the hour grew late enough that even Howell's fervor had diminished, she left. First, in case someone was watching, she went to her hotel. After waiting a few hours, she went to Mount Royal Palace. Dawn was not far off when she arrived.

"I need to speak with Queen Elizabeth," she told the astonished duty guard.

"The Queen is getting her much needed rest," the guard said. "You may leave a message and if her schedule can accommodate you . . ."

"Please!" Marrou interrupted. "I must speak with her."

"I don't have the authority to awaken the Queen for anything less than an act of war," the guard said stubbornly.

Marrou played her trump card. "Please! This has to do with what happened with Padraic Dover early today."

Her blindness felt smothering. She wished she could see the guard's expression, but she forged on. Remembering the young man hovering at the Queen's shoulder that evening, she pleaded:

"If I can't talk with the Queen, let me speak with Justin Zyrr."

This seemed to decide the guard. Putting her into a small, soundproofed waiting room, he placed a call. Sometime later, she was escorted to another room. The flatness of the noise around her told her that this room was also soundproofed.

The scent of the room held rich upholstery fabrics and some type of incense; the carpet underfoot was thick and plush. At least she was not in a holding cell. After a time, during which she was offered refreshments, she heard the door slide open.

Two people entered. One of them her computer identified as Justin Zyrr; the other was a stranger.

Zyrr spoke, "Ms. Marrou? I don't believe— Oh, yes! You're the member for South Shore, aren't you. You asked to speak with me?"

"Yes."

His words reminded her that she was a person of some small influence—nothing to a Queen or Prince Consort-to-be, but still someone. She held her head high.

"May I ask for an introduction to the person with you?"

A rasping voice, a slight chuckle underlying its notes, answered, "I'm Daniel Chou. I'm with PGS. Today I helped save Justin's life when he was attacked by Padraic Dover. I'd certainly like to know how you knew that something had happened to Dover. We've put a complete blackout on the incident."

"He didn't show up for a meeting," Marrou said firmly.

Chou's voice told her that he was at least as good at reading people as she was. She sincerely hoped that he would be able to tell that she was telling the truth.

"A meeting," Chou said. "Why don't you tell us more?"

And so she did, sparing nothing, not even her own part in the conspiracy. Apart from occasional gasps of surprise from Zyrr or a brief request that she clarify some point, they let her speak without interruption.

"When I overheard Gwinner and Seltman talking," she concluded, "I realized their motives and mine were not as closely linked as I had believed. Honestly, I feared for my own life if they came into power, but I also feared for the Star Kingdom."

"That's been your motive all along," Chou said, almost teasingly, "if we're to believe your story. You feared what King Roger would do to the Star Kingdom; then you feared your own allies. Do you have any proof of this rather extraordinary tale?"

"You can check the places and dates I mentioned," Marrou said. Her hand dropped to the computer at her waist and, feeling as if she were newly blinding herself, she detached it. "This contains a complete record of both our last meeting and the conversation I overheard between Gwinner and Seltman."

A hand accepted the device. Without the visual link, she had no idea who, but she imagined it was Zyrr.

"This could be falsified," Chou said.

"It isn't," Marrou interrupted, "but I have an idea how you can prove my good faith."

"How?" Zyrr asked.

"I know something about Sphinx treecats," she said. "I visited there some years ago. My sensors give me information enough to navigate, but I hoped that I would be adopted and that the 'cat's senses would augment my own."

Her shoulders drooped as she recalled the rejection. "None would have anything to do with me, but I did get a strong impression that they could read emotions. Perhaps the Queen's 'cat . . ."

"Ariel could," Zyrr answered, and Marrou wondered at his slight emphasis on the word "Ariel." "I'll talk to Beth."

"She needs to know this in any case," Chou agreed. "Go and find her. While you do so, I'll sit with Ms. Marrou here.

We can listen to her recording. Then I'll copy it so she can have her device back."

Jean Marrou could almost hear his smile. "It's quite a remarkable device. It must be of inestimable value to you."

"It is," she said.

Then the long wait began.

There was nothing extraordinary about Willis Kemeny being summoned before the Queen. His new nomination to the Regent's council and almost certain confirmation made such a meeting inevitable.

It was rather more interesting that Baroness Gwinner and Mr. Marvin Seltman, MP, should also be summoned. Although their summons came quietly, through very discreet channels, they reached the ears of the Earl of North Hollow.

Sitting in his grav chair, his bulk billowing around him, he considered this bit of news, combined it with certain other information, and smiled greasily.

Calling his secretary, he handed her four invitations and directed that they be sent only after his spies reported that the four addressees had departed Mount Royal under their own power.

Then he returned to the work of the moment. Somehow, he suspected that Earl Howell would not be confirmed onto the Council of Regents. Sending out messages, he began to agitate for Baron High Ridge to take Howell's place. High Ridge's membership in the Conservative Association might make him less palatable to the new Queen than a Crown Loyalist, but with Howell out of the running, he might just squeak in. And North Hollow had some very interesting material on High Ridge in his files, material that might come in useful if the Regent's council needed a bit of directing.

Happily, the Earl of North Hollow went about his morning's work.

When Ariel had finished confirming Jean Marrou's essential honesty and Queen Elizabeth had heard the recordings, the Queen retired to her privy chamber and requested that Chou, Justin, and Duchess Winton-Henke meet with her there.

"I," she said pithily when all were gathered and Duchess Winton-Henke had heard the full story, "want their heads."

Ariel, bristling in her lap, telegraphed the intensity that Elizabeth would not permit herself to put into her voice. Monroe, lying on the chair next to Justin, raised his head and hissed.

Neither Chou nor Justin said anything, their gazes turning to the duchess.

"Then all of this must become public," Caitrin said.

"Yes," the Queen said. "What of it? They have conspired to assassinate the King—and succeeded. Two of them are Havenite minions. All are treasonous."

"They must be given a trial."

"Must they?" Elizabeth's dark eyes glinted angrily. "Did *they* give my father the benefit of the legal fashion in registering protests?"

"If you have them privately executed," Caitrin said evenly, "you are as much in violation of our Constitution as they are themselves. Would you like to give Haven's other allies an opportunity to bring action against you? If you are impeached, then Prince Michael takes over a kingdom in chaos. Haven will certainly strike then."

Justin Zyrr raised his hand in question. "What's wrong with a trial? Daniel and I have found some evidence, but Marrou's confession and her recordings make conviction a certainty."

"Perhaps." The duchess steepled her fingers and looked over them, her eyelids half-closed. "Before I continue, let me state that I agree with Elizabeth. I want these bastards' heads. You may forget, Beth, but Roger was my big brother, my buddy, my—"

Her voice broke. Sipping water, she steadied herself with admirable poise.

"I am only too aware of the consequences of a public trial," she continued. "First of all, Howell is one of the three or four most important Crown Loyalists. Public doubt placed on him will weaken the authority of the party—and, don't forget, they are Cromarty's most reliable allies outside of his own Centrists.

"Secondly," she continued, "publicly trying Havenite spies— both of whom are members of Parliament—will most certainly start a witch hunt within our government. Members of the Lords hold their seats by inheritance, but those in the Commons are elected. And the Commons, if I may remind you, tend to support Crown policy. If incumbents can be challenged on their imagined Havenite leanings, the upset may lead to members being elected who will not tend to support the Crown."

Chou nodded, "And open a way for Haven to get more of its lackeys into Parliament."

"Exactly," the duchess agreed. "Who would accuse members elected on an anti-Haven platform of being a spies themselves?"

Queen Elizabeth listened, her mahogany face stiff, but dark spots of color on either cheek making her anger readily apparent. Duchess Henke glanced at her, read her mood, but continued relentlessly.

"Thirdly, Marrou would almost certainly be let off with only minor penalties. Her testimony is needed to condemn the others. Although she has not once hinted that she would plea bargain—"

Chou interrupted. "I hinted that the opportunity would be open to her and she simply looked affronted. She's ready to take her licks."

"No matter," Caitrin Winton-Henke said remorselessly. "Marrou's role in the trial cannot help but make her something of a hero in the public eye. Even if she is barred from holding office thereafter, as a private citizen she still will be in a position to influence others. Politically, her primary interests are domestic. She is actively opposed to our foreign policy. If we help to make a hero of her, we will be creating a powerful adversary."

The Queen opened her mouth, but her aunt's eyes locked on hers and her voice, cold with hard-held self-control, marched on across whatever she might have said.

"And finally, there are the foreign policy implications of making all this public. If we accuse the People's Republic of having ordered its paid agents to plan Roger's assassination and then convict those agents of that crime in open court, the very least that could happen would be severance of all diplomatic relations. And, yes, there's nothing I'd like better than to punch the bastards who paid for this right in the eye. But we're not *ready* yet, Beth. That's what Roger was doing, the reason they wanted him dead before he could *get* us ready. They don't want to hit us yet. We're too far away, and they've got too many problems closer to home. Besides, they probably figure they can use stooges like Seltman and Gwinner to keep undercutting our efforts to build up any effective opposition. But if it comes to a shooting war now, the odds are very, very good that we'd lose. If we avenge Roger's death, we risk losing the very thing he died to achieve."

Queen Elizabeth hit the flat of her palm against the table. Ariel's tail lashed back and forth.

"You make your points very well, Aunt Caitrin, but I cannot accept that these people will be permitted to go free. If a trial is unacceptable, I must take refuge in our Code Duello."

"Beth!" Justin gasped. "You couldn't!"

"Is the Queen not permitted the same recourse as a private citizen?" she responded angrily.

"Can you fire a pistol?" Chou asked, his tone one of idle curiosity, but his eyes burning.

"I can," Elizabeth said proudly. "My father made certain that both Michael and I had training."

"And how would you challenge them without making public the reasons for the challenge?" Duchess Henke said. "Remember, each one must accept your challenge. I do not believe Marvin Seltman could be so goaded. He knows that you have too much to lose if this becomes public."

"I will offer . . ." Elizabeth's voice faded, her eyes flooded with tears.

"And Marrou would have every reason to request a champion," Daniel Chou added. "And the opportunity for an enemy to offer her the use of a skilled specialist is too great to ignore."

Justin leaned across the table and took Elizabeth's hands in his, ignoring Ariel's growled threat.

"Beth, you'd be killed and for nothing. The end results of a duel would be sufficient to severely weaken the Star Kingdom."

Queen Elizabeth stayed silent for a long while, her downcast eyes studying the tabletop as if reviewing her options. When she spoke, her voice was hoarse with unshed tears.

"I most sincerely hope that I am never forced to refuse any of my subjects the choice you have taken from me today. I never realized that the Queen would be less protected by the law than the least of her subjects."

Caitrin Winton-Henke touched her arm. "Why do you think Roger so enjoyed dangerous sports? The monarch is given great power and privilege, but the cost is so high no sane person would pay it."

"Why should I then?" Elizabeth asked, her voice calm.

"Because you're a Winton," Caitrin answered, "and we all understand our duty."

"Give me your advice then," the Queen said, freeing one hand from Justin's grasp to blot the tears from her eyes, "on how we should handle this mess."

When the summons to Mount Royal came, Marvin Seltman considered taking advantage of one of the escape plans he had in place. Something about the little old man with the drooping mustaches who brought the invitation, rather than the more obvious threat of the two burly "bodyguards" who accompanied him, made him decide that such an attempt would be unlikely to succeed.

When they arrived at Mount Royal, the sight of his three co-conspirators quashed the vague hopes he had been nourishing that this was unrelated to his recent extra-legal activities. Swallowing a sigh, he permitted himself to be offered a seat and put his mind to salvaging what he could from the situation.

The group gathered in the council chamber did not offer a great deal of hope for a happy ending. There gathered were the Queen, Queen Mother Angelique, Crown Prince Michael, Dame Eliska, Duchess Winton-Henke, Justin Zyrr, and the little, wizened man who had brought him to the palace.

Queen Elizabeth's expression was cold as space, but the lashing tail of the treecat who crouched on the back of her chair gave lie to her calm.

"This meeting," the Queen began without further ceremony, "is to be regarded as a state secret, its minutes to be sealed until at least a century after my death. To speak of the proceedings will be considered treason—not that I expect that threat to trouble any of you greatly."

Her words were a beautiful bit of irony. They could be interpreted as meaning that she would not believe any here gathered capable of contemplating treason . . . or that she knew that several of them already were guilty of it. She continued:

"I am fully aware of—and possess incontrovertible, legally admissible *proof* of—the roles the four of you and the late Padraic Dover played in the death of King Roger the Third. In case you're curious, Padraic Dover met his death when he attempted to assault my promised husband. Through great good luck, my father's treecat was with Justin and saved his life."

Her words gave menace to the treecat growling at her own shoulder, but with a thrill of delight, Marvin Seltman realized that the 'cat was growling from frustration rather than because it intended to attack. His terrified fantasy that he would meet his death as had Dover vanished and he leaned back in his chair, crossing his legs with renewed confidence.

Queen Elizabeth's next words stole some of that confidence from him.

"Ms. Marrou and Earl Howell, from what I have learned, your crimes grew from a misplaced belief that our people were seriously threatened by King Roger's plans to expand the Star Kingdom's sphere of influence. That you turned to murder to right these wrongs rather than working within our established government was your folly. You are traitors, no doubt, but traitors who are, oddly enough, still loyal to the system you would circumvent.

"Mr. Seltman and Lady Gwinner, you have no such excuse for your actions. Not only are you murderous traitors, but we have undeniable proof that you are both in the pay of the People's Republic of Haven."

Gwinner made a small sound, as if she would, even at this late date, try to offer some excuse. The Queen's dark gaze silenced her:

"Don't try to tell us how you were led astray by Mr. Seltman. Your stock portfolio records reveal some very interesting additions that cannot be easily explained. You have had ample time to reconsider any 'bad influence.'"

Earl Howell stared at his former allies, the expression on his aristocratic features an undisguised mixture of horror and revulsion. His mouth shaped words that protocol would never permit him to speak aloud:

"I never knew. I never even suspected."

Elizabeth might have pitied him, but the memory of her father's twisted body, her mother's anguished scream, kept her hard.

"For reasons I do not intend to discuss," Queen Elizabeth continued, "I do not care to bring this matter to trial. Nor, although you have forfeited the protection of the law, will I have you quietly executed. Instead, I have other offers for you."

The dark eyes sought Howell. The man who sat there was a poor mockery of the bold politician who a few hours earlier had directed plans for his ascendance to the Regency.

"Willis Kemeny, I cannot strip you of your titles without the type of lengthy explanation I am certain both you and I would both prefer to avoid. Therefore, I request that you voluntarily renounce your seat in Parliament and pass it to your eldest daughter, Maralise. As she is a minor, a Regent will need to be appointed for her. I am certain that both you and I would be satisfied with LeBrun taking on that responsibility."

Aware that the Queen's offer would permit him to salvage both his life and his reputation, Howell rose to the occasion.

"Your Majesty," he said in his deep orator's voice. "I am most sincerely concerned about my health if I remain active in public life. The shock of learning that two of my associates were conspiring with the People's Republic of Haven has been the final blow to my constitution. I will obey your recommendations with alacrity."

The Queen nodded. "To make certain that you attend to

your health as you should, you will be required to report to a physician whose name will be given to you."

"I understand, Your Majesty."

"Jean Marrou."

"Your Majesty."

"In many ways, your crime, unlike that of the others gathered here, was motivated by principle and personal experience, not raw ambition. However, you did violate the oath to uphold the Constitution and the Crown that you swore when you took office, so your treason is no less heinous. Yet, in committing your crimes you neither violated a noble's particular vassalage to the Crown, nor treated with foreign powers."

Seltman, hearing the Queen rationalize for Marrou, was certain the blind bitch had bargained for her freedom. There was no way to confirm his suspicions . . . at least not now. Just give him time! Then Marrou would learn what it meant to cross him!

The Queen was continuing: "Nonetheless, I cannot permit you to retain your seat in Parliament. If you persist, there are subtle ways that I can make my disfavor known."

Marrou nodded solemnly. "I understand. Perhaps like Earl Howell, I should resign."

"I think that would be wise. Your popularity in the Commons is such that I would be more comfortable if you would relocate to a district where you are less well-known. Earlier, you made mention of your interest in Sphinxian treecats. My suggestion is that you relocate to one of the forest reserves and pursue your desire to acquire a companion."

Blind eyes wide, Marrou managed a polite, "Thank you, Your Majesty!"

"I must warn you," the Queen continued, "that your life will not be entirely safe. Remember that *all* treecats are empaths . . . and that I believe they're much more intelligent than even the 'experts' guess. You will not be able to fool *them* about who and what you are, and they may choose to take vengeance for the pain your actions helped cause Monroe."

A guttural growl from Ariel seemed to confirm this warning.

"However," the Queen went on, "if you are willing to take the risk, a place will be found for you."

Marrou held her head high. "Will I be permitted to take my family?"

"If they wish to go. However, I remind you that you may not speak of these matters to them."

"I understand. Will I also have a 'physician' to report to?"

Queen Elizabeth nodded. "You will, but my greatest assurance of your fidelity will be the treecats themselves."

"Will Monroe be returning to Sphinx?" Reasonably, Marrou looked rather frightened at the prospect.

"No." For the first time, Elizabeth smiled. "In the process of saving Justin's life, it appears Monroe has adopted him. They are both getting accustomed to the idea, but Monroe will be remaining with him."

Justin Zyrr touched her hand. "And what a wedding ours will be with two treecats as attendants!"

The Queen squeezed his fingers, but the coldness returned to her features as she surveyed the remaining two conspirators. For the first time, some of the anger she must feel surfaced.

"I can hardly express the disgust I feel for you," she said to Gwinner and Seltman. "These two plotted out of misplaced loyalty to the Star Kingdom. *Your* only reason was greed and ambition.

"For the safety of the Star Kingdom, you must be removed to where you cannot serve Haven's interests. Fortunately, Duchess Winton-Henke has suggested an ideal location for you. Basilisk is under our administration, yet it is far enough away that you will be unable to effectively influence Manticoran politics.

"Mr. Seltman, your business acumen and personal ambition are so well-known that no one will question your leaving to take a Crown-granted concession on Medusa."

"And if I refuse?" Seltman tried to sound menacing.

"Dame Eliska has done some analysis on this."

Dame Eliska consulted her screen and spoke as precisely as a computer: "A conservative analysis says that your refusal, combined with strategic placement of rumors, would destroy your political career quite neatly. You are up for re-election next year, are you not?"

Seltman nodded. He had held his seat for so long he had forgotten how easily it could be taken from him.

"Moreover," Paderweski said, "your business associates will hear those rumors. Projections say that there would be an immediate downturn. Following your failure to be re-elected, your profit base would be diminished by half and fall further thereafter. We would also make certain that your little 'extra' income was cut off entirely. And, of course, your Peep employers might well decide to tie up a loose end once you were no longer of use to them."

"And if I insisted on a trial?" Seltman roared.

"For what?" the Queen said coldly. "No one is accusing you of anything. The Crown is simply offering you a job."

Seltman crumpled, beaten, but even as he accepted the Queen's politely worded exile he was planning his comeback. They would forget him in time. Haven had agents on Medusa; he could contact them. Yes. . . .

The Queen had turned her attention to Paula Gwinner.

"You are somewhat more difficult to deal with," she said, "as I cannot remove your titles. However, I am also offering you a job on Basilisk as assistant to Daniel Chou."

The wiry old man straightened and gave Gwinner a casual wave. His mustaches flopped.

"Liaison to the natives," he said, "in a really lonely district. We probably won't see another human for months at a time. They don't even trade with humans. They're good folks, though. Smell a bit funny, but they are fiercely honorable."

"Mr. Chou will also be in a position to help Mr. Seltman with his new business venture, although I plan to assign him a partner in the concession. There are many loyal servants of the Crown who would be delighted with the opportunity."

Seltman glanced at Gwinner. Paula was clearly in shock. She probably didn't even hear the Queen's next words.

"Your vote, Lady Gwinner, will be handled by proxy. The only difficulty with your somewhat fluid voting record is that you have no strong allies. However, I am certain that Lord Jacob Wundt would be honored to transmit pertinent data to you and forward your votes."

Lady Gwinner straightened. Perhaps, Seltman thought, like him she assumed where there was life and freedom, there was hope.

"Your Majesty, I would be delighted to accept both your offer to relocate and your choice of a proxy."

Her words were spoken so gracefully and with such a genteel flourish that only the glint in her eyes belied them.

"Very good," the Queen said. "Due to the sensitive nature of this meeting, I am assigning all of you bodyguards. You will not know who they are, but I assure you, they will be there. You have my permission to leave."

Escorted by Daniel Chou, the four left.

"I hope the restrictions we've placed on them will be enough," Duchess Winton-Henke said.

"Hope is all we have," Elizabeth said. "Hope that the checks and balances of our system will preserve it. Isn't that what you've been telling me?"

"Precisely, dear." The duchess smiled. "And it's about time for lunch. I don't know about you, but I'm famished!"

❖   ❖   ❖

The Earl of North Hollow found himself wishing his son Pavel wasn't away on active service. He would have liked to tuck him behind a curtain somewhere and show him how a masterstroke was delivered.

Three of those he had summoned to him had come at his call. Only Jean Marrou had declined, sending a message that she was "relocating to Sphinx and retiring from public life."

No matter. Despite her brilliance in some areas, she was a small fish indeed. Seltman, Gwinner, and Howell, however, studied him as his butler passed around tea and cakes. Howell's eyes were dull, as if he had taken a mortal blow. Seltman and Gwinner, though . . . they were still sharp and suspicious.

When they were settled and the room sealed (except for his own recording equipment, of course), he rubbed his fat hands together, a parody of the jovial fat man.

"I have gathered you here to note that through my own channels I have become aware of certain of your actions."

He outlined their meetings, their connection with Padraic Dover, the purchasing of certain obscure electronic parts, Seltman's secret trip into the wilds on the day of King Roger's death. Unknown even to himself he provided more data than even Daniel Chou had ferreted out (although in fairness to Chou, Dover's actions had made such ferreting unnecessary).

When he had finished, he paused, pleased with himself.

"I could make this data public," he said, "but I feel that such is a Crown prerogative."

He chuckled greasily. "However, it could come to certain ears in a privy fashion. . . . Perhaps to LeBrun, Earl Howell? I simply wanted you to know this, in case I need you to be, shall we say, of service."

"I am retiring from Parliament," Howell said firmly.

"But an aristocrat never really retires, does he?" He favored Gwinner with a leer. "Or she."

Gwinner barred her teeth in a parody of a smile. "Sadly, my duty to the Crown takes me to Basilisk." *And none too soon, you old letch*, her eyes seemed to add.

"Lovely," the Earl purred. "Perhaps I shall call on you if I am out that way. Any more tea or cakes? I see that we understand each other. Do be thoughtful now, won't you? For now, my interest parallels that of the Crown. I would hate to see its policies jeopardized."

He centered his thin smile on Seltman. "King Roger was so very popular. I'm certain that any proof that you had a hand in his death might have unfortunate consequences."

Seltman shuddered, a thousand plots for his political res-
urrection dying under that chilly gaze.

"Of course," he said. "Your interests and those of the Crown
are as one."

The Earl of North Hollow looked around his sumptuously
appointed study. "The People's Republic of Haven doesn't care
for aristocracies, nor for personal ambition. I rather do, and
so will my son, Pavel, when I pass on. Remember that, won't
you?"

When another offer of tea and cakes was refused, he had
the butler show them to the door. Another day's work well
done.

Only when lunch was over and the servants dismissed, did
Elizabeth finally relax her stiff shoulders. Taking one each of
her mother and her brother's hands, she said in a small voice:

"Did I handle that all right? Can you forgive me for not
getting better vengeance for Dad?"

Queen Angelique, still in shock from the revelations of the
previous hour, could only nod proudly. Michael, however,
squeezed her hand tightly.

"You did the right thing, Beth. After watching you be Queen,
I don't think the Navy is going to be hard at all."

Elizabeth kissed him. "I'm glad you've made up your mind."

"Cousin Mike helped," Michael admitted bluntly. "She made
the Navy sound so good I can hardly bear the thought of not
making it in!"

"The people who help are the most important of all." Elizabeth rose from her chair. "Without Justin's willingness to listen to my worries, none of this might have been solved."

"Marrou might have confessed in any case," Justin admitted honestly.

"Perhaps, but indirectly Dover's attacking you was what made
her nervous and sent her from the viewing early enough to
overhear Gwinner and Seltman. And Dover attacked because
you questioned him." She took his arm. "Don't deny me the
pleasure of thanking you."

"Then thank Monroe, too," Justin said. "And I can't help
but feel that Daniel is getting poor reward for his service."

"Don't," Dame Eliska said surprisingly, stirring her coffee
with a fingertip. "Daniel is getting old and was beginning to
feel useless. This assignment will make his final years fruit-
ful and keep him from doing something self-defeating like
retiring."

Queen Elizabeth surveyed her loyal circle. "Aunt Caitrin is

almost certain to be confirmed as Regent. If not, I'm just too tired to worry about what we do next."

"My early indicators," Paderweski said, "and those of Duke Cromarty indicate that she will be."

Elizabeth smiled. "Tonight is my father's funeral. After that, we can begin again."

Queen Mother Angelique nodded and raised her glass in toast: "To new beginnings!"

Coffee mugs and crystal met with a soft chime as the rest took up the Queen Mother's toast:

"To new beginnings!"

The Hard Way Home

David Weber

"Look! Look up there!"

Ranjit Hibson twisted in his seat and leaned out over the chartered air bus's aisle, bending his head sharply and trying to see out the window on the far side as his sister pointed excitedly through it. The scenery was spectacular as the pilot took them up the Olympus Valley at an altitude well below that of the towering peaks on either side, but it had been equally so out of his own window. The stupendous mountains which thrust their huge caps of blindingly bright snow high and sheer against the painfully blue winter sky of Gryphon were awe inspiring, especially for someone who'd spent the last two years aboard an orbital habitat, but Ranjit couldn't see anything over there to explain the suddenness of her excitement.

"What?" he asked. "It's just more mountains, Susan."

She turned her head to show him an expression of exasperation dusted with reproach, and he gave himself a mental shake, for his comment had come out in an older brother's deflating tone, and he hadn't meant it to. At seventeen, he was five years older than Susan, and as his mother had just finished pointing out to him a few weeks ago (in a rather painful conference), he'd gotten into the habit of ditching his kid sister whenever he and his friends had something "interesting" to do.

It had been an accurate accusation, and that had hurt, because he loved Susan and he knew he truly had been brushing her off and shooing her away as if she'd become some

233

sort of inconvenience. And she could *be* an inconvenience, he admitted. But so could he, and so could anyone else, under the right—or wrong—circumstances. And the fact that Manticore Mineralogy and Mining, Ltd., which employed both their parents, had assigned them to the job of evaluating exploratory asteroid cores for the Hauptman Cartel in Manticore-B's Unicorn Belt for the past two years had only made it worse.

For all its massive resource wealth, the Unicorn could be a decidedly boring place to grow up. At least the Hibsons were assigned to Unicorn Eleven, one of the newer of the widely scattered orbital habitats Hauptman's had built to provide housing for its employees, and Unicorn Eleven had the most up to date living and recreational facilities imaginable. But most of its permanent work force tended to be very young—brand new geologists passing through for evaluation and final training before they were assigned to their own field teams, or equally young processing and R&D personnel just starting their way up *those* career ladders—with only a small, hard core of senior station training and management personnel. Kalindi and Liesell Hibson were two of the rare exceptions to that rule: the sort of specialist analysts who were too valuable to use in the field but who were most useful close to the actual exploration sites, where turnaround time could be minimized. For the last few years, Hauptman's teams had been working what had turned out to be an exceptionally rich portion of the Unicorn, and the need for extra hands was one reason Hauptman's had picked them up from Three-M on retainer to augment Unicorn Eleven's normal work force. As consultants from outside Hauptman's normal career tracks, they fell right in the middle of the gap in the age spread aboard the station: younger than the permanent senior personnel, but older than the transient newbies. As a result, they felt just a bit awkward whenever they tried to socialize with either, and the fact that they weren't officially part of the "Hauptman team" tended to exacerbate that problem.

What was true for them was twice as true for their kids, however. There simply weren't many children on Unicorn Eleven, and that was one area in which the invention of the prolong anti-aging treatments didn't help a lot, either. Prolong was tending to erase a lot of the age-based divisions which had always been humankind's lot, which would probably be a good thing once civilization fully adjusted to the consequences. Of course, first they'd have to have prolong long enough to figure out what all those consequences *were*, Ranjit supposed. It had been available in the Star Kingdom for only sixty-four years. To someone his age, that seemed like forever, but it was less than an eye-blink in terms of a culture's adjustment to so monumental a change. One immediate effect was readily apparent, however: people were waiting considerably longer, on average, to have children. His own parents had rushed things more than many of their contemporaries in that regard, because both of them loved children and they'd wanted to get started early, but that was increasingly rare. Which meant that, despite a total population on the order of eight thousand, there were less than three hundred kids on Unicorn Eleven, and those who were present tended to be the children of the senior personnel and so, on average, older themselves. At seventeen, Ranjit himself was below the median age of the children aboard the station, whereas Susan, at twelve, was actually the youngest one of all.

Worse, the station was far enough out from Gryphon, the inhabited planet of the Manticore Binary System's G2 secondary component, that the light-speed transmission lag between them was very noticeable. At the moment, it ran to just over twelve minutes each way, and it was growing steadily longer as the relative motions of Unicorn Eleven and Gryphon took them further and further apart, which made it impractical for station personnel to tie into the Gryphon planetary education net as they would normally have done. The Hauptman Cartel had set up an excellent school system within the habitat, and Ranjit rather enjoyed the novel experience of having direct, physical access to his human instructors. But the lack of any real-time link to the planetary net meant Susan had been denied even the electronic friendships with classmates she might have enjoyed under other circumstances. She'd made a couple of long-distance friends aboard Unicorn Nine and Unicorn Ten, the closest pair of Hauptman habitats to their own, but that was it, and Ranjit knew his sister had grown increasingly lonely. She hadn't needed her own big brother making it worse, but that was exactly what he'd done. Which was the reason he had assured his parents that if they allowed Susan to come along on the field trip Mr. Gastelaars, Unicorn Eleven's chief administrator, had arranged, he would keep an eye on her.

His father, especially, had been hesitant to let her go, for several reasons. For one, she would be the youngest student on the trip, and it would be the first time she had ever been allowed to make such a lengthy trip unaccompanied by at least one of her parents. For another, the Hibsons were natives of Manticore itself, and the capital planet was a warm world where skiing opportunities were rare. Susan had been only a beginner-level skier (on snow, anyway) when her parents were assigned to Unicorn Eleven, and she'd had precious little opportunity for practice since, but Kalindi Hibson had a pretty shrewd notion that his headstrong daughter would insist she was more experienced than she actually was unless someone sat on her firmly. And for yet a third, he knew that all of Ranjit's friends would also be along—including Monica Gastelaars, the chief administrator's strikingly attractive daughter, who also happened to be seventeen years old—and questioned just how much time Ranjit would truly devote to keeping an eye on Susan.

Their mother had come down on Ranjit and Susan's side, however. Liesell had insisted that Susan was old enough for the trip and pointed out that the group would be accompanied by six adults, most of whom were child care professionals and *all* of whom were experienced skiers. Moreover, the Athinai Resort, the largest and best known on Gryphon (which meant in the Manticore Binary System) was accustomed to this sort of field trip. That was one of the main reasons it had been chosen when the outing was planned, and the Hauptman Cartel had arranged for the resort to provide full-time instructors, all experienced with young people, to ride herd on their youthful charges on the actual slopes. It was unlikely that even their inventive daughter would be able to put much over on that many veteran kid-watchers, she'd suggested. And if Susan *could*, then her parents needed to find out about it now so that they could take proper precautions— like locking her in her room until she was twenty. Besides, it was past time Susan got a chance to meet some other youngsters her own age. Then Liesell had sealed the deal by unscrupulously extracting an explicit promise from Ranjit that he would *not* allow his own interests to distract him from maintaining a close watch on Susan. He'd given her his word, but not without a certain sinking feeling which suggested to him that he had, in fact, been planning on spending just a little less time with his sister than he'd originally tried to allow his parents (and himself) to believe he had in mind.

Which was how he came to find himself looking out Susan's window and mentally kicking himself for raining on her parade.

"I mean they look a lot like the ones on this side," he told her now, waving a hand at the peaks beyond the armorplast and making his tone an apology for his earlier dismissiveness. "They're pretty spectacular, but—"

"I didn't mean the *mountains*," Susan said. "Look! See the pinnaces?"

"Pin—?"

Ranjit unlatched his seat harness and crossed the aisle to kneel beside Susan's seat in order to get a better look through her window, and his eyebrows rose. She was right. Those *were* pinnaces up there—six of them, in fact, all in Navy markings. They were headed in the opposite direction at what appeared to be (barely) subsonic speed, with their variable geometry wings mostly swept, and their shadows raced across the snowy summits beneath them.

"What are they doing?" he wondered aloud.

"Making a drop," Susan said promptly. She didn't—quite—add "of course," but he heard her anyway and jabbed a *"sure they are"* sideways glance at her, then darted his eyes back to the pinnaces.

He could see more details of the sleek, hungry-looking craft now, and his pulse went just a bit faster as they scorched over the peaks. They were paralleling the valley's long axis, heading down it on a direct reciprocal of the air bus's course, but at a considerably higher altitude to clear the four and five thousand-meter summits of the valley's walls. They were also flying a nape-of-the-earth profile that was much tighter than they could have managed in pure air foil mode, because they were bouncing up and down over peaks as if they were tennis balls. Ranjit was pretty sure they had to be riding their counter-grav hard to pull off some of those maneuvers, and his stomach lurched in sympathy as he tried to imagine what it must be like for their passengers. Some of the other members of the ski group had seen them now, and he heard other voices repeating his own question about their intentions. And then, suddenly, the pinnaces turned to sweep out across the valley. Their flight path angled well astern of the air bus, but the bus pilot obviously knew they were back there and had decided to give his youthful customers a little extra treat. The vehicle turned sharply, then went into hover, offering a magnificent view down the snow-and-stone vista of the deep, narrow river valley which also kept the pinnace flight in clear sight.

No, Ranjit realized. Not just a single pinnace flight. Another half-dozen of the sleek craft must have been coming down his side of the valley at the same time without his even noticing their presence. Now they came shooting out to meet the ones Susan had spotted, and as their vectors crossed, all twelve of them slowed abruptly and distance-tiny figures spilled from them. The figures were too far away for Ranjit to tell whether or not they wore battle armor, but he felt a thrill of excitement as they plummeted towards the valley floor. Then they slowed magically as their grav canopies popped, and he watched raptly as they continued drifting downward with deceptive gentleness.

"*Told* you they were making a drop," Susan said with exasperating complacency, and Ranjit gave her another, sharper look. She only smiled sweetly, then batted her sea-green eyes at him, and, despite himself, he felt his own lips twitch in an answering grin.

"You were right this time," he conceded, "but I think it was a lucky guess."

"Lucky guess?" Susan repeated, then tossed her head with a snort. "If you'd been paying attention," she told him pityingly, "you'd've noticed that those were the new Mark Twenty-Six Skyhawks. Didn't you see the extra pulser under the nose and the ventral and after gun turrets? Or the extra underwing hard points?" She snorted again, harder. "I bet you didn't even notice the new chaff dispensers or the ECM pod on the vertical stabilizer!"

"Ah, no," Ranjit admitted. "I must have missed those somehow."

"Well you shouldn't have," she said severely. "Because if you'd happened to recognize what they were, you might have recalled that according to my last issue of the *Royal Marine Institute Record*, the Mark Twenty-Sixes've been specifically optimized for the Marine Corps' use."

"They had *Navy* markings, Sooze," Ranjit pointed out, but there wasn't much hope in his voice. Susan was only an average student in most of her courses, but she had a mind like a docking tractor when her interest was truly engaged, and she was seldom wrong about anything to do with one of her pet obsessions, however trivial her information might have seemed to any normal person. In fact, if he wanted to be honest about it, he couldn't actually recall the last time she *had* been wrong about one of them. Not that he intended to bring that up at this particular moment.

"Well of course they did," Susan said, turning to give him the full advantage of her pitying expression. "Every pinnace and shuttle in inventory belongs to the Navy . . . officially. But the Corps were the ones who really wrote the requirements for the new Skyhawks, because they wanted a better combined delivery and fire support platform for space-to-ground assaults; the Navy just paid for 'em and built 'em. Well, they provide the ships to carry them around, too, of course, but that's what chauffeurs are for." She wrinkled her nose in tolerant contempt for such useless sorts, then shrugged. "But if a bunch of pinnaces designed to double as light assault shuttles are flying around in the middle of the Attica Mountains playing NOE with mountain peaks, what do *you* think they're up to? Photo mapping for a new spaceport?"

"You know, you can be amazingly irritating when you put your itty-bitty mind to it," Ranjit observed, and she grinned.

"You only say that when I prove you're a doof," she shot back. "Of course, that *does* seem to happen a lot, doesn't it?"

"Just take your victory and go home with it while you still can, kid," he advised her, and punched her shoulder lightly.

"Ha! One of my *many* victories, you mean!"

Ranjit smiled again, but he also let it drop. He'd had too much experience arguing with her to do anything else.

Much as he loved his sister, he was convinced that her genetic code must have dropped a stitch somewhere. She was a slight, slender child who shared with Ranjit the dark complexion they'd both inherited from their father, but unlike her brother, she had their mother's green eyes to go with it, which made for a startling contrast even (or especially, perhaps) after so many centuries of genetic homogenization. That was what people always noticed first about her; it was only later that they realized her design schematic included nothing remotely resembling a reverse gear. Susan Hibson had a whim of steel and absolutely no idea of how to give in—gracefully or otherwise—to anyone, anywhere, over anything, and Ranjit couldn't remember the last time she'd truly set her mind on a goal and failed to achieve it.

It was, perhaps, unfortunate that she persisted in setting those goals to suit her own idiosyncratic interests. Devoting just a little of that determination (one might even say obstinacy, if one were careful to say it quietly enough that she couldn't hear one) to academic endeavors might have produced a radical improvement in her grades, for example. But that simply wasn't an area of particular concern for her. No, all of *her* attention was focused, for some reason no one else had ever been able to fathom, on the Royal Manticoran Marines.

It *had* to be something genetic, Ranjit mused. Some previously unsuspected mutation which had been nurtured by the Star Kingdom's ongoing military buildup against the People's Republic of Haven. Certainly no one else in the family had ever been especially interested in a military career, and if Susan simply had to be bitten by the military bug, why couldn't she at least have decided she hungered for the Navy? The Marines, even more than the Royal Army, were one of the areas of military service in which size and physical strength still mattered, and Susan was never going to be a big woman. Kalindi Hibson was wiry and muscular, but he also stood just under a hundred and sixty-three centimeters tall. Ranjit, who favored their mother's side of the family more than Susan did, was already over one-eighty, but Susan took very much after her father when it came to size and bulk, and he doubted she would ever break one-fifty-five. Yet where Ranjit had no particular desire to embrace the rigors of a military lifestyle—especially not if, as the alarmists insisted was likely in light of the Peeps' expansion in the Star Kingdom's direction, he might also someday get to enjoy the experience of having ill-intentioned strangers actually shooting at him—and found the very thought of boot camp revolting, Susan actually looked *forward* to the experience.

It was all profoundly unnatural, Ranjit thought, settling back into his own seat and fastening his harness once more. And if he were honest, it was a little frightening, too. He was young enough to have trouble truly believing in his own mortality, but the thought of having those ill-intentioned strangers shooting at his kid sister instead of at him was a chilling one. Which was probably one reason he didn't let himself consider it very much.

At least it'll be another four-plus T-years before she can legally enlist, even with parental approval, he thought now. *In the meantime, I guess I'll just have to go along with Dad and hope that it's a "phase" she'll grow out of. Of course*—he grimaced out his own window—*I don't recall her ever having grown out of any* other *phases, but hey! There's always a first time, right? Yeah, sure. Right.*

He snorted to his reflection in wry amusement and returned his attention to the craggy mountain walls.

"I thought it went better than last time, Ma'am," Lieutenant Hedges said.

The young, blond-haired lieutenant smiled hopefully at HMS *Broadsword*'s tall executive officer, but his smile faded as the Exec returned his look dispassionately. The prick-eared treecat on her shoulder cocked his head, whiskers quivering as his grass-green gaze joined his person's chocolate-brown, almond eyes in their contemplation of the heavy cruiser's boat bay officer, and Hedges fought an urge to swallow. Lieutenant Commander Harrington had been one of the Star Kingdom's

first third-generation prolong recipients, and the later generations of the life-extending treatments had a pronounced tendency to stretch out the physical maturation process. As a
result, she looked almost indecently young for her present rank,
especially with the close-cropped hair style she favored, and
she was also a quiet, soft-spoken sort. He had never heard her
so much as raise her voice or use even the mildest profanity,
and he supposed some unwary souls might have added that
to her youthful appearance and decided she was unsure of
herself.

Upon better acquaintance, however, those individuals would
quickly discover that her triangular face, with its strong patri-
cian nose and severe, sharply carved features, made an excellent mask for whatever she happened to be thinking at any
given moment. It could also freeze the hardiest malefactor in
his tracks without so much as a word, and if Hedges had never
heard her raise her voice, he *had* heard that same, calm soprano
sound as if it were shaving off slivers of battle steel while its
owner . . . discussed some unfortunate's shortcomings. Captain Tammerlane, *Broadsword*'s commanding officer, was a
genial, almost paternal soul. No one who'd ever served under
him could doubt his competence, but he was definitely considered an easy-going CO. Which was what made Harrington
the perfect exec for him. She was patient, just, and fairminded,
and she would go light-seconds out of her way to help or
support anyone whom she was convinced was genuinely trying to do his job. But she had zero tolerance for fools or
gratuitous stupidity . . . and somewhat less than that for anyone
she considered a slacker. She had *Broadsword* running like a
fine chrono, and no one would ever *dare* let himself become
part of a problem the Exec had no choice but to bring to the
Captain's attention.

Now those level brown eyes continued to consider Hedges
for several short eternities, and he felt his hands try to flut-
ter nervously, as if to check for some minor flaw in his appearance—like an open trousers fly or a large, crusty blotch of dried
egg on his tunic—which he'd somehow failed to notice for
himself.

"Well, yes," she said finally. "I suppose it *was* better. At least
there were no mid-airs, were there?"

Her voice was perfectly conversational, but Hedges winced.
The barely averted mid-air collision between one of *Broadsword*'s pinnaces and two from HMS *Cutlass* which had been
the focal point of yesterday's exercises had been almost entirely
his fault, and he knew it as well as the exec did.

She let him reflect upon that for several more seconds, then smiled slightly.

"In fact, I believe every one of our birds got home without a hull scratch or even a single last-minute evasion maneuver, and *Halberd* and *Cutlass* report the same."

"Yes, Ma'am." Hedges winced again, but only inwardly this time, and her smile grew.

"Not only that, but every one of Major Stimson's squads hit within fifty meters of its exact drop point. In snow, in the Attica Mountains, in winter, no less. I wouldn't want to suggest that we're establishing any trends here, Mister Hedges, but I suppose we *could* call that an improvement if we really wanted to." She paused one more beat, and then her smile became something suspiciously like a grin as she added, "The Captain certainly called it that when he discussed the drop-ex with Commander Nouaya Tyumen, at any rate."

"He did?" Hedges couldn't keep himself from blurting out the question, and his face went magenta as Harrington chuckled. Her 'cat's cheerful bleek of laughter echoed her amusement, and Hedges blushed even darker before his own sense of humor came to his rescue and he grinned back.

"Yes, he did, Johnny," she said, and gave him a gentle pat on the shoulder. She didn't do that often, and he beamed at her as he savored the rare sign of approval.

"On the other hand," she added more warningly, "we've still got another week of exercises. Plenty of time for us to screw up thoroughly if we put our minds to it. So let's not do that, right?"

"Aye, aye, Ma'am!" Hedges assured her, still grinning. "I'll have those birds running as regularly as Andermani air buses, Ma'am. And my coxswains will put those Marines down anywhere you want to aim them—guaranteed!"

"Good, Johnny. Very good." She patted his shoulder again, then reached up to scratch her 'cat's chin. "But you've got a lot to do to make good on all those boasts, I imagine. So let's be about it, shall we?"

"The beginners' slope," Susan Hibson said in tones of profound disgust. "'*Kiddy Hill!*' Can you *believe* that?"

Her breath smoked in the morning sunlight, and she kicked viciously at a bank of piled snow the maintenance remotes had swept from a walkway. A chunk of ice exploded into the air and disintegrated into a rainbow-spray, and she glowered at it angrily.

"I did warn you, you know," Ranjit said in a cautiously

neutral voice, then shrugged as she glared up at him. "It's their job, Sooze."

"They could at least let me *try* the intermediate runs," she protested, and he shook his head.

"They're not going to let you go out and break your neck on a slope you're not ready for no matter what you say."

"I am so ready for the intermediate slopes!"

"Oh?" He cocked his head at her. "And just how well did you do in the sim this morning?"

"That's not fair! Besides, everybody knows sims aren't really like the real thing!"

"Didn't ask that," he told her. "I asked how well you did in it."

"Not well enough—obviously," she admitted through gritted teeth. She looked as if she wanted to hit something, but Ranjit's smile held too much sympathy to make him a legitimate target, so she kicked the snow again. Harder.

"It's not fair, anyway," she grumbled. "Nobody told us they'd have sims at all! Or that they'd use the stinking things this way, either."

"No, they didn't. On the other hand, I can't help wondering if maybe Ms. Berczi didn't know all about it."

"Huh!" Susan stopped kicking snow to consider that, then grunted. "I bet you're right. It's just the kind of thing she *would* do, isn't it?"

Her tone did not suggest that she thought well of Berczi at that particular moment, but Ranjit was sure that would pass. Csilla Berczi was the head chaperone for their trip. She was also in charge of the history curriculum for Unicorn Eleven and one of Susan's favorite teachers, which probably had something to do with the fact that she had attained the rank of major in the Marines before a training injury pushed her into early retirement. She obviously liked Susan, and she'd become a source of discreet support for the girl's military ambitions, but she was hardly the sort to put up with any nonsense where her own responsibilities were concerned.

That was why Ranjit was privately certain that she had, indeed, known all about the Athinai Resort's simulators. He'd been surprised by their sophistication himself, although he didn't intend to admit that to Susan; an older brother had a certain image to live up to, after all, and managing that with Susan for a sister was already harder than it ought to be. But it would appear Athinai's cash flow supported a much more capable installation than he'd expected, for the simulators' VR had been as good as or better than any full-sensy he'd been allowed to play around in, which put it several cuts above the plebeian, barely adequate "instruction grade" sim he'd anticipated. Indeed, the combination of late-generation sensory input, physical interaction with "skis" which had produced a totally convincing illusion of unlimited mobility in all axes, and judicious use of counter-grav and a cunning wind-tunnel effect had sucked him in completely. Within the first ten seconds, he had completely forgotten that he wasn't truly on the slopes of Mount Pericles, high above Athinai, and he grinned wryly as he recalled his own high-pitched shouts of glee and wondered what the sim operators had thought of them.

He could see where it made excellent sense to allow patrons to dust off their skiing skills (if necessary) in the safety of the simulators before letting them loose on the actual slopes, and he was grateful that such a training device would be available to him. (He also intended to ask Mr. Gastelaars if Unicorn Eleven might not be able to find the budget for one or two of them back home, as well, which was something else he didn't plan on discussing with Susan just now.) But the resort had also used it to sort out the real skill levels of its youthful charges, and his mother had been right. Susan *hadn't* been able to talk her examiners into passing her for the more challenging slopes.

"It's not the end of the world, kiddo," he offered after a moment. "We're here for ten days, you know, and you're a fast learner. They'll let you off the beginner slopes a lot sooner than you may think right now."

"Yeah. Right," Susan snorted, then stabbed him with a sharp-edged green gaze. "And just what skill level did they assign *you?*"

"Advanced-intermediate," he replied without thinking, and then swore at himself mentally as something flickered behind her expression. Susan might complain bitterly when she was held back from something she wanted to do, and she was capable of arguing her points with unendurable tenacity and earnestness, but one thing she did not do was sulk or go hunting for sympathy. Which didn't mean Ranjit hadn't learned to recognize the times when a part of her wanted to do those things. He'd seen that same flicker in her eyes before, often enough to know it for a sure sign of her refusal to whine, and he reached out to lay a hand on her shoulder.

"Hey, just because they said I could go advanced-intermediate if I wanted to doesn't mean I do want to," he told her. "I almost busted my butt twice on the sim run for that difficulty level. It wouldn't hurt me a bit to start out on the beginner slopes myself when it's for real—at least until I'm sure I've got myself sorted out. For that matter, it'd probably hurt a lot *less* to do it there, now that I think about it!"

"You don't have to do that just to keep me company," Susan muttered. "I'm not a baby, Ranjit."

"Didn't say you were," he said, and gave her shoulder a squeeze. "A pain in the butt, and the neck, and several other places I can think of, yeah. *That* you are. But a baby?" He shook his head, and her lips twitched as she fought not to grin up at him. "But you're my kid sister, too, and I'm serious about wanting to ease back into things myself, so why not kill two birds with one stone? I'll keep you company on the beginners' slopes, for the first day or so, anyway, until I'm fairly sure I won't break something I'll need later. By that time, they may've cleared you for something a little tougher on your own. And even if they haven't, you'll probably have made a bunch of new friends amongst the other 'retards,' right?"

"Do you really want to do that?" she demanded, eying him suspiciously, and he shrugged.

"Heck, no! That's why I only suggested it after you stuck a pulser in my ribs!" She laughed, and he grinned, then went on more seriously. "I'm not saying I'd want to spend the whole trip stuck there, of course. But I can spare a day or two to keep my sister company in her exile without wrecking my entire social calendar, you know. And *that* part of it I do want to do. Okay?"

"Okay," she said almost shyly, then dropped her gaze to the snow at her feet for a long moment. "And . . . thanks, Ranjit," she added after a moment in a gruff little voice, and gave him a fierce, rare hug before she went scampering off.

" . . . so the weather looks like it's thinkin' about bein' more than a little 'iffy,' " Commander Anthony Agursky, Fourteenth Baron of Novaya Tyumen, drawled, and let his eyes sweep around the officers in the briefing room aboard *Broadsword*. The commander had been pulled out of his comfortable office at the Bureau of Ships and sent out to take charge of the Skyhawk evaluation program, and the brand new heavy cruiser was the senior ship of the small squadron the Navy and Marines had assembled for that purpose. She also had the most room for extra personnel and the biggest (and most comfortable) briefing rooms . . . and visiting officer's quarters. Those qualities would have made *Broadsword* the inevitable choice for someone like Novaya Tyumen, even if Captain Tammerlane hadn't been the impromptu squadron's senior officer. After all, he *was* an Agursky of Novaya Tyumen. In fact, one might say he was *the* Agursky of Novaya Tyumen—a point he rarely chose to allow anyone to forget—and that made the newest and best ship available no more than his just due.

The commander was a man of average height and build, but with coal-black hair and a complexion that was intensely pale, almost pallid. He also had a particularly pronounced version of the exaggerated drawl some segments of the more recent generations of the Star Kingdom's aristocracy had begun affecting. Coupled with a certain supercilious air and a taste for dandyism when it came to the tailoring of his uniforms, that drawl had inspired many an unwary soul to mark him down as some sort of over-bred, self-absorbed, slow-witted drone who'd gotten this far solely on the basis of his prominent family's undoubted political enfluence.

Which, Honor Harrington reminded herself, *could be a very unfortunate mistake for someone to make, because one thing he* isn't *is "slow-witted." On the other hand,* she allowed herself a mental grimace, though no sign of it showed on her face, *three out of four isn't all that bad.*

"Yes?" Novaya Tyumen asked now, as a hand rose.

"You said 'iffy,' Sir," Lieutenant Hedges said. "Does that mean we may drop below approved minimums?"

"If we dropped below approved minimums, then the weather would scarcely be 'iffy' any longer, now would it, Lieutenant?" Novaya Tyumen observed in that irritating drawl. "In that case, conditions would be definitely unacceptable, and the mission would be scrubbed, no?"

"Ah, yes, Sir." Hedges glanced at his own superior from the corner of one eye, but Honor simply sat there, her expression one of composed attentiveness. She and Novaya Tyumen had enjoyed two or three icy exchanges already. She liked Hedges, and she didn't intend to leave him twisting in the wind if what she expected happened, but she did intend to choose her ground with care. She might be *Broadsword*'s executive officer, but she was also junior to Novaya Tyumen, and BuShips and BuPlan had placed him in command of the evaluation exercise. That made for a somewhat convoluted chain of command, and she'd already discovered that Novaya Tyumen was one of those officers who always pushed the outer limit of his current authority to the max.

Hedges wasn't aware of everything that was happening between her and Novaya Tyumen, but he'd obviously figured out there was something more than showed on the surface.

Now he glanced at her again, as if seeking some sort of sign, then cleared his throat.

"What I meant to inquire, Sir, was whether or not we should plan for the possibility that we might have to scrub if weather conditions do worsen even further."

"I see." Novaya Tyumen tipped back in his chair and regarded the lieutenant for several seconds, then swiveled his eyes to Honor. She gazed back at him calmly, but the treecat perched on the back of her chair lashed the very tip of his tail back and forth.

Hedges doubted Novaya Tyumen could see that tail from where he sat, yet there was something ominous about his outwardly neutral expression as he gazed at Hedges' immediate superior. Some sort of unspoken hostility seemed to lie between him and Harrington, like dark, black swamp water over a bog of quicksand. As far as Hedges could tell, it came primarily from Novaya Tyumen's side, although it was hard to be sure. The very qualities of self-possession and poise which served Harrington so well in other ways made her emotions damnably hard to read when she chose to conceal them.

"I should hope, Lieutenant," the baron said after a moment, projecting his voice to the entire briefing room yet never taking his eyes from Honor's face, "that every officer in this compartment *always* plans for the possibility of havin' a mission scrubbed. Or revised. Or any one of the other thousand-and-one things that can change between a final briefin' and an operation's actual execution. Is there some special reason you or your ship might find this a little more difficult than the rest of us?"

Hedges inhaled sharply, and the temperature in the compartment seemed to drop several degrees. He felt other officers stiffen in their chairs at the unexpected, contemptuous bite in the commander's drawl, and fought down a sudden, dangerous desire to tell this aristocratic ass just what he truly thought of him. But Novaya Tyumen was not only his superior officer; he was also the son of one of the clique of nobles who ran the Conservative Association in the House of Lords. Someday he would pass his barony on to his own heir and replace it with his father's earldom, and everyone in the compartment knew it. Worse, the baron struck Hedges as precisely the sort of person who would delight in using the enormous political pull his birth gave him to swat an irritating junior, and his tone suggested that any answer to his question would be the wrong one.

Hedges started to answer it anyway, if with rather more

circumspection than he truly wanted to exert, but another voice spoke before he could.

"I believe that what Lieutenant Hedges intended, Sir," Honor said coolly, her crisp Sphinx accent cutting across Novaya Tyumen's drawl like a chill alpine wind, "was to ask you, as the primary mission coordinator, to share your own contingency planning with us all. Since you've had the weather information longer than any of the rest of us, your thoughts on the subject are undoubtedly more . . . complete than our own." She smiled slightly, but her eyes were dangerous and she heard a soft popping sound as Nimitz's extended claws penetrated the fabric of her chair back. "I'm sure we'd all find them a most useful starting point for our own thinking," she added.

There was nothing overtly challenging in her tone or choice of words, but no one missed the implication, and Hedges suddenly found himself wishing he had never opened his mouth. Novaya Tyumen's dark eyes flashed angrily in his pale face, his lips tightened, and his right hand—the only one visible, since the left was in his lap—clenched into a fist on the briefing room conference table as those eyes locked with Harrington's.

"I see," he said after a moment, and his drawl was in total (if transitory) abeyance. Then he twitched his shoulders and smiled. It wasn't a very convincing smile, more of a grimace that bared his teeth at Honor, but his voice sounded closer to normal when he spoke again. "In that case, Commander Harrington, I suggest we continue with the briefin'. Perhaps his questions will be answered in passin'. And if they aren't, there should be plenty of time to discuss them afterward, don't you agree?"

"I feel confident of it, Sir," Honor replied. Her level soprano was unruffled, but once again Hedges seemed to sense the clash of bared steel between his superiors, and he wondered just what the devil he had stumbled into the middle of.

"Very good. In that case, I'll ask Ensign Haverty to give us the full weather brief," Novaya Tyumen said, "and we'll follow that up with the mission parameters. Ensign Haverty?"

He nodded to the ensign, then leaned back in his chair, his expression outwardly affable, but his hard, dark eyes never wavered from Honor Harrington's face.

Huge clouds swirled across the surface of the planet Gryphon. From orbit, an observer could clearly see the storm front's ominous cloud wrack flowing up the long, deep trough of the Olympus Valley like some dangerous river, probing for openings in the mighty rampart of the Attica Mountains, and Ensign Yolanda Haverty, RMN Bureau of Ships, watched it with wary respect. Gryphon's axial tilt of almost twenty-seven degrees always made for . . . interesting weather patterns, but this one promised to be unusually lively even for Gryphon, and it was Haverty's job to keep an eye on it for Commander Novaya Tyumen.

She grimaced at the thought, for she didn't much care for the baron. She would far rather have served under someone like Lieutenant Commander Harrington, although, to be fair, Harrington was daunting enough in her own way. She didn't seem the sort to indulge in the sort of sharp-tongued goading which appeared to amuse Novaya Tyumen, but she clearly demanded the very best of her people, and there was something detached about her. Not as if she didn't care about her people, for she obviously did, but more of a sense of . . . watchfulness. An impression that there was something poised and cat-like behind her eyes, observing every single thing that happened but reserving judgment and eternally considering options and alternatives and responsibilities.

But how much of that is real and how much of it comes from the fact that I know she's got a treecat? Haverty mused. The six-limbed, empathic 'cats were very rare off their native planet of Sphinx. Indeed, Harrington was the only person Haverty had ever actually met who had been adopted by one of them, and the ensign wondered if the 'cat's presence had somehow shaped her own perception of the lieutenant commander's personality.

I don't think so, though, she reflected after a moment. *And even if the 'cat does make me see her a bit differently, it doesn't change the fact that she* leads *her people instead of kicking them from behind!*

Standards. That was the word for it. Harrington set the standards which she required of herself at levels which were considerably higher than anyone else would have demanded of her . . . then went right ahead and met them. That was what made her daunting. Not because she would jump down someone's throat for failing to hold themselves to the same rigorous measure, but because she *challenged* them to meet it without fanfare or goading, and that made it unthinkable to disappoint her in the first place.

Novaya Tyumen wasn't like that, unfortunately. His attitudes might seem almost perfunctory to the casual observer, especially covered by the drawling pretense of boredom which he projected so well, but the truth was very different. He, too, watched everyone about him, but he was more spider than cat. Rather than challenge people to meet the standards he demanded of *himself*, he watched and waited until someone failed to meet the standards he demanded of *them* and then turned himself into the worst nightmare that person had ever had. That languid, aristocratic accent could cut like a razor, and he used it with the precision of a surgeon's scalpel. It wasn't so much the words he chose as it was the ineffable contempt with which he infused them, his obvious belief that only an imbecile could possibly have misunderstood any instructions that *he* gave, and that any failure in executing them could only be the consequence of abject stupidity or willful negligence. Worse, he obviously relished the opportunity to slice and dice anyone unfortunate enough to give him the chance. He *enjoyed* slamming people who couldn't slam back, and he would never have dreamed of risking the ire of one of his own superiors to defend or protect one of his juniors the way Harrington had deflected him from Hedges.

That clearly apparent contempt for anyone he considered his inferior was the worse of the only two real failings Ensign Haverty had so far detected in him. (*Professional* failings, that was; the list of things she detested in him on a personal level grew longer with each passing day.) The other was a tendency to ignore the unlikely in his planning and depend on his natural intelligence and ability—both of which were considerable, she admitted—to wiggle out of trouble if it persisted in happening anyway. He wouldn't tolerate that sort of approach in anyone else, and Haverty was a recent enough product of the Academy to feel outraged by his willingness to adopt it for himself, but she had to admit that so far it seemed to have always worked for him.

And however much she might dislike that trait, it was far less disruptive and demoralizing than the contemptuous (and public) verbal flayings he was in the habit of handing out. Like the way he'd started in on Lieutenant Hedges. It wasn't that Novaya Tyumen wasn't good at his job, for in many ways he performed at a high level of competence. Indeed, Haverty had already realized that there were very few officers who could have taught her more about the inner workings of their joint BuShips specialization than he could. It was just that he could be so . . . so *nasty* about the lessons he chose to impart and how he taught them.

The ensign grimaced wryly at the weather front, then frowned. It was already a rough night down there, and from the look of things, it was going to get rougher. She really ought to bring it to Novaya Tyumen's attention, but she hated the very thought of that. He was undoubtedly sound asleep at the moment, which meant he would start out by tearing a strip off of her for disturbing him. And it would be even worse if he thought the fact that the weather was, indeed, headed for the wrong side of "iffy" might make him seem less than on top of things after the morning's discussion. He would undoubtedly take *that* out on her, as well, and after that, he'd make everyone else on his field test staff totally miserable by dragging them all in and demanding that they produce the contingency plans (which, Haverty knew, didn't actually exist, whatever he might have implied) for canceling or modifying the drop. And they'd have to put them all together within the next five or six hours so that he could casually (and triumphantly) produce them for people like Harrington and Hedges.

She checked the readouts again. *Still within parameters so far,* she noted, comparing them to the notes Novaya Tyumen had jotted down for her. *Of course, it's going to come an awful lot closer to exceeding them before the night is over, but I don't think it's actually going to bust the outside limit he set. Even if it does, he specifically told me not to bother him until conditions did just that. He'll probably say something really ugly if I bug him early and then they* don't *exceed the mission parameters after all, and if they do. . . .*

She frowned again. Maybe if her boss had been Harrington instead of Novaya Tyumen she would have gone ahead and made the call now. But she didn't work for Harrington. She worked for Novaya Tyumen, and she was covered by his logged instructions not to wake him until the storm did reach unacceptable levels. *And if executing his own orders makes him look bad, well, that's hardly* my *fault, now is it?* the ensign thought. She hesitated for one more moment, then smiled a remarkably nasty smile for someone of her tender years and meticulously logged the wind velocities and snowfall, noted that both were still within acceptable bounds as stipulated in her orders, and went on about her other duties.

HMS *Broadsword* swung in her orbit around Gryphon, tranquil and still in the peaceful vacuum of space, while far, far below her, the late-season blizzard howled up the Olympus Valley and hurled itself upon the Athinai Resort with seventy-five-kilometer winds.

"Ohhh, *look* at it!" Susan Hibson exulted as she and Ranjit joined the flow of people towards the grav lifts that served the slopes. "Isn't it *gorgeous?*"

Ranjit laughed out loud, and she looked up at him with dancing eyes. Susan rarely gushed, but she'd found the storm which
had moaned and howled about the resort last night exciting.
Well, Ranjit had, too, he supposed. A belter habitat didn't offer
its inhabitants any genuine weather at all, much less a shrieking
blizzard, and he'd felt the wild power of the wind singing in
his own blood.

He'd tried not to let it show, but Susan hadn't shared his
own determination to avoid looking like some bumpkin kid
from the back of beyond. She'd roamed around the main lodge,
staring out the double-paned windows at the wind-tortured
snow in wide-eyed delight and chattering to anyone unwary
enough to pause within her range. Some of that still simmered
within her, and made her even more appreciative of a winter-
scape unlike anything she had ever seen on warmer, sunnier
Manticore, far less Unicorn Eleven. The tracks and paths which
had marred the snow around the resort's buildings had disappeared magically, swept away by over a meter of fresh white.
Huge drifts of even deeper white had been piled wherever an
obstruction broke the wind, and the resort staff had told them
that the slopes had been given an average of better than eighty
centimeters of fresh powder. Although Ranjit fully intended
to spend the next day or so with Susan on the beginners' slopes,
he was looking forward to what all that fresh snow meant for
the more difficult runs, as well. Yet right this moment, all of
that was secondary to the sheer beauty of the crystal clear
morning and the almost painful perfection of the white mantle
which covered everything in sight.

"Well it *is* gorgeous!" Susan told him firmly as he chuckled, and he nodded.

"Yes, it is," he agreed, and draped his left arm around her
while he balanced two sets of skis on his right shoulder. "This
should be fun," he added, and she nodded eagerly.

High above the Olympus Valley's floor, uncountable of tons
of fresh snow lay smooth and white under the brilliant sun,
and the only sound was the faint sigh of the wind that swept
swirling snow devils across the pristine peaks. The snow pack
was always deep in the Atticas, but it was deeper than usual
this year, although the sun had been unseasonably warm for
the last few weeks. The overburden of fresh snow lay on a
base which had been weakened and softened ever so slightly
by that warmth, and no one knew it at all.

Honor settled into the copilot's couch aboard *Broadsword*'s

Number Three Pinnace and checked her safety harness. She really ought to be staying aboard, but Captain Tammerlane had only smiled indulgently when she told him she intended to accompany the drop. She was certain the Captain thought it was just her way of sneaking off to get in a few extra flight hours—he and Admiral Courvosier, Honor's old Academy mentor, were friends, and Tammerlane had let drop his awareness of her reputation as a hot pilot—but that wasn't her real motive at all.

She grimaced as she admitted that to herself, and a soft almost-scold sounded gently in her ear. She turned her head, and her normal dispassionate on-duty expression softened into an urchin-like grin as Nimitz cocked his head at her from the back of her couch. The treecat waited until he was certain he had her attention, then reached out one deceptively delicate-looking true-hand and brushed it lightly over her cheek.

"It's all right, Stinker," she told him. They were alone on the flight deck for the moment while they awaited the pinnace's assigned coxswain, and she raised her hand to return the caress.

The 'cat made a chittering sound and shook his head in an unmistakable gesture of disagreement with her statement, and her grin turned wry. She never had been able to fool Nimitz. The two of them had been together for over twenty T-years, and she relied upon the empathic 'cat's reactions to others as a barometer and evaluation system most people never even realized she had, but there were times when their adoption bond could be a drawback. Or, no, not a *drawback*. Never that! But there were times when it could have . . . inconvenient consequences, and this was one of them, for Nimitz knew precisely how she felt about Anthony Agursky. Unfortunately, the 'cat also knew *why* she felt that way . . . and why Baron Novaya Tyumen hated her, as well.

Nimitz made another sound, softer this time, with a dangerous edge of darkness. Honor had never been certain exactly how deep into her own emotions he could see. She suspected that his sensitivity went deeper than even most "'cat experts" believed, just as she felt stubbornly certain that there were times when she hovered on the very brink of sensing *his* emotions in return. She never had, of course. No human had ever been able to duplicate a treecat's empathy, not even those fortunate few who, like Honor, had been bonded to and adopted by one of them. On the other hand, some people could at least feel the existence of the empathic bond, and Honor was one of them. She had no word for the sensation—not surprisingly, she supposed, since it used none of the senses humans had

ever assigned names to—but she could always point unerringly
to wherever Nimitz was, whether she could see him or not.
She might be wrong about the distance between them; she was
never wrong about the bearing.

Then again, she wasn't exactly typical, even among adoptees.
Childhood adoptions like hers were extremely rare, just for start-
ers. More than that, her family's association with the 'cats went
back literally to the very first adoption. Indeed, Honor's middle
name memorialized the first Harrington adoptee, who had also
been the first human being even to suspect the 'cats existence.
Not content with that, she'd gone on to reorganize the Forestry Commission from the ground up and write (literally;
Honor had seen her handwritten first draft) the Ninth Amendment to the Star Kingdom's Constitution, which recognized the
treecats as Sphinx's indigenous sentient species and guaranteed their corporate claim to just over a third of Sphinx's
surface in perpetuity. She'd campaigned long, hard, and vic-
toriously to get the amendment enacted, and then spent the
rest of her lengthy life enforcing it, and the extensive Harrington clan which had followed her probably boasted the
highest percentage of adoptees of any single family on Sphinx.

An awful lot of those adoptees had been compulsive jour-
nal-keepers, and Honor had viewed every scrap of information any of her ancestors had ever recorded about their
relationships with their 'cats. She was also an only child, and
that meant she and Nimitz had been allowed an extraordinary
amount of time to themselves when she was a girl. Not even
her parents knew everything the two of them had gotten into,
just as they didn't know that she had accompanied Nimitz home
to meet the rest of his clan on more than one occasion. All
of which meant that, despite her relative youth, she probably
knew more about treecats, on a practical level, at least, than
almost anyone else in the Star Kingdom. But for all that, she
could no more have explained how the 'cats' empathy worked,
or precisely how and why they bonded with humans—or why
with one particular group of humans and not another, or just
exactly what Nimitz did to help her cope with stress and
anxiety—than she could have flown.

Yet she didn't have to be able to explain those things to
understand the 'cat's hatred for Novaya Tyumen. Treecats were
direct, uncomplicated souls, so she supposed she should count
the fact that she'd at least convinced Nimitz not to hiss and
bare his fangs at the commander as a victory, especially since
she was well aware that what he *really* wanted to do was
reduce that pale, supercilious face to slashed ruins. If she were

honest about it, that was what *she* really wanted him to do, as well, but that was probably a little excessive of her. After all, she and Novaya Tyumen had never even met until they wound up assigned to the Skyhawk evaluation exercise.

Perhaps not, but their first, brief conversation on the day he came aboard *Broadsword* had been enough to tell her he was another of Pavel Young's allies. She'd run into several of them over the years, and she'd never enjoyed the experience. Young would never forgive her for beating him bloody in the Academy showers that dreadful night, just as *she* would never forgive *him* for trying to rape her in the first place. Unfortunately, Young was the eldest son and heir of the powerful Earl of North Hollow. The very thought that anyone with that much influence behind him might face any meaningful consequences for his actions had been laughable, and Honor had known it. Any effort to see him punished would only have created a scandal the Academy didn't need, and she'd told herself that the beating she'd administered had been punishment enough. Even at the time, she'd wondered if she were trying to convince herself of something which wasn't really true because she'd known she would never tell a soul what had actually happened. She hadn't known the answer to that question even then, and she hadn't come any closer to finding it since, but it was certainly true that he'd walked away with no additional punishment other than a sizable dose of humiliation. She'd expected no more, and she'd even managed to accept it—after a fashion—as one of those horrible, unfair things people simply had to put up with in an imperfect universe. But it hadn't ended there for either of them. Young's later actions had made it abundantly clear that he intended to use his own and his family's connections both within and without the Service to cripple Honor's career in any way he could . . . and he and Anthony Agursky were second cousins.

Novaya Tyumen couldn't have cared less how the bad blood between Honor and his cousin had begun. Like the Youngs, the Agurskys belonged to that fortunately minority portion of the aristocracy which used power and influence with ruthless arrogance to get whatever it wanted, regardless of the consequences for anyone else. The two families had also intermarried for generations, to the point that it was sometimes difficult for an outsider to keep who belonged to which of them straight, and Novaya Tyumen had clearly signed on to help crush the upstart commoner who had dared to frustrate his cousin's desires.

It was small, petty, and disgusting, but Honor had learned

to cope with it. She shouldn't have had to, and she hadn't enjoyed her frequently painful lessons in just how low Young and his allies would stoop, but she'd had eight Manticoran years—almost fourteen T-years—in which to digest those lessons and armor herself internally against her enemies. What filled her with fury, and what she had *not* learned to accept, were the instances in which Young or his cronies tried to use other people to get at her. Like Novaya Tyumen's caustic response to John Hedges' perfectly appropriate question of the day before. She'd seen entirely too much of that, and she suspected that she'd see more of it before this evaluation program was over.

And that was the real reason she would be flying co-pilot for Chief Zariello today. The bad weather of the night before had put them over four hours behind schedule, and Novaya Tyumen had been like a hexapuma with a toothache over the delay. The fact that everyone in *Broadsword* had known he'd been caught totally unprepared for it had only made it worse, of course. His harried, furious efforts to reorganize on the fly had made him look like an imbecile after his exchange with her the day before, and knowing that had only made him even more furious.

Given his personality, Honor had no doubt at all that he was looking for anyone upon whom he might vent some of his self-inflicted spleen, nor did she doubt that that venting would be even more satisfactory to him if he could somehow use it to take a few cheap shots at her. So she intended to be right there, on the spot, throughout the day's entire ops schedule, because if a piece of aristocratic trash like Novaya Tyumen thought he could get away with victimizing her pinnace pilots, or her Marines, or any of her subordinates, as part of a quarrel with *her*, then he had another thought coming. She was confident Captain Tammerlane's backing would be there if she needed it, but she also planned to have every detail of today's operations at her fingertips from first-hand experience, and the first time Novaya Tyumen opened his mouth or even looked like he intended to unfairly criticize one of her people, she meant to cut him off at the knees.

And I'll enjoy *it, too*, she admitted unrepentantly, and heard Nimitz's soft bleek of agreement in her ear.

Ranjit eased the skis on his shoulder and pushed back his new souvenir knit cap, with the resort's Old Earth owl logo, to wipe his forehead. It was late in the ski season, and the crowds was unusually dense, even for a resort with Athinai's reputation. That meant long lines and slow movement, especially at the access points for the lift towers, and the early morning had gotten away while he and Susan shuffled their way slowly along the lengthy line. Despite all the fresh snow, the current outdoor temperature had actually risen above freezing as the sun shone down from the cloudless sky, and it was downright hot here in the covered concourse at the base of the lift. His one-piece ski suit's thermo-reactive fabric maintained most of his body at a comfortable twenty-two degrees, but it didn't keep the bright sun shining through the crystoplast roof from making the top of his head hot.

The lift tower rose above them like a squat, massive cylinder of bright alloy. He was a little surprised that the resort's owners hadn't gone for something more "traditional" looking, in keeping with the high-peaked roofs of the chalet architecture they'd favored for the rest of its buildings. Maybe they'd simply decided there was no way to make a forty-meter wide sphere set atop a cylinder sixty meters tall and fifteen in diameter look like anything but an old pre-space water tank and decided to spare themselves the effort, he thought with a grin. Or maybe they'd deliberately chosen to go for the sharpest contrast they could get.

Either way, the lift—one of four serving the Athinai Resort's slopes—was the focal point of several converging lines of skiers, each proceeding down its own crystoplast-roofed concourse. The lift cars settled atop the tower two at a time, then each pair slid down the guides to the tower's base, accepted their own loads of passengers, and lifted effortlessly into the sky once more to deliver them to the designated slopes. The drifting bubbles of alloy and crystoplast glittered and glistened like magic jewels as they caught the sun, and he wondered if that, too, was deliberate. It certainly turned them into eye-catching attractions, and their stately movement—like the measures of some huge, elaborate dance—probably helped distract people from how long they had to wait in line for them during peak demand periods.

He watched the most recent pair of cars lift away, following the invisible aerial pathways the ground based countergrav/presser plates within the lift tower laid down for them, and then tugged his cap back down. The first car of the next pair was scheduled for the beginner-level slopes, and he and Susan should make it aboard easily.

"You're sure you don't need me to tag along?"

He glanced over his shoulder, and Csilla Berczi smiled and quirked an eyebrow at him. The history teacher was a tallish, slender woman with short-cut auburn hair and gray eyes, and he'd never gotten used to how quietly she moved. Especially since he knew she was one of the people regen didn't work for and that one of her legs—the right, he thought, but he wasn't certain—had been replaced with a prosthetic after the accident that retired her from the Marines. It wasn't that she was *sneaky* or anything; she just moved like a hunting cat all the time. But that didn't keep him from liking her a lot, and he shook his head as he gave her an answering smile.

"Sooze and I'll be just fine, Ma'am," he assured her. "I promise we'll report in to the instructor as soon as we get up top."

"I wasn't thinking about *you*, young man," Ms. Berczi informed him with a twinkle. "Or not directly, at any rate. I was wondering whether or not Susan might like me to come along to help ride herd on you!"

"Oh, I think I can manage him," Susan said. "He's actually pretty easily led, once you figure out the right buttons to push."

"Oh, *thank* you!" Ranjit muttered, and she giggled.

"In that case, I think I really will leave the two of you to your own devices," Ms. Berczi said much more seriously. "Mr. Fleurieu drew the Krepson twins *and* Donny Tergesen in his group." She rolled her eyes. "Even with Monica to help out, he's going to need all the zoo-keepers he can get with *that* crowd. You two have fun—and be careful!"

She waved a finger at them with a sternness only slightly marred by the gleam in her eyes, then turned and marched away, and Ranjit and Susan exchanged eloquent looks. The Krepson twins all by themselves would have been enough to keep three adults fully occupied, and Donny Tergesen's classmates had voted him the boy most likely to validate Darwin by opening an airlock without checking his helmet seal. Ranjit didn't envy Mr. Fleurieu or Ms. Berczi one little bit, and he was moderately flattered by the implicit compliment Ms. Berczi had just paid him—and his sister—by deciding to trust them on their own.

Which, now that he thought about it, was actually a pretty sneaky way of making sure that they were trustworthy. It was much harder to disappoint someone who expected good things out of you than it was to confirm the expectations of someone who figured you'd screw up anyway.

He chuckled at the thought, and then stepped forward eagerly as the lift car settled and the doors slid open.

✧   ✦   ✧

"Bravo Leader, this is Broadsword Control. You are cleared to begin insertion."

"Broadsword Control, Bravo Leader copies cleared for insertion. I am beginning my run now."

Honor listened to the crisp voices in her earbug and gave a mental nod of approval. Hedges was back aboard *Broadsword*, coordinating the shuttles from all three cruisers for the troop insertion while Novaya Tyumen watched over his shoulder. Officially, that was to free the baron from detail concerns while he watched and evaluated the exercise. Actually, she suspected, it was because Novaya Tyumen preferred not to get up off his lazy backside and exert himself when it could be avoided . . . not to mention the pleasure he undoubtedly took from looming ominously over Hedges' shoulder. On the other hand, she knew her intense dislike for the man could be affecting her judgment. Despite his irritating mannerisms and current foul temper, he did have a reputation as an officer who got things done, and there was a limit to how much the Service would allow even someone with his exalted connections to get away with depending on his subordinates to carry the load for him.

But whatever Novaya Tyumen was thinking, Hedges seemed to have things well in hand. He'd waited a few minutes longer than Honor would have to release the pinnaces for their runs, but that was a pure judgment call, and at the moment, he had access to much better tracking data on the other ships' pinnaces than she did. Now she watched her heads-up display, hands resting loosely on her chair arms but poised to go for the controls in an instant if Chief Zariello needed her. Lieutenant Freemantle, flying Bravo Leader for the exercise, led the ship's pinnaces, slashing down into atmosphere at the head of the drop force, and Honor looked up past her HUD as the Attica Mountains and the axe-sharp cleft of the Olympus Valley swelled rapidly through the cockpit canopy.

High on the southern face of the rift humans had named the Olympus Valley, a runnel of snowmelt, trickling down from the wet, heavy blanket of new snow as the sun probed at it, washed away a small lump of clay. In and of itself, it was a negligible lump, little more than a couple of centimeters across, which simply collapsed as its core of pebbles and tiny stones separated from one another. But that small lump was the keystone of an entire bed of pebbles and gravel which, in turn, helped shore up a field of loose stone . . . and that loose stone was under almost intolerable pressure as the massive weight of snow crushed down upon it. When the lump of clay disappeared, it allowed two of its neighbors to shift, and they, in turn, let still more bits and pieces of rock and mud wiggle and squirm.

By itself, it probably wouldn't have mattered very much. But it wasn't by itself, for the Athinai Resort lay on the flank of Mount Pericles, and an unsuspected branch of the Olympus Fault ran along the foot of the mountain. No one had ever realized it was there, and it was only a very minor fault. Yet it was enough. The tremor which ran through it that morning was scarcely enough to register, but the field of stone was already in slow, dreamy motion when the vibration hit. For just an instant, it seemed not to have had any effect at all . . . but then the first real boulder moved grindingly in its bed and nudged another rock aside. It was all quite invisible under the concealment of the innocent-looking white snowpack, and even if a single human in the Olympus Valley had had the slightest clue of what was happening, it was already far too late to do a thing about it.

Ranjit Hibson hid a smile as Susan unwrapped a second stick of gum and shoved it into her mouth. He didn't know where she'd picked up that particular habit—certainly their parents had done all they could to discourage it!—but it was a pretty reliable barometer of her mood. When she started shoving in extra sticks, she was apprehensive, excited, angry, or some combination of all three. At the moment, he figured it was probably ninety percent excitement and ten percent apprehension, for they were three-quarters of the way up to the beginners' slope landing.

For all her vocal disgust at being restricted to "Kiddy Hill," Susan had to be as aware of her inexperience as anyone else could possibly be. She was also aware that there was a world of difference between any simulator, however realistic, and the reality of a fast downhill run on real skis. So however much she might resent the restrictions she faced, she knew it was still—

He could never remember, later, what interrupted his train of thought. Not the first thing, at any rate. There had to have been *something*, some tiny clue his conscious mind didn't grasp at the time and never managed to get its hands on later, but he had absolutely no idea what it had been. One moment his thoughts were sliding along in their normal channels, and the next they simply stopped. Just like that. As if someone had thrown a switch in his brain that jerked his eyes away from his sister and to the sheer wall of snow-ribbed black rock sliding past just beyond the lift car's windows.

It was rough, that wall, with icicle-anchoring cracks and crevices which had caught and held shallow dustings of snow. He'd been fascinated when he first saw the striations across the rock face, but he'd also become quickly accustomed to them. Yet there was something different about them now, and his brow furrowed as he tried to figure out what it was. Then he had it. Fine sprays of snow and ice crystals—almost like snow devils, but not quite—had begun to swirl above the pockets of snow.

But there's not any wind, he thought in puzzlement. *Or not that much, at least. And what's that sound? It's almost like—*

He looked up through the crystoplast roof of the car, and his heart seemed to stop.

Csilla Berczi's head jerked up as the first dull rumble vibrated through her ears and the soles of her feet. She didn't recognize the sound, but something about it rang warning signals in the primitive, cavewoman side of her brain. Her eyes snapped around the horizon, sweeping it for threats, and then she sucked in as if someone had just punched her in the stomach.

The entire mountainside above the Athinai Resort seemed to heave and shudder. It was a dropping motion, at first, a slow-motion movement at the very peak of Mount Pericles that seemed to have nothing at all to do with the buildings and people at the mountain's foot. But that changed with terrifying speed. The slow-motion quickened, sliding faster and faster, and as it quickened, it spread. More and more of the mountain seemed to crumble, curling over like the top of some monstrous ocean wave while a spume of snow blew high above it. Boulders and rock outcrops and the dense dark green of evergreen trees vanished into the accelerating maw of the avalanche, and Csilla Berczi heard herself crying out in horrified denial as a lethal wall of rock and snow and splintered trees—and human beings—engulfed the lift towers and exploded across the resort.

Like all modern ski resorts, especially on Gryphon, the Athinai had the very latest in seismic monitoring equipment. Gryphon's weather was frequently violent and always difficult to predict very far in advance, and the mountainous planet was also the most tectonically active of the Star Kingdom's three inhabited worlds. That combination was enough to create avalanche hazards often, particularly in late winter or spring, when sharp temperature changes were common, and Athinai's management had no intention of allowing itself to be caught by surprise if it happened to them. Remote listening stations and temperature monitors reported back to the resort's central data processing station on a real-time basis. That data also went out to the Gryphon Mountain Data Interface, which had begun as a private venture over two T-centuries before, where it was joined by satellite imagery which allowed GMDI to track accumulations and search for even the tiniest signs of instability on a planet-wide basis. In the last fifty years, the planetary government had gotten involved—Gryphon's resort attractions accounted for almost twenty percent of its foreign exchange, and the local government reasoned that allowing paying guests to be squashed would do unfortunate things to the tourist trade—and GMDI routinely spotted avalanche conditions even as they formed.

Whenever that happened, steps were taken either to relieve the conditions or to evacuate all of the threatened resorts' guests until the danger had passed. Given the capabilities of modern counter-grav, tractors, and pressers, it was usually possible to deal with the threat before it materialized, and perhaps that was part of the reason for what happened. Perhaps the human beings behind those monitors and all the sophisticated technology for intervening and forbidding avalanches had become too confident, too certain of their own ability to control the raw fury of nature. Or perhaps it was even simpler than that, for the sensor density in the critical area was lower than it ought to have been. No one had known the minor fault line geologists would later name the Athinai Switch even existed, and the detection net's designers had skimped just a bit on what everyone "knew" was a stable area and chosen to devote more of their resources to known fault areas. What they had installed around Mount Pericles met the seismologists' specs— barely—but it was spread thin, and no one would ever know if the fault had given any previous signs of its existence that better instrumentation might have detected.

And what someone might or might not have known was utterly irrelevant anyway as the entire side of the Mount Pericles snowpack broke loose and went thundering downward like the icy white breath of Hell.

"Oh my God!"

Honor didn't recognize the voice on the net. She knew it wasn't one of her people—or she thought it wasn't, anyway, she corrected herself almost instantly, for she really wasn't sure. The shock and horror which suffused the words could have disguised anyone's voice.

She exchanged a sharp glance with Chief Zariello, and then automatically ran her eyes over the icons in her HUD, making certain all of her pinnaces were where they were supposed to be. But the check was pure reflex. Some part of her already knew whatever was happening had nothing to do with the drop exercise.

"Look!" someone else gasped. "Holy Mithra, *look at the valley!*"

Honor's head snapped up and around, and Chief Zariello automatically rolled the pinnace to give her a better look through the roof of the armorplast canopy. Her eyes swept out, looking for whatever had prompted that horrified exclamation. Then she saw it, and her face went blank with horror of her own as she watched the tidal wave of snow, stone, rock, and earth come smashing down the valley like the Apocalypse itself.

Athinai's sensors might not have seen it coming far enough ahead of time for an evacuation, but the resort's designers had allowed to the best of their ability for that possibility. Alarms began to wail throughout the compound, and massively reinforced panels of alloy snapped up to cover the huge expanses of crystoplast built into the viewing galleries and restaurants and shops. Lift towers locked down and threw up barrier panels of their own, and immensely powerful presser beams snarled to life. No one could have built an effective wall of pressers all around the resort, but the designers had stationed the generators at strategic points. They didn't try to build a wall; instead, they projected a series of angled pressers, like baffles or coffer dams that strove to divide the flowing megatons of snow and stone like the prows of ships and divert them from the resort's critical points. But the engineers who designed and built those generators had expected more time to bring them on-line. That was the reason all those monitoring systems existed: to give time for remedial measures, or for evacuation, or at the very least to spin the generators fully up before they had to take the load.

Only this time there was no warning . . . or not enough, anyway. Almost all of the barrier panels slammed into position, and most of the pressers came up before the avalanche hit them, but they were still spinning up to full power. Those intended to protect the slopes themselves were closer to the threat. They had less time to reach full power, and most of them failed completely under the sudden, enormous load, while many of those meant to protect the resort facilities themselves were only partially successful at their designed function.

The lift towers for the advanced and intermediate slopes survived undamaged, as did three-quarters of the resort's other buildings and promenades. But almost seven hundred morning skiers found themselves squarely in the path of thundering death with no more than a few minutes warning. Some were lucky; they were on the fringes of the avalanche and managed to get clear of its outriders. Others had brought individual counter-grav belts with them as a means to avoid the lines at the lifts, and most of those managed to activate their belts and lift out of the way in time. Still others turned and skied as they never had before, racing madly to outrun destruction, and some of those managed to get clear, too. But over four hundred people were unable to escape, and the churning wall of snow and boulders smashed over them mercilessly.

Those in position to see it watched in horror as one tiny cluster of figures after another was overtaken, overwhelmed, and pounded under, and *still* the avalanche thundered onward. It hit the first of the inner perimeter of baffles, and spouts of snow spumed upward. Impossible concentrations of moving mass rammed the beam generators back on their reinforced foundations like pile drivers, but somehow they held, and the horrified spectators felt a tiny surge of hope. If one baffle had held, perhaps all of them would.

But all of them didn't, and the avalanche seemed to have a malevolent life of its own, a sort of bestial sentience which sought out the chinks in the resort's armor like a hexapuma stalking a wounded Sphinx tri-horn. And when it found those chinks, it sent torrents of destruction lunging brutally through them, smashing and crushing everything in their path.

Just like the torrent that crashed over the beginners' slopes, and the lift tower serving them, in a wave of snow-white death.

"My God."

Honor didn't realize for almost a second that the whisper had been her own. The scanner tech riding in the pinnace's tac section had gotten the on-board sensors reconfigured from navigational to tactical analysis mode without orders, and Honor stared in numb horror at the holo projections before her. The lethal tide of destruction had slammed deep into the perimeter of the resort below her. At least a half dozen structures had been completely buried, and her stomach tightened as she wondered how many people had been on the slopes when that monster hit. Honor Harrington was from Sphinx, and Sphinx was the coldest of the Star Kingdom's three habitable planets. She knew all about what an avalanche could do, and she keyed her com.

"Bravo Leader, this is Bravo Three," she said, and at least she *sounded* as if she were coming back on balance, for her voice was calm and crisp once more. "I am assuming control of the flight."

"Three, this is Leader," the relief in Lieutenant Freemantle's voice was unmistakable. "The flight is yours, Ma'am. What do we do?"

"First, we come round to starboard," Honor told him. "We'll make a sweep down the path of the slide, from top to bottom. I want a full tac scan. Heat sources as small as people are going to be hard to spot through snow, but—"

"Bravo Flight, this is ExCom," another voice cut in angrily. "Return to profile immediately!"

Honor grimaced and made herself strangle a burst of fury as Novaya Tyumen's words rattled in her ear bug. She recognized personal anger when she felt it, and this was no time for it.

"ExCom, Three," she said instead, forcing herself to speak normally. "There are injured civilians down there. The people digging them out are going to need the best data they can get, and—"

"I didn't ask for your advice, Bravo Three!" Novaya Tyumen snapped. "It's more important that we reorganize properly before we just go chargin' in, so that we can use our resources most effectively. Now return to profile and prepare to reverse course!"

"Negative, ExCom," Honor said flatly. "I am assuming control of all Bravo assets. Bravo Flight, form on me. Bravo Three, out."

"Goddamn you, Harrington!" Novaya Tyumen shouted, his usual supercilious hauteur brushed aside by the hatred festering between the two of them. "I've had just about enough of you! Now you get your ass back into formation and the fuck back up here before I come down there and ki—"

"ExCom, this is Captain Tammerlane," a deep, coldly furious voice said suddenly, and Novaya Tyumen's tirade chopped off in mid-syllable. Tammerlane was using the squadron ops net rather than using *Broadsword*'s internal communications to speak to Novaya Tyumen. That meant every pinnace in the exercise could hear every word he was saying, and Honor felt her lips purse in a silent whistle at the public slap in the face her skipper had just given the baron. "I am formally notifying you that the exercise has been scrubbed. Commander Harrington has my authorization to reassume command of this ship's pinnaces immediately, since it would appear that she—unlike some people—actually has a clue about what to do with them now, not three hours from now. Do you have a *problem* with that, ExCom?"

"Uh, no, Sir," Novaya Tyumen said quickly. "Of course not. I only wanted to avoid the sort of command confusion and, ah, impetuosity which might prevent us from makin' optimum use of our resources."

Honor glanced over at Chief Zariello. She shouldn't have, of course. It was prejudicial to authority, if nothing else. But she couldn't help herself, and she saw the same contempt flicker in the chief's eyes. Not that either of them had ever had any intention of obeying Novaya Tyumen. Bravo Three was already buffeting heavily as she sliced down into atmosphere, headed for the avalanche site at high mach numbers, and every one of *Broadsword*'s other pinnaces followed right behind her while they listened to their coms and waited for their captain's response.

"No doubt that's a worthy ambition, ExCom," Tammerlane said, still coldly, "but the people who just got buried need help *now*—even if it's not the best organized rescue effort we could possibly arrange—one hell of a lot more than they need a well-organized effort after they've already died of suffocation or hypothermia. Don't you agree?"

"Yes, Sir. Of course!"

"Good. I'm delighted to hear that, ExCom. And since we're in agreement, why don't you just turn the rest of your pinnaces over to Commander Harrington until you can get 'reorganized' dirtside yourself?"

"Of course, Sir." Novaya Tyumen sounded as if he were chewing ten-centimeter iron spikes, but there really wasn't much else he could say. "Bravo Three," the commander went on after a moment, and Honor didn't need any empathy to recognize the barely contained hate smoking in that grating tone, "you are in command until ExCom can move dirtside. All other pilots, Bravo Three is in command until you hear differently from me."

"Understood, ExCom." Honor tried very hard to keep any trace of triumph out of her own voice, but she knew she'd failed, and somehow, as she listened to the acknowledgments of the other section leaders, she couldn't seem to make herself care as much as she should have.

"All pinnaces will form on Bravo Three," she continued on more crisply. "Charlie Section, I want you out on my starboard wing. Hotel, you take port. We'll start with a line abreast flight down the main path of the slide with a full tac sweep. Drive those thermal sensors hard, people. All the junk that avalanche brought down with it is going to play hob with our sonar and DIR, so the thermals are probably going to be the best we have today. Then—"

She went on, giving her orders in a clear, strong voice, yet as she looked out at the vast swath of destruction below her, she knew deep inside how very likely it was that all their efforts would be useless for anyone who had been caught in its path.

"Ranjit? *Ranjit?*"

Ranjit Hibson groaned as a small hand shook his shoulder. His eyes slid open and he blinked, trying to orient himself.

His head was in his sister's lap. She was hunched over him, her shadowed face peering anxiously down at him, and he managed to pat her knee with his right hand before he rolled his head to look about him. The lift car was tilted at a crazy angle, he noted muzzily, and the light was all wrong. It wasn't sunlight through crystoplast, and it was dim, little more than a murky twilight. Then his mind cleared with almost painful suddenness. No wonder the light was dim! It came from a single one of the lift car's small emergency lighting elements somewhere behind Susan.

He tried to sit up, and cried out sharply at the sudden, wrenching stab of agony. Susan's hand had locked on his shoulders the instant she realized he was trying to move, and she pushed him back down hard.

Wish she'd figured out what I was doing just a little sooner, he thought with queer detachment, even as he locked his teeth against the groan of anguish still rattling about in his throat. The grotesque discrepancy between how much he hurt and the clarity of the thought made him want to laugh, although for the life of him he couldn't see why he thought it was so funny, and he made himself pat Susan's knee again.

"All—" He stopped and coughed. "All right, Sooze. I'm . . . all right."

"No you aren't," she told him, and the mixture of terror and determination to hang onto her self-control which quivered in her voice twisted his heart. "Your legs are both trapped. And I think the right one's broken. And I don't know where we are or . . . or what to do, and—"

She made herself stop and drag in a ragged breath as she felt her hard-held discipline begin to crumble. She stared down into her brother's pain-hazed eyes in the dim shadows and bit her lip for a moment. Then she made herself go on.

"And I think all the others are . . . are dead," she got out quietly, and Ranjit's hand clenched on her knee.

He stared up at her, trying to make his mind work, and then it was his turn to swallow hard as he remembered the tidal bore of snow and rock which had leapt out from the mountainside at the lift car. He couldn't recall any details after that, only a confused impression of shock and savage motion and screams of terror from the car's passengers as the avalanche batted it out of the air like a cat batting away a pellet of paper. Perhaps it was a good thing that he couldn't remember details, he thought, still with that queer sense of detachment.

Shock? he wondered. *Could be. 'Cause Sooze is sure as hell right about my right leg. Maybe my left, too, the way they feel.*

But he remembered enough to feel dull surprise that anyone in the car had survived, and a terrible sense of gratitude crushed over him as he realized that Susan must be mostly unhurt, since she'd been able to get his head into her lap in the first place.

"Help . . . help me sit up," he said after a moment.

"No! Your leg—"

"I've gotta see, Sooze," he told her through locked teeth. "Just help ease me up. I'll . . . let you lift me. Won't use my legs or stomach muscles at all. Promise."

He managed a white-faced smile. Fortunately, he had no idea how ghastly it looked in the dim emergency lighting, but Susan did. She stared at him dubiously for several seconds, remembering his breathless scream when he'd tried to move on his own, and her stomach churned at the thought of inflicting still more hurt on him. But at the same time, she knew how desperately she needed for her big brother to be in charge, to take the burden of solitary decision from her shoulders. And on the heels of that knowledge came an ugly little worm of self-contempt for wanting Ranjit to make the decisions when he was so badly hurt. Yet he was almost half again her age, and she *needed* him to help her decide what to do, and she was terrified, however hard she fought not to show it.

"All right," she said finally. "But you let me do *all* the lifting, Ranjit! You hear me?"

"Yes, Ma'am," he got out in an almost normal voice, and managed another smile.

"All right," she said again, and slid around, shifting position to get both her hands under his shoulders. He was much taller and heavier than she, but she'd signed up for the phys-ed martial arts elective taught by Csilla Berczi over a year ago, as part of her determination to pursue a career in the Marines. Now, for the first time, she drew seriously on that training, closing her eyes and concentrating on her breathing as she focused herself on her task. And then, smoothly and with a strength even she had never guessed she possessed, she raised her brother into a sitting position on the crazily tilted floor of the lift car.

Ranjit's eyes flared wide as the small hands raised him. He'd promised not to use his muscles, but he'd been privately certain he would have no choice, even though he'd known—or feared he knew—how much it would hurt when his thigh muscles tightened. He'd been wrong. Susan boosted him smoothly, if not as easily as he might have lifted her, and then she was kneeling behind him, bracing him upright while her hands moved to rest on his shoulders and hug him tightly against her.

"Thanks, Sooze," he said, and then sucked in another shocked breath as he saw the rest of the lift car at last.

It was crushed. Its structure had never been designed to endure the abuse it had suffered, and one entire side had crumpled like tissue paper. Snow had poured in through the shattered crystoplast windows, and Ranjit's mind flinched away as he saw the huge branch or tree trunk which had come from somewhere up-slope to slam into the car like a battering ram. It had smashed in one entire side of the car, and crushed and lifeless bodies marked its path. There were at least three of them, he thought, but there could have been more. There was too much blood and mutilation for him to tell for certain.

He looked around in disbelief. There had been over twenty people in the car with him and Susan. Surely *someone* else had to be alive!

As if his thought had summoned it, a hand moved feebly down beside the tree trunk.

"Sooze! Did—"

"I saw it," she told him before he could finish the question.

"You've gotta go check," he told her.

"But—" Susan swallowed, trying to cling to the sense of focus she had summoned to lift Ranjit's shoulders. If she moved, he would have to support himself—if he could, with the car tilted this way. That would be bad enough. But she would also have to go over there by the tree trunk. By the broken bodies, and the blood. The prospect was enough to make her want to cry out in refusal, and the thought of what she might find attached to that feeble hand—the damage she might see, the dying she might have no way to prevent or ease—screamed at her to say no. But she couldn't.

"You need me to hold you up," she said instead.

"Find something and prop me," he replied, and put his hands on the tilted floor behind him. He leaned his weight on them and looked back at her, facial muscles tight with the fresh pain even that movement sent crashing through him. "I can hold myself up for a few minutes. Find something, Sooze."

"I— All right. Don't you move, though!"

She slid herself cautiously back, watching to be sure he truly could support himself, and then started fumbling through the wreckage. Within seconds, she had found several skis, including one of her own, and she dragged them back to him. It took her only a few more seconds to figure out how to wedge them between two of the stanchions (one now badly twisted) to which standing passengers had held for balance when the car was moving, and Ranjit gave a half-sigh and half-moan of relief as he let himself slump back against the support they offered.

"Great, Sooze. This is great. Now go check."

She nodded, not trusting her voice, and crawled slowly towards the moving hand. She had to pick her way with care, for the lift car's floor was badly buckled, with rents which could easily have swallowed her up to the waist, and she could hardly even see them in the dim light. Worse, she seemed to feel the car quivering. She told herself that was just her imagination, that the car was buried immovably under an unknown depth of snow. It *couldn't* be moving with all that piled on top of it! Yet it didn't feel that way, and whether it was real or not, that quiver—a vibration, like the potential for movement—was one more ripple of terror to wash at her jaggedly held self-control.

She reached the tree trunk at last, trying very hard not to think about the mangled human limbs and the smell of blood as she inched her way down it. She squashed her awareness down into a hard little shell, an armored citadel where nothing could reach it, and concentrated on what she had to do because she *did* have to do it. Because Ranjit certainly couldn't, and that meant there was no one but her.

She made her careful way down the trunk to the hand that had moved. It was a small hand, not much larger than her own, protruding from a wash of snow, and it moved again, weakly, as she reached it. She drew a deep breath and leaned forward to touch it, and then almost screamed as it twisted around like a snake to lock upon her wrist. It clutched with desperate strength, pulling frantically, demanding rescue, and the force it exerted jerked her off-balance. Her forehead slammed into the tree trunk, and she heard herself cry out as the impact bloodied her nose. But the shock also seemed to help somehow, as if the familiarity of the pain had broken through her sense of unreality and horror, and she heaved back. She managed to yank free, and the hand flailed frantically while a muffled sound came from the snow through which it emerged.

A part of Susan wanted to stamp on the hand's fingers for frightening her that way, but it was only a tiny part, for most of her understood only too well the terror which had driven it. And so instead of striking back at it, she simply avoided it and began digging into the snow with her own hands. She'd lost her gloves somewhere, and the snow quickly numbed her fingers, but it didn't take long. She was able to make a good estimate of where the rest of the hand's body was from the angle of the arm, and she quickly excavated downward to reach the shoulder. The hand stopped its flailing, making it easier for her to work, as its owner realized someone was digging away the snow, and long, snow-matted golden hair gleamed palely in the dim light as she uncovered it. She worked her way cautiously higher, and then a head flung itself upward the moment she'd shoved enough snow aside.

"Oh *God!*" The ragged, gasping cry seemed to fill what remained of the lift car, and Susan stared into huge, terrified blue eyes. The girl before her was about midway between her and Ranjit in age, and probably would have been quite pretty under other conditions. But these weren't "other conditions," and she blinked and squinted up at Susan from a face twisted with fear.

And no wonder, Susan thought. The other girl must have been pinned face-down when the tree trunk crashed into the car, and only the fact that she'd managed to curl her right arm under as she hit had held her face and chest just a little clear of the car floor, forming an air space until Susan dug her out.

"What— What hap—" the blonde began, then chopped herself off rather than ask the excruciatingly obvious question. That was the first thing about her of which Susan unreservedly approved, and she smiled tightly.

"Who are you?" the blonde asked instead.

"Susan Hibson," Susan replied, and jerked her head back

over her shoulder. "My brother Ranjit is back there. He can't move either. Who're *you* and how bad are you hurt?"

The blonde blinked at her, then craned her neck, trying to push herself up far enough to look past Susan at Ranjit. It was little more than a reflex action, and she couldn't complete it anyway with all the weight piled atop her, and she shook herself.

"Andrea," she said after a heartbeat. "I'm Andrea Manders."

"How bad're you hurt?" Susan asked again.

"I . . . don't know," Andrea said. "I don't think I'm hurt at all. I just can't move."

"That's all?" Susan pressed.

"I think so. I can feel my feet and my legs and everything. I just can't move them, and—*hneeeek!*"

Susan jumped at Andrea's sudden, totally unexpected squeal. "What?" she demanded. "*What?*"

"Someone—someone *touched* me!" Andrea gasped. "There's someone else under all this stuff! Someone's holding my ankle!"

Susan flinched at the very thought and stared desperately at the massive barrier of wood and snow and crumpled alloy blocking her from whoever else might be alive underneath it all. There was no way in the world she could dig her way through all of that, and her soul cringed as she imagined someone else, trapped even more completely than Andrea or Ranjit, alone in the suffocating dark and cold while they ran out of air and warmth.

"We've got to get them out!" Andrea was saying. "We've got to—"

"I know!" Susan interrupted harshly. "I just don't know *how.*" She bit her lip, wiping unconsciously at the blood still trickling from her mashed nose, and thought hard for several seconds. "Look," she told Andrea finally, "I've gotta go talk it over with Ranjit. Then I'll see what I can do."

"Don't go!" Andrea gasped.

"I've *got* to," Susan repeated.

"*Please!*" Andrea whispered. "Don't leave me alone!"

"You're not alone," another voice said. It was Ranjit, his words harsh-edged with his own pain and fear. "I'm here too— Andrea, was it?" he went on. "But Sooze is right. She's the only one of us who can move. She and I have to talk. But you're not alone, okay?"

"O-okay," Andrea got out after a moment, still shaky but no longer hovering on the edge of panic, and Susan bent down to pat her shoulder gently and then started climbing back up to Ranjit.

Her brother looked worse when she got back to him, but he smiled at her. He didn't mention that he thought his right leg was bleeding under the wreckage that trapped it, or that a deadly chill was creeping into the limb despite his ski suit's best efforts.

"How is she?" he asked quietly, jerking his head in the direction of the girl he couldn't actually see from his position.

"Okay, I think," Susan replied, equally quietly. "But she's scared, Ranjit—even more scared than I am!" Her lips produced a trembling smile.

"Is there any way you can dig her out? So maybe the two of you could get whoever else is under there out?" Ranjit hated to ask the question and drop the responsibility for an answer on her, but no one else *could* answer it. He watched her bite her lip, but she shook her head without hesitation.

"No way," she said, and he heard her self-anger in the flatness of her tone. "She's caught under a branch of that tree or whatever it is. I can't shift it to get her out, and I can't get past it to dig whoever else is under there out. Too much snow and metal and rocks and junk are all mashed up together with the tree, Ranjit. I don't see how anyone *can* be alive under there . . . or how they can last very long if we don't get them out quick."

"I see." Ranjit closed his eyes against his own pain and fear and sucked in deep, dragging draughts of air. Susan was right, he thought. None of them could know what conditions were like on the far side of that tree, but the lift car hadn't been all that big to begin with. The open space they knew about and the mass of stuff they could see took up at least two-thirds of its original volume, and that meant anyone trapped beyond the tree was already living on borrowed time. For that matter, so was he, if the way his leg felt was any indication. Even Andrea might be wrong about her own condition—Ranjit hadn't realized how badly *he* was hurt until he tried to move, after all—and they had no way to know if more than one person was trapped on the other side of the car. But Susan couldn't dig whoever it was out. And that meant. . . .

"Have you checked out this end of the car, Sooze?" he asked finally.

"This end?" she repeated, then shook her head. "I've been kinda busy," she added pointedly, and he surprised both of them with a breathless, pain-curdled chuckle.

"I guess you have," he agreed, and turned his head to meet her eyes. "But you're gonna have to check now, Sooze. This is the upper end of the car. That means it's the one closest to the surface."

"Closest to—?" Susan began, then cut herself off, and her eyes widened with a new, fresh fear as she realized what he meant.

Honor Harrington stood with her hands jammed deep in the pockets of her Navy-issue parka, and despite her total lack of expression, a fury far colder than Mount Pericles' snow blazed within her as she watched Commander Novaya Tyumen wave his hands and snap orders at the Marines and Navy ratings around him. It hadn't taken the baron long to get himself dirtside after Captain Tammerlane's brutal assessment of operational realities, and he had immediately snatched command back from Honor.

A part of her had wanted to let him have it without a struggle, for she was appalled by the scale of the destruction. The Star Kingdom hadn't seen a natural disaster like this one or such a heavy loss of civilian lives in decades, and very little in her Navy training had taught her how to cope with civilian death and devastation on such a scale. But even as that ignoble sliver of her had wanted to cringe away and let someone else decide how to deal with it, her own stubborn sense of responsibility had rebelled against Novaya Tyumen's authority. Partly, she knew, it was that she didn't trust his ability to cope with the situation, but there was more to it. Honor had been raised in the Copper Wall Mountains of Sphinx. She might never have seen a catastrophe of these dimensions, given Sphinx's sparser population, but she knew avalanches, and she'd pulled her share of the load in a couple of avalanche rescues before she left Sphinx for the Naval Academy at Saganami Island. But Novaya Tyumen was from Manticore, and she very much doubted he had ever even come close to anything as arduous and risky as something like this.

Besides, she told herself with brutal frankness, *I know perfectly well that deep down inside I'm convinced I can do just about* anything *better than he can, now don't I?*

She snorted at the thought, and Nimitz bleeked reprovingly from her shoulder. Insalubrious as humans might find the current weather conditions, the 'cat was quite comfortable. Gryphon weather might be more fractious and changeable than that of Sphinx, but Sphinx's winters were far colder, and Nimitz was equipped with the long, silky coat to survive them. Yet if the weather didn't worry him, the empathic 'cat had been savagely battered by the emotions of the humans around him. The worst combers of panic had passed, which helped, but rescuers had already dug out and brought in over fifty injured people. The echoes of pain coming from those who had been hurt, mingled with the desperate determination of those trying frantically to find still more injured in time, remained more than sufficient to keep him off balance and edgy. Yet he was getting on top of it once more, and his bleek scolded her for the sharp edge of self-condemnation in her thoughts.

She reached up to caress his ears, but she never took her eyes from Novaya Tyumen. The baron hadn't bothered with a single word of approval for anyone since he grounded, but he'd acted with dispatch and at least an outer appearance of being in command of both the situation and himself. He'd quickly taken the scanner data Honor had gathered on her approach to the resort (and plotted on an overlay from file sensor passes made earlier in the course of the exercise), and shouted for the senior member of the Athinai staff.

He hadn't had to shout. If he'd bothered to ask Honor, she could have introduced him to the man, because the resort's manager had been standing right beside her. The two of them had already agreed upon the rough outlines of a plan to use the Navy-gathered data to guide and coordinate search and rescue operations, and they'd been working out the best way to make use of the Marines and ratings aboard the pinnaces when Novaya Tyumen intervened.

Not that the baron had cared about anything Honor might have worked out. He didn't even ask about it. He'd simply begun giving the resort manager orders, as if the man were a boot spacer on his first deployment or one of the Agursky family's lackeys back on Manticore, and Honor had seen the fury blazing even behind the manager's frantic concern for the scores of guests and employees still unaccounted for. The man had looked at her for a moment, his face stark with his desire to appeal to her, but she had shaken her head minutely. She was fairly certain Novaya Tyumen hadn't seen her gesture— not that she'd really cared particularly. But the manager had, and after an instant, he'd nodded back ever so slightly. Finding and rescuing people mattered more than who got the credit for it—to the two of them, at least—and Novaya Tyumen was clearly capable of obstructing any rescue efforts which didn't bear his own personal stamp of approval.

And so Honor had found herself shunted aside. Technically, as the second ranking naval officer present, she was Novaya Tyumen's second-in-command. In fact, he'd chosen to completely—and pointedly—ignore her. He'd cut her entirely out of the loop and made it perfectly clear that he was about as likely to cut off his own right hand as he was to give her

any share of the "glory" which might flow from the operation. It sickened her that anyone could be so petty as to think
about stupid personal vendettas—especially vendettas which had
nothing at all to do with anything anyone had ever done to
them in the first place—when innocent lives were at risk. But
Novaya Tyumen clearly could be and was, and furious though
she was at the calculated insult, she had no intention of fighting
him over it. As *Broadsword*'s executive officer, she supposed
she might have ignored him where her own people were concerned, but only a third of the pinnaces and personnel assigned
to the drop exercise had come from her ship, and he obviously assumed that everything assigned to the exercise was still
his to command. Honor was fairly certain that if she'd appealed
to Captain Tammerlane again, her CO would have slapped
Novaya Tyumen down once more . . . but she couldn't be
certain. Novaya Tyumen *was* the senior officer present, after
all. Under the circumstances, it made a lot of sense to leave
him alone as long as he got the job done, however infuriat-
ing Honor might find his treatment of her or her people. And
it was also true that the Service remembered an officer who
made a habit of going over a superior's head or behind her
back. However justified her actions, anyone who got a name
for stabbing her superiors in the back could expect to pay the
price for it down the road. Not that Honor would have let
that stop her. Or she didn't think she would have, anyway.
It was just that she had no desire to get Tammerlane involved
once more. She didn't need any glory, and she refused to
hamper operations by fighting some sort of turf war at a
moment like this.

*Better one person in command, even if he's not the best person
for the job, than two of us fighting each other and getting even less
done,* she thought bitterly. *But—*

"Excuse me, Commander."

The voice came from behind her, and she turned quickly.

The woman who had spoken had dark auburn hair, only a
little longer than Honor's, and gray eyes in a face whose high
cheekbones promised more than a dash of Old Earth's Slavic
inheritance. The left side of her face was a mass of bruises,
the eye on that side was swollen almost shut, and she listed
to port as she stood there, clearly favoring her left hip. But
the unbruised side of her face was tight, almost desperate, and
Honor heard Nimitz make a soft, muttery-snarly sound as the
other woman's emotions hammered at him.

"Yes?" Honor replied cautiously.

"Are you Commander Harrington?" the woman asked.

"Yes. Yes, I am." Honor knew she sounded surprised by the question, because she was, but the other woman nodded as if in grim satisfaction and thrust out her right hand.

"Berczi," she said as Honor took it. "Major Csilla Berczi, late of Her Majesty's Marines."

"Ah." Honor returned her firm grip, then cocked her head to one side. "What can I do for you, Major?"

"What I'd like best would be for you to lend me a pulser and let me have three seconds alone with that pompous, arrogant, mind-fucking son-of-a-*bitch*," Berczi said, jerking her head contemptuously to where Novaya Tyumen stood giving his orders. The glare she turned upon the commander for a long, poisonous moment was not one Honor would have liked to see directed at herself, but then the other woman shook herself and forced a humorless grin. "Short of your assistance in culling the human genotype, however, I need your help getting around the asshole, Commander."

"*My* help getting around him?" Honor gazed into the other's eyes and quirked an inquiring eyebrow.

"Yes." Berczi bit the word off, then flushed, as if ashamed of herself for showing her anger, and drew a deep breath. "Frank Stimson was one of my platoon commanders when he was a brand new lieutenant, Commander," she said, pointing with her chin—much less violently, this time—to where the commander of *Broadsword*'s Marine detachment had set up his own CP to pass on Novaya Tyumen's orders. "When I asked him if there was anyone reasonable involved in managing this cluster fuck, he told me to talk to you."

"About?" Honor asked coolly, refusing to allow herself to be drawn into agreeing (openly, at least) with Berczi's obvious opinion of Novaya Tyumen.

"The beginners' slopes," Berczi said, and this time there was a raw, urgent note in her voice. "They're back that way—" she waved a hand in the direction of the avalanche's worst devastation "—and I can't get that *bastard*"—fresh venom crackled in her voice as she jabbed a thumb at Novaya Tyumen—"to even authorize search parties for them!"

"What?" Honor blinked.

"He says he doesn't have the *resources*," Berczi said viciously. "According to him, there's no chance anyone survived over there, and he 'can't afford to divert' his efforts from areas where there may actually be someone to rescue. The resort has some people searching, but they don't have gear as good as the Navy or the Corps, and your precious Novaya Tyumen—" she made the title a mockery "—is insisting on telling *them* what to do, as well. As if *he* could find his own ass with both hands and a flashlight!"

"I see." Honor's soprano was colder than the mountain wind, and she felt Nimitz's quivering anger as he clung to her shoulder while she turned suddenly arctic eyes to sweep the area Berczi had pointed to. A part of her could follow Novaya Tyumen's argument, for they did have limited resources. But those resources would begin to grow as the emergency response teams from other resorts arrived. The three nearest ones were already here; within hours, there would be special alpine SAR units here from all over the planet. When that happened, Novaya Tyumen would probably find himself shouldered aside by the experts, and she couldn't quite help wondering if that was part of the reason for his present autocracy. Did he want to make perfectly certain that *his* name was firmly stamped on any credit that might emerge from the rescue operations before someone else arrived to supplant him?

But whatever he was thinking couldn't change reality, and the reality was that saving lives in a situation like this was enormously dependent on the speed with which victims could be found . . . and that Novaya Tyumen had chosen to organize his available personnel and equipment in a way Honor would never have accepted. She'd had personal experience of the incredible, improbable ways in which human beings could survive something like this. She'd seen men and women dug out of ten and even fifteen meters of snow, still alive and— somehow—breathing. But she also knew from that same experience how critical it was that such people be found and retrieved before hypothermia or exhaustion or untreated injuries killed them anyway.

But Novaya Tyumen didn't have her experience, and he had detailed the bulk of his Navy and Marine personnel into simple labor gangs, digging into areas where there were known survivors, whereas only a relatively small percentage of his strength was assigned to hunting for other victims. Now that she considered his operational patterns in the light of Berczi's savage comments, she realized things were even worse than she'd thought before. Even the pinnaces he had flying overhead were concentrated on a limited area, searching the portions of mountainside where the damage was less total and avoiding the areas of maximum devastation.

There was such a thing as refusing to throw away resources by reinforcing failure, Honor admitted, but now that Berczi's description had focused her thoughts and pulled them away from how Novaya Tyumen had shoved her aside, it was suddenly clear to her that he had completely written off those more devastated areas. If the resort employees wanted to divert *their* efforts, or if any of the other civilian rescue teams cared to search those areas as they arrived, that was fine with him, but he himself wasn't interested.

She tried to force herself to give him the benefit of the doubt. To remind herself that he was with BuShips—an engineering specialist more accustomed to a bureaucratic environment than finding himself at the sharp end of the stick. She even reminded herself of her own earlier thoughts about the need to avoid fragmenting command of the operation. But none of that really mattered to her any longer. Not compared to the fact that he had chosen to write off a third of the total resort area and make no effort at all to search for anyone who might be out there and alive. And not, she admitted with scathing self-honesty, now that she realized how her preoccupation with personal concerns and slights had prevented her from realizing sooner that he had.

"You mentioned the beginners' slopes, Major?" she said to Berczi.

"Yes." Berczi's eyes were locked to Honor's face. "There were six lift cars that I know of in the air on their way up the mountain when the slide hit. One of them, the one that was furthest up-slope when the slide hit, was discovered over there—" she pointed to a spot over five hundred meters from the demolished stump of lift tower still poking out of the churned snow "—almost immediately. Most of the people in it were kids. A third of them were dead." She swallowed, then drew a deep breath. "But I'm here with a field trip from the school I currently teach in, Commander, and there are at least five more lift cars out there. One of them had two of *my* kids and twenty or so other people aboard it." She turned to face Honor squarely. "That's bad enough, but their parents are already on board a fast transport inbound from the Unicorn Belt. I don't have an ETA yet, but it can't be more than a few hours from now, and if they get here and discover that the asshole idiot in charge refuses even to *look* for their children—"

She chopped herself off, staring at Honor in stark, simple appeal, and Honor nodded slowly. She understood Berczi's desperation now, and she supposed some people might have called it personal. Well, no doubt it was. But that made it no less valid, and Honor respected her no less for her determination to do something about it.

"I see, Major," she said, and her lips curled in what might have been called a smile. "I see indeed. We'll just have to see to it that they don't have to deal with that, won't we?"

"I don't know if I can, Ranjit," Susan said in a small voice. She hated herself for admitting it—more for admitting it to *herself* than for admitting it to him—but she couldn't help it. She knelt on the floor of the lift car, staring through the twisted opening which had once held a crystoplast window, and the hole she'd gouged out of the wall of snow beyond it with a salvaged ski pole looked back at her.

"I know it's scary, Sooze," Ranjit said, fighting to keep his growing pain and weakness out of his voice. "But it's the only way you can get out, and we don't have enough time to wait for them to find us." He managed not to add "*If* they find us," but from the way she turned her head to look at him, he knew she'd heard it anyway.

"I know," she said after a moment, and managed a weak smile. "I just wish I knew how stinking far down we are."

"I do too," he told her, trying to match her smile while his heart wept for the courage she clung to with both hands.

"Well, at least it's not packed as hard as it could be, I guess," she sighed. She knelt there a moment longer, then raised her voice. "Andrea?"

"Yes?" the older girl's strained voice floated up out of the shadows.

"You take good care of Ranjit while I'm gone, hear?" Susan called, trying to smile at her brother again. "He's a doof, but I kinda like him."

"I'll do my best," Andrea promised, and Ranjit blinked on tears as Susan nodded to him.

"Be back as soon as I can," she told him quietly, and climbed out through the window, taking her ski pole with her. She pushed herself up into the hole she'd already dug, and Ranjit turned his head as far as he could, watching more snow fall through the shattered window onto the lift car's floor. It fell quickly at first, then more slowly . . . and then not at all as Susan tunneled higher into the underbelly of the avalanche, burrowing her way through it, and the snow she excavated packed the tunnel behind her. He pictured her forcing her way through the cold, terrifying darkness, all alone in her tiny, moving airspace as she burrowed towards the sun like some small, blind creature, and he closed his eyes and prayed as he had never before prayed in his life.

✧   ✧   ✧

"Don't be stupid, Commander!" Novaya Tyumen snapped. "Nothin' could possibly have survived over there!" He swept an angry arm at the area around the broken-off lift tower. "If we're goin' to find *anyone* alive, it'll be out *there!*" He jabbed an index finger at the zone in which he had concentrated his efforts.

"With all due respect, Sir, I disagree," Honor said. No one but her had to know how hard it was to keep her words level and dispassionate, but her eyes bored into Novaya Tyumen's. "We've already recovered one lift car that was in the area in question at the time the avalanche hit, and the majority of the people aboard it were still alive. On that basis, I don't believe we can ignore the possibility that others might have survived the initial disaster, as well. And—"

"You don't believe? *You* don't believe?!" Novaya Tyumen glared at her. "Well fortunately, Commander, it doesn't matter what *you* believe, because *I* happen to be in command here!"

"I have no desire to undermine your authority or the chain of command," Honor said. *At least half of that statement is true, anyway*, she reflected acidly. "My sole concern is to point out that there may be people alive in that area, and that they *won't* be alive for long if someone doesn't find them and dig them out."

"Which is also true out there!" Novaya Tyumen shot back, pointing once more at his chosen area of operations.

"No doubt, Sir, but you have people getting in one another's way 'out there,'" Honor said coldly, pointing in turn at two squads of Marines who were crowded tightly enough together to hamper one another's efforts as they tried to dig out around the shell of one of the buildings which had not survived. The rescuers were restricted to shovels and only light tractors and pressers, because even with the tactical sensors from the pinnaces and the Marines' skinsuits, they could only see a couple of meters into the snow with any clarity. That meant they couldn't afford to use more efficient means of excavation for fear of killing the very people they were trying to rescue. "Under the circumstances, you should be able to detail more people to search operations so that civilians now en route will at least know where to dig when they get here!"

"And just how do you propose to search that area?" Novaya Tyumen demanded contemptuously, and shook a sheaf of hardcopy in her face. "These are your own tac readouts, Commander. There's so much junk and garbage—rocks and tree trunks and pieces of buildin's and God only knows what—buried out there even deep-imagin' radar can't see shit! So you

tell me just how in hell we're supposed t' find anythin' out
there even if we tried!"

"We can start by trying to identify some of the garbage as
such so that we can then ignore it and concentrate on the
rest of the targets, Sir." Honor's voice was still controlled, but
it was also ice cold, and its very control made it a slap in
the face after Novaya Tyumen's choleric outburst. "Certainly
there's a lot of wreckage out there to confuse the DIR, but if
we can at least locate the biggest pieces, we can use snow
probes to find them and get microphones down there to listen for any sounds from trapped people. Human beings spent
centuries finding avalanche victims before anyone ever thought
of deep-imaging radar or sonar, Sir, and if we don't start looking
soon—"

"I refuse to discuss this any further, *Commander*," Novaya
Tyumen told her with chill, sneering precision. "I've made my
decision, and I'm not squanderin' resources on some stupid,
glory-grabbin' officer's quixotic lunacy when there are lives to
save right here! Now stand aside and let me get on my with
job before I file formal charges for insubordination."

"'Insubordination'?" Honor repeated. She didn't recognize
her own voice. It was much too calm and reasonable to belong
to her at that moment. She heard Nimitz's deep, sibilant hiss
of disdain as the 'cat glared at Novaya Tyumen, and then she
smiled a cold, dangerous smile. "You file whatever you want
to file, *Sir*," she told him, and turned and walked away.

Novaya Tyumen glared after her, and his face went apoplectic
purple as she pulled an ear bug and attached boom mike from
her parka pocket, clipped it into place, and spoke briefly into
the mike. She listened for a few seconds, her head cocked to
one side, then said something else into the mike, turned on
her heel, and strode directly to Major Stimson.

Novaya Tyumen's eyes blazed with fury as she headed for
the Marine, for there could be no mistaking her purpose,
whatever he might have ordered. He couldn't believe the sheer
gall of her, and rage boiled within him as Stimson looked up
at her approach. Ensign Haverty was saying something to the
baron, but he waved the young woman aside and went stamping
through the snow after Honor.

"—start right there," she was saying to the Marine when
Novaya Tyumen reached them. She pointed at a corner of the
crumpled lift tower. "From the tac system overlays, it looks
like the main thrust of the avalanche must have been roughly
in *this* direction," she turned, sweeping her arm to illustrate
her sentence, "and that checks with where Major Berczi tells

me the one recovered car was found, so we'll want to head northeast. We'll go with a half-klick DIR sweep by two of the pinnaces first, then follow up with your people's skinsuit sensors and snow probes on anything they turn up. If we get a solid hit, we'll—"

"What the *hell* d'you think you're *doin'*?" Novaya Tyumen bellowed. "Goddamn it, I *ordered* you—"

"Now just one minute, you—" Major Stimson's head had snapped up as Novaya Tyumen approached, and his eyes flashed as he began a furious reply, but Honor's raised hand stopped him. She watched the Marine's face for a moment, as if to be certain he had himself under control, and then turned to Novaya Tyumen with what a casual observer might have called an attentive expression. Only the small muscle twitch at the corner of her mouth gave any overt lie to that impression, but the baron flinched involuntarily under the disgust in her dark eyes.

"I believe I was speaking to Major Stimson, not to you, Sir," she told him coldly.

"And just what were you talkin' to him *about?*" Novaya Tyumen sneered.

"Doing our job," Honor said flatly.

"Well whatever orders you were givin' him are counter-manded right now, Commander!" Novaya Tyumen told her in a low, vicious tone. "And you can just report your ass back aboard ship under arrest!"

"I'm afraid I can't do that, Sir," Honor told him. Something about her expression rang an alarm bell in his mind at last, but he was too enraged to heed it.

" 'Can't *do* that'?" he mimicked savagely. "Well that's too fuckin' bad! Major Stimson!" he wheeled to the Marine. "You will place this officer under close arrest and escort her immediately back to her ship!"

"I'm afraid the Major can't do that, either, Sir." Honor told him, and her smile looked like a Sphinx neo-shark rising out of deep water as she looked over Novaya Tyumen's shoulder at someone behind him. "I believe Ensign Haverty is trying to get your attention," she observed.

Novaya Tyumen glared at her, confused, despite his fury, by the apparent *non sequitur.* Almost despite himself, he turned and looked in the direction of her gaze, and his confusion grew greater as he saw the ensign struggling through the snow towards them.

"What the fuck d'*you* want?" he barked as Haverty reached him.

"I was trying to tell you, Sir," the ensign replied. "You've got a com message back at the CP." Haverty's eyes strayed towards Honor, despite her best effort to keep them locked on Novaya Tyumen's face. "It's from Captain Tammerlane, Sir. You are to report back aboard immediately."

"What?" Novaya Tyumen goggled at her. "But—but what about the operation down here?" he demanded.

"All I know is what the Captain told me, Sir," Haverty said. "When I told him you were away from the CP, he told me to find you, tell you to report back aboard *Broadsword* immediately, and inform you that Commander Harrington is now in command of all SAR operations."

"But I'm in command of—"

"You are in command of the Skyhawk evaluation exercise," Honor told him flatly, "and that is *all* you are in command of. This is no longer an evaluation exercise, and you are no longer in command of it. So get out of the way, Commander. Now."

He stared at her, his eyes sick as he realized who she had been speaking to on her earbug mike. It hadn't been Stimson after all. She'd been tied into the com aboard her pinnace, sneaking around and talking to Tammerlane behind his back, and—

"Excuse me, Sir?" He turned as if in a daze and found himself face-to-face with Chief Zariello. "Lieutenant Hedges just informed me that I'm to transport you back to *Broadsword*, Commander," the CPO told him. Novaya Tyumen blinked at him, and Zariello nodded respectfully to the waiting pinnace. "If you'll come this way, Sir, we'll have you aboard in no time," he said, and there was no expression in his voice at all.

Eternity crawled as Susan Hibson clawed her way upward through a shifting, icy world. Her ski suit kept her body warm, but her soul was another matter, and the darkness and closeness and fear drove a dreadful chill deep into the heart of her. She had no light, no guide but her sense of up and down, and she wanted more than she had ever wanted anything before to curl up into a ball and just huddle where she was until someone found her. But she couldn't do that. Ranjit was hurt—worse than he wanted her to believe, she knew—and Andrea Manders was trapped, and so was whoever had gripped Andrea's ankle, and that meant she couldn't stop.

She closed her eyes, feeling the ice against her cheeks as she reached forward once more in the dark, driving her gloveless fingers into the snow ahead of her and dragging herself through it like some sightless worm. She'd lost her broken ski pole, and her hands were like frozen iron claws at the ends of her arms, she could barely feel them now, but she knew they'd been abraded bloody long since. Not that there was anything she could do about it, and she tried not to think about it, just as she tried not to think about how much air she had, or whether the snow would let more air pass through. She didn't think it would, but she didn't know, and it wasn't something she could afford to worry about now anyway.

Her thrusting hands hit something hard, ramming into it with enough force to make her cry out in pain and shock. She snatched them back against her, hugging them to her chest and whimpering while she waited for the hurt in her fingers to subside. It seemed to take forever, but at last she uncurled a little and reached out once more, tentatively. It was another rock, she thought. It wasn't the first she'd encountered, but as her hands tried to explore it and find a way around it, she realized it was the largest so far. There was only one way around it, she told herself, and braced her hand against its support, then arched her back. The snow was just loose enough that she could wedge it away from her, packing it more firmly, using her own body to shape the tiny, moving open space she carried with her, and she arched her back again and again, panting through gritted teeth as she forced the all-enfolding snow to conform to her desires. At last she let herself slump back, pressing her forehead against the rough, icy surface of the rock she had never seen while she sucked in air. She was so tired. So very, very tired. But at least the space about her was big enough now, and she rose on her knees and reached over her head with aching, exhausted arms. She drove her hands into the snow directly above her and felt it shower down. It fell with frightening speed now that she was digging vertically through it, and she bit her lip, forcing herself not to sob with terror as she visualized hitting a looser patch of snow, having it lose its cohesion and come rushing down like crystalline quicksand, filling her tiny space, sealing her mouth and nose alone in the dark—

Susan Hibson moaned, fighting to shut her mind down, clinging to the memory of her brother, and made herself dig onward.

"This may be one of the lift cars here, Ma'am. According to the DIR, anyway." Major Stimson's finger jabbed at a blur of light in the holograph generated by the deep-imaging radar mounted in the shuttle hovering overhead. The DIR was intended to probe for underground bunkers and similar installations, but it should have been equally useful for work like this. Except that the avalanche had carried so much debris down with it that they could never be certain exactly what they were looking at. It could have been a lift car . . . or a boulder . . . or a section of the lift tower.

"What about sonar?" Honor asked.

"No more definitive," Stimson said unhappily. "Whatever it is, it's about thirty meters down, and resolution is crap with both systems. Thing is, if DIR is right and it *is* a lift car, sonar ought to be indicating a void inside it, and it isn't. Of course, thirty meters is a long reach for a skinny's sonar. We really need more of the big units the alpine SAR people use. But still—"

He shrugged unhappily, and Honor forced her face to show no expression as she nodded. She knew what he meant, of course. Even if it was a lift car, there could be at least one very simple reason why neither the DIR nor sonar had revealed any open air spaces within it.

"All right, Frank," she said after a moment. "I want a squad working on it anyway. Get one of the pinnaces over and use its tractors and belly fans to clear the first ten or fifteen meters for them, then they can go in with the hand tractors and shovels."

"Aye, aye, Ma'am." The Marine nodded and began speaking into his own boom mike, and Honor turned away to survey the snow field.

More civilian rescue personnel were arriving now, but most of them were concentrating on the ski slopes higher up the mountain. That made sense, she supposed, given that at least half the missing had been on the slopes when the avalanche hit. Others had taken over the areas in which Novaya Tyumen had concentrated his efforts, digging down into buried buildings and freeing the people trapped inside them. She couldn't really fault their priorities, and her pinnaces were busy everywhere, moving people and equipment wherever they were needed and bringing their tac sensors to bear in response to requests from rescue teams. But she herself and all of her Marines were committed to the area here around the beginners' slope lift and the neighboring intermediate slope lift. Major Berczi was with them, limping painfully around with a face like beaten iron, as they drove themselves into exhaustion trying to find the children death had snatched away from them. At least there were enough other rescue personnel present now to let them concentrate their efforts here without ignoring other needs, and she tried to feel grateful that it was so.

They'd been at it since late morning, and the shadows of

early evening were stretching out across the churned snow. The winter mountain twilight wouldn't last long, and the temperature was dropping, too. By morning, all the snow softened by the sun would have frozen hard, making their task that much more difficult. But, of course, by morning anyone who was still alive underneath this wilderness of hostile white would almost certainly be dead, anyway, she thought grimly.

Nimitz made a soft sound on her shoulder, and she reached up to comfort him. He pressed against her gloved palm for a moment, but then, to her surprise, he leapt lightly down. He landed in the snow and crouched there for a long moment, whiskers quivering and ears cocked, and then he began to move slowly away from her. She stared at him, her weary mind trying to figure out what he was up to, and he looked back over his shoulder at her. He flirted his tail and bleeked up at her, and then went bounding away into the shadows.

"Ranjit? *Ranjit!*"

Ranjit's eyes snapped open as the sudden panic in Andrea's voice penetrated his hazy thoughts. He blinked hard, then rubbed his face weakly, trying to scrub himself back to wakefulness. It didn't work very well, and his mouth moved in a parody of a smile as he realized why. It wasn't simple fatigue or sleepiness reaching out for him; it was blood loss from his damaged leg and the cold biting into him where his ski suit must have been rent and torn.

"Yes?" he said after a moment, and noted the hoarseness of his voice with a sort of dull bemusement.

"I—" Andrea paused. "I was afraid you'd passed out," she finished after a moment, and he astounded them both with a dry, coughing burst of laughter.

Passed out? I don't think so, he thought. *You were afraid I'd gone and died on you, Andrea. But I haven't. Not yet.*

"'S okay," he said finally, when the laughter had released him. "'M just tired, you know? Sleepy. G'on talkin' to me. It'll keep me awake."

"Are you sure?" The voice of the girl he couldn't remember ever having seen came back to him from the dimness, and he nodded.

"Positive," he said. The word came out sounding like a drunk he'd once heard, with a sort of exaggerated, woozy precision. He wanted to giggle some more at the thought, but he managed not to.

"All right," Andrea said. "You know, this was the first time I ever came to the Atticas for the skiing. We always went to the Black Mountains before. I don't know why. Just closer, I guess. Anyway—"

She went on talking, hearing the thin veneer of calm holding her own words together like glue against the terror quivering deep inside her. She'd never said anything so inane and pointless in her life, she thought. Yet somehow, however disjointed and pointless it might have been, it was also the most important thing she'd ever told anyone.

Because it proved she was still alive, she thought, just as the weakening grip on her ankle told her at least one other person still lived beyond the barrier which pinned her, and just as Ranjit's occasional responses to her questions proved *he* was still alive.

For now.

Susan's hands were more than simply abraded now. She'd been forced to work her blind, agonizing way through and around a tangle of broken limbs the avalanche had carried down from above with it, and she'd injured her right hand badly when she caught it in the angle of two of the branches. She couldn't tell how badly it was bleeding, and she was terrified of meeting another, worse tangle—one she couldn't find a way past.

She was weeping now. She couldn't stop. Every muscle and sinew ached and throbbed and burned, and she wanted so badly to make it stop. Just to make it end. But she couldn't. Ranjit depended on her, and so she drove her exhausted body upward.

How far down am *I?* she wondered in the small corner of her mind which had any energy to spare from the brutal task of pushing herself on. *Surely I should be seeing some sign of daylight coming down from above by now, shouldn't I? Am I even still going up? Or did I get turned around somehow by those limbs? Have I started digging downward again?*

She didn't know. She only knew she couldn't stop.

"What is it, Stinker?" Honor asked. She knelt beside Nimitz in the gathering twilight, and the 'cat sat up on his rearmost limbs, reaching up to pat her chest urgently. His eyes bored into hers like augers, and she knew he was trying to tell her something, but she couldn't quite bring herself to believe the most logical explanation. Treecats had been used over the years in search and rescue efforts on Sphinx, but not as often as one might have expected, for the range at which they could sense human beings they'd never met before appeared to be limited. There had been instances of 'cats who were able to home in on total strangers at distances of up to a hundred or even two hundred meters, even under the most adverse conditions, but such cases were extremely rare—more the stuff of rumors and legends than recorded fact. More to the point, perhaps, Honor couldn't recall ever having seen any indication from Nimitz that *he* might be capable of such a feat. Besides, they were over three hundred meters beyond the line the alpine SAR teams had calculated as the furthest any of the lift cars might have been carried from the lift tower. The shouts and machinery sounds of the rescue effort were small and lost here, little stronger than the whine and moan of the gathering wind, and she looked around, trying to see anything that might have brought him here.

The 'cat made a sound, half-pleading and half-commanding, that dragged her attention back to him. He captured her eyes once more, and then he took his right true-hand from her chest and made an unmistakable gesture with it. A gesture that pointed straight down into the snow.

"*Here?*" As well as she knew him, Honor couldn't quite keep the doubt out of her voice. "You think there's someone down there?"

Nimitz bleeked loudly, then chittered at her and nodded hard. She looked around once more, back to where the stump of the lift—the better part of two kilometers from where she knelt—poked up out of the snow, tiny with distance. There was no way a lift car could have been carried this far, she told herself. Was there? Yet Nimitz seemed so positive. . . .

"All right, Stinker," she sighed. "What do we have to lose?"

The 'cat bleeked again, even louder, as she keyed her com once more. And then, as she started to speak into it, he turned and began to burrow into the snow himself. Snow tunnels were a game he and Honor had played often during her childhood on Sphinx, and it was remarkable how rapidly a six-limbed creature with centimeter-long claws could tear through snow. By the time Honor was done speaking on the com, he was two meters down and going strong.

Susan froze. For a moment, her mind was too foggy and confused to tell her why it had stopped her, and then she realized she'd heard something. It seemed impossible, after so long sealed up alone with the sound of her own breath roaring in her ears, yet she was certain she truly had heard something. She strained her ears, and then her heart gave a tremendous lurch. She *had* heard it! A scraping, scratching sound, like something moving through snow—something moving towards *her!*

She screamed, lunging suddenly in her dark little world, thrusting towards the sound, fighting her way up out of the endless blackness. She punched and kicked and ripped at the snow, and then, suddenly, her right fist broke through some final barrier into open air and she froze once more, unable to move, paralyzed with a strange terror which dared not believe she might actually have clawed her way back into the upper world at last. She wanted to shout, to move, to cry out for help, to do *something* . . . and she couldn't. She couldn't move at all, and so she simply lay there.

But then something touched her hand. Strong, wiry fingers closed on her wrist, holding it, and something soft and silken pressed against her torn and bleeding palm. A half-heard, half-felt croon of comfort burned into her, and Susan Hibson went limp, sobbing in a sudden torrent of relief like agony as the reassurance of that touch filled her.

"Where do you want us, Ma'am?" Sergeant Wells panted as she and her squad slithered to a halt beside Honor. The sergeant carried a powerful hand lamp against the gathering darkness, and her people carried hand tractors and pressers and shovels. Honor ran her eyes over them once, then nodded for them to follow her.

"Over this way," she said, leading the way back towards Nimitz.

"We're a long way beyond the search line, Ma'am," Wells pointed out diffidently, and Honor nodded.

"I know. Call it a hunch."

"A hunch, Ma'am?"

"That's right, but it's not really mine. It's—"

She stopped dead, so abruptly Wells almost ran into her, but neither of them really thought about that. They were staring down into the hole burrowed into the churned white surface, to where a small, dark-skinned hand, torn and bloodied, thrust out of a wall of snow and a cream-and-gray treecat cradled it against his chest while his eyes blazed like green fire in the glow of the sergeant's lamp.

Ranjit Hibson's eyelids fluttered open.

For a long moment he simply lay there, drowsy and content and warm. For some reason it seemed wrong for him to feel that way, but he couldn't quite remem—

"Susan!"

His eyes flew wide, and he jerked up in the bed. Susan! Where was—?!

"It's all right, Ranjit," a familiar voice said, and his head snapped around as someone touched his shoulder. "I'm fine," the voice told him, and he gasped in terrible relief as his sister sat down on the edge of his bed and smiled at him. It was her old, indomitable smile—almost . . . with just a shadow of remembered darkness behind it—and he reached out to touch her bruised face with gentle, wondering fingers.

"Sooze," he half-whispered, and her green eyes gleamed with suspicious wetness as she caught his hand and held it to her cheek. Her own hands were heavily bandaged, and his mouth tightened as he saw how carefully she touched him. But she saw his borning frown and shook her head quickly.

"It's not that bad," she reassured him. "I skinned them and cut them some and broke one finger, but the quick heal's already working on them. They'll be all better a long time before your legs will. And speaking of legs," a spark of true anger glittered in her eyes, "why didn't you *tell* me you were bleeding like that!"

"I didn't know for sure that I was," he replied, still drinking in her face and the fact that she was alive. "Besides, there wasn't anything you could've done except what you did do— go for help—so why should I have worried you with it? You had enough on your mind, Sooze."

"Yeah," she said after a moment, and lowered her eyes to his hand. "Yeah, I guess I did, at that."

"Indeed she did," another voice said, and Ranjit's head snapped around toward the hospital room's door. Kalindi and Liesell Hibson stood there, each with an arm around the other, and Kalindi's smile seemed to waver just a bit as he tried to keep his voice steady. "You both did. And we're proud of you both. Very proud."

"Mom—Dad—" Ranjit stared at his parents and, to his horror, heard his own hoarseness and felt the hot burn of tears. He was too old to bawl like a baby, he told himself, and it didn't do any good at all as he felt his face crumple. Horrible embarrassment engulfed him, but there was nothing he could do about it . . . and a moment later, it didn't matter, for his mother was there, with her arms around him, hugging him close while he sobbed into her shoulder. Her hands stroked his back, and he heard her murmuring the words of comfort he was much too old to need . . . and needed anyway. He raised his head, staring at her through his tears, and his father

reached across her shoulder to ruffle his hair as he had when
Ranjit was only a boy.

"I-I'm sorry," he got our finally. "I promised . . . promised
I'd take care of Sooze, and instead—"

"Forgive me for intruding," another voice said dryly from
the open door, "but I tend to doubt they expected your promise
to be binding on a mountain, Ranjit."

He blinked on his tears, and Csilla Berczi smiled at him.
The teacher's expression commiserated with his wounded
adolescent pride, yet it also congratulated him for having the
good sense to ignore it.

"May I come in?" she asked.

"It's Ranjit's room," Liesell said with a small smile, and
looked at her son.

"Of course you can!" he said quickly, and Berczi chuckled
and stepped into the room. She seemed unsteady on her feet,
but she only grimaced at Ranjit's quick look of concern.

"Don't worry about it," she told them. "The wiring and a
couple of servos in my replacement took a hit during the
excitement, but it's nothing they can't adjust back on Unicorn
Eleven. At the moment, though, I've brought another visitor
along with me."

She grinned at her students' expressions, but she also lowered herself into a bedside chair and waved a hand at the door
as yet another head poked around the frame and peeked into
the room.

"Come on in, Andrea," Berczi invited, and laughed as Ranjit
suddenly sat up straighter in bed. The girl in the doorway was
taller than he'd somehow expected, with a lovely oval face and
dark blue eyes. She moved a bit stiffly, as if she had her own
share of bruises, but the smile she gave him and Susan was
blinding, and Liesell and Kalindi looked at one another with
wry, resigned expressions .

"Hi," she said just a bit shyly. "I, uh, told Ms. Berczi I
wanted to meet you two—actually *meet* you, that is. Because
I wouldn't be here without you, and I know it."

"Without Sooze, you mean," Ranjit corrected, feeling his face
blaze scarlet as he made himself meet her gaze.

"Maybe, but I'd never've had the nerve to climb out into
that stinking snow without you, Ranjit," Susan said stoutly.

"Yeah, but—" Ranjit began, only to be cut off by their
teacher.

"There's plenty of credit to go around, people," she told them
both. "I'm proud of you both—very proud—and so are your
parents."

"Indeed we are," Kalindi agreed firmly. "We would appreciate it if both of you could see your way to giving us a little less cause for such, um, *traumatic* pride for the next little bit—like, oh, the next fifty or sixty years, you understand. But we've heard how you handled yourselves." He smiled, but his eyes and voice were serious. "A parent is always proud when his or her child rises to meet a challenge, but your mother and I are most pleased with you both, and the courage and resourcefulness you showed bring much honor upon you."

"And don't you forget it, either," Berczi said as Ranjit and Susan flushed with mingled pride, pleasure, and embarrassment under their father's praise. "You not only got yourselves out, but you got Andrea here and four other people from the other side of the lift car, as well. And finding your car indicated that we'd been much too conservative in our estimates of where we should have been looking in the first place, so we widened the search. Which is how we found two more cars the same night."

"I'm glad you did," Ranjit said slowly, but his eyes had darkened as he did the mental math. "But Sooze and Andrea and I make three, and you said there were only four more?" He stared at the teacher, begging her to tell him he'd misunderstood her, but she only shook her head with gentle compassion. "Only seven" he whispered.

"Only seven," she confirmed quietly, and Ranjit felt his mother's grip tighten comfortingly about him once more. "You kids were lucky—gutsy and smart as hell, too, but lucky clear through," the teacher went on. "The newsies are calling this the worst avalanche in the Star Kingdom's history, at least in terms of loss of life. So far—" She paused and drew a deep breath, then continued. "So far, we've confirmed three hundred and sixty dead, and the toll's still going up. Odds are that it'll at least double before it's all over."

"And us? The other kids?" Ranjit asked tautly.

"All in one piece, more or less," Berczi said with unfeigned gratitude. "You and Susan were the only ones we had headed for the beginners' slopes. Donny Tergesen got banged up pretty bad—he'll be in the body and fender shop longer than you will, Ranjit—but we didn't have anyone else actually out on the slopes yet, and none of the other lifts got hit anywhere near as hard as yours did."

"That's for sure," Andrea put in, and smiled crookedly as Ranjit looked her way. "My mother and sister were waiting for the lift to the advanced slopes, and they hardly even got shaken up over there," the blonde told him. "We were the ones who got walloped."

"Yes, you were," Berczi agreed. "But the three of you came through it intact, and that's the important thing for you to remember—all of you. I'm sure you'll have your share of nightmares over it. That's normal, and there's nothing anyone can do to prevent it. But don't let yourselves feel guilty somehow because you made it and other people didn't. You didn't kill anyone, and nothing that happened to anyone else was your fault. You got home the hard way, but you got there, and along the way, you managed to save some lives that would have been lost without you. That's what it's important to remember."

She looked deep into three young sets of eyes in turn, holding each of them until their owners nodded solemnly.

"Good." She leaned back in her chair and nodded at the older Hibsons. "Your parents and I have already discussed the need to schedule a few sessions with a counselor for all of you, but if you want someone else to talk to about it, come to me. And that includes you, Andrea, assuming I'm anywhere in com reach."

"I will, Ma'am," the blonde began, "and—"

"Excuse me. Is this a private party, or are drop-ins welcome?" a crisp soprano voice inquired.

Ranjit turned his head as the speaker stood in the open doorway. She was tall for a woman, with broad shoulders and short-cropped brown hair, and she wore the space-black and gold of the Royal Manticoran Navy with the cuff stripes of a lieutenant commander. All of that registered, but only at the corners of his mind, for she also had something else that reached out and seized his attention. It couldn't be what it looked like! He'd wanted to see one of them for as long as he could remember, dreamed of being adopted by one, but he'd never really expected ever to *meet* one of them, and especially not off Sphinx!

The fluffy-coated, six-limbed creature on the officer's shoulder turned its head to meet his own goggle-eyed stare. There was a moment of silence, and then the treecat bleeked and twitched its whiskers at him, obviously delighted by his stunned reaction to its presence.

"Commander Harrington!" Berczi said, and Ranjit's parents stiffened, as if they recognized the name. His mother released him to stand up as the teacher started to push herself awkwardly to her feet, but the woman in the doorway waved her back into her chair.

"Stay where you are, Major. I just dropped by for a word

with Susan. And—" she glanced speculatively at Kalindi and Liesell "—her parents?"

"Yes. Yes, we are," Liesell said, and stepped forward to take the newcomer's hand in both of hers. "Thank you, Commander. *Thank you.* We can never repay you for what you've done."

"There's no need to repay me for anything, Ms. Hibson," the tall woman said gently. "It was Nimitz here who found Susan, you know, not me. If you want to thank anyone, thank him—and the people who actually dug Ranjit and Andrea out, of course. But to be perfectly honest, Susan would have done the job without me or Nimitz. She was less than five meters down when he sensed her, and there was no way five measly meters of snow were going to stop your daughter, Ma'am."

Susan blushed a bright, blazing scarlet—a hue so hot she could have used it to melt her way to rescue if it had been available at the time, Ranjit thought—and Liesell reached out and wrapped her arm tightly around her daughter's shoulders.

"I believe you're correct, Commander," she said with a wry smile. "Her father and I have noticed before that she can be just a bit on the stubborn side."

"So I've heard," Commander Harrington agreed. "Which brings me to the rather delicate matter of what I wanted to speak to her about."

"With me, Ma'am?" Susan said, and her tone was almost as big a surprise for Ranjit as the treecat's appearance. He'd become accustomed to the way his sister always spoke of the Navy—as the "chauffeurs" and "deck jockeys" whose sole job was to move important people like Marines around—but there was no sign of that now. She had addressed the tall officer in tones of profound respect, and as he heard it, Ranjit sensed that there was a great deal about their rescue that he hadn't been told yet.

"Yes." The tall woman looked consideringly down at Susan, and the 'cat on her shoulder joined her, cocking his head to peer thoughtfully at Ranjit's sister. "I thought you'd like to know what I just heard over at the CP," the woman said. "If your parents don't mind, of course."

"Mind what, Commander?" Kalindi asked.

"Well, I'm afraid it has to do with that stubbornness your wife just mentioned, Sir," Harrington said. "You see, the newsies are swarming all over the resort looking for human interest stories, and I'm afraid your daughter here is rapidly turning into the central heroine of the entire disaster. The quickie interview they did with her last night has gone out on live feeds and in all the 'faxes, and we've already heard back from Manticore about her."

"From Manticore?" Susan repeated. "About *me?*"

"Yes. You know, you really impressed everyone with the rescue teams. We all feel you showed a lot of nerve and determination, and you did a good job of helping us backtrack your tunnel to find Ranjit and Andrea, too."

She paused, and Ranjit watched bemusedly as Susan blushed yet again. The woman with the 'cat smiled ever so slightly, almond eyes gleaming as she enjoyed Susan's atypical tongue-tied silence. She let it stretch out for several seconds, then cleared her throat.

"It just happens," she went on, "that Major Stimson and Major Berczi are old friends, and the Major explained your, um, military ambitions to us. I believe you also said a little something about them to the newsies, didn't you?"

Susan darted an agonized look at her parents, then nodded, and Harrington shrugged. "Well, Major Stimson had already mentioned them to me, and *I* mentioned them to Captain Tammerlane—he's the skipper of my ship—and *he* passed them on up the chain in turn, and then the interview imagery hit the capital news net, and, well—"

She shrugged, grinning, and Susan turned her eyes to her brother in agonized embarrassment. She stared at him pleadingly, and he shook himself.

"And *what*—Ma'am?" he asked finally.

"Well, I understand that somehow your sister's plans got bucked all the way up the chain to the Commandant of the Corps," Commander Harrington told him.

"All the way—?" Ranjit's jaw dropped, and twisted back around to stare at his Susan.

"Yes, indeed. And according to the traffic over at the CP, General Ambristen was rather taken with her exploits himself. Sufficiently so, in fact, that on the recommendation of Major Berczi, Major Stimson, and myself, the Corps has already reserved a slot for her at OCS, assuming—" Harrington darted a moderately severe glance at Susan "—that she gets her grades up, of course."

"*Really?*" The word burst out of Susan like an explosion, and Harrington nodded with a chuckle.

"Really," she assured the girl. "But it really is contingent on your passing the academic requirements, too. May I assume that you'll be doing a little something about those grades Major Berczi mentioned to me?"

"Yes, Ma'am! I mean— Yes, of course I will!"

"Good. In that case, maybe you and I will serve together sometime."

"I'd . . . I'd like that, Ma'am," Susan said, suddenly almost painfully shy. "I'd like that a lot."

"Stranger things have happened," Harrington observed. Then she nodded to Andrea and Ranjit, shook hands once more with both of Susan's parents, sketched an abbreviated salute to Berczi, and disappeared.

Ranjit stared after her for a long, endless moment, then looked at his parents, but they weren't looking at him. They were looking at each other, with expressions that mingled resignation, pride, bittersweet laughter, and the admission that their long effort to divert Susan from the Marines had just turned into an abject failure. It was going to take them a while to deal with that and once more begin paying any attention to the rest of the world, and Susan was in even worse shape. She was simply standing there, staring off into space, and her entire face was one huge, beatific smile. There wasn't so much as a hint of intelligence in her bemused eyes, and Ranjit shuddered. She was going to be extremely difficult to live with for the next few weeks, or months—*or years*, he thought wryly—once she resumed interactive contact with the world about her. But that wasn't going to happen for a while, so he turned to Csilla Berczi.

"Who *was* that?" he demanded.

"She's the one who dug the lot of you out of the avalanche," the teacher replied. "Well, she and a squad of Marines under her command. Her treecat found Susan."

"Yeah, it was great!" Andrea chipped in. "Commander Harrington says he must've sensed her emotions or something and led them straight to her. They were wonderful about getting all the rest of us out, too. But I can hardly believe she went to the trouble of telling her captain Susan wanted to be a Marine and then actually came clear over to the hospital just to tell her!"

"Believe it, young lady," Berczi told her. "There are never enough good officers to go around. Commander Harrington knows that—which shouldn't be too surprising, since she's one of the good ones herself!—and she recognized the same things in our Susan that I've been looking at for the last couple of years. Although," she added judiciously, glancing sidelong at the younger girl's gloriously bemused expression, "we could all be excused for not seeing them just at the moment, I suppose."

"Well I'm happy for her," Andrea said firmly. "Aren't you?"

"Of course I am," Berczi agreed, "and—"

She stopped speaking as Ranjit's deep, heartfelt groan suddenly interrupted her. He, too, had been staring at his sister, but now his eyes were fixed on his parents, and Berczi cocked an eyebrow at him.

"What?" she asked. "Are your legs bothering you all of a sudden, Ranjit?"

"No, no," he shook his head, but his expression was that of someone in intense pain, and she looked a question at him. "It wasn't that," he assured her. "It wasn't that at all."

"Then what *was* it?" she demanded, and he looked at her mournfully.

"It's just that I really did promise to keep an eye on Susan if Mom and Dad let her come on the trip," he told her, "and I just realized. They may not be going to blame me for the avalanche, but when they come back up for air, they're gonna *kill* me for letting *this* happen!"

Deck Load Strike

Roland J. Green

ONE

If maps could sneer, Major Shuna Ryder would have expected the one facing her to do so. Or maybe something even less polite, such as spitting in her eye.

It certainly displayed as fine a collection of discouraging data as she had ever seen, at least since the efficiency report filed on her when she got crosswise with the detachment commander aboard *Warspite*. Her career had survived that report, however. So her mission on Silvestria ought to survive the map.

The map was a flat-board digital display, several generations behind even the most primitive holo, but the best that the Canmore Republic could make available to its Manticoran "advisers." But then, the Republic was only a few generations removed from paper maps, and she'd even seen one in the Guard Museum that was supposed to be inked on a fish bladder.

All five million people of Silvestria's two nations were perversely proud of the length and depth of their neo-barbarian period. However, Ryder doubted that on a planet with so many trees, they had ever lost the art of papermaking. Although since fish were as thick in the sea as trees were on land, maybe somebody actually *had* used fish organs.

Certainly both fish and trees were well on their way to restoring a technological civilization on Silvestria. In another generation, the Canmore Republic and the Kingdom of Chuiban would have been able to decide on their own whether to roll out the red carpet for off-world allies, or toss them unceremoniously into the nearest body of water (which was seldom far away, in either nation).

Unfortunately, Silvestria was close enough to the Erewhon Wormhole Junction to be of interest to anyone concerned about the status of Erewhon. This naturally included the Erewhonese, the more so in that they imported vast quantities of aquacultural and forestry products from Silvestria in a fleet of massive bulk carriers that made a highly visible component of the Erewhon Merchant Marine.

(Not so highly visible, but not escaping the Manticorans, was that some of the bulk carriers were rather over-built for their work, with features that smelled ever so slightly of Solarian League naval dockyards. A bribe to the Erewhonese, a reserve in case the Sollies ever needed troop lift in this area, or something else entirely?)

Still more unfortunately, Silvestria wasn't going to get that generation. A T-year and a half ago, the long expansion of the People's Republic of Haven had run so hard into the obstinate independence of the Star Kingdom of Manticore that long-simmering tension had flared into open war.

Erewhon's allies and patrons, the Solarian League, had also coveted the Manticore Junction. Although the Sollies were a little less crude about it than the Peeps, there was little love lost between the Assembly on Old Earth and the Star Kingdom, and they were definitely neutral in a way that let them transfer technology to the Peeps. Perhaps even worse, from Manticore's viewpoint, the League's security concerns made it extremely nervous about anyone intervening anywhere close to any of the Junctions that it already claimed or—as in the case of Erewhon—controlled indirectly through military and economic treaties.

So even when it became obvious that the Peeps were putting down a mission in the Kingdom of Chuiban, the Star Kingdom could not intervene as openly. Fortunately, it didn't have to. One of the Admiralty's secret assets, carefully saved up for just such a situation as this, was covert advisers like Major Ryder and her team.

"Break ranks and gather round," the major said. It took a moment for the other Royal Marines and the Royal Navy contingent to stop looking around for the vast multitude that Ryder seemed to be addressing. Thirty men and women sitting in chairs could hardly form ranks in the first place!

"We were all there for Exercise Juno," she said, when the team had formed a semi-circle around the map. "Those of us who weren't with the shore party made the inland run. What do the Republic's prospects look like to you? Anyone?"

Master Chief Sick Berth Attendant Loren Bexo replied first, which did not surprise Major Ryder. He knew more about healing casualties than any other two SBA's she'd ever known. He also knew more than he would usually admit about inflicting the casualties in the first place. Why he was no longer an Assault Marine was his personal business, but that background made him even more invaluable to the Silvestria mission than he would have been otherwise.

"If the next mobile force to get ashore anywhere within two hundred klicks north or south of Port Malcolm is real, instead of simulated, the Republic is hip deep in hexapuma shit," Bexo said. "Anything brigade-sized stands a good chance of encircling the city and cutting off all three passes to the Highlands."

"What about the guns at the passes?" a Navy lieutenant (j.g.) said. "Couldn't they keep the passes open?"

"Not against targets in the forest, unless they had very good aerial observation," Ryder said. *Probably not even then*, she added mentally. Silvestria was short of heavier metals like iron; steel was expensive. The Guard's best artillery was assigned to the coastal defenses of Port Malcolm; what was left to hold the passes would not have raised eyebrows on an Old Earth battlefield centuries before the Diaspora.

"The Guard can block the roads to the Highlands by cutting down trees across them," a Marine sergeant pointed out. "As a matter of fact, I understand that's part of the plan anyway."

Ryder had a visceral reaction to both wagging tongues and dressing down subordinates in public. The two reactions fought to a standstill, giving an ache to her stomach and an edge to her voice.

"A thoroughly *secret* part, unless I've forgotten our briefing from the Director of the Guard. Which he was courteous enough to give us personally."

"Ah, well—I got a personal—briefing—from somebody who's on the tree-chopping crew. And she pointed out the problem, too. There's not enough air lift to get the Malcomers upland, let alone the rest of the Lowlands. They'd have to go by road, and fallen trees would block any ground vehicles, not just a mobile enemy."

And the one railroad could be broken by blowing any one of five bridges from the air or even from orbit. Ryder sighed. It looked as if the sergeant had fraternized but given no more than he gained—which was not a bad way for such an affair to go, and besides, she was not really in a position to throw stones.

"I have to agree," Ryder said. "No harm done this time,

Sergeant, but everybody remember about mistimed curiosity. If we didn't have the goodwill of the Guard, we wouldn't be even close to having six hundred combat-ready Sea Fencibles. The Republic is giving us everything they can afford and maybe a little more. We all have some sort of body armor, but half their artillery crews are still wearing fatigues and helmets!

"So don't let's us embarrass them unnecessarily, all right?"

Everyone agreed enthusiastically, maybe even sincerely, but she saw the reservations on every face. It would take more than cooperation, it would take miracles, to give the Canmore Republic some sort of offensive capability before Carl Euvin-ophan's private army was ready to cross the Central Sea and become that non-simulated mobile brigade.

Then the red on the map would be a trail of equally non-simulated bodies. It almost helped that the oldest tradition of the Marine advisers (nearly ten years old) was to be among the corpses when the smoke cleared. That meant fewer hard decisions to make during the fighting, and none at all after-ward.

The Kingdom of Chuiban's main western port was not blacked out. That would have made no sense, even if the Canmore Republic had possessed a halfway-decent satellite network or even a reliably friendly eye aboard the orbital freight station. A satellite net or the station would have been over Buwayjon several times before the tanks was were safely under cover, and tanks gave off impressive heat signatures even from orbit.

Fortunately, the freight station was under the control of the foolish, decadent, elitist, and obstinately neutral Erewhonese. They kept it as neutral as they were. Also, they had not sold either contender on Silvestria more than a few basic weather satellites.

When somebody on Silvestria suddenly flourished a satel-lite network, it would be the Kingdom of Chuiban. And the satellites would *work*—Citizen People's Commissioner Jean Testaniere had handpicked the models himself, then person-ally run the diagnostic and maintenance tests on them. It might be considered dangerously elitist for a People's Commissioner to exhibit so much technical competence, but it was simply dangerous to trust one's life to electronics left in the hands of people who did not know one piece of diagnostic nanoware from another.

The first tanks were now turning off the pier and rolling

up Mongkut Avenue, from which all civilian traffic had been barred by white-gloved Field Police. There were too many of them to all be from the city's modest Royal Army garrison; some of warlord Euvinophan's own Field Police company had to have arrived with the vehicle convoy.

A challenge floated through the thin mist, and a response came back. The challenger was the Commissioner's bodyguard, Citizen Sergeant Pescu of the State Security; the response came from Citizen Captain Paul Weldon, of the People's Navy.

Testaniere wondered how long Weldon had been in town. The commissioner hadn't heard the pinnace land, and both Weldon and his two pilots were fond of making a noisy entrance.

"Greetings, Citizen Captain," Testaniere said. They shook hands, the greeting of equals, although privately Testaniere wondered if the Citizen Captain would ever have risen above Lieutenant Commander under the Legislaturalist regime.

Testaniere was sure that he himself would have risen at least to foreman if he had stayed at the shop long enough. He had always had the self-confidence which comes with mastering a particular body of knowledge—which he was elitist enough to know was hardly universal among the ranks of the People's Commissioners, State Security, or even the armed forces of the People's Republic!

"Fraternal greetings to you, Citizen Commissioner," Weldon replied. He sniffed the air. "A fine night for our work, eh?"

"I could wish it were not quite so fine," Testaniere said. "A good thick fog would hide us from eyes closer than the Republic's."

"You doubt the loyalty and discretion of the people looking forward to the day of liberation from a *monarchy*?" Weldon's incredulity was not entirely an act.

Testaniere sighed. They had been over this ground often enough that he had lost his sense of humor about it. He would have to be careful, however, or he might become one of the first People's Commissioners to be informed on by his military counterpart! Ninety-nine times out of a hundred it went the other way, but they were many light-years from Nouveau Paris and Silvestria was an even bigger political joke than Testaniere's briefings had led him to expect.

In careful detail, he reminded Weldon that the monarchy was highly revered, and that much of Carl Euvinophan's support came from his blood connection with the royal house. Furthermore, it was possible to have legitimate doubts about how much liberating of anything Euvinophan was likely to do without a decisive victory over the Canmores to wave in the face of his enemies.

"Remember that on his mother's side he's descended from a king and on his father's from an Andermani soldier of fortune. That's not what I would have picked as a heritage for the perfect revolutionary."

That was stronger than Testaniere would have put it without the rumble and squeal of the tanks to cover his voice. He only hoped that Citizen Captain Weldon would not quote him anywhere it might be overheard. A vital part of using somebody like Carl Euvinophan as a puppet was to make sure that he never saw the strings until you had replaced them with unbreakable monofilament and preferably shoved a pulse rifle into his belly to make sure he didn't try to untie the monofilament.

The citizen commissioner wondered what his superiors had been thinking of when they decided that the People's Republic should work with Euvinophan. Among other things, he had a good many Andermani comrades, some his own and some left over from his father, and the Andermani were no friends to the People's Republic unless they could see a profitable war in it. In Testaniere's opinion, Gustav Anderman had used hyper to fly back to the Dark Ages, and most of his people were still living there!

The last tank of the first company had passed, and Testaniere saw the tail lights of the earlier ones, turning off to the assembly area and dumps in the industrial park at the south end of the city. Each of the six tank companies had eighteen tanks, old San Martin models marginally survivable on a really modern battlefield, but still generations ahead of anything Silvestria could have produced locally. The full force of these track-borne antiques mounted a hundred and eight 10-cm plasma guns, two hundred and sixteen flex-mounted pulsers, and several hundred launchers for grenades, flares, smoke bombs, and chaff.

They could carry all of this on a battlefield at up to seventy klicks an hour, with turbines burning anything from diluted tar or wood alcohol up to the hydrogen-enriched synthetics already in the dump. They even had silent low-speed electric drives for stealth operations, running off power packs rechargeable from any commercial electric grid.

They and the similarly-powered armored personnel carriers were two legs of the tripod on which the fall of the Canmore Republic would be mounted. The third was an air arm, consisting of six converted refrigerated-cargo freighters and Captain Weldon's pinnace. They were intended more for scouting and airlift than for close support, but the freighters all had racks for ten tons of homemade iron bombs or an equivalent load of troops and supplies. The pinnace mounted two heavy bow-mounted tribarrel pulsers, a single three-centimeter laser (primarily for space use), and ventral hard points for up to forty assorted short-range missiles.

The People's Republic had given Carl Euvinophan the firepower to break up any concentrated resistance the Canmore Republic could offer, and as much freedom from fuel shortages, that ancient curse of armored troops, as the People's forces could spare for a backwater like Silvestria.

Another tank company was rolling up Mongkut Avenue. Testaniere wondered if when the three infantry battalions came in they would make a show riding on the tanks (as long as they didn't fall off), staying snugly out of the night mist in the carriers, or marching on foot. As might have been expected from anyone with even a trace of Andermani blood, Carl Euvinophan had polished the close-order drill and parade marching of his private army.

One could only hope that this had not been at too much cost to their tactical proficiency.

Citizen Captain Weldon watched another tank company roll past, then signaled to his Navy escort. "We'd better get back and relieve the guard on the pinnace," he said.

"Euvinophan hasn't detailed any of his Field Police to help you?" People's Commissioners weren't supposed to sound confused, but Testaniere couldn't help it. The security arrangements had been made more than one of Silvestria's thirty-five-day months ago.

"The ground troops aren't coming in until just a few days before the strike force moves out," Weldon said. "Tank crews and maintenance techs are coming in by rail in a few days, to have the vehicles on line, but the ground pounders are still back in the Royal City."

Now Testaniere knew that he was not merely confused but hallucinating. "I assume there is some logic behind this," he said quietly. This should really not be discussed in the open, although if the three infantry battalions weren't leaving Royal City until who knew when, it would not be a secret long.

"I don't know if Euvinophan has any plans he isn't telling us about," Weldon said. "But his message to me said that he wanted to avoid conflicts or leaks connected with the local population. A lot of the fishermen have been friendly to their opposites across the Central for centuries."

This was sufficiently true that if there'd been another port besides Buwayjon on the west coast of the Kingdom suitable for loading the strike force Testaniere would have proposed using it. Also, the main training camp for Euvinophan's troops was near Royal City.

Still, having all the heavy weapons out on a limb like this . . .

"I'll see what I can do about helping with security for the pinnace. Maybe I can spare a few State Security people to keep your people's noses out of the dirt."

"I'd be grateful," Weldon said. He almost saluted before he turned away.

Weldon was not likely to have much of a chance to be grateful. Testaniere had a "protective mission" of thirty State Security people nominally under his orders, although several of them were probably the local links in a chain of spies that ran all the way back to gloomy little offices in Nouveau Paris. Still, most of them knew enough about soldiering to give friendly advice to the Field Police—not the royal ones, who were fairly reliable, but Euvinophan's, who were one step up from street brawlers.

He'd been spared any SS people of that low caliber, which made him wonder if perhaps somebody higher up really hoped the mission to Silvestria would succeed. SS people who knew the basics of field soldiering were not unknown, but neither did they grow on bushes.

First step, a talk with Citizen Sergeant Pescu. Everybody listened to him (he could break bones if they didn't) and he knew most of his counterparts in Euvinophan's local Field Police. Advice would go over better, coming from him.

Then get an up to date map of what was parked where. The Canmores had no offensive capability that could handle even the Field Police, but sabotage by fishermen or royalist sympathizers was another matter.

Concentrate, concentrate, concentrate our heavy weapons. The fewer places we have to guard, the better.

The tourist guide hadn't listed the Hadrian's Wall as having private baths, but Shuna Ryder heard a shower running when she let herself into the room.

She was tempted to join Fernando under the spray, but half the fun of that vanished if it wasn't a surprise, and her lover had ears like a cat. He'd probably heard her come in even over the running water.

Ryder put down her overnight bag, sat down on the bed, and pulled off her boots. They were civilian, like the rest of her clothing, and a good deal more comfortable than anything the Admiralty had issued in her time in the Royal Marines. The Republic got a surprising amount of leather off its scruffy little cattle and big fluffy sheep, not to mention some domesticated local ungulates, and they had either remembered or rediscovered the art of making really sybaritic boots.

The bed was so comfortable that Ryder lay back and closed her eyes. What saved her from falling asleep was a few drops of water hitting her in the face. She opened her eyes and contemplated the well-muscled form of Fernando Chung.

Chung was also in civilian clothes—if a towel around his waist could be called clothing—but if he'd been in uniform he would have been recognized as a Lieutenant Colonel in the Erewhon Army. A sophisticated observer would have recognized Assault, Intelligence, and Ordnance qualification badges as well.

It would have taken someone with inside information to realize that he was Ryder's Erewhonese counterpart, the head of a somewhat smaller group of "advisers" sent to the same place on the same mission as Ryder's Manticorans. The exact genesis of Chung's assignment remained a bit hazy, given his government's official support for the Solarian League's "neutral" position, but his presence was a clear indication that the Erewhonese were rather more concerned over Peep ambitions in their direction than their Solarian allies. Or, as Ryder had quipped when they discovered one another's missions, "Great minds wobble and weave down the same gutter."

Fernando Chung had thrown that quip back at her on another occasion, the evening that they realized they were attracted to each other *and* were neither far apart in rank nor in the same chain of command. This didn't entirely kill the thrill of thumbing noses (and other parts) at distant superiors, but with proper security precautions they thought the companionship and the cooperation going literally hand in hand would harm no one.

An observer able to bug the room would have seen Shuna Ryder's normally sober look change to a broad grin at Chung's appearance. She put her right hand up to grip one of Chung's while her left hand reached for the towel.

He took the first hand, but backed hastily out of reach of the left.

"What's this, Sir? Do you need me to rinse your back?"

Chung did not smile. Ryder 's own grin faded. Her first thought was that someone at the Hadrian's Wall had recognized one or both of them. Port Malcolm had a good many small hotels and inns whose owners had civilized attitudes toward unmarried lovers, unlike too many of the Republicans, and so far she and Fernando had been lucky, but had their luck finally run out?

"I hate to break the rule about no business," Chung said. "But we have a situation." The tone made it clear that "we" meant the two advisory missions to the Canmore Republic, not Fernando and Shuna, the unlikely but ardent lovers.

"The Peeps?" Ryder looked around the room, batting her eyes in what she hoped would be taken as a seductive manner if anybody had a video bug hooked up.

"In a way," Chung said. He poked a foot under the bed and moved something back and forth. It sounded plastic-covered and heavy, and Ryder realized that Chung had probably brought a scrambler to counter any bugs. It would be a good one, too; the Erewhon mission had access to state-of-the-art Solarian League technology.

Unfortunately, so did the Peeps.

Ryder groaned. Nobody would mistake the sound for ecstasy. Indigestion or arthritis, possibly, but not any kind of serious pleasure.

"It's an opportunity as well as a problem," Chung said, knotting the towel in place and sitting down on the bed. He had not quite dried himself, and Ryder had visions of a soggy bed even if they finished the business quickly.

"I've heard that ancestral quotation at least fifty times," Ryder said.

"Not from me."

"No, it was a favorite of my senior tactical officer at the Staff College."

"Ah, he recognizes the wisdom of the ancient Chinese, then."

"If you don't either explain yourself or take off that towel, nobody will recognize a certain young Chinese-Latino Erewhonese. Not even your own mother."

"You would lose face with her by violence," Chung said. "Otherwise, I am sure she would approve of you, if only because I am finally not living like a eunuch—"

"That can be arranged," Ryder said. She sat up, with a look on her face that made Chung jump up and back hastily away from the bed.

"Your pardon, honored lady," Chung said. "I will be brief. The private army of the Peep's pet warlord is on the move. The heavy equipment is coming into Buwayjon, a shipload at least every night. It is being secured by Euvinophan's Field Police."

"Not his infantry?"

Chung looked like a treecat contemplating a new litter of healthy kittens. "No. The ground troops are still in the Capitol."

Ryder took a moment to assimilate this fact. "Guarding the White Elephant?"

"I don't think His Majesty would let Euvinophan's brawlers within ten klicks of the Elephant Temple," Chung said. "I have an alternative theory."

"He wants to pull a quick shuffle, keeping the components of his assault force separated so we won't recognize what they are until it's too late."

"Bravo!" He bent down and kissed her. She was tempted to grab for the towel, but refrained. She smelled more coming.

"That tactical officer could teach more than ancient Chinese sayings," Ryder said tartly. Then, slowly, she added, "I see what you mean by an opportunity. Without their ground component—"

"The heavy equipment is vulnerable to the kind of offensive your Sea Fencibles could launch."

"They're not *my* Sea Fencibles. If they're anybody's other than the Republic's they're as much yours as mine. Or was it another man of the same name who developed those conversion kits to make their assault rifles up to date, at least for cartridge weapons?"

"Guilty," Chung said. "Now, if you don't mind tactical planning as pillow talk . . . ?"

Usually, Ryder did. But somewhere in the last minute, it had struck her that this might be the last time together for her and Chung. Neither of them was the kind to stay in the rear when the people they had trained went into battle, for all the secrecy surrounding both their missions. Besides, if the Crown's forces helped Erewhon pull this particular basket of nuts out of the Peep fire, the Erewhonese would probably do their best to repair any minor leaks.

So she and Fernando need not hold back, either now or when the raid set out.

She stood up, flexing her knees so that she could kiss his lips instead of his nose.

TWO

Silvestria was a long way from Old Earth in the days of cryogenic colony ships and not a short haul even when would-be emigrants could hyper out and hope to reach their destination—or some destination—alive. This did not keep it from suffering the not-uncommon fate of a good many planets—two colonies, the one that started out first arriving second, and the one that started out second being down on the ground before the first hit planetary orbit.

However, *both* expeditions managed to run into trouble. The Pechili Consortium whose people founded the Kingdom of Chuiban sent them out in a ship whose cryogenic suspension killed two-thirds of the voyagers. The Conforming Wee Free Kirk which sent out a hypership to found the Canmore Republic bought the latest in ships and skimped on the supplies, so that the engine trouble which prolonged the voyage left the ancestors of the Republicans a short step from cannibalism. Weakened by hunger and facing a Silvestria winter, two-thirds of them also died with depressing speed.

Whatever the survivors knew about (and this shortly included each other), what they could build at once was on the level of black-powder rifles and sailing ships, for some centuries. However, one can catch a lot of fish from a sailing lugger and cut down a lot of trees with a simple steel axe or saw.

The Silvestrians' widely differing cultural traditions kept them from uniting. So did a mostly amiable pride in having each survived the neo-barbarian period largely on their own. But slowly life on the planet passed from survival to comfort, and from there to the accumulation of a capital surplus for investment in modern technology.

The population increase was also slow at first; the harsh climate was deadly to more children and old folk than anyone in later years cared to remember in too much detail. Then out-system trade and better nutrition began to work their customary magic, and Silvestria was no more than a generation from introducing orbital industries and life prolong when the Manticore-Haven war reached the stage that made both sides interested in planets they might otherwise have ignored for another century.

None of which explained to Shuna Ryder why the Canmore Republic called its military chief by the unwarlike name of Director of the Guard but still cultivated that most martial of instruments, the Highland pipes. Or why the Kingdom of Chuiban had gone so far as to bring several live cow white elephants and a large cryo-frozen supply of fertilized ova all the way from Old Earth? (She had seen the estimated cost for the interstellar elephant migration, and the Royal Navy could have built, equipped, stored, and crewed a superdreadnought for somewhat less.)

The Director of the Guard was named Jonathan Stuart Simpson. He listened to Ryder and Chung present their Staff

Appreciation of the best way to deal with Euvinophan's threat with great attention, in total silence, and showing not so much as a tic or a blink while they were speaking. If this was a technique intended to intimidate them into fluffing key lines, it failed—at least with Colonel Chung.

Chung managed to pick up the pace nearly every time Major Ryder even thought of stumbling. This wasn't the first time that he'd made her wonder if he was as empathic as a treecat; remembering some of the other occasions would have made her blush, if she hadn't been facing the stony visage of the Director.

"I observe that you do not include much tactical air support, if indeed you mentioned any at all," was the Director's first remark when the two advisers concluded their presentation.

"No," Ryder said. This was an area where she had both strong opinions and, technical competence. "In the first place, your handful of armed atmosphere fighters are needed for defending the coast and the passes, in case we don't bring this off.

"In the second place, no air strike has ever been as really surgical as we'll need to be, for this job. We have to take out an objective well inside a city of sixty-five thousand friendly or neutral people, without any collateral damage beyond broken windows, cracked chimneys, and frightened children.

"Your pilots are good. They are not—" She stopped before she said "God," which would definitely put her on the wrong foot with an Elder of the Kirk. "They are not trained for close-support work. They would get a bomb wrong somehow, and hand Carl Euvinophan and the Peeps a whole bundle of support, free of charge."

Simpson nodded, in a way that seemed to close the matter. "I find it more than slightly marvelous that the Peeps find it possible to work with both a monarchy and an aristocratic mercenary," he said.

There Chung was more at home. Erewhon had always been closer to Silvestria, so its intelligence on the planet had been more complete. Chung also seemed to have had more civilian contacts in both nations than Ryder. *And I wonder if any of those contacts were female*? she asked herself, as the ghost of her gawky youth returned to hiss jealousy in her ear.

"The Peeps have a rigid ideological standard," Chung said. "But the farther from Nouveau Paris, the better a shrewd adviser team's chances of adjusting the doctrine to the situation. The Kirk is sudden death on adultery, but can they watch every couple a thousand klicks beyond the Dunedin Pass?"

For a moment Ryder thought that Chung had really stepped in the toxics, as Simpson's face twitched. Then she realized the Director was trying not to laugh.

"Do you know this from personal experience, either of you?" he finally asked.

"No," Chung said, with great decision. "The only woman I have known since coming to Silvestria is standing here beside me."

That gun nut is *an empath!*

"Have you taken the old oath of the Sacred Band of Thebes?" Simpson asked. Now he was actually smiling.

"Not precisely," Ryder said. "For one thing, we're a man and a woman. Or we were, the last time it mattered.

"Also, we can't lock shields because we don't use them on most battlefields anymore. Although I'd like to learn your shield and claymore technique, if I have time."

"The best instructor in the Republic happens to be the Guard's Deputy Director for Physical Training," Simpson said. "He is one of the people I will be consulting on the general strategic concept you have presented. Are you in a position to present more details of the forces you will require, if asked?

"You see, we have not waged offensive warfare outside the Republic since the Landing. Even the Sea Fencibles the Manticorans have trained are for counterattacking seaborne raids. The political harmony we have enjoyed with the Kingdom depends very heavily on their not seeing us as a threat."

"It also depends on putting Carl Euvinophan out of business, even if he isn't a pistol in the Peeps' pocket," Ryder said. She nearly got tangled in the p's, and saw that the Director was again trying not to laugh.

"Even if he doesn't turn the Republic over to the Peeps, he could set up as an independent ruler, bribing Chuiban subjects or Andermani immigrants with pieces of your economy. Once he had a power base in the ex-Republic, he might even use his mother's rights to try for the throne."

"Exactly," Chung said. "Then you'd have neo-barbarism all over again, until somebody intervened. At worst it would be the Peeps, at best Erewhon, with the Solar League and the Star Kingdom somewhere in the middle."

"You, Sir, speak as one not without wisdom," Ryder said, also trying hard not to laugh.

"Neither of you lacks wisdom," Simpson replied, standing up and reaching out a hand. Ryder noticed that it shook slightly, and the knuckles were red and enlarged. Simpson had to be less than eighty T-years, but Ryder knew she wouldn't look as old as he did until she reached her third century—if she lived that long.

They shook hands and left, picking up their escorts on the way out. Both of them trusted the Republic and the Guard to take all the standard precautions, but the Canmore Republic had not had to deal with suicidal assassins in the lifetime of any of its citizens. Neither Erewhon nor Manticore had been so fortunate.

Citizen Commissioner Testaniere was at his desk when Sergeant Pescu knocked and entered, followed shortly by another knock signaling the arrival of Citizen Captain Weldon.

Testaniere decided to deal with both men at once. It would be a good test of Weldon's commitment to egalitarian values, being briefed along with a sergeant. Both of them were also discreet. Or if they weren't, then the mission was a lost cause and word to that effect was doubtless already on its way homeward from one of the SS types.

Besides, dealing with both men at once was politer than asking them both to wait until he got out of the bathroom. The diet in western Chuiban ran more heavily to fish than anyone except the wealthy had been able to afford on the older worlds of the People's Republic for centuries. It was doubtless ultimately healthy, and Testaniere could recognize a cook's skill even if he didn't like the results.

Meanwhile, however, one of those results was a mild case of diarrhea.

"The tank crews are arriving," Weldon said at once.

"How many?"

"Enough for ten tanks."

Testaniere's stomach churned from the news even more than from lunch. "I presume that many can at least keep the tanks running?"

Weldon nodded. He even smiled at the spectacle of a People's Commissioner recognizing a military concept. "Also, if the tanks are detected moving, ten will look like only enough for a raid. Not an invasion."

"If we want to make the threat of a raid credible, we have to keep that pinnace and the freighters in one piece," Testaniere reminded his counterpart. "No pinnace, no raid, and somebody with no more than a grenade launcher or a ring charge could do for the pinnace as nicely as you please. Have you thought about hangering and defueling it, until the infantry come in?"

Pescu's red face wore an almost pleading expression, for the citizen captain to agree, but Weldon ignored it. "We have to show the flag and raise the consciousness of the Chuibans concerning modern weaponry," he said. "Besides, the troop movements seem to be—a little behind schedule, let us say."

Testaniere did not groan. Neither did Citizen Sergeant Pescu. But they exchanged looks.

Pescu wore the expression of a man being asked to scrub the barracks with a toothbrush. He would do so well that the floor would be clean enough to eat from when he was finished, but he did not promise to enjoy the process.

Testaniere wondered what was showing on his face. Within, he knew how the financial bureaucrats had felt before Haven began its interstellar expansion, trying to provide more and more benefits to more and more Dolists from a shrinking budget.

He would have to ask Pescu privately how the retraining of the Field Police was coming. They might still be slow to come in out of the rain, but at least they were *here* and not somewhere else.

To Major Ryder, Director Simpson looked years older than he had three days ago, which was impossible. Or maybe not. She looked at the other three faces on the Director's side of the table, and decided that if she had spent three days in conference with any, let alone all, of them, she might have looked her chronological age!

The Deputy Directors for Physical Training, Tactical Training, and Supply were as grim and granite-faced a lot as Ryder had never wished to see this side of the Final Judgement. Did the Conforming Free Kirkers end up looking stern because they spent too much time thinking about that Judgement? Theology had never been one of Ryder's strong points; she hoped to conclude her mission on Silvestria before it became a survival skill.

Simpson nodded to the Supply Deputy. She brushed her graying auburn hair back from a forehead that must have once been seriously burned, and frowned.

"You are asking for an odd mix of resources. Not excessive, I think, but I would like you to explain the reason for each component."

Ryder looked at Chung. They exchanged smiles, for reasons that they could never tell these earnest Republicans. They had worked out the Table of Organization and Equipment, after consulting with their own people, on a portable computer. They'd propped the computer up at one end of the bed and themselves at the other. In between was a take-out fish and chips dinner. Their clothing lay on the floor, beside an insulated bucket with three liters of chilled ale.

It was quite the most comfortable planning session that Ryder had ever attended. A few more of them, and she might even be reconciled to combining briefings and pillow talk.

The four elements of the proposed force were two hundred fifty picked Sea Fencibles, a dozen fishing boats, two fish-factory ships, and enough air freighters, small enough to land on the decks of the factory ships, to carry the Sea Fencibles three hundred klicks to Buwayjon.

The air freighters would be borrowed from the fishing industry, which got priority in modern technology whenever possible. They were slow, clumsy, and low-ceilinged, with robust hulls of local aluminum alloy and fiberglass built around imported power plants and electronics. But like anything built to haul cargo bulky in proportion to its value, they also had payload capacity to spare.

"Unless somebody sees them all together, they won't connect them with the idea of a raiding force," Chung said. "So we are going to march—or in this case, sail—divided, and attack united."

"Won't a new fishing fleet look suspicious all by itself?" the PT Deputy asked. He was bullet-headed but not, as far as Ryder could tell, bull-headed—or at least no more so than his colleagues. And she'd seen a tape of him working out with claymore and sword; she anticipated bruises in her first few—or first few dozen—sessions with him.

"Not with the cover story we're going to circulate," she put in now. "The Erewhon consul is circulating stories of a new agreement with Broadman Imports for exploiting the icefish grounds off the Strathspey Islands. That means recommissioning a whole bunch of the old turtlebacks, which can hide just about anything below decks."

"The correct noun of association for ships is squadron or fleet," the PT Deputy said firmly. "And as one who hauled nets from one of those turtlebacks as a boy, I can assure you that soldiers riding aboard them will be practicing mortification of the flesh."

"I don't believe this is being organized as a pleasure cruise," the Supply Deputy said. "But I really must ask. Will two hundred and fifty people be enough?"

"If we have surprise, half that many could do the job," Ryder said. "If we lose surprise, or Euvinophan's infantry are in place, twice that many won't be enough."

That reduced everyone to silence. *Including me*, Ryder realized. *I hope they don't have any more questions, because I'm damned if I could answer them.*

Then three graying and one bald head nodded. "We will authorize in the name of the Republic all resources for this mission, as you have requested," Simpson said. "May the Lord Mighty in Battle watch over you, keep you in His hand, and give you the courage and skill you will need to bring victory in His cause."

Now, if I was just as sure as these people are, that we did have God on our side. . . .

THREE

The big truck backed in under the camouflage net and squealed to a stop. Half a dozen Sea Fencibles ran up to lift off the crates of potatoes that hid the crates of ammunition. Then Director Simpson himself climbed out of the cab.

Shuna Ryder's first thought was to call SBA Bexo. Simpson didn't look fit to be out of bed, let alone this far north in the late summer, with so much water dripping off the trees that you couldn't tell if it was raining or not.

But he smiled as he came up and shook her hand. Most of the Sea Fencibles stopped, nodded, and went back to work. They were grasping the notion of when to salute and when not to, as well as a few other military skills. She only hoped the improvement in their marksmanship hadn't cost the Republic more of its ammunition reserve than it could afford.

Ryder pushed aside the blackout curtain and led Simpson to the observation platform, overlooking the covered hundred meters of creek that served as a workshop. Five of the wooden-hulled turtleback fishing boats were moored to the banks, with more Sea Fencibles and a few selected boatyard workers swarming over them. Saws, sanders, and paint sprayers buzzed, whined, and hissed, and through the hatch of one boat the glow of a welding torch suggested work on the engine or one of the steel tanks being converted for heads.

"I worked in a boatyard after I left school," Simpson said, his mouth nearly touching Ryder's ear so that she could hear him over the din. "I remember working on some of these boats, converting them from steam to diesel. It is good to see them doing more than rot in the rain, even if this were not God's work they will be about."

Ryder could have wished that God or somebody had made the boats larger or the Sea Fencibles smaller. Only two hundred twenty-seven people with their personal weapons and gear would be riding in the disguised boats. The other twenty-five would have to ride by air, along with most of the heavy weapons.

But the demolition charges were going in the turtlebacks. The Sea Fencibles were not going to be separated from their personal weapons or the explosives. Not if they had to swim in with them on their backs!

"I hope we bring back not only the people but the transport," Ryder said. "God will not feed families when the fishermen can't bring home their catch."

Apparently this was not heresy. Simpson nodded. "We can cut back on our catch for export, if necessary. Indeed, the war itself may make this necessary. If the godforsaken Havenites are really going to commission privateers, we may be living plain and short once again, until there is peace."

He took Ryder's hands in his, which somehow were not shaking and felt stronger than they had looked. "Even if nothing came back but yourselves, it would be worth the cost. Our people are hardy, but if Euvinophan held Port Malcolm and the passes, he would have four-fifths of our industry and two-thirds of our people hostage. Guerrilla warfare under those circumstances might cost us more than even Peep tyranny—if King Bira allowed the Peeps a free reign in the first place."

Ryder wanted to suggest that the Republicans consider ways of playing off a victorious Carl Euvinophan against the Peeps, so that King Bira would have to intervene all the sooner. But that would sound defeatist, and besides, the Republicans were surely canny enough to think of that for themselves.

"Now I had better take a cup of tea and be ready to ride the truck back," Simpson said. "I am supposed to be in a clinic for an examination. Better that I not turn the cover story into the truth."

A hovercraft armored personnel carrier nosed down into a shallow ditch, sprayed up water and weeds crossing the stream at the bottom, then lunged up the near slope. As the APC's nose appeared above the edge, two streaks of fire darted from a clump of bushes three hundred meters to Jean Testaniere's left. His first thought was Infiltrated *saboteurs*!

Then the two anti-tank rockets hit the hovercraft's bow plating. Smoke billowed and paint splattered from the dummy warheads. Citizen Sergeant Pescu rose from beside Testaniere and waved to the hovercraft, which stopped. He and the crews of the two rocket launchers walked over to the hovercraft. When Pescu returned, he was actually smiling.

"I estimate one penetrating hit and a probable mission kill on the second. Anybody riding that hover would be walking the rest of the way, if they weren't on a stretcher."

Testaniere tried to hide his surprise. "You've been working them hard, Citizen Sergeant. I didn't think they were up to hitting a hovercraft."

"Hitting anything's easy when there's no return fire. I hope to work out something with the tank people for simulating that in a few days. If not, I can at least run everybody through one firing with a live warhead on a stationary target."

"Excellent."

Under Pescu's firm hand, the Field Police were giving the armored forces practice in facing missile-armed infantry, while learning to play that role themselves. Testaniere didn't expect many fighting vehicles on the other side of the water, but wrecked trucks made good road blocks, and anti-tank missiles had a long history as good "bunker-busters."

If one was going to fight a war with the technology of the past, one could at least take advantage of the lessons already taught by long-ago wars!

Fernando Chung looked at his watch. "Almost time," he whispered.

Shuna Ryder grabbed the wrist and lifted the hand to her lips, then moved the kiss up Chung's arm until she got a mouthful of wet battledress.

"Ptah!"

"I never said I was a man of excellent taste—"

He broke off to take her in his arms. Then they hugged hard, and Ryder knew so well that this was their last private moment, maybe forever, that heart and head fought a short battle.

What kept her from pulling Fernando behind the nearest bushes and then down on top of her was not discipline. It was the thought of the wet leaves and wetter ground, and the folly of leading a major operation with a howling cold. The mission's supply of antivirals was running low, and would have to be saved for something worse than the CO's sniffles!

They slowly stepped back to arm's length. Chung patted her cheek. "You are getting to be a habit with me, you know."

"Better a habit than a vice."

"Yes, but a habit is harder to give up."

"I will—I'll think about ways of not—of our not having to give up. Fair enough?"

"Completely."

They hadn't gone more than fifty meters down the slope toward the waiting boats, when several torches glowed, each held under a thermal umbrella to hide the heat signature. Then Sea Fencibles by the dozens and scores stepped out of the trees, applauding and cheering.

Ryder flushed. It was hard to see what Chung was doing, but he did glare, when Bexo joined the crowd. Ryder now saw among the audience some of the Sea Fencibles who'd come north to work on the boats in the hope of earning a slot in the raiding force, or even offered hefty bribes.

"Thank you," she said. "But let's not tempt fate. Hold the applause for when we come back. Then we can have a proper torchlight ceremony."

"By then it will be autumn," Bexo said, "then it rains even harder."

FOUR

If autumn meant rain, then it had already come to this stretch of the Central Sea two hundred klicks south of the Strathspey Archipelago. Fortunately the half-gale that had blown the past two days had died as the rain came to take its place. Ryder would not have cared to transfer twenty-odd Sea Fencibles from a sinking turtleback with the waves sending green water over the cockpit forward.

She braced herself against the cockpit coaming and gripped the back of the helmsman's seat with one aching wrist, the windscreen with the other. She thought that the windscreen might as well be blown away, considering that it was opaque with caked salt.

A thud and a clatter rose from below as somebody opened the port hatch. A familiar sound followed, fortunately not accompanied by a familiar smell. The rain drowned it, and the seasick Fencible's stomach was quickly empty anyway.

Not as many people were seasick as she'd feared, but enough, and enough of those badly, that Bexo had issued the antinausea pills wholesale. It would not do for fifty Fencibles to reach their target so weak that they couldn't even carry their loads, let alone run, climb, or shoot.

The rain wrapped Ryder's command boat and the other three visible ones in a gray murk, relieved only by the dim riding lights. In this weather, nobody would see them from above; the problem would be finding their way to the rendezvous.

The hatch had stayed open, to let in fresh air. Over the hiss of the rain and the rumble of the diesel, Ryder heard someone reading aloud from Chung's manual on Peep weaponry. He'd digested his files into a printed manual of enemy weapons, one copy for each squad, even though he'd acquired some of the knowledge on an exchange tour with the Technical Section of Solarian League Intelligence.

Ryder wondered if he'd done that for personal reasons, as well as professional. Did he want to be tossed out of the Erewhonese forces on his ear, for revealing confidential material, so that he could then freely emigrate to the Star Kingdom?

It would be pure Hell all around, if Chung did on his own something Ryder would never have dared ask him to do, then couldn't emigrate because the Sollies or the Erewhonese would put pressure on the Star Kingdom not to accept him! Then, when both adviser groups got shipped out from a (hopefully) neutral Silvestria, where could she and Fernando be—other than many light-years apart?

There was much wisdom in the old saying about not playing where you worked. It was just as true that she and Fernando were no longer playing.

The last tank whined and rattled into the sprawling warehouse complex that was now the vehicle park and supply dump for the armored battalion and infantry carriers. Four of Euvinophan's Field Police presented arms to Jean Testaniere and Citizen Sergeant Pescu, and the door closed behind the tank.

Thanks to the last few days' work on the tanks and rain on the door, the door made more noise than the tank. It hadn't been that way before the Peep advisers took in hand all the Euvinophan troops that they could talk to.

"One regrets the absence of the live firing practice," Testaniere said. "But I will not criticize you for being unable to control the weather."

"No, and this gives us a few days to screen the rounds. Corporal—Citizen Corporal Randall used to work for a chemical company. He's built a testing set and some tools for stripping the charges out of dud rounds. He thinks we can get maybe fifty to eighty extra satchel charges for house-to-house work, allowing for the usual percentage of duds."

"Citizen Corporal Randall can look for a commendation. And so can you, and everyone else you think deserves one."

"Thank you, Citizen Commissioner. But I'd be even more grateful for an easing up in this soggy weather. As long as it lasts, Euvinophan's pets aren't going to move out of their cozy barracks and start soldiering."

The two fish-factory ships would have looked innocent to anyone who didn't know their purpose. Their decks were maybe a little clearer than usual, but they were within fifty klicks of known fishing grounds, and their crews had manned both the side cranes and the stern ramp as if ready to start unloading the fishing boats' catch. Finally, it would be hard to believe that anything smelling like the two ships could be an instrument of anything remotely warlike . . . unless it was bacteriological warfare.

Ryder stood in the cockpit and waved across a hundred meters of heaving, oily sea to Chung, whom she hadn't seen or spoken to in a week. Radio silence had been complete, which hadn't kept the fishing boat skippers from navigating the Sea Fencibles to the rendezvous.

The only problem was that it was two hours after the planned arrival of the air lift, and the sky was still empty (except for thick gray clouds that promised more rain) and silent (except for an occasional distant muttering gust of wind).

Ryder put a hand on the wheelman's shoulder. He twitched it irritably, as if to say *I know my job without Manties pawing me.*

The wind to the west seemed to gust harder as Ryder's boat and Chung's approached one another. Looking over the side, Ryder expected to see a fluff of whitecaps sprouting from the waves, but the swell was as modest, even monotonous, as ever.

Then it came into sight—six dark-painted air freighters, all flying just above the wave tops.

Six, when there should have been seven.

The first one overflew the more distant factory ship, circled the second, then went to vertical lift and descended on the handling deck amidships. The crew lowered the booms out of the way just in time. Three more made equally smooth landings in quick succession. The pilots had all done this scores or hundreds of times; getting fresh fish to the markets or frozen fish to the container ports depended on their skill. But the fifth one faced trouble that went beyond the pilot's skill.

As it shifted to vertical flight, the counter-gravity failed. The pilot had enough altitude that even with a full load, he didn't plummet straight on to the factory ship. He even managed to claw the nose up before the tail smashed into the water.

Explosive bolts flung hatches away from both sides of the cockpit area, and the people aboard the freighter erupted into the open. Ryder managed to draw about three deep breaths before the water around the up-thrust nose of the freighter was dotted with bobbing black heads.

Then with a rumble and a hiss, the freighter sank.

Two down, including God knew how much equipment and how many people.

Ryder was glad that she hadn't endorsed the notion of this being a mission from God. If it was, He was definitely having an off day.

By now, Chung was in hailing distance.

"And here I thought we weren't going to have to wait around to recalculate any more loads!" he said.

It was just as well that he was out of reach. If he was as blithe as he sounded, Ryder would cheerfully have thrown him overboard.

FIVE

"This isn't an automatic abort," Chung said.

Ryder saw a few of the Republicans wince at the colonel's choice of words. The Conforming United Wee Free Kirk had its crotchets in the area of reproductive rights.

After that one slip, they looked relieved. Not that aborting the mission wouldn't have been simpler, but if simplicity had governed human affairs, a lot of institutions, including war and sex, would never have come into existence.

The air lift had come in two hours late because one freighter's navcomputer had gone out, then down. They'd had to find a handy piece of no more than damp ground to transfer ten Fencibles and several tons of weapons and stores. Then the cripple had flown off homeward, while the other six flew on.

Losing the second freighter reduced the lift capacity by a serious number of tons. It also took to the bottom of the Central Sea a portion of every item of supplies, from mortars to clean socks, but only two people.

They could now lift in the full assault team, or a partial team with the heavy weapons. Not both. Which, and how?

Meanwhile, the fish-factory crews had been pulling nets (camouflage and fishing varieties) over the deck load of freighters. They would still look peculiar, nearly filling the decks of both *Nautilus* and *Sir Patrick Spens*, but they would not signal "commando raid" to anyone not coming alongside.

The turtlebacks had transferred their Sea Fencibles to the two ships, and all the officers to *Sir Patrick*. Then flags, lights, and loud voices harried all of them into a loose formation that looked almost as if it belonged in these waters, around these two ships. Nobody who wasn't already paranoid would suspect the fleet of intending harm to anybody except fish.

Of course, if they're short of paranoia over to the east, I can always loan them some of mine. Ryder shook herself out of that mood, saw on the chart display that the fleet was on an innocuous course to the south, and got ready to listen or speak as necessary.

Captain Biddle of *Nautilus*, the older of the two factory ships, saved everybody a great deal of time—once they took him seriously.

"Now look, good people," he said. "I've an old ship not safe for more than another season at most. I can think of a better end for her than tied up to rot at a pier, smelling of fish guts until the beggars complain!

"Put your confounded mortars and rockets aboard *Nautilus*. We'll cover them with tarps, then run in at night. About the time you hit Buwayjon, we can be in range. If you can leave the gunners aboard too, we'll not stint—"

The leader of the heavy weapons platoon let out a howl of protest. Three glares—Chung, Biddle, and Ryder—reduced him to muttering things probably not approved of by the Kirk. He sounded no happier than before at the prospect of missing the fight ashore.

"As I said," Biddle went on, "we can steam through the night and be within range about the time you're keeping the fellows ashore too busy to notice us. Then tell your gunners where to shoot, and we'll put them where they can."

It wasn't wholly lunatic; just nearly so. The 120-mm mortars and the 150-cm rockets could reach out twenty thousand meters, although with reduced accuracy beyond twelve thousand. The supply of precision-guided rounds was less than half of what they'd hoped for, but the Sea Fencibles or at least their Marine advisers did have a reasonable quota of terminal-guidance lasers.

"We'd have to strike the vehicles below deck to dismount the heavy weapons, or else wait and dismount them after the ground assault flies off," Chung said. This time the weapons platoon leader said nothing, because he was obviously trying to think of an intelligent answer. It was Ryder's turn to want to glare or mutter curses.

Was agreeing so fast smart?

If we don't have time to spare and don't intend to abort, yes.

That had been a short mental debate, but long enough for the weapons platoon officer to answer. The vehicles would have to be struck below to avoid crowding the deck unacceptably, so once below, they might as well be worked on.

Further calculations showed that *Nautilus* was strong enough to stand the recoil. Built in an archaic style called "composite," with heavy wooden planks on a steel frame, she was nearly a century old and originally built for two steam reciprocating engines instead of her current diesels. If she had survived a century of storms, stresses, and heavy loads, and could still support the weight of loaded freighters on her handling deck, she could undoubtedly survive a few hundred rounds' worth of recoiling mortars and rocket tail-flares.

Still more calculations declared that reducing the airlift requirements by the weight of the heavy weapons and their ammunition would let the ground assault take all the ammunition they still had for their own weapons. Except that a couple of those were staying behind, too—a light machine gun and the one Erewhonese pulser the raiders had brought along.

"Otherwise," Ryder said, "the Peeps could fly out in a tourist air bus and drop grenades on your deck. If they hit the ammunition, it could ruin your taste for whiskey forever."

Everybody was carefully not mentioning the pinnace, although with Peep-quality piloting it might not be much good at low altitude. Ryder carefully did mention one non-trivial problem, which was the legal status of *Nautilus* and her crew.

"I don't think I can commission you in the Canmore Republic Navy," Ryder began. "But if you don't have some military status, the Peeps could shoot you, and King Bira might let them. Never risk being the victim of an atrocity you can't live to laugh over."

"Any positive suggestions?" Chung said. Captain Biddle looked as if he would rather say something stronger.

"Would and your crew—and *Sir Patrick's* people—like to volunteer for the Sea Fencibles? We do have our Personnel Officer with us, believe it or not. She leads the Boat Maintenance gang in her spare time. I think she can print up enough certificates to cover everybody."

"Like a tarpaulin," Chung said. This time he got Captain Biddle's dirty look.

✧ ✧ ✧

Testaniere peered out into a night completely opaque with fog. If the port finally had been blacked out, it could hardly have been any darker. All that told Citizen Commissioner Testaniere that he wasn't looking into the depths of the Central Sea was a dim glow from the tank workshop.

Citizen Sergeant Pescu coughed behind the commissioner, then went on coughing. Testaniere reached for the teapot and poured two cups.

"Warm your throat, please. That's not an order. But you are the last person I want catching a cold from this soggy soup."

"Thank you." Pescu drank, then put the half-empty cup down. "A girl has disappeared."

"We are not an Office of Missing Persons," Testaniere said. "Is there anything particular about her?" He picked up his cup and drank.

"She was—ah, friendly—with several of the Navy ratings. Not any of our SS, to my knowledge, but they wouldn't be telling on themselves."

Since "lack of revolutionary virtue" could mean a labor camp or worse, Pescu was probably right. "Are you implying that one of them killed her?

"Maybe. Or maybe one of the local gangs didn't like her going with off-worlders. Or—"

"She could have been spying?" Testaniere filled in.

Pescu nodded.

"Not impossible. But impossible to tell for whom. We can't terminate agents from the Royal Army's Counter-Intelligence Office, let alone from Euvinophan's staff."

He did not like the timing, though, in spite of the fog. "I suggest that we propose a stand-to for dawn tomorrow. Tank crews, security, Field Police, and our Navy friends. I'll sweeten Weldon if you can work on everybody else."

"I can alert the dawn duty watch, and be there myself. Everybody else may be a bit busy then. The first of the infantry are coming in. Five hundred of them, by truck."

Testaniere nearly choked on his tea. "You might have told me this first."

"I'm sorry, Citizen Commissioner. But after so long, it's hard to believe that it's actually happening."

The raiders' reprieve from disaster lasted until Claymore Flight entered both darkness and fog. Maintaining electronic silence meant dubious navigation, worse station-keeping, and eventually total loss of contact with Claymore Three. At that point Ryder and Chung risked IR signals to bring the remaining four freighters down on the first convenient island that offered enough flat surface.

Fortunately, Claymore Three contained only forty people and a single light scout car. The raiders still had more than a hundred and fifty Sea Fencibles, thirty assorted advisers, three scout cars, and an adequate load of everything else needed for light infantry combat and heavy demolitions work.

"It's a good thing you handed out the material on Peep weapons," Ryder said, as she and Chung stood beside a freighter. A four-Fencible security patrol walked past, feeling their way cautiously forward on the fog-slick rock. "We may be using them!"

"That would solve the heavy weapons problem nicely," Chung said. "And if we can bag the pinnace and their air lift as well, only the Peeps will complain."

It would need more than captured heavy weapons to be sure of striking the local air base before anything could get off. It would need a force large enough to carry out the original plan of simultaneously striking both the ground-forces depot and the air base. They no longer had that.

But if Chung said that he would try it, he would—and do as well as anyone could. Ryder leaned back into her lover's arms.

"I am losing my enthusiasm for yachting," he said, into her ear. "When I knew I was going to try for Manticore, I thought of a vacation on a rented sailboat. You and me, a well-stocked galley, days of wearing nothing but sun screen—"

"You, Sir, assume a good deal."

"It would be better than a good deal, good lady. Furthermore, I am only assuming that if the idea repelled you, you would have pushed me off a cliff into the sea or otherwise discouraged me some time ago."

Unfortunately, Ryder had no reply to that. Of course, that was because there was none.

SIX

The four surviving freighters ran in at such low altitude and high speed that the sea was a gray glaze rushing toward Ryder as she stood in the cockpit of Claymore One. The other freighters were leaving visible wakes, and an agile treecat could probably have jumped from sea level into an open hatch of any of the freighters—if they'd dared open a hatch at this speed.

They still hadn't heard from Claymore Three, which suggested either disaster or complete radio discipline. Ryder was betting on the second, and not only to keep up morale. They'd heard a good deal of radio traffic, much of it commercial, some of it in low-grade Peep codes easily broken on the freighter's computer. None of it suggested that anyone ashore knew about Claymore Three, *Nautilus*, or the four grim gray darts now flinging themselves across the sea toward Buwayjon.

Ryder turned away from the cockpit to start applying her camouflage cream. It was one of Chung's ideas; he'd pointed out that warpaint was as old as war, and did things for your morale and to the enemy's. Even in Old Earth's post-industrial wars, one warrior band had been known as "the devils with green faces."

Except that Ryder had never been able to put on makeup without at least three tries, and had always thanked God for regulations that strictly limited it for female officers on duty. She had succeeded in making her face into something that scared her when she glimpsed it in the mirror, and was trying to sort it out when she felt gentle fingers touching her cheeks from behind.

This was almost too public a touch even from Chung, but she was still not going to slam her elbow back into his stomach. Instead she sighed, not caring if he thought that meant pleasure, and a moment later she realized that it did. Chung was not only spreading the camouflage cream more evenly, his touch was taking a few of the knots out of her stomach.

"Just practicing for the sun lotion," he whispered, when he was finished.

Before she could turn to thank him, he was gone, and the pilot was waving for her attention.

"We've picked up a clear signal, with a Peep Navy call sign. Reports they're heading south to investigate a suspected raid south of Point Luchuin."

The map display was late Neolithic digital but it made at least the distance evident. "That could be Claymore Three," she said. "Keep a passive watch for the pinnace. "If it's airborne, we may have to take evasive action suddenly."

Peep piloting might still let them evade at low level, but the pinnace would be more likely to be carrying air-to-air than air-to-ground weapons, let alone anti-ship ones. This raid could still end in a futile disaster: the Canmore Republic striking the first blow without gaining anything by it.

Then the white cliffs north of Buwayjon thrust above the horizon. Fishing boats of all sizes and colors whipped past to either side. Ryder motioned the pilot to climb a little to avoid being impaled on a mast.

A black hull with a dirty yellow superstructure and a white funnel, off to the right—*Nautilus*! The pilot jumped as Ryder blasted the word triumphantly into his ear.

"Just keep cool, Ma'am, and we'll have you on the ground in a minute."

The minute seemed to last a millennium, and it didn't help that the pinnace switched to scrambled communications but kept talking, obviously on the track of *something* that had the people aboard excited. Ryder managed thirty seconds to check her gear and lock and load her assault rifle, then they were over the breakwater, below the top of the lighthouse, from which a woman in a nightgown stared as if she couldn't believe what her eyes showed her.

They raced over treetops, turned at the foot of the cliffs, saw the air base briefly as they banked—no pinnace in sight—and then slowed to come down on the Subinaro Esplanade next to the warehouse district.

As the noses came up and the counter-gravity on, the pilot swore. "I forgot to drop the damned leaflets!"

That was a planned propaganda move—dropping thousands of leaflets telling the port's citizens to stay under cover, for the Republic had a quarrel only with the traitorous Carl Euvinophan and the imperialistic Peeps.

"I don't imagine that will do any harm," came Chung's voice, "unless Buwayjon is short of toilet paper."

Then the landing gear groaned and squealed, hatches and ramps slammed open even before power died, and everybody was yelling "Go, go, go!" so loudly that Ryder knew she was shouting too only because she could feel her throat vibrating.

"He did *what*?" Jean Testaniere said. If it would have relieved his feelings, he would have shouted, even screamed. Since that would only have added to what already seemed a first-class panic, he replied in as normal a tone as he could manage, with the erupting din of battle in his ear.

"The pinnace has gone south, to investigate and if necessary attack a Republican raiding force south of Point Luchuin. Citizen Captain Weldon went with it, in personal command."

Citizen Sergeant Pescu looked as if he wouldn't mind being killed, as primitive tradition allowed with the bearers of bad news, if only to get him out of this embarrassing situation. However, it was so far only embarrassing. It was not yet fatal. Five minutes ago, the first three truckloads of Carl Euvinophan's troops had pulled into the Training Barracks Compound. In another five minutes, they could be out of their trucks and on the way to the tank depot and supply dump.

The whole five hundred would have been better, but convoy discipline, at night, on the kingdom's mountain roads, would have taxed anyone's ability. Fifty could fight at least a delaying action against any number of Manty puppets who could have ridden in four air freighters. And the Manties would be fighting in two directions at once, because forty Field Police and ten SS people were already on watch to defend their target.

"I'm going out to the air base," Testaniere said. "It has the best command facilities, and it's where Weldon will come if he has the sense to return in time. Deploy all StateSec personnel to guard the depot at all costs, and—"

"What about a message to Euvinophan's men?"

Testaniere slammed his fist down on the table. A calculator and an electronic notepad fell to the floor. The SS and Field Police knew Pescu; they would obey him if they obeyed anyone. But Euvinophan's infantry wouldn't recognize any local People's authority other than Testaniere himself, and if they wasted time arguing—

"I wasn't trying to run out," Testaniere said.

"No, and neither was Citizen Captain Weldon. Just be glad you didn't make as big a mistake."

Then they were both pounding down the stairs, with Pescu shouting back over his shoulder to start securing files. If even the clerks were going to be needed on the firing line, there was no reason to leave anything lying around for hostile or even curious eyes.

Ryder popped out an empty magazine and pushed a fresh one into her assault rifle. It was amazing how fast you went through ammunition, even if you had the sense and training to fire in three-round bursts. Some of the Sea Fencibles seemed to have forgotten even the abbreviated Royal Marine fire-discipline training they'd received. The use of those Peep weapons was looming closer every moment, as the raiders' ammunition supply shrank with gruesome speed.

At least it was gruesome for both sides, maybe a little more so for the enemy. Right now the raiders had the edge in numbers and firepower. The surviving SS and Euvinophan Field

Police troops defending the tanks, armored personnel carriers, and supplies were getting very much the worst of the firefights.

They weren't giving up, however. Bullets whined and rattled on either side of Ryder, and a Sea Fencible doubled up, to fall screaming and writhing.

Welcome to the Fraternal Order of Those Who Know Bullets Hurt.

Ryder's radio squalled in her ear. "This is Claymore Red Leader. I'm in the middle of a firefight. What is it?"

Chung's reply was cool enough to calm without reproaching. "We have some of Euvinophan's infantry detrucking at the old Training Barracks. They seem to be armed, but not yet deploying. Also, *Nautilus* is within range and wants targeting data for the air base."

"Tell them we have no observation on the air base. Negative observation, negative firing. Can you call them in on Euvinophan's goons?"

"If I can't, a lot of taxpayers got cheated on Erewhon and Manticore!"

"Less joking and more shooting, if you please."

"Feeding data—now!"

That ought to do some good—the heavy weapons platoon leader was not only one of the more promising Sea Fencible officers, he had three of the best heavy-weapons Marine sergeants Ryder had ever known. They were the kind who, if you told them to hit a specific house, would ask, "Which room?"

Euvinophan's people were in trouble. If they broke and ran, even better—they wouldn't add to the body count and they would destroy their own reputation, also their leader's. Then it wouldn't matter what happened to the vehicle park, because nobody would follow Carl Euvinophan across the street for a beer, let alone across the ocean to fight the Canmore Republic.

"Major!"

It was the junior Marine of the advisory team, a buck sergeant with a demolitions specialty.

"We've secured the fuel dump and the Sea Fencibles have it rigged to blow. Four charges. But we can't do anything. There's a school full of kids on the other side of the wall. Right in range of the fireball."

Ryder thought rude things about the Kingdom of Chuiban's urban planners, then nodded.

"All right. You and the Fencibles watch the charges. Disarm them if you're in danger of being overrun. Wait for my signal—'Hallucination' will be the code word."

"Hallucination. Yes, Ma'am. I kind of wish it was one, too."

"You aren't the only one, Marine."

SEVEN

Ryder sprinted after the demolitions sergeant, found herself at the base of a low wall, and scrambled up on top of it before anybody or anything (including her own second thoughts) could stop her. Nobody shot at her, but about fifty pairs of large, mostly brown, eyes stared up at her out of as many faces.

"Evacuate the school!" Ryder shouted. She would have given ten years off her life for a loudspeaker, to be heard inside. The school had a tile roof, a timber frame, and dozens of glass windows. The blast wave would slaughter everyone inside when it hit, even without the fireball's help.

She wanted to scream, but realized that might cause a panic. Instead she pointed at the exit. "Run, now!" she called. "The fuel dump is on fire and might explode. Get out of the school now and keep on running."

The children turned slowly and walked off toward the exit still more slowly. Ryder wondered if they somehow thought that the Sea Fencibles were firefighters, who would provide a grand spectacle whether or not they put out the fire before the explosion.

Two bits of luck saved the children. One was the first incoming round from *Nautilus*. It was an air-bursting smoke round, timed to detonate three hundred meters up. It made a bang audible all over town, even over the firing, and left a cloud of white and purple smoke big enough for a low-yield nuke. Ryder hoped that it would, in the words of an old drill instructor, "warn everybody to keep their heads down and their mouths and—ah, sphincters—shut."

Seeing and hearing the explosion started the children on the playground hurrying. It brought more of them out of the school, followed by a teacher shouting at them to get back inside and sit down!

The teacher went on shouting until she caught sight of Major Ryder, standing on top of the wall, dripping with weapons, hands and face black as fresh tar, and altogether looking like something sprung from Hell. The teacher let out a shriek that must have sounded like the noon lunch whistle in factories halfway across town and darted for the exit with an alacrity that did credit to her condition if not her courage.

She not only swept most of the children out of the exit along with her, her scream brought other teachers out—and Ryder's warning finally got through to them. In five minutes the school was empty, and the street beyond its gates crowded with children and teachers, all of them still moving.

Chung came on the radio, to say that the first round had got some of the Euvinophan people moving, and "in a retrograde direction," but not all of them, and three more truckloads had just pulled up. *Nautilus* was going to drop a couple more rounds on the hillside behind the Esplanade, but if that didn't discourage loitering, she was going to have to fire for effect.

"If we clear the Euvinophan people out of their assembly area, we'll have a clear shot at Blue Temple Avenue, which takes us straight out to the air base," he concluded.

Personally, Ryder thought they would do better to hold Market Square, which would block any counterattacks by either the Euvinophan people at the training barracks or the Peep Navy types at the air base. But Chung was definitely offensive-minded, and if he could capture any local vehicles, he might just bring it off.

"All right. Just be careful going through Market Square," Ryder said. "Street merchants are bad people to have mad at you. They'll slick up the pavement with spoiled fruit if they can't do anything else!

Jean Testaniere could only hope that the second convoy of Euvinophan's infantry wouldn't follow the example of the first. It would probably help them to take a few casualties, so that they would have somebody to be angry at. They could not possibly be as angry at anyone as he himself was at Paul Weldon, but it would be a start.

The second salvo from the sea was only another demonstration of firepower. The sixty-odd infantry looked in all directions, and most of them turned as pale as their complexions allowed. They neither charged nor fled. Some of them actually unslung their rifles and started loading, while a couple of adequately loud NCO's started forming squads.

That was all Testaniere saw before Citizen Captain Weldon finally replied.

"People's Will Flight One to People's Will Ground One. We have sighted, bombed, and destroyed a Republican air freighter. One major secondary explosion, and minor ones continuing.

Any hostile personnel in the area have taken evasive action and are under cover. I intend to search and strafe."

"I do not advise that," Testaniere said. The words came out like an order, rather than advice, but he could not have used any other tone to save his life. He wanted to scream, "Get that piece of tin and your useless behind back here half an hour ago!" but managed to avoid that extreme as well.

"Major hostile attack on Buwayjon," he said instead. "Air-lifted Manticoran puppet forces in company strength or above, with offshore fire support. Repeat, I recommend an immediate return to the city and that you make your first priority target the bombardment vessel. Black hull, yellow superstructure, white funnel, older vessel."

"A surface ship, in broad daylight? Can't you engage it with the tanks?" Weldon sounded genuinely bewildered.

Testaniere hated to admit the truth. "The vehicles and dump were the first hostile target. The puppet troops have made the area inaccessible, until the Euvinophan reinforcements now arriving permit us to counterattack."

A long silence with only the background noise of the pinnace's engines, then, in eloquently perfect diction:

"You, Citizen People's Commissioner Testaniere, are an ass."

Testaniere wanted to laugh. He doubted he would stop if he began, so he only said, "Like calls to like, Citizen Captain Weldon. We can divide up the blame for this mess once we've cleaned it up. That still needs you and your pinnace here, now!"

"On the way."

Several Sea Fencibles and the Marine demolitions sergeant joined Ryder on the wall before the last of the children was out of range of the explosion (or so she hoped).

"Are they ready to blow?" she asked.

"Not quite," the sergeant replied. "They're salvaging a whole bunch of Peep ammo that we can use—satchel charges, rocket launchers for anti-tank rounds, a couple of vehicle-mounted tribarrels with power packs—all sorts of stuff."

"Tell them to hustle," Ryder said. "If we don't blow the main dump, we'll have to blow the tanks individually. We may not have that much time."

"Oh, they're already putting demo or satchel charges under each tank," the sergeant said. "Double fuses and everything else. I don't think those youngsters have ever had so much fun in public."

Then the sergeant's eyes widened and he shouted, "Get down!"

Ryder was already moving; she'd seen the green fatigues of
Euvinophan troops at the playground exit. Neither she nor the
sergeant was down before one of the enemy let fly. The burst
only hit the sergeant with three rounds, but one of them
knocked off his helmet and another hit him in the throat, so
that he was mortally wounded twice over when he hit the
bricks head first.

Ryder and the Sea Fencibles returned fire, shooting low to
keep overs from hitting the children. The children immediately
started running again, and the soldiers seemed to have enough
nerve to attack—at least for about ten seconds.

After that, more than a dozen of them were down, one of
them propped up against a swing set, choking on his own blood.
Ryder suspected that she would see that man in her nightmares for a while.

Then some of the school windows blew out, and more hostile fire smashed a Sea Fencible off the wall. A moment later an
explosion tore a hole in the playground wall to the left. As bricks
crashed down and the dust blew away, one of Euvinophan's Peep-
surplus tanks came grinding improbably across the rubble.

Still more improbably, it swung its turret and let fly with
both its plasma cannon and the ball-mounted bow tribarrel at
the school's upper floor. Both were firing at maximum eleva-
tion, but that was enough. Suddenly the school had much less
of an upper floor than before, and bricks, tiles, timber, furniture, and bodies (all adult-sized and in uniform, mercifully)
rained down on to the playground.

A scout car with a ring-mounted Peep tribarrel followed the
tank over the rubble. It cleared its field of fire just as several
Euvinophan troops hurried in the gate, brave enough to try
rescuing their fallen comrades. Their courage did not keep them
alive against tribarrel fire, but some of them got off shots, and
one of them actually hit Shuna Ryder.

It didn't penetrate the armor, and anyway she had been
described as well-padded in the relevant area. She did pick up
a selection of bruises and scrapes when she hit the ground,
not to mention what felt like a couple of cracked ribs. She
also knew that she would be standing up when awake and
lying on her stomach when asleep, until the bruise healed.

Somehow an SBA was beside her even before she tried moving. Before the SBA finished, Fernando Chung was standing
over her, looking unprofessionally concerned.

"Would you believe where I was shot?" Ryder muttered.

"I see where the painkiller is going in," Chung said. "I will
modify my massage techniques."

Ryder felt more like blushing from that remark than she did from having her pants around her knees.

When the painkiller had taken hold and the scan showed no fractures or internal injuries, the SBA let her stand. "I really think a medevac is—"

"Going to have to wait," Chung interrupted. "I want to get a few more tanks out, if we have time. The power packs for the plasma guns only hold about ten full shots apiece, but that's enough direct fire that we won't need *Nautilus* risking a miss. I wish we could block the access road, but that would mean pushing tanks out too far—"

A sonic boom sent glass cascading out of windows. Ryder wiped a suddenly stinging cheek, and her hand came away smeared with a grisly mixture of blood, sweat, and camouflage paint.

The SBA laid a field dressing over the demolitions sergeant's face, and watched the silver shape of the pinnace race overhead.

Her eloquent curse spoke for everyone.

Testaniere saw the Navy people from the airbase drive up just as he saw Citizen Sergeant Pescu leading a handful of ragged SS survivors from the direction of the vehicle park. Then everybody stopped to stare or cheer as the pinnace blasted the city with its sonic boom.

Testaniere doubted that the People's Republic would appreciate the bill for the chimneys, roofs, and windows broken by the supersonic approach, but he would take his share of the responsibility for it. After all, he had ordered the pinnace to hurry.

The pinnace was now slowing and banking, to let its on-board fire control systems pick out the enemy bombardment ship and paint an accurate picture of it for the missiles. The commissioner hoped that Weldon had not shot off too much of his ammunition, and that he would not go in close, to grab glory and also come within range of any air-defense weapons the ship might have. Those, he suspected, would be Manticore-supplied; the precision of the incoming fire and the modern ammunition would have been beyond the primitive technology that their Kirk imposed on the Canmore Republic.

Meanwhile, the SS personnel had their personal weapons and some ammunition, and Pescu was no longer the only one who looked like a warrior. The Navy people looked scared half out of whatever wits their training had left them, but all were armed and they had brought several crated anti-tank missiles as well. Two of them were even driving a hover truck with a light plasma gun in a fixed bow mount.

Testaniere wondered how Weldon had managed to acquire the extra weaponry. But that was a question that would not need answering until after they had saved the People's mission to liberate Silvestria.

Or at least kept it from being driven from the field in its first battle.

Testaniere knew that was defeatism, but in the privacy of his own mind he could refuse to observe political propriety when it didn't match the facts. The leaders of the People were not only going to have to learn that all over again, they were going to have to teach it to a great many of their fighters and workers.

"We have the resources for a quick counterattack. If somebody can have Euvinophan's people reform on the left flank, and the next trucks bring their people around to reinforce us, and somebody gets at least one freighter airborne with a bombload—"

"The Royal Army has put a no-fly order into effect until further notice, and they have a tracked missile-launcher bearing on the air base," a citizen petty officer said. She looked and sounded as if she would rather have confessed to child molesting.

Testaniere understood how she felt. He swallowed. "We can still make a useful ground counterattack with what we have here or can rally."

"Won't that make us a big target?" the citizen petty officer asked. She had a rocket crate slung across her back, a helmet on her cropped head, and an assault rifle in her hands, so he knew this was not a coward asking.

"If we form out here, the enemy won't dare strike us for fear of hitting the city. Once we've closed in, they'll be afraid of hitting their own people. No reactionaries or elitists can be superhuman."

He thought he heard someone mutter, "Neither can the People's fighters," but all his attention was suddenly elsewhere. As the pinnace raced overhead, white smoke and some kind of silver vapor suddenly filled the sky ahead of it. The pinnace banked, increased speed, shredded the smoke and vapor clouds with its slipstream, then vanished to the south.

For once Testaniere did not suspect Weldon of cowardice. He didn't know what the raiders had suddenly sprung, either. He hoped that in the pinnace, Weldon would have a better view and the weaponry to handle it.

✧   ✧   ✧

Ryder had seen the tank suddenly hurl smoke grenades and chaff into the sky, and the pinnace's reaction. She'd hoped to see the pinnace's turbines simply ingest debris and fall out of the sky that way, but either there wasn't any solid debris or the pilot was both smart and lucky.

Then the tank's turret hatch opened, and Fernando Chung stuck his head out.

"I told you we were going to need some Peep hardware. What's more, we've been lucky. The San Martinos built all the weapons on these things with anti-air capabilities, and high-elevation mounts, and either the Peeps left well enough alone or one of their ordnance software people has the brains God gave cave slugs."

"Is everybody out of the buildings?" Ryder shouted. She wanted to say something to Fernando, but knew that her voice might not be quite steady for anything but orders. A tank-vs.-pinnace duel was both unavoidable and mortally dangerous.

Besides, it was time to haul her aching posterior and everybody else's out of the range of any fuel dump explosion, since it might no longer wait for the demolition charges. Peep air-to-ground equipment was usually marginal and their training worse; they could barely hit a building if they hovered over the skylight.

"Move, move, move!" Ryder yelled. So did all the NCO's, then everybody in hearing took up the cry. She called to her radio operator to take over relaying data to *Nautilus*, because if the pinnace had to fight the tank it couldn't attack the ship, and the mortars and rockets might be able to hit the depot once the raiders were clear of it.

Then it would be house-to-house fighting until they reached the open country or met the Royal Army, which had to be alerted and sending *somebody* besides Field Police to see what was going on. As long as the Royal Army wouldn't turn them over to Euvinophan's people, that would be coming out on top. Even if Euvinophan did catch up with them, his people might be slow to push home an attack, and the Royal Army might break up the fight before the raiders exhausted their ammunition.

But damn it, we are taking everybody who can walk or be carried when we go!

That was the Royal Marine tradition, but there was no harm in spreading the gospel to other peoples' forces.

Then too much happened too fast. The pinnace came back,

and Chung's turret-mounted launchers went to rapid, automatic
fire, throwing out a stream of anti-laser grenades on the bearing
to its airborne enemy. The cloud of aerosol hung between it
and the Peeps, depriving the pinnace of the laser which was
its sole light-speed weapon. The pinnace still had its pulsers,
but the probability of a kill on a vehicle as heavily armored
as the tank were poor, whereas the tanks' plasma cannon would
blow right through the aerosol . . . and kill any pinnace ever
built with a single clean hit.

But whoever was piloting that pinnace knew what he was
about. He came in fast and low, using the city's buildings to block
Chung's line of fire on the approach. The Sea Fencibles' net of
ground sensors told the Erewhonese colonel where the pinnace
was, while the pinnace knew only the tank's approximate location. That meant the pilot would have to pop up and stay high
long enough to acquire the tank. But the pinnace was vastly more
maneuverable than the tank. It could dodge and weave on its
approach, which meant Chung could bring his main armament
to bear only on the general threat axis. He had to wait for direct observation before he could actually target his foe, while the
pinnace carried missiles which could be launched even off-bore
in fire-and-forget mode. If the pilot had long enough to lock
Chung up at all, the missiles would do the rest whatever happened to the pinnace . . . unless the San Martin vehicle's point
defense could stop modern, short range, hyper-velocity missile
fire, and that simply wasn't going to happen.

Which meant it all came down to a crap shoot. Both com-
batants knew what they had to do, and what their enemy had
to do, and roughly where to look for one another. The question of who would survive came down to how quickly each
of them could generate a firing solution and get his shot off.

All of that flashed through Shuna Ryder's mind in a flicker
of an instant, and then the pinnace popped up and came
screaming in on them, and Chung had laid his main armament almost perfectly. But the tank held its fire. It simply sat
there, tracking the enemy without firing while eternities flashed
by in the unbearable dragging of fractions of seconds until Ryder
was screaming at her lover to shoot.

Something in her mind screamed back that he was trying
not to shoot down the pinnace in the city, where its crash
would slaughter civilians.

But then the pinnace spewed missiles—eight at least—from
its ordnance racks. They plummeted at their target with accel-
erations that made their flight an eye-blink affair, and Chung
no longer had the option of waiting.

The missiles began hitting at the same moment the tank's turret gun slashed a melon-sized plasma charge into the root of the pinnace's right wing. The pinnace staggered once from the hit and a second time from the blast as the fuel dump erupted in a fireball a hundred meters high, then fell off on the shredded wing, fighting to stay in the air with all air-foil lift destroyed.

It was still airborne when it passed the edge of town; then its counter-grav failed as well, and it crashed into the hillside, not far from where the second warning salvo had hit. The fuel and ammunition still aboard made another respectable fireball, but one harmless to anything except the landscape.

Ryder forced herself up off her face, coughed to clear smoke and heat from her lungs, and looked at the nearer wreckage. Euvinophan's vehicle park and dump were completely enveloped in smoke where they weren't spewing flame. Bits of smoking debris made an ugly fringe around the area, and over the roar of the flames she could hear the satchel charges and ammunition cooking off.

Hydrogen-enriched fuels are useful both for propelling armored fighting vehicles and for demolishing them. She reminded herself to include that in any book of tactical tips she ever had published by the Admiralty House Press.

She saw no point in looking for Chung's tank. The playground had been well inside the fireball area. Even the ruins of the school were half-invisible, and the other half was thoroughly on fire.

Please, God. Let the blast wave have killed him before he had time to burn alive.

She was going to cry if she went on with thoughts like that, and she had more than a hundred of her people close enough to see her do it, which was bunching up too much if the bad guys had anything left—

"Spread out, you damned sheep!" she yelled. "Tactical formations, *now*. This isn't over and it won't be a carnival even when it is!"

The shriek of an incoming rocket made her whirl, with one ghastly moment of thinking *second pinnace* before she saw the Peep counterattack. It was StateSec and Navy people, with a handful of Euvinophan's greenies looking as if they were tagging along because they were too afraid to do anything else.

The first rocket hit one of the scout cars, flinging it over on its side. The raiders' tribarrel had already been dismounted, though, and the its crew was setting up. Now they dodged behind a half-ruined wall and returned fire.

The com tech was dragging Ryder toward something she couldn't recognize but which looked solid. They ducked behind it just as a second rocket hit five meters to the major's right.

Her rifle flew out of her hand. A rock smashed into her right cheek, and she sprawled out from behind cover. She was rolling back toward the com tech, who was huddled over his equipment, when a storm of solid rounds punched her all over, and a plasma pulse charge ripped at her legs.

Suddenly the painkillers weren't working. Neither, it seemed, was shock. She hurt terribly in several places, tried to roll toward where her rifle had been without knowing what she was going to do when she reached it, but passed out from the pain before she rolled over more than twice.

The last thing she thought she heard was mortar rounds, crashing down on top of the Peep counterattack.

EIGHT

Shuna Ryder decided that she was hurting too much to be dead, so she wasn't. When she tried to move, she hurt even more. She didn't quite keep silent, so all at once Chief Bexo was standing over her stretcher.

"Good . . ." she said.

"You ought to feel pretty awful," Bexo said in a flat voice.

"I mean . . ." She had meant that it was good to see him alive and on duty, not that she felt at all good. She felt considerably worse than awful.

Then she felt worse still, because Bexo and another SBA— a Sea Fencible—had to move her to treat her, and the pain won another victory over the drugs. This time she screamed.

"We're all out," Bexo said, almost whispering, as if a loud voice would add to Ryder's pain. "Everybody we could find, even the dead. You're aboard *Nautilus*. We're going home."

Nautilus? Wasn't there a famous submarine by that name? A long time ago, and back on Old Earth, maybe. This wasn't it. The deck was wood and smelled of fish. She smelled other things too. She vaguely remembered that they were sick bay smells.

Well, if she hurt this much, it only made sense for her to be in sick bay.

She also remembered that it was a good place for catching up on your sleep.

❖   ❖   ❖

Citizen Commissioner Testaniere's counterattack lasted through the second salvo from the puppet bombardment ship. At the first salvo, the Euvinophan soldiers fled. Some of them didn't abandon their weapons, though they all "abandoned the field," in the old phrase from elitist history books.

"The ones who hung on to their rifles probably thought their chief was going to take it out of their pay," Citizen Sergeant Pescu muttered. He had half a dozen minor wounds and burns but looked ready to go on fighting all day.

The Navy people held until a shell from the second salvo blew their CPO—whose name Testaniere wished he had learned—into bits. The same shell also wounded Citizen Sergeant Pescu in the stomach and both legs. His fight was over, and the last Field Police followed the Navy.

At that point, Testaniere ordered a withdrawal out of range, leaving the bodies but bringing the wounded. The handful of surviving People's fighters had three vehicles. Perhaps they could reach open country, make contact with the incoming Euvinophan troops, and at least find a temporary sanctuary in the warlord's camp on the other side of the mountains.

But the Royal Army was at last out in force, and the fugitives met the first roadblock before they'd gone two klicks. Testaniere signaled everyone else to stay in the vehicles, dismounted, and walked toward the roadblock with his hands open and empty. He would have waved the traditional white handkerchief, if everything he was wearing or carrying hadn't been black with soot and dirt.

"I surrender, on condition of medical care for our wounded," he said.

For a moment he thought the sergeant in command either didn't speak Standard English or was refusing the request.

"We are combat soldiers of the People's Republic of Haven," he said. "We are entitled to honorable treatment. The Royal Army has suffered few losses today, but this might change if you do not accept our surrender."

Several gun muzzles rose, but a first lieutenant stepped out of one of the vehicles and approached Testaniere. "Of course, we accept your surrender under those conditions." He pulled a radio from his belt and spoke rapidly in the Chuiban dialect Testaniere knew well enough to recognize as a call for medics.

Then he stepped up to Testaniere, so that only the People's Commissioner could hear him. "Our treatment will be honorable even for you, but recall that when you return to your homeland, it may be otherwise."

That was a large understatement, Testaniere thought. He was a dead man, and his family and friends might die with him, or at best see the inside of a prison or labor camp for more years than they could survive.

Now the lieutenant was holding out his own sidearm, a solid-shot caseless-cartridge pistol, butt-first. "The honor you have shown to all here, and that we wish to show to you, allows a solution. I hope you are not too filled with 'revolutionary consciousness' or any other such nonsense to have forgotten what it is."

Testaniere decided not to force the lieutenant to do the shooting himself, which might make for bad relations between the Royal Army and the People's survivors. Instead he turned, saluted his fighters and the lieutenant, then walked fifty meters down the nearest alley before he put the pistol in his mouth.

They'd pulled Fernando's body out of the burning tank. He looked dreadful, but he was alive and smiling. He even had the strength to reach into his breast pocket and pull out a small insulated packet.

"Close to my heart, as I said it always would be when you weren't," he said. "But for now, you'd better take it. I don't want the medics staring at it."

She understood then. It was his quite flattering tri-D shot of her, wearing what he'd called "recreational undress uniform." He was quite right about not letting it become public knowledge.

She reached for the packet, but his hand fell back and the packet disappeared. Suddenly he was completely still, apparently unwounded but terribly pale. Too pale— she could see the grass (and why grass, in an industrial area?) through him.

He was gone. She lifted a hand to wipe her eyes—nobody here to see her cry—and saw the grass *through her own hand*. She stood up, and could see it through her feet and legs, too.

But she could still move them. Instead of wiping her eyes, she brought her hand up to the salute.

A Marine officer always saluted the quarterdeck, coming aboard.

All of Shuna Ryder's vital signs had flat-lined when Chief Bexo came back. He had suspected that she wouldn't be able to hear the news that the Royal Army was releasing Claymore Three, after fining them for trespass and malicious damage (three dead pigs). He hoped she'd heard the cheering when the news came in.

Then he looked down at the visible portion of Ryder's face. It didn't exactly show a smile—too much pain, then too many drugs, for that. But it looked as though the last thing she'd heard had been something that took her attention off her mortal wounds for a little while.